THE LYING LIFE OF ADULTS

THE LYING LIFE
OF ADULTS

ELENA FERRANTE

*Translated from the Italian
by Ann Goldstein*

THORNDIKE PRESS
A part of Gale, a Cengage Company

Copyright © 2019 by Edizioni e/o.
Original title: *La vita bugiarda degli adulti.*
Translation by Ann Goldstein. Translation copyright © 2020 by Europa Editions.
Thorndike Press, a part of Gale, a Cengage Company.

Thorndike Press® Large Print Core.
The text of this Large Print edition is unabridged.
Other aspects of the book may vary from the original edition.
Set in 16 pt. Plantin.

LIBRARY OF CONGRESS CIP DATA ON FILE.
CATALOGUING IN PUBLICATION FOR THIS BOOK
IS AVAILABLE FROM THE LIBRARY OF CONGRESS.

ISBN-13: 978-1-4328-8054-5 (hardcover alk. paper)

Published in 2020 by arrangement with Europa Editions.

Printed in Mexico
Print Number: 01   Print Year: 2020

THE LYING LIFE OF ADULTS

I

1.

Two years before leaving home my father said to my mother that I was very ugly. The sentence was uttered under his breath, in the apartment that my parents, newly married, had bought at the top of Via San Giacomo dei Capri, in Rione Alto. Everything — the spaces of Naples, the blue light of a frigid February, those words — remained fixed. But I slipped away, and am still slipping away, within these lines that are intended to give me a story, while in fact I am nothing, nothing of my own, nothing that has really begun or really been brought to completion: only a tangled knot, and nobody, not even the one who at this moment is writing, knows if it contains the right thread for a story or is merely a snarled confusion of suffering, without redemption.

2.

I loved my father very much; he was an unfailingly courteous man. A refined manner perfectly matched a body so slender that his clothes seemed a size too large, and this, to my eyes, gave him a look of inimitable elegance. His features were delicate, and nothing — deep-set eyes with long lashes, impeccably engineered nose, full lips — spoiled their harmony. With me he had an air of cheerfulness on every occasion, whatever his mood or mine, and he never shut himself in his study — he was always studying — unless he got at least a smile out of me. He especially liked my hair, but it's hard to say, now, when he started praising it, maybe when I was two or three. Certainly, during my childhood we had conversations like this:

"What lovely hair, so fine, so shiny — will you give it to me?"

"No, it's mine."

"How about a little generosity."

"If you want I can lend it to you."

"Excellent, then I just won't give it back to you."

"You already have yours."

"What I have I took from you."

"That's not true, you're lying."

"Check for yourself: yours was too pretty and I stole it."

I would check but just to play along, I knew he would never steal it. And I laughed, I laughed a lot; I had much more fun with him than with my mother. He always wanted something of mine, my ear, my nose, my chin: they were so perfect, he said, he just couldn't live without them. I loved that tone, which proved to me over and over again how indispensable I was to him.

Naturally, my father wasn't like that with everyone. At times, when he was really caught up in something, he tended to frantically mash together sophisticated arguments and uncontrolled emotions. At other times, instead, he was curt, resorting to brief, extremely precise phrases, so dense that no one could refute them. These were two fathers very different from the one I loved, and I had started to discover their existence at the age of seven or eight, when I heard him arguing with the friends and acquaintances who on occasion came to our house for meetings that could become very heated, on issues I knew nothing about. In general, I stayed with my mother in the kitchen and paid little attention to the squabbling just a little ways off. But sometimes, when my mother was busy and closed herself in her

11

room, I was left alone in the hall playing or reading — mostly reading, I would say, because my father read a lot, and my mother, too, and I loved being like them. I didn't listen to the arguments, I broke off my game or my reading only when there was a sudden silence and those alien voices of my father's arose. From then on he would dominate, and I waited for the meeting to end to find out if he had gone back to his usual self, the one with the gentle and affectionate tones.

The night he made that statement he had just learned that I wasn't doing well in school. It was something new. I had always done well, since first grade, and only in the past two months had started doing badly. But it was very important to my parents that I be successful in school, and at the first poor grades my mother, especially, was alarmed.

"What's going on?"

"I don't know."

"You have to study."

"I do study."

"And so?"

"Some things I remember and some I don't."

"Study until you remember everything."

I studied until I was exhausted, but the

results continued to be disappointing. That afternoon, in fact, my mother had gone to talk to the teachers and had returned very unhappy. She didn't scold me, my parents never scolded me. She merely said: the mathematics teacher is the one who is most dissatisfied, but she says that if you want to you can do it. Then my mother went into the kitchen to make dinner, and meanwhile my father came home. All I could hear from my room was that she was giving him a summary of the teachers' complaints, and I understood that she was bringing up as an excuse the changes of early adolescence. But he interrupted her, and in one of the tones that he never used with me — even giving in to dialect, which was completely banned in our house — let slip what he surely wouldn't have wanted to come out of his mouth:

"Adolescence has nothing to do with it: she's getting the face of Vittoria."

I'm sure that if he'd known I could hear him he would never have used a tone so far removed from our usual playful ease. They both thought the door of my room was closed, I always closed it, and they didn't realize that one of them had left it open. So it was that, at the age of twelve, I learned from my father's voice, muffled by the effort to keep it low, that I was becoming like his sister, a woman in whom — I had heard him say as long as I could remember — ugliness and spite were combined to perfection.

Here someone might object: maybe you're exaggerating, your father didn't say, literally, Giovanna is ugly. It's true, it wasn't in his nature to utter such brutal words. But I was going through a period of feeling very fragile. I'd begun menstruating almost a year earlier, my breasts were all too visible and embarrassed me, I was afraid I smelled bad and was always washing, I went to bed lethargic and woke up lethargic. My only comfort at that time, my only certainty, was that he absolutely adored me, all of me. So that when he compared me to Aunt Vittoria it was worse than if he'd said: Giovanna used to be pretty, now she's turned ugly. In my house the name Vittoria was like the name of a monstrous being who taints and infects anyone who touches her. I knew almost nothing about her. I had seen her only a few times, but — and this is the point — all I remembered about those occasions was revulsion and fear. Not the revulsion and fear that she in person could have provoked in me — I had no memory of that. What frightened me was my parents' revulsion and fear. My father always talked about his sister obscurely, as if she practiced shameful rites that defiled her, defiling those around her. My mother never mentioned her, and in fact when she intervened in her husband's outbursts tended to silence him, as if she were afraid that Vittoria, wherever she was, could hear them and would immediately come rushing up San Giacomo dei Capri, striding rapidly, although it was a long, steep street, and deliberately dragging behind her all the illnesses from the hospitals in our neighborhood; that she would fly into our apartment, on the sixth floor, smash the furniture, and, emitting drunken black flashes from her eyes, hit my mother if she so much as tried to protest.

Of course I intuited that behind that tension there must be a story of wrongs done and suffered, but I knew little, at the time, of family affairs, and above all I didn't consider that terrible aunt a member of the family. She was a childhood bogeyman, a lean, demonic silhouette, an unkempt figure lurking in the corners of houses when darkness falls. Was it possible, then, that without any warning I should discover that I was getting her face? I? I who until that moment had thought that I was pretty and assumed, thanks to my father, that I would remain so forever? I who, with his constant affirmation, thought I had beautiful hair, I who wanted to be loved as he loved me, as he had accustomed me to believing I was loved, I who was already suffering because both my parents were suddenly unhappy with me, and that unhappiness distressed me, tarnishing everything?

I waited for my mother to speak, but her reaction didn't console me. Although she hated all her husband's relatives and detested her sister-in-law the way you detest a lizard that runs up your bare leg, she didn't respond by yelling at him: you're crazy, my daughter and your sister have nothing in common. She merely offered a weak, laconic: what are you talking about, of course she isn't. And I, there in my room, hurried to close the door so as not to hear anything else. Then I wept in silence and stopped only when my father came to announce — this time in his nice voice — that dinner was ready.

I joined them in the kitchen with dry eyes, and had to endure, looking at my plate, a series of suggestions for improving my grades. Afterward I went back to pretending to study, while they settled in front of the television. My suffering wouldn't end or even diminish. Why had my father made that statement? Why had my mother not forcefully contradicted it? Was their displeasure due to my bad grades or was it an anxiety that was separate from school, that had existed for years? And him, especially him, had he spoken those cruel words because of a momentary irritation I had caused him, or, with his sharp gaze — the gaze of someone who knows and sees everything — had he long ago discerned the features of my ruined future, of an advancing evil that upset him and that he himself didn't know how to respond to? I was in despair all night. In the morning I was convinced that, if I wanted to save myself, I had to go and see what Aunt Vittoria's face was really like.

3.

It was an arduous undertaking. In a city like Naples, inhabited by families with numerous branches that even when they were fighting, even when the fights were bloody, never really cut their ties, my father lived in utter autonomy, as though he had no blood relatives, as if he were self-generated. I had often had dealings with my mother's parents and her brother. They were all affectionate people who gave me lots of presents, and until my grandparents died — first my grandfather and a year later my grandmother: sudden deaths that had upset me, had made my mother cry the way we girls cried when we hurt ourselves — and my uncle left for a job far away, we had seen them frequently and happily. Whereas I knew almost nothing about my father's relatives. They had appeared in my life only on rare occasions — a wedding, a funeral — and always in a climate of such false affection that all I got out of it was the awkwardness of forced contact: say hello to your grandfather, give your aunt a kiss. In those relatives, therefore, I had never been much interested, also because after those encounters my parents were tense and forgot them by mutual consent, as if they'd been involved in some second-rate performance.

It should also be said that if my mother's relatives lived in a precise place with an evocative name, Museo — they were the Museo grandparents — the space where my father's relatives lived was undefined, nameless. I knew only one thing for certain: to visit them you had to go down, and down, keep going down, into the depths of the depths of Naples, and the journey was so long it seemed to me that we and my father's relatives lived in two different cities. And for a long time that appeared to be true. We lived in the highest part of Naples, and to go anywhere we had inevitably to descend. My father and mother went willingly only as far as the Vomero, or, with some annoyance, to my grandparents' house in Museo. And their friends were mainly in Via Suarez, Piazza degli Artisti, Via Luca Giordano, Via Scarlatti, Via Cimarosa, streets that were well known to me because many of my schoolmates lived there as well. Not to mention that they all led to Villa Floridiana, a park I loved, where my mother had brought me for fresh air and sunshine when I was an infant, and where I had spent pleasant hours with my friends of early childhood, Angela and Ida. Only after those place names, all happily colored by plants, fragments of the sea, gardens, flowers, games, and good manners, did the real descent begin, the one my parents considered irritating. For work, for shopping, for the need that my father, in particular, had for study, encounter, and debate, they descended daily, usually on the funiculars, to Chiaia, to Toledo, and from there went on to Piazza Plebiscito, the Biblioteca Nazionale, to Port'Alba and Via Ventaglieri and Via Foria, and, at most, Piazza Carlo III,

19

where my mother's school was. I knew those names well, too — my parents mentioned them frequently but didn't often take me there, and maybe that's why the names didn't give me the same happiness. Outside of the Vomero, the city scarcely belonged to me, in fact the farther it spread on that lower ground, the more unknown it seemed. So it was natural that the areas where my father's relatives lived had, in my eyes, the features of worlds still wild and unexplored. For me not only were they nameless but, from the way my parents referred to them, I felt they must be difficult to get to. The times we had to go there, my mother and father, who usually were energetic and willing, seemed especially weary, especially anxious. I was young, but their tension, their exchanges — always the same — stayed with me.

"Andrea," my mother would say in a tired voice, "get dressed, we have to go."

But he went on reading and underlining books with the same pencil he used to write in a notebook he had beside him.

"Andrea, it's getting late, they'll be angry."

"Are you ready?"

"I'm ready."

"And the child?"

"The child, too."

My father then abandoned books and notebooks, leaving them open on the desk, put on a clean shirt, his good suit. But he was taciturn, tense, as if he were rehearsing mentally the lines of an inevitable role. My mother, meanwhile, who wasn't ready at all, kept checking her own appearance, mine, my father's, as if only the proper clothing could guarantee that we would all three return home safe and sound. In sum, it was obvious that, on each of those occasions, they believed they had to defend themselves from people and places of which they said nothing to me, so as not to upset me. But still I noticed the anomalous anxiety, or, rather, I recognized it, it had always been there, perhaps the only memory of distress in a happy childhood. What worried me were sentences like this, uttered in an Italian that, for one thing, seemed — I don't know how to say it — splintered.

"Remember, if Vittoria says something, pretend you didn't hear."

"You mean if she acts crazy I say nothing?"

"Yes, keep in mind Giovanna's there."

"All right."

"Don't say all right if you don't mean it. It's a small effort. We're there half an hour and we come home."

I remember almost nothing of those forays. Noise, heat, distracted kisses on the forehead, dialect voices, a bad smell that we probably all gave off out of fear. That climate had convinced me over the years that my father's relatives — howling shapes of repulsive unseemliness, especially Aunt Vittoria, the blackest, the most unseemly — constituted a danger, even if it was difficult to understand what the danger was. Was the area where they lived considered risky? Were my grandparents, my aunts and uncles, my cousins dangerous, or just Aunt Vittoria? Only my parents seemed to be informed, and now that I felt an urgency to know what my aunt was like, what sort of person she was, I would have to ask them in order to get to the bottom of it. But even if I asked them, what would I find out? Either they would silence me with a phrase of good-humored refusal — you want to see your aunt, you want to visit her, what's the point? — or they would be alarmed and try not to mention her anymore. So I thought that, at least for a start, I'd have to find a picture of her.

4.

I took advantage of an afternoon when they were both out and went to rummage in a dresser in their bedroom where my mother kept the albums containing, in an orderly arrangement, the photographs of herself, my father, and me. I knew those albums by heart. I had often leafed through them: they mostly documented my parents' relationship and my almost thirteen years of life. And so I knew that, mysteriously, there were a lot of pictures of my mother's relatives, very few of my father's, and, among those few, not a single one of Aunt Vittoria. Still, I remembered that somewhere in that dresser was an old metal box that held random images of my parents before they met. Since I'd hardly ever looked at them, and always with my mother, I hoped to find in there some pictures of my aunt.

I found the box in the bottom of the wardrobe, but first I decided to re-examine conscientiously the albums that showed the two of them as fiancés, the two of them as bride and groom frowning at the center of a small wedding party, the two of them as an always happy couple, and, finally, me, their daughter, photographed an excessive number of times, from birth to now. I lingered in particular on the wedding pictures. My father was wearing a visibly rumpled dark suit and was scowling in every image; my mother, beside him, not in a wedding dress but in a cream-colored suit, with a veil the same shade, had a vaguely excited expression. I already knew that among the thirty or so guests were some friends from the Vomero they still saw and my mother's relatives, the good grandparents from Museo. But still I looked and looked again, hoping for a figure even in the background that would lead me somehow or other to a woman I had no memory of. Nothing. So I moved on to the box and after many attempts managed to get it open.

I emptied the contents onto the bed: all the pictures were black and white. The ones of my parents' separate teenage years were in no order: my mother, smiling, with her classmates, with her friends, at the beach, on the street, pretty and well dressed, was mixed in with my father, preoccupied, always by himself, never on vacation, pants bunching at the knees, jackets whose sleeves were too short. The pictures of childhood and early adolescence had instead been put in order in two envelopes, the ones from my mother's family and those from my father's. My aunt — I told myself — must inevitably be among the latter, and I went on to look at them one by one. There weren't more than about twenty, and it struck me immediately that in three or four of those images my father, who in the others appeared as a child, a boy, with his parents, or with relatives I'd never met, could be seen, surprisingly, next to a black rectangle drawn with a felt-tipped pen. I immediately understood that that very precise rectangle was a job that he had done diligently and secretly. I imagined him as, using a ruler that he had on his desk, he enclosed a portion of the photo in that geometric shape and then carefully went over it with the marker, attentive not to go outside the fixed margins. I had no doubts about that painstaking work: the rectangles were deletions and under that black was Aunt Vittoria.

For quite a while I sat there not knowing what to do. Finally, I made up my mind, went to the kitchen and found a knife, and delicately scraped at a tiny section of the part of the photograph that my father had covered. I soon realized that only the white of the paper appeared. I felt anxious and stopped. I knew that I was going against my father's will, and any action that might further erode his affection frightened me. The anxiety increased when at the back of the envelope I found the only picture in which he wasn't a child or a teenager but a young man, smiling, as he rarely was in the photos taken before he met my mother. He was in profile, his gaze was happy, his teeth were even and very white. But the smile, the happiness weren't directed toward anyone. Next to him were two of those precise rectangles, two coffins in which, at a time surely different from the cordial moment of the photo, he had enclosed the bodies of his sister and someone else.

I focused on that image for a long time. My father was on a street and was wearing a checkered shirt with short sleeves; it must have been summer. Behind him was the entrance to a shop, all you could see of the sign was –RIA; there was a display window, but you couldn't tell what it displayed. Next to the dark patch appeared a bright white lamppost with well-defined outlines. And then there were the shadows, long shadows, one of them cast by an evidently female body. Although my father had assiduously eliminated the people next to him, he had left their trace on the sidewalk.

Again I began to scrape off the ink of the rectangle, very gently, but I stopped as soon as I realized that here, too, only the white appeared. I waited a moment or two and then started again. I worked lightly, hearing my breathing in the silence of the house. I stopped for good only when all I managed to get out of the area where once Vittoria's head must have been was a spot, and you couldn't tell if it was the residue of the pen or a trace of her lips.

5.

I put everything back in order and tried to repress the threat that I looked like the sister my father had obliterated. Meanwhile I became more and more distracted, and my aversion for school increased, scaring me. Still, I wanted to go back to being a good girl, the way I'd been until a few months earlier: it was important to my parents, and I thought that if I could get excellent grades again I would be pretty again, too, and good. But I couldn't; in class my mind wandered, at home I wasted my time in front of the mirror. In fact looking at myself became an obsession. I wanted to know if my aunt really was peeking out through my body, and since I didn't know what she looked like I searched for her in every detail that marked a change in myself. Thus, features that I hadn't noticed before became evident: thick eyebrows, eyes that were too small and dull brown, an exaggeratedly high forehead, thin hair — not at all beautiful, or maybe not beautiful anymore — that was pasted to my head, big ears with heavy lobes, a short upper lip with a disgusting dark fuzz, a fat lower lip, teeth that still looked like baby teeth, a pointed chin, and a nose, oh what a nose, how gracelessly it extended toward the mirror, widening, how dark the caverns on the sides. Were these elements of Aunt Vittoria's face or were they mine and only mine? Should I expect to get better or get worse? Was my body — the long neck that seemed as if it might break like the filament of a spider web, straight bony shoulders, breasts that continued to swell and had dark nipples, thin legs that came up too high, almost to my armpits — *me* or the advance guard of my aunt, her, in all her horror?

I studied myself and at the same time observed my parents. How lucky I had been, I couldn't have had better ones. They were good-looking and had loved each other since they were young. My father and mother had told me the little I knew of their romance, he with his usual playful distance, she sweetly emotional. They had always felt such pleasure in being with each other that the decision to have a child had come relatively late, given that they had married very young. When I was born my mother was thirty and my father had just turned thirty-two. I had been conceived amid countless anxieties, expressed by her aloud, by him to himself. The pregnancy had been difficult, the birth — June 3, 1979 — torturous, my first two years of life the practical demonstration that my entering the world had complicated their lives. Worried about the future, my father, a teacher of history and philosophy in the most prestigious high school in Naples, an intellectual fairly well known in the city, beloved by his students, to whom he devoted not only the mornings but entire afternoons, had started giving private lessons. Worried, on the other hand, about the present — my constant nighttime crying, rashes that vexed me, stomachaches, ferocious tantrums — my mother, who taught Latin and Greek in a high school in Piazza Carlo III and corrected proofs of romance novels, had gone through a long depression, becoming a poor teacher and a very distracted proofreader. These were the problems I had caused when I was born. But then I had become a quiet and obedient child, and my parents had slowly recovered. The phase in which they tried in vain to spare me from the evils that all human beings are exposed to had ended. They had found a new equilibrium, thanks to which, even if love for me came first, second place was again occupied by my father's studies and my mother's jobs. So what to say? They loved me, I loved them. My father seemed to me an extraordinary man, my mother a really nice woman, and the two of them were the only clear figures in a world that was otherwise confused.

A confusion that I was part of. Sometimes I imagined that a violent struggle between my father and his sister was taking place in me, and I hoped that he would win. Of course — I reflected — Vittoria had already prevailed once, at the moment of my birth, since for a while I had been an intolerable child; but then — I thought with relief — I turned into a good little girl, so it's possible to get rid of her. I tried to reassure myself that way and, in order to feel strong, forced myself to see my parents in myself. But especially at night, before going to bed, I would look at myself in the mirror yet again, and it seemed I had lost them long ago. I should have had a face that synthesized the best of them and instead I was getting the face of Vittoria. I was supposed to have a happy life and instead an unhappy period was starting, utterly without the joy of feeling the way they had felt and still did.

6.

I tried to find out, after a while, if the two sisters, Angela and Ida, my trusted friends, were aware of any deterioration, and if Angela, in particular, who was the same age as me (Ida was two years younger), was also changing for the worse. I needed a gaze that would evaluate me, and it seemed to me that I could count on them. We had been brought up in the same way by parents who had been friends for decades and had the same views. All three of us, to be clear, had not been baptized, all three didn't know any prayers, all three had been precociously informed about the functioning of our bodies (illustrated books, educational videos with animated cartoons), all three knew that we should be proud of being born female, all three had gone to first grade not at six but at five, all three always behaved in a responsible manner, all three had in our heads a dense network of advice useful for avoiding the traps of Naples and the world, all three could turn to our parents at any time to satisfy our curiosities, all three read a lot, and, finally, all three had a sensible disdain for consumer goods and the tastes of our contemporaries, even though, encouraged by our teachers, we were well informed about music, film, television programs, singers, and actors, and in secret wanted to become famous actresses with fabulous boyfriends with whom we shared long kisses and genital contact. Of course, the friendship between Angela and me was closer, since Ida was younger, but she could surprise us, and in fact read more than we did and wrote poems and stories. And so, as far as I remember, there were no conflicts between them and me, and if there were we could speak to each other frankly and make peace. So, considering them reliable witnesses, I questioned them cautiously a couple of times. But they didn't say anything unpleasant: in fact, they seemed to appreciate me quite a bit, and for my part I thought they seemed to keep getting prettier. They were well proportioned, so carefully modeled that just the sight of them made me feel a need for their warmth, and I hugged and kissed them as if I wanted to fuse them to myself. But one night when I was feeling down they happened to come for dinner at San Giacomo dei Capri with their parents, and things got complicated. I wasn't in a good mood. I felt especially out of place, gangling, lanky, pale, coarse in every word and gesture, and therefore ready to pick up allusions to my deterioration even when there weren't any. For example Ida asked, pointing to my shoes:

"Are they new?"

"No, I've had them forever."

"I don't remember them."

"What's wrong with them."

"Nothing."

"If you noticed them now, it means that *now* something's wrong."

"No."

"Are my legs too thin?"

We went on like that for a while, they reassuring me, I digging into their reassurances to find out if they were serious or hiding behind good manners the ugly impression I'd made. My mother intervened in her weary tone, saying: Giovanna, that's enough, you don't have skinny legs. I was ashamed and shut up immediately, while Costanza, Angela and Ida's mother, emphasized, you have lovely ankles, and Mariano, their father, exclaimed, laughing: excellent thighs, they'd be delicious roasted with potatoes. He didn't stop there, but kept teasing me, joking constantly — he was that person who thinks he can bring good cheer to a funeral.

"What's wrong with this girl tonight?"

I shook my head to indicate that nothing was wrong, and tried to smile but couldn't; his way of being funny made me nervous.

"Such nice hair, what is it, a sorghum broom?"

Again I shook my head no, and this time I couldn't hide my annoyance, he was treating me as if I were a child of six.

"It's a compliment, sweetheart: sorghum is a plump plant, part green, part red, and part black."

I responded darkly:

"I'm not plump, or green, or red, or black."

He stared at me in bewilderment, smiled, spoke to his daughters.

"Why is Giovanna so grim tonight?"

"I'm not grim."

"Grim isn't an insult, it's the manifestation of a state of mind. You know what it means?"

I was silent. He again turned to his daughters, pretending to be despondent.

"She doesn't know. Ida, you tell her."

Ida said unwillingly: "That you have a scowl on your face. He says it to me, too."

Mariano was that sort of person. He and my father had known each other since their university days, and because they'd stayed

34

friends he had always been present in my life. A little heavy, completely bald, with blue eyes, he had impressed me since I was a small child because his face was too pale and slightly puffy. When he showed up at our house, which was often, he would talk with his friend for hours and hours, inserting into every sentence a bitter discontent that made me nervous. He taught history at the university and contributed regularly to a prestigious Neapolitan journal. He and Papa argued constantly, and even though we three girls understood little of what they were saying, we had grown up with the idea that they had assigned themselves a very difficult task that required study and concentration. But, unlike my father, Mariano didn't merely study day and night, he also railed loudly against numerous enemies — people in Naples, Rome, and other cities — who wanted to prevent them from doing their work properly. Angela, Ida, and I, even if we weren't able to state a position, were always for our parents and against those who didn't like them. But, in the end, in all their discussions the only thing that had interested us since childhood was the bad words in dialect that Mariano uttered against people who were famous at the time. That was because the three of us — especially me — were not only forbidden to use swear words but also, more generally, to utter a syllable in Neapolitan. A useless ban. Our parents didn't prohibit us from doing anything, but even when they did, they were indulgent. So, under our breath, just for fun, we repeated to each other the names and last names of Mariano's enemies accompanied by the obscene epithets we had heard. But while Angela and Ida found that vocabulary of their father's merely amusing, I couldn't separate it from an impression of spite.

Wasn't there always something malevolent in his jokes? Wasn't there that evening as well? I was grim, I had a scowl on my face, I was a sorghum broom? Had Mariano merely been joking or, joking, had he cruelly spoken the truth? We sat down at the table. The adults started a tedious conversation about some friends or other who were planning to move to Rome, we suffered our boredom in silence, hoping that dinner would be over quickly so we could take refuge in my room. The whole time I had the impression that my father never laughed, my mother barely smiled, Mariano laughed a lot, and Costanza, his wife, not too much but heartily. Maybe my parents weren't having fun like Angela and Ida's because I had made them sad. Their friends were happy with their daughters, while they were no longer happy with me. I was grim, grim, grim, and just seeing me there at the table kept them from feeling happy. How serious my mother was and how pretty and happy Angela and Ida's mother. My father was now pouring her some wine, he spoke to her with polite aloofness. Costanza taught Italian and Latin; her parents were very wealthy and had given her an excellent upbringing. She was so elegant that sometimes my mother seemed to be studying her, in order to imitate her, and, almost without realizing it, I did the same. How was it possible that that woman had chosen a husband like Mariano? The brilliance of her jewelry, the colors of her clothes, which always looked perfect, dazzled me. Just the night before I had dreamed that with the tip of her tongue she was lovingly licking my ear like a cat. And the dream had brought me comfort, a sort of physical well-being that for several hours after I woke up had made me feel safe.

Now, sitting at the table next to her, I hoped that her good influence would drive her husband's words out of my head. Instead, they lasted for the whole dinner — I have hair that makes me look like a broom,

I have a grim face — intensifying my nervousness. I went back and forth between wanting to have fun by whispering dirty expressions in Angela's ear and a bad mood that wouldn't go away. As soon as we finished dessert, we left our parents to their conversation and shut ourselves in my room. There I asked Ida, without turning around:

"Do I have a scowl on my face? Do you think I'm getting ugly?"

They looked at each other, they answered almost simultaneously:

"Not at all."

"Tell the truth."

I realized that they were hesitant, Angela decided to speak:

"A little, but not physically."

"Physically you're pretty," Ida emphasized, "only you look a little bit ugly because you're anxious."

Angela said, kissing me:

"It happens to me, too. When I'm anxious I turn ugly, but then it goes away."

7.

That connection between anxiety and ugliness unexpectedly consoled me. You can turn ugly because of worries — Angela and

Ida had said — and if the worries go away you can be pretty again. I wanted to believe that, and I made an effort to have untroubled days. But I couldn't force myself to be calm, my mind would suddenly blur, and that obsession began again. I felt an increasing hostility toward everyone that was difficult to repress with false good humor. And I soon concluded that my worries were not at all transient, maybe they weren't even worries but bad feelings that were spreading through my veins.

Not that Angela and Ida had lied to me about that, they weren't capable of it: we had been brought up never to tell lies. With that connection between ugliness and anxieties, they had probably been talking about themselves, and their experience, using the words that Mariano — our heads contained a lot of concepts we heard from our parents — had used, in some circumstance or other, to comfort them. But Angela and Ida weren't me. Angela and Ida didn't have in their family an Aunt Vittoria whose face their father — *their father* — had said they were starting to take on. Suddenly one morning at school I felt that I would never go back to being the way my parents wanted me, that cruel Mariano would notice it, and my friends would move on to more suitable friendships, and I would be left alone.

I was depressed, and in the following days the bad feelings regained strength; the only thing that gave me a little relief was to stroke myself continuously between my legs, numbing myself with pleasure. But how humiliating it was to forget myself like that, by myself; afterward I was even more unhappy, sometimes disgusted. I had a very pleasant memory of a game I played with Angela, on the couch at my house, when, in front of the television, we would lie facing each other, entwine our legs, and silently, without negotiations, without rules, settle a doll between the crotch of my underpants and the crotch of hers, so that we rubbed each other, writhing comfortably, pressing the doll — which seemed alive and happy — hard between us. That was another time, the pleasure didn't seem like a nice game anymore. Now I was all sweaty, I felt deformed. And so day after day I was repossessed by the desire to examine my face, and went back even more relentlessly to spending time in front of the mirror.

This led to a surprising development: as I looked at what appeared to me defective, I started to want to fix it. I studied my features and, pulling on my face, thought: look, if I just had a nose like so, eyes like so, ears like so, I'd be perfect. My features were slight flaws that made me sad, touched me. Poor you, I thought, how unlucky you've been. And I had a sudden enthusiasm for my own image, so that once I went as far as to kiss myself on the mouth just as I was thinking, forlornly, that no one would ever kiss me. So I began to react. I moved slowly from the stupor in which I spent the days studying myself to the need to fix myself up, as if I were a piece of good-quality material damaged by a clumsy worker. I was I — whatever I I was — and had to concern myself with that face, that body, those thoughts.

One Sunday morning I tried to improve myself with my mother's makeup. But when she came into my room she said, laughing: you look like a Carnival mask, you have to do better. I didn't protest, I didn't defend myself, I asked her as submissively as I could:

"Will you teach me to put on makeup the way you do it?"

"Every face has its own makeup."

"I want to be like you."

She was glad to do it, complimented me, and then made me up very carefully. We spent some really lovely hours, joking, laughing with each other. Usually she was quiet, self-possessed, but with me — only with me — ready to become a child again.

Eventually my father appeared, with his newspapers; he was happy to find us playing like that.

"How pretty the two of you are," he said.

"Really?" I asked.

"Absolutely, I've never seen such gorgeous women."

And he shut himself in his room; on Sunday he read the papers and then studied. But as soon as my mother and I were alone she asked me, as if that space of a few minutes had been a signal, in a voice that was always a little weary but seemed to know neither irritation nor fear:

"Why did you go looking in the box of pictures?"

Silence. She had noticed, then, that I had been rummaging through her things. She realized that I had tried to scrape off the black of the marker. How long ago? I couldn't keep from crying, even though I fought back the tears with all my strength. Mamma, I said between my sobs, I wanted, I believed, I thought — but I was unable to say a thing about what I wanted, believed, thought. I gasped, sobbing, but she couldn't soothe me, and as soon as she said something with a smile of sympathy — there's no need to cry, you just have to ask me, or Papa, and anyway you can look at the photos when you like, why are you crying, calm down — I sobbed even harder. Finally, she took my hands, and it was she herself who said gently:

"What were you looking for? A picture of Aunt Vittoria?"

8.

I understood at that point that my parents knew that I had heard their conversation. They must have talked about it for a long time, maybe they had even consulted with their friends. Certainly, my father was very sorry and in all likelihood had delegated my mother to convince me that the sentence I'd heard had a meaning different from the one that might have wounded me. Surely that was the case — my mother's voice was very effective in mending operations. She never had outbursts of rage, or even of annoyance. When, for example, Costanza teased her about all the time she wasted preparing her classes, correcting the proofs of silly stories and sometimes rewriting entire pages, she always responded quietly, with a transparency that had no bitterness. And even when she said, Costanza, you have

43

plenty of money, you can do what you like, but I have to work, she managed to do it in a few soft words, without any evident resentment. So who better than her to remedy the mistake? After I calmed down, she said, in that voice, we love you, and she repeated it once or twice. Then she started on a speech that until then she had never made.

She said that both she and my father had made many sacrifices to become what they were. She said: I'm not complaining, my parents gave me what they could, you know how kind and affectionate they were, this house was bought at the time with their help; but your father's childhood, adolescence, youth — those for him were truly hard times, because he had nothing at all, he had to climb a mountain with his bare hands, and it's not over, it's never over, there is always some storm that knocks you down, back to where you started. So finally she came to Vittoria and revealed to me that, non-metaphorically, the storm that wanted to knock my father down off the mountain was her.

"Her?"

"Yes. Your father's sister is an envious woman. Not envious the way others might be, but envious in a very terrible way."

44

"What did she do?"

"Everything. But above all she refused to accept your father's success."

"In what sense?"

"Success in life. How hard he worked at school and university. His intelligence. What he has constructed. His degree. His job, our marriage, the things he studies, the respect that surrounds him, the friends we have, you."

"Me, too?"

"Yes. There is no thing or person that for Vittoria isn't a kind of personal insult. But what offends her most is your father's existence."

"What kind of work does she do?"

"She's a maid, what should she do, she left school in fifth grade. Not that there's anything bad about being a maid, you know how good the woman is who helps Costanza in the house. The problem is that she also blames her brother for this."

"Why?"

"There's no why. Especially if you think that your father saved her. She could have ruined herself even further. She was in love with a married man who already had three children, a criminal. Well, your father, as the older brother, intervened. But she put that, too, on the list of things she's never forgiven

45

him for."

"Maybe Papa should have minded his own business."

"No one should mind his own business if a person is in trouble."

"Yes."

"But even helping her was always difficult, she repaid us as destructively as possible."

"Aunt Vittoria wants Papa to die?"

"It's terrible to say, but it's true."

"And there's no way to make peace?"

"No. To make peace, your father, in Aunt Vittoria's eyes, would have to become a mediocre man like the ones she knows. But since that's not possible, she set the family against us. Because of her, after your grandparents died we couldn't have a real relationship with any of the relatives."

I didn't respond in a meaningful way, I merely uttered a few cautious or monosyllabic phrases. But at the same time I thought with revulsion: so I am taking on the features of a person who wants my father dead, my family ruined, and the tears flowed again. Noticing, my mother tried to stop them. She hugged me, murmured: there's no need to feel bad, is the meaning of what your father said clear now? Eyes lowered, I shook my head energetically. So she explained to me softly, in a tone that was suddenly amused: for us, for a long time, Aunt Vittoria has been not a person but a locution. Sometimes, when your father isn't nice, I scold him jokingly: be careful, Andrea, you just put on the face of Vittoria. And then she shook me lovingly, repeated: it's a playful expression.

I muttered darkly:

"I don't believe it, Mamma, I've never heard you talk like that."

"Maybe not in your presence, but in private, yes. It's like a red signal, we use it to say: look out, it would be all too easy for us to lose everything we wanted for our life."

"Me, too?"

"No, what are you talking about, we'll never lose you. You are the person who matters most in the world to us, we want all the happiness possible for your life. That's why Papa and I are so insistent about school. Now you're having some little difficulties, but they'll pass. You'll see how many great things will happen to you."

I sniffled, she wanted to blow my nose with a handkerchief as if I were still a child, and maybe I was, but I avoided it, and said:

"What if I stopped studying?"

"You'd become ignorant."

"So?"

"So ignorance is an obstacle. But you've

already gotten back on track with studying, haven't you? It's a pity not to cultivate one's intelligence."

I exclaimed:

"I don't want to be intelligent, Mamma, I want to be beautiful, like the two of you."

"You'll be much more beautiful."

"Not if I'm starting to look like Aunt Vittoria."

"You're so different, that won't happen."

"How can you say that? Who can I ask, to find out if it's happening or not?"

"There's me, I'll always be here."

"That's not enough."

"What are you proposing."

I almost whispered:

"I have to see my aunt."

She was silent for a moment, then she said:

"For that you have to talk to your father."

9.

I didn't take her words literally. I assumed that she would talk to him about it first and that my father, as soon as the next day, would say, in the tone I loved best: here we are, at your orders, if the little queen has decided that we have to go meet Aunt Vittoria, this poor parent of hers, albeit with a noose around his neck, will take her. Then he would telephone his sister to make a date, or maybe he would ask my mother to do it, he never concerned himself in person with what annoyed or irritated or grieved him. Then he would drive me to her house.

But that's not what happened. Hours passed, days, and we scarcely saw my father. He was always tired, always torn between school, some private lessons, and a demanding essay that he was writing with Mariano. He left in the morning and returned at night, and in those days it was always raining: I was afraid he'd catch cold, get a fever and have to stay in bed till who knows when. How is it possible — I thought — that a man so small, so delicate, has fought all his life with Aunt Vittoria's malice? And it seemed even more implausible that he had confronted and kicked out the married delinquent with three children who intended to be the ruin of his sister. I asked Angela:

"If Ida fell in love with a delinquent who was married with three children, what would you, the older sister, do?"

Angela answered without hesitation:

"I'd tell Papa."

But Ida didn't like that answer, she said to her sister:

"You're a snitch, and Papa says a snitch is

the worst thing there is."

Angela, miffed, answered:

"I'm not a snitch, I'd only do it for your own good."

"So if Angela is in love with a delinquent who's married with three children, you won't tell your father?"

Ida, as an inveterate reader of novels, thought about it and said:

"I would tell him only if the delinquent is ugly and mean."

There, I thought, ugliness and meanness are more important than anything else. And one afternoon when my father was out at a meeting I cautiously returned to the subject with my mother:

"You said we would see Aunt Vittoria."

"I said you had to talk about it with your father."

"I thought you talked to him."

"He's very busy right now."

"Let's go the two of us."

"Better if he takes care of it. And then it's almost the end of the school year, you have to study."

"You two don't want to take me. You've already decided not to."

My mother assumed a tone similar to the one she'd used until a few years earlier when she wanted to be left alone and would propose some game that I could play by myself.

"Here's what we'll do: you know Via Miraglia?"

"No."

"And Via della Stadera?"

"No."

"And the Pianto cemetery?"

"No."

"And Poggioreale?"

"No."

"And Via Nazionale?"

"No."

"And Arenaccia?"

"No."

"And the whole area that's called the Industrial Zone?"

"No, Mamma, no."

"Well, you have to learn, this is your city. Now I'll give you the map, and after you've done your homework you study the route. If it's so urgent for you, one of these days you can go by yourself, to see Aunt Vittoria."

That last phrase confused me, maybe it hurt me. My parents wouldn't even send me by myself to buy bread down the street. And when I was supposed to meet Angela and Ida, my father or, more often, my mother drove me to Mariano and Costanza's house and then came to pick me up. Now, suddenly, they were prepared to let me go to unknown places where they themselves went unwillingly? No no, they were simply tired of my complaining, they considered unimportant what to me was urgent, in other words they didn't take me seriously. Maybe at that moment something somewhere in my body broke, maybe that's where I should locate the end of my childhood. I felt as if I were a container of granules that were imperceptibly leaking out of me through a tiny crack. And I had no doubt that my mother had already talked to my father and, in agreement with him, was preparing to separate me from them and them from me, to explain to me that I had to deal with my unreasonable, perverse behavior by myself. If I looked closely behind her kind yet weary tone, she had just said: you're starting to annoy me, you're making my life difficult, you don't study, your teachers complain, and you won't stop this business about Aunt Vittoria, ah, what a fuss, Giovanna, how can I convince you that your father's remark was affectionate, that's enough now, go and play with the atlas and don't bother me anymore.

Now, whether that was the truth or not, it was my first experience of privation. I felt the painful void that usually opens up when something we thought we could never be separated from is suddenly taken away from us. I said nothing. And when she added: close the door, please, I left the room.

I stood for a while in front of the closed door, dazed, waiting for her to give me the street atlas. She didn't, and so I retreated almost on tiptoe to my room to study. But, naturally, I didn't open a book; my head began to pound out, as if on a keyboard, plans that until a moment before had been inconceivable. There's no need for my mother to give me the map, I'll get it, I'll study it, and I'll walk to Aunt Vittoria's. I'll walk for days, for months. How that idea seduced me. Sun, heat, rain, wind, cold, and I who was walking and walking, through countless dangers, until I met my own future as an ugly, faithless woman. I'll do it. Most of those unknown street names that my mother had listed had stayed in my mind, I could immediately find at least one of them. Pianto especially went around and around in my head. A cemetery whose name meant weeping must be a very sad place, and so my aunt lived in an area where one felt pain or perhaps inflicted it. A street of torments, a stairway, thorn bushes that scratched your legs, wild, mud-spattered stray dogs with enormous drooling jaws. I thought of looking for that place in the street atlas, and I went to the hall, where the telephone was. I tried to pull out the atlas, which was squeezed between massive telephone books. But as I did so I noticed on top of the pile the address book in which my parents had written down the numbers they habitually used. How could I not have thought of that. Probably Aunt Vittoria's number was in the address book, and if it was there, why wait for my parents to call her? I could do it myself. I took the book, went to the letter "V," found no Vittoria. So I thought: she has my last name, my father's last name, Trada, and I immediately looked at the "T"s; there it was, Trada Vittoria. The slightly faded handwriting was my father's, the name appeared amid many others, like a stranger.

For seconds my pulse raced, I was exultant, I seemed to be facing the entrance to a secret passage that would carry me to her without other obstacles. I thought: I'll phone her. Right away. I'll say: I'm your niece Giovanna, I need to meet you. Maybe she'll come get me herself. We'll set a day, a time, and meet here at the house, or down at Piazza Vanvitelli. I made sure that my mother's door was closed, I went back to the telephone, I picked up the receiver. But just as I finished dialing the number and the phone was ringing, I got scared. It was, if I thought about it, after the photographs, the first concrete initiative I'd taken. That I was taking. I have to ask, if not my mother, my father, one of them has to give me permission. Prudence, prudence, prudence. But I had hesitated too long, a thick voice like that of one of the smokers who came to our house for long meetings said: hello. She said it with such determination, in a tone so rude, with a Neapolitan accent so aggressive, that that "hello" was enough to terrorize me and I hung up. I was barely in time. I heard the key turning in the lock, my father was home.

10.

I moved a few steps away from the telephone just as he came in, after setting the dripping umbrella on the landing, after carefully wiping the soles of his shoes on the mat. He greeted me but uneasily, without the usual cheerfulness, in fact cursing the bad weather. Only after taking off his raincoat did he concern himself with me.

"What are you up to?"

"Nothing."

"Mamma?"

"She's working."

"Did you do your homework?"

"Yes."

"Is there anything you didn't understand and want me to explain?"

When he stopped next to the telephone to listen to the answering machine, as he usually did, I realized that I had left the address book open to the letter "T." He saw it, he ran a finger over it, closed it, stopped listening to the messages. I hoped he would resort to some joking remark, which would have reassured me. Instead, he caressed my head with the tips of his fingers and went to my mother. Contrary to his usual practice, he closed the door behind him carefully.

I waited, listening to them discuss in low voices, a hum with sudden peaks of single syllables: you, no, but. I went back to my room, but I left the door open, I hoped they weren't fighting. At least ten minutes passed, finally I heard my father's footsteps again in the hall, but not in the direction of my room. He went to his, where there was another telephone, and I heard him telephoning in a low voice, a few indistinguishable words and long pauses. I thought — I hoped — that he had serious problems with Mariano, that he must be discussing the usual things that were important to him, words I'd heard forever, like politics, value, Marxism, crisis, state. When the phone call ended, I heard him in the hall again, but this time he came to my room. In general he would go through innumerable ironic formalities before entering: may I come in, where can I sit, am I bothering you, sorry, but on that occasion he sat down on the bed and without preliminaries said in his coldest voice:

"Your mother has explained to you that I wasn't serious, I didn't mean to hurt you, you don't resemble my sister in the least."

I immediately started crying again, I stammered: it's not that, Papa, I know, I believe you, but. He didn't seem moved by my tears, he interrupted me, saying:

"You don't have to explain. It's my fault, not yours, it's up to me to fix it. I just telephoned your aunt — Sunday I'll take you to see her. All right?"

I sobbed:

"If you don't want to, let's not go."

"Of course I don't want to, but you do and we'll go. I'll drop you off at her house, you'll stay as long as you want, I'll wait outside in the car."

I tried to calm down, I stifled my tears.

"You're sure?"

"Yes."

We were quiet for a moment, then he made an effort to smile at me, he dried my tears with his fingers. But he couldn't do it unaffectedly, he slid into one of his long, agitated speeches, mixing high and low tones. Remember this, Giovanna, he said. Your aunt likes to hurt me. I've tried in every way to reason with her, I helped her, I encouraged her, I gave her as much money as I could. It was useless, she's taken every word of mine as bullying, every kind of help she has considered a wrong. She's proud, she's ungrateful, she's cruel. So I have to tell you this: she will try to take your affection away from me, she'll use you to wound me. She's already used our parents that way, our brothers and sisters, our aunts and uncles and cousins. Because of her, nobody in our family loves me. And you'll see that she'll try to get you, too. That possibility — he said, tense as I had almost never seen him — is intolerable to me. And he begged me — he really begged me, he joined his hands and waved them back and forth — to calm my anxieties, anxieties with no basis, but not to listen to her, to put wax in my ears like Odysseus.

I hugged him tight, as I hadn't in the past two years, ever since I'd wanted to feel grown up. But to my surprise, to my annoyance, I smelled on him an odor that didn't seem like his, an odor I wasn't used to. It gave me a sense of estrangement that provoked suffering mixed incongruously with satisfaction. It was clear to me that though until that moment I had hoped that his protection would last forever, now, instead, I felt pleasure at the idea that he was becoming a stranger. I was euphoric, as if the possibility of evil — what he and my mother in their couple's language claimed to call Vittoria — gave me an unexpected exuberance.

11.

I pushed that feeling away, I couldn't bear the guilt. I counted the days that separated me from Sunday. My mother was attentive, she wanted to help me get as much homework done for Monday as possible so that I could face the encounter without the worry of having to study. And she didn't confine herself to that. One afternoon she came into my room with the street atlas, sat down beside me, showed me Via San Giacomo dei Capri and, page by page, the whole journey to Aunt Vittoria's house. She wanted me to understand that she loved me and that she, like my father, only wanted me to be happy.

But I wasn't satisfied with that small topographical lesson and in the days that followed devoted myself secretly to maps of the city. I moved with my index finger along San Giacomo dei Capri, reached Piazza Medaglie d'Oro, descended by Via Suarez and Via Salvator Rosa, reached Museo, traversed all of Via Foria to Piazza Carlo III, turned onto Corso Garibaldi, took Via Casanova, reached Piazza Nazionale, turned onto Via Poggioreale, then Via della Stadera, and, at the Pianto cemetery, slid along Via Miraglia, Via del Macello, Via del Pascone and so on, with my finger veering into the Industrial Zone, the color of scorched earth. All those street names, and others, became in those hours a silent mania. I learned them by heart as if for school, but not unwillingly, and I waited for Sunday with increasing agitation. If my father didn't change his mind, I would finally meet Aunt Vittoria.

But I hadn't reckoned with the tangle of my feelings. As the days laboriously passed, I surprised myself by hoping — especially at night, in bed — that for some reason the visit would be postponed. I began to wonder why I had forced my parents in that way, why I had wanted to make them unhappy, why I hadn't considered their worries important. Since all the answers were vague, the yearning began to diminish, and meeting Aunt Vittoria soon seemed to me a request both extravagant and pointless. What use would it be to know in advance the physical and moral form that I would likely assume. I wouldn't be able to get rid of the face or the chest anyway, and maybe I wouldn't even want to, I would still be me, a melancholy me, an unfortunate me, but me. That wish to know my aunt should probably be inserted into the category of small challenges. In the end, wasn't it ultimately just another way to test my parents' patience, as I did when we went to a restaurant with Mariano and Costanza and I always ended up ordering, with the attitude of an experienced woman, and charming little smiles addressed mainly to Costanza, what my mother had advised me not to order because it cost too much. I then became even more unhappy with myself, maybe this time I had overdone it. The words my mother had used when she told me about her sister-in-law's hatreds returned to mind, I thought again of my father's worried speech. In the dark, their aversion for that woman was added to the fear instilled by her voice on the telephone, that fierce "hello" with its dialectal cadence. So Saturday night I said to my mother: I don't feel like going anymore, this morning I got a lot of homework for Monday. But she answered: now the appointment is set, you don't know how angry your aunt will be if you don't go, she'd blame your father. And since I wasn't convinced, she said that I had already fantasized too much, and even if I backed off now, the next day I would have second thoughts and we'd be right where we started. She concluded, with a smile: go and see what and who Aunt Vittoria is, so you'll do all you can not to be like her.

After days of rain, Sunday was beautiful, with a blue sky and occasional little white clouds. My father made an effort to return to our usual lighthearted relationship, but when he started the car he became silent. He hated the ring road and got off it quickly. He said he preferred the old streets, and as we made our way into another city, made up of rows of small bleak apartment buildings, faded walls, industrial warehouses and sheds, gashes of green overflowing with garbage of every sort, deep puddles filled by the recent rain, putrid air, he became increasingly somber. But then he seemed to decide that he couldn't leave me in silence, as if he had forgotten about me, and for the first time mentioned his origins. I was born and grew up in this neighborhood here — he said with a broad gesture that embraced, beyond the windshield, walls of tufa, gray, yellow, and pink apartment buildings — my family was poor, we didn't even have two cents to rub together. Then he drove into an even bleaker neighborhood, stopped, sighed with irritation, pointed to a brick building whose façade was missing large patches of plaster. Here's where I lived, he said, and where Aunt Vittoria still lives. I looked at him, frightened; he noticed.

"What's wrong?"

"Don't go."

"I won't move."

"What if she keeps me?"

"When you're tired, you'll say: I have to go now."

"What if she doesn't let me go?"

"I'll come and get you."

"No, don't, I'll come."

"All right."

I got out of the car, went through the entrance. There was a strong odor of garbage mixed with the aroma of Sunday sauces. I didn't see an elevator. I climbed up uneven, broken steps, beside walls showing broad white wounds, one so deep it seemed like a hole dug out to hide something. I avoided deciphering obscene sayings and drawings. I had other urgencies. My father had been a child and a boy in this building? I counted the floors, on the third I stopped, there were three doors. The one on my right was the only one that displayed a surname, and pasted to the wood was a strip of paper on which was written in pen: Trada. I rang the bell, held my breath. Nothing. I counted slowly to forty: my father had told me some years earlier that whenever you're in a state of uncertainty you should do that. When I got to forty-one I rang again, the second electrical charge seemed exaggeratedly loud. A shout in dialect reached me, an explosion of hoarse sounds, and goddammit, what's the hurry, I'm coming. Then decisive steps, a key that turned four times in the lock. The door opened, a woman dressed all in blue appeared, tall, with a great mass of very black hair arranged on her neck, as thin as a post, and yet with broad shoulders and a large chest. She held a lighted cigarette between her fingers, she coughed and said, moving back and forth between Italian and dialect:

"What's the matter, you're sick, you have

to pee?"

"No."

"So why'd you ring twice?"

I murmured:

"I'm Giovanna, aunt."

"I know you're Giovanna, but if you call me aunt again, you'd better turn right around and get out of here."

I nodded yes, I was frightened. I looked for a few seconds at her face, without makeup, then stared at the floor. Vittoria seemed to me to have a beauty so unbearable that to consider her ugly became a necessity.

II

II

1.

I learned to lie to my parents more and more. At first I didn't tell real lies, but since I wasn't strong enough to oppose their always well-ordered world, I pretended to accept it while at the same time I cut out for myself a narrow path that I could abandon in a hurry if they merely darkened. I behaved like that especially with my father, even though his every word had in my eyes a dazzling authority, and it was exhausting and painful to try to deceive him.

It was he who, even more than my mother, hammered into my head that you shouldn't ever lie. But after that visit to Vittoria lying seemed unavoidable. As soon as I came out of the entrance door I decided to pretend that I was relieved, and I ran to the car as if I had escaped a danger. When I got in, my father started the car, glancing bitterly at the building of his childhood, and pulled away too suddenly, which caused him instinctively to extend an arm to keep me from hitting my forehead against the windshield. He waited for me to say something soothing, and a part of me wanted nothing more, I suffered seeing him upset; yet I was obliged to be silent, I was afraid that even a wrong word would make him angry. After a few minutes, keeping one eye on the street, one on me, he asked how it had gone. I said that my aunt had questioned me about school, had offered me a glass of water, had wanted to know if I had friends, had had me tell her about Angela and Ida.

"That's it?"

"Yes."

"Did she ask about me?"

"No."

"Never?"

"Never."

"About your mother?"

"Not her, either."

"For a whole hour you talked only about your friends?"

"Also about school."

"What was that music?"

"What music?"

"Music at a very high volume."

"I didn't hear any music."

"Was she nice?"

"A little rude."

70

"Did she say nasty things?"

"No, but she's not very nice."

"I warned you."

"Yes."

"Is your curiosity satisfied now? Do you realize she doesn't look like you at all?"

"Yes."

"Come here, give me a kiss, you're beautiful. Do you forgive me for the stupid thing I said?"

I said I had never been mad at him and let him give me a kiss on the cheek even though he was driving. But immediately afterward I pushed him away laughing, I protested: you scratched me with your beard. Although I had no desire for our games, I hoped we would start joking around and he would forget about Vittoria. Instead he replied: think of how your aunt scratches with her mustache, and what immediately came to mind was not the faint dark down on Vittoria's lip but the down on mine. I said softly:

"She doesn't have a mustache."

"She does."

"No."

"All right, she doesn't. The last thing we need is for you to get an urge to go back and see if she has a mustache."

71

I said seriously:

"I don't want to see her again."

2.

That wasn't a lie, either, I was scared to see
Vittoria again. But already as I uttered that
sentence I knew on what day, at what hour,
in what place I would see her again. In fact,
I hadn't parted from her, I had her every
word in my head, every gesture, every
expression of her face, and they didn't seem
things that had just happened, it all seemed
to be still happening. My father kept talking, to show me how much he loved me,
while I saw and heard his sister, I hear and
see her even now. I see her when she appeared before me dressed in sky blue, I see
her when she said to me in that rough
dialect: close the door, and had already
turned her back, as if all I could do was follow her. In Vittoria's voice, or perhaps in
her whole body, there was an impatience
without filters that hit me in a flash, as
when, holding a match, I turned on the gas
and felt on my hand the flame shooting out
of the burner. I closed the door behind me,
I followed her as if she had me on a leash.

We took a few steps into a place that
smelled of smoke, without windows, the

only light coming from an open door. Her figure moved out of sight beyond the door, I followed her into a small kitchen whose extreme orderliness struck me immediately, along with the smell of cigarette butts and filth.

"You want some orange juice?"

"I don't want to be a bother."

"You want it or not?"

"Yes, thank you."

She ordered me to a chair, changed her mind, saying it was broken, ordered me to another. Then, to my surprise, she didn't take out of the refrigerator — a yellowish-white refrigerator — an orange drink in a can or a bottle, as I expected, but picked out from a basket a couple of oranges, cut them, and began to squeeze them into a glass, without a squeezer, by hand, with the help of a fork. Without looking at me she said:

"You didn't wear the bracelet."

I got nervous:

"What bracelet?"

"The one I gave you when you were born."

As far as I could remember, I had never had a bracelet. But I sensed that for her it was an important object and my not having worn it could be an affront. I said:

"Maybe my mother had me wear it when

73

I was little, until I was one or two, then I grew up and it didn't fit anymore."

She turned to look at me, I showed her my wrist to prove that it was too big for a newborn's bracelet, and to my surprise she burst out laughing. She had a big mouth with big teeth, and when she laughed her gums showed. She said:

"You're smart."

"I told the truth."

"Do I scare you?"

"A little."

"It's good to be afraid. You need to be afraid even when there's no need, it keeps you alert."

She put the glass down in front of me; juice had dripped down the outside, while bits of pulp and white seeds floated on the bright orange surface. I looked at her hair, which was carefully combed, I had seen hairdos of the type in old films on television and in photos of my mother as a girl, a friend of hers wore her hair like that. Vittoria had very thick eyebrows, licorice sticks, black lines under her large forehead and above the deep cavities where she hid her eyes. Drink up, she said. I immediately took the glass in order not to upset her, but drinking repulsed me, I had seen the juice run across her palm, and, besides, with my mother I would have insisted that she take out pulp and seeds. Drink up, she repeated, it's good for you. I took a gulp while she sat on the chair that a few minutes earlier she had considered not to be solid. She praised me, but keeping her brusque tone: yes, you're smart, you immediately found an excuse to protect your parents, good. But she explained to me that I was off track, she hadn't given me a baby bracelet, she had given me a big girl's bracelet, a bracelet she was very fond of. Because, she emphasized, I am not like your father, who is attached to money, attached to things; I don't give a damn about objects, I love people, and when you were born I thought: I'll give it to the child, she'll wear it when she grows up, I wrote that in the card to your parents — give it to her when she's grown up — and I left it all in your mailbox, imagine me coming up there, your father and mother are animals, they would have thrown me out.

I said:

"Maybe thieves stole it, you shouldn't have left it in the mailbox."

She shook her head, her black eyes sparkled:

"What thieves? What are you talking about, if you don't know anything. Drink your orange juice. Does your mother

75

squeeze oranges for you?"

I nodded yes, but she didn't acknowledge it. She talked about how good orange juice is, and I noticed the extreme mobility of her face. She could smooth in a flash the folds between nose and mouth that made her grim (precisely that: grim), and the face that until a second earlier had seemed long under the high cheekbones — a gray canvas stretched tight between temples and jaw — colored, softened. My mamma, rest her soul, she said, when it was my saint's day brought me hot chocolate in bed, she made it into a cream, it was frothy as if she had blown into it. Do they make you hot chocolate on your saint's day? I was tempted to say yes, even though a saint's day had never been celebrated in my house, and no one had ever brought me hot chocolate in bed. But I was afraid she would figure it out, so I made a sign to indicate no. She shook her head, unhappy:

"Your father and mother don't respect traditions, they think they're someone, they don't lower themselves to make hot chocolate."

"My father makes caffe latte."

"Your father is a jerk, imagine him trying to make caffe latte. Your grandmother knew how to make caffe latte. And she put in two spoonfuls of a beaten egg. Did he tell you how we had coffee, milk, and zabaglione when we were children?"

"No."

"You see? Your father is like that. He's the only one who does good things, he can't accept that others do, too. And if you tell him it's not true, he erases you."

She shook her head unhappily, she spoke in a distant tone, but without coldness. He erased my Enzo, she said, the person I was most fond of. Your father erases everything that might be better than him, he's always done that, he was already doing it as a child. He thinks he's smart, but he's never been smart: *I* am smart, he's only clever. He can become by instinct a person you can no longer do without. When I was a child, the sun stopped shining if he wasn't there. I thought that if I didn't behave the way he wanted, he would leave me all alone and I'd die. So he made me do everything he wanted, he decided what was good and what was bad, for me. Just to give you one example, I was born with music in my body, I wanted to be a dancer. I knew that was my destiny, and only he would have been able to persuade our parents to give me permission. But for your father a dancer was bad, and he wouldn't let me do it. For

77

him, only if you always show up with a book in your hand do you deserve to stay on the face of the earth, for him if you haven't gone to school you're nobody. He said to me: what do you mean dancer, Vittò, you don't know what a dancer is, go back to studying and shut up. At that time he was making some money with private lessons, so he could have paid for dancing school for me instead of always and only buying books for himself. He didn't do it, he liked to take significance away from everything and everybody, except himself and his things. With my Enzo — my aunt concluded suddenly — first he let him think they were friends and then he took away his soul, he tore it out and cut it into tiny pieces.

She said words like that but more vulgar, with a familiarity that disoriented me. In no time at all her face cleared then clouded, troubled by diverse feelings: remorse, aversion, rage, melancholy. She covered my father with obscenities I'd never heard. But when she mentioned that Enzo, she broke off because of the emotion, and, head down, dramatically hiding her eyes with one hand, she hurried out of the kitchen.

I didn't move, I was in a state. I took advantage of her absence to spit into the glass the orange seeds I'd held in my mouth.

A minute went by, two, I was ashamed that I hadn't reacted when she insulted my father. I have to tell her it's not right to talk like that about someone everybody respects, I thought. Meanwhile some music began softly and in a few seconds exploded at high volume. She shouted to me: come on, Gianni, what are you doing, sleeping? I jumped up, went from the kitchen toward the dark entrance. A few steps and I was in a small room with an old armchair, an accordion left on the floor in a corner, a table with a television, and a stool with the record player on it. Vittoria was standing in front of the window, looking out. From there she could surely see the car in which my father was waiting for me. In fact she said, without turning, alluding to the music: he's got to hear that singer, so he'll remember. I realized she was moving her body rhythmically, small movements of feet, hips, shoulders. I stared at her back, bewildered.

"The first time I saw Enzo was at a dance party and we danced this dance," I heard her say.

"How long ago?"

"Seventeen years on May 23rd."

"A long time has gone by."

"Not even a minute has gone by."

"Did you love him?"

She turned.

"Your father hasn't told you anything?"

I hesitated, she was as if frozen, for the first time she seemed older than my parents, even though I knew she was a few years younger.

"I know only that he was married and had three children."

"Nothing else? He didn't say he was a bad person?"

I hesitated.

"A little bad."

"And then?"

"A delinquent."

She burst out:

"The bad person is your father, he's the delinquent. Enzo was a police sergeant and he was even nice to the criminals, on Sunday he always went to Mass. Imagine, I didn't believe in God, your father had convinced me that he doesn't exist. But as soon as I saw Enzo I changed my mind. A man more good and more just and more sensitive has never existed on the face of the earth. Such a lovely voice he had, and he sang so well, he taught me to play the accordion. Before him, men made me vomit, after him anyone who came near me I drove away in disgust. Everything your parents told you is false."

I looked uneasily at the floor, I didn't

answer. She pressed me:

"You don't believe it, eh?"

"I don't know."

"You don't know because you believe more in lies than in the truth. Giannì, you're not growing up well. Look how ridiculous you are, all in pink, pink shoes, pink jacket, pink barrette. I bet you don't even know how to dance."

"My friends and I practice whenever we see each other."

"What are your friends' names?"

"Angela and Ida."

"And are they like you?"

"Yes."

She scowled with disapproval and leaned over to start the record again.

"Do you know how to do this dance?"

"It's an old dance."

She made a sudden movement, grabbed me by the waist, held me tight. Her large bosom gave off an odor of pine needles in the sun.

"Climb on my feet."

"I'll hurt you."

"Come on."

I climbed on her feet, and she whirled me around the room with great precision and elegance, until the music ended. She stopped but didn't let go of me, she held me tight, and said:

"Tell your father that I made you dance the same dance that I danced for the first time with Enzo. Tell him that, word for word."

"O.K."

"And now that's enough."

She pushed me away forcefully, and, suddenly deprived of her warmth, I muffled a cry, as if I'd felt a sharp pain somewhere but was ashamed to show myself weak. It seemed wonderful that after that dance with Enzo she hadn't liked anyone else. And I thought she must have preserved every detail of her unique love, so that maybe, dancing with me, she had relived it moment by moment in her mind. I thought it was thrilling, I wanted to love, too, immediately, in that absolute way. Surely she had a memory of Enzo so intense that her bony organism, her chest, her breath had transmitted a little love into my stomach. I said softly, dazed:

"What was Enzo like, do you have a picture?"

Her eyes shone:

"Good, I'm glad you want to see him. Let's make a date for May 23rd and we'll go: he's in the cemetery."

3.

In the days that followed, my mother tried delicately to carry out the mission my father must have entrusted to her: to find out if the encounter with Vittoria had succeeded in healing the involuntary wound that they themselves had inflicted. This kept me constantly alert. I didn't want to show either of them that I hadn't disliked Vittoria. So I forced myself to hide the fact that, although I continued to believe in their version of things, I also believed a little in my aunt's. I carefully avoided saying that Vittoria's face, to my great surprise, had seemed so vividly insolent that it was very ugly and very beautiful at the same time, and so now I was hovering between the two superlatives, puzzled. Mainly I hoped that I wouldn't give away by some uncontrollable sign or other — a flash in the eyes, a blush — the appointment in May. But I had no experience as a deceiver, I was a well-brought-up child, and I felt my way blindly, sometimes answering my mother's questions with excessive prudence, sometimes taking things too lightly and in the end talking recklessly.

I made a mistake that very Sunday, in the evening, when she asked me: "How did your aunt seem to you?"

"Old."

"She's five years younger than me."

"You look like her daughter."

"Don't make fun of me."

"It's true, Mamma. You and she are very far apart."

"About that there's no question. Vittoria and I were never friends, even if I did all I could to love her. It's hard to have a good relationship with her."

"I noticed."

"Did she say nasty things?"

"She was testy."

"And then?"

"Then she got a little angry because I didn't wear the bracelet she gave me when I was born."

I said it and immediately regretted it. But anyway it had happened, I felt myself blush, and immediately tried to figure out if mentioning the jewelry had made her uneasy. My mother reacted in a completely natural way.

"A bracelet for a newborn?"

"A bracelet for an older girl."

"That she supposedly gave to you?"

"Yes."

"I don't think so. Aunt Vittoria never gave us anything, not even a flower. But if it interests you, I'll ask your father."

That upset me. Now my mother would report the story to him, and he would say: so it's not true that they talked only about school, about Ida and Angela, they also talked about other things, of many things that Giovanna wants to hide from us. How stupid I'd been. I said confusedly that I didn't care about the bracelet and added in a tone of disgust, Aunt Vittoria doesn't wear makeup, doesn't wax her facial hair, has eyebrows this thick, and when I saw her she wasn't wearing earrings or even a necklace; so if she ever gave me a bracelet it was probably very ugly. But I knew that any dismissive remark was now pointless: from here on, whatever I said, my mother would talk to my father and would report to me not her true response but the one they had agreed on.

I didn't sleep well, at school I was often scolded because I was distracted. The bracelet came up again when I was sure that my parents had forgotten about it.

"Your father doesn't know anything about it, either."

"About what?"

"The bracelet Aunt Vittoria says she gave you."

"I think it's a lie."

"That's for certain. Anyway, if you want

to wear one, look through my things."

I really did go and rummage through her jewelry, even if I knew it by heart — I had played with it since I was three or four. The objects didn't have much value, especially the two bracelets she had: one gold-plated with little angel charms, the other silver with blue leaves and pearls. As a child I loved the first and ignored the second. But lately I'd grown to really like the one with the blue leaves, even Costanza had once praised its craftsmanship. So, to let it be understood that I wasn't interested in Vittoria's gift, I began to wear the silver bracelet at home, at school, and when I saw Angela and Ida.

"It's so pretty," Ida exclaimed once.

"It's my mother's. But she said I can wear it when I want."

"My mother doesn't let us wear her jewelry," said Angela.

"What about that?" I asked, indicating a gold necklace she was wearing.

"It's a present from our grandmother."

"Mine," said Ida, "I got from a cousin of our father's."

They often spoke of generous relatives, some of whom they were very fond of. I had had only the nice grandparents in Museo, but they were dead and I had a hard time remembering them, so I had often envied

Angela and Ida their relatives. But now that I had established a relationship with Aunt Vittoria it occurred to me to say:

"My aunt gave me a bracelet much nicer than this."

"Why don't you ever wear it?"

"It's too precious, my mother doesn't want me to."

"Show it to us."

"Yes, sometime when my mother's out. Do they make you hot chocolate?"

"My father has let me taste the wine," said Angela.

"Me, too," said Ida.

I explained proudly:

"My grandmother made me hot chocolate when I was little and even until right before she died: not normal chocolate, my grand-mother's was all frothy, really good."

I had never lied to Angela and Ida, that was the first time. I discovered that lying to my parents made me anxious, while lying to Angela and Ida was fun. They had always had toys more exciting than mine, clothes more colorful, family stories more surprising. Their mother, Costanza, who came from a family of goldsmiths from Toledo, had boxes full of jewelry, all of it valuable, countless gold and pearl necklaces, earrings, and piles of bracelets and bangles, a couple that she wouldn't let them touch, and one that she was extremely fond of and wore often, but for the rest — for the rest she had always let them play with it, and I was allowed to play with it, too. So as soon as Angela stopped being interested in hot chocolate — that is, almost immediately — and wanted some more details about the very precious piece of jewelry from Aunt Vittoria, I described it in great detail. It's pure gold with rubies and emeralds, it sparkles — I said — like the jewelry you see in movies and on television. And just as I was talking about the truth of that bracelet, I couldn't resist and also claimed that once I had looked at myself in the mirror without anything on, only some earrings and a necklace of my mother's, and the marvelous bracelet. Angela looked at me enchanted, Ida asked if I had at least left my underpants on. I said no, and the lie gave me such relief that I imagined if I really had done it I would have tasted a moment of absolute happiness.

So one afternoon, to prove that, I transformed the lie into reality. I undressed, put on some of my mother's jewelry, looked in the mirror. But it was a painful sight, I saw myself as a small, faded green plant, debilitated by too much sun, sad. Even though I had made myself up carefully, what an insignificant face I had, the lipstick was an ugly red stain on a face that looked like the gray bottom of a frying pan. I tried to understand, now that I had met Vittoria, if there really were points of contact between us, but the more I persisted the more useless it was. She was an old woman — at least in the eyes of a thirteen-year-old — I a young girl: too much disproportion between the bodies, too great an interval of time between my face and hers. And where in me was that energy of hers, the warmth that lit up her eyes? If I was really starting to look like Vittoria, my face lacked the essential, her force. So on the wave of that thought, while I was comparing her eyebrows with mine, her forehead with mine, I realized that I wished she really had given me a bracelet, and I felt that if I had it now and wore it, I would feel more powerful.

That idea immediately infused me with a cheering warmth, as if my depressed body had suddenly found the right medicine. Certain words that Vittoria had said before we parted, walking me to the door, came to mind. Your father — she was angry — has deprived you of a big family, of all of us, grandparents, aunts and uncles, cousins, because we're not intelligent and educated like him; he cut us off with a hatchet, he forced you to grow up in isolation, for fear we'd ruin you. She spewed bitterness, and yet those words now brought me relief, I repeated them in my mind. They affirmed the existence of a strong and positive bond, they demanded it. My aunt hadn't said: you have my face or at least you look something like me; my aunt had said: you don't belong only to your father and mother, you're mine, too, you belong to the whole family that he came from, and anyone who belongs to us is never alone, is charged with energy. Wasn't it because of those words that, after some hesitation, I had promised her that on May 23rd I would skip school and go with her to the cemetery? Now at the idea that, at nine in the morning on that day, she would wait for me in Piazza Medaglie d'Oro beside her old dark-green Fiat 500 — so she had told me imperatively, saying good-bye — I began to cry, to laugh, to make terrible faces in the mirror.

4.

Every morning the three of us went to school, my parents to teach, I to learn. My mother usually got up first: she needed time to make breakfast, to dress and put on her makeup. My father instead got up only when breakfast was ready, because as soon as he opened his eyes he started reading, and writing in his notebooks, and he continued even in the bathroom. I got up last, although — ever since that story began — I'd demanded to do as my mother did: wash my hair frequently, put on makeup, choose with care everything I wore. The result was that both of them were continuously rushing me: Giovanna, how far along are you; Giovanna, you'll be late and we'll be late. And meanwhile they rushed each other. My father pressed: Nella, hurry, I need the bathroom, my mother answered calmly, it's been free for half an hour, you haven't gone yet? But those were not the mornings I preferred. I loved the days when my father had to be at school for the first period and my mother for the second or third or, even better, when she had the day free. Then she simply made breakfast, from time to time called, Giovanna, hurry up, devoted herself serenely to her many domestic duties and the stories she corrected and often rewrote. On those days, everything was easier for me: my mother washed last and I had more time in the bathroom; my father was always late and, apart from the usual jokes with which he kept me laughing, left in a hurry, dropped me at school, and drove off without the watchful lingering of my mother, as if I were grown up and could face the city by myself. I did some calculations and discovered with relief that the morning of the 23rd was of this second type: it would be my father's turn to take me to school. The night before I got out my clothes for the next day (I eliminated pink), something that my mother always urged me to do but that I never did. And I woke up very early in the morning, in a nervous state. I ran to the bathroom, made myself up very carefully, put on, after some hesitation, the bracelet with blue leaves and pearls, appeared in the kitchen when my mother had barely got up. How in the world are you already up, she asked. I don't want to be late, I said, I have Italian homework, and, seeing that I was agitated, she went to hurry my father.

Breakfast went smoothly, they joked with each other as if I weren't there and they could gossip about me freely. They said that if I wasn't sleeping well and couldn't wait to get to school, surely I was in love, I gave them little smiles that said neither yes nor no. Then my father disappeared into the bathroom, and this time it was I who shouted to him to hurry up. He — I have to say — didn't waste time, except when he didn't find clean socks or forgot books he needed and ran back into his study. In short, I remember that it was exactly seven-twenty, my father was at the end of the hall with his bag loaded, I had just given the obligatory kiss to my mother, when the doorbell rang violently.

It was surprising that someone should ring at that hour. My mother quickly shut herself in the bathroom with a vexed expression, and said: open the door, see who it is. I opened it, and found myself facing Vittoria.

"Hi," she said, "lucky you're ready, come on, we'll be late."

I felt my heart burst in my breast. My mother saw her sister-in-law in the frame of the door and cried — yes, it was really a cry — Andrea, come here, it's your sister. At the sight of Vittoria — his eyes widening in surprise, his mouth incredulous — he exclaimed: what are you doing here? Fearful of what would happen in a moment, in a minute, I felt weak, I was covered with sweat, I didn't know what to say to my aunt, I didn't know how to explain to my parents, I thought I was dying. But it was all over in a moment and in a way as surprising as it was clarifying.

Vittoria said in dialect:

"I'm here to get Giannina, it's seventeen

years today since I met Enzo."

She added nothing else, as if my parents should understand immediately the good reasons for her appearance and were obliged to let me go without protesting. My mother, however, objected in Italian.

"Giovanna has to go to school."

My father, instead, without addressing either his wife or his sister, asked me in his cold tone:

"Did you know about this?"

I stood with my head down staring at the floor and he insisted, without changing his tone:

"Did you have a date, do you want to go with your aunt?" My mother said slowly:

"Are you serious, Andrea, of course she wants to go, of course they had a date, otherwise your sister wouldn't be here."

He said only: if that's the case, go, and with his fingertips signaled to his sister to move aside. Vittoria moved aside — she was a mask of impassivity set atop the yellow patch of a light dress — and my father, looking ostentatiously at his watch, ignored the elevator and took the stairs without saying goodbye, not even to me.

"When will you bring her back," my mother asked her sister-in-law.

"When she's tired."

They coldly negotiated the time and agreed on one-thirty. Vittoria held out her hand, I gave her mine as if I were a child, it was cold. She held me tight, maybe she was afraid I would escape and run home. Meanwhile, with her free hand she called the elevator under the eyes of my mother, who, standing in the doorway, couldn't bring herself to close the door.

A word more, a word less, that's how it went.

5.

Our second encounter left an even deeper impression than the first. Just to start with, I discovered that I had a space inside me that could swallow up every feeling in a very short time. The weight of the lie discovered, the disgrace of the betrayal, all the pain for the pain I had surely caused my parents lasted until the moment when, through the glass doors of the iron cage of the elevator, I saw my mother close the door of the apartment. But as soon as I was in the hall and then in Vittoria's car, sitting next to her as, immediately, she lighted a cigarette with trembling hands, something happened that very often occurred later in my life, sometimes bringing me relief, other times demoralizing me. The bond with known spaces, with secure affections, yielded to curiosity about what might happen. The proximity of that threatening and enveloping woman captivated me, and here I was, already observing her every move. Now she was driving a repugnant car that stank of smoke, not with my father's firm, decisive control or my mother's serenity but in a way that was either distracted or overanxious, made up of jerks, alarming screeches, abrupt braking, mistaken starts on account of which the engine almost always stalled and insults rained down from impatient drivers to which, with the cigarette between her fingers or her lips, she responded with obscenities that I had never heard uttered by a woman. In other words, my parents were relegated effortlessly to a corner, and the wrong I'd done them by making an arrangement with their enemy vanished from my mind. In the space of a few minutes I no longer considered myself guilty, I felt no worry even about how I would confront them in the afternoon, when all three of us returned to the house on Via San Giacomo dei Capri. Of course, anxiety continued to dig away at me. But the certainty that they would always love me no matter what, the helter-skelter motion of the little green car, the increasingly unknown city that we were crossing, and Vittoria's jumble of words forced me to an attention, to a tension, that functioned like an anesthetic.

We went up along the Doganella, parked after a violent quarrel with an illegal parking attendant who wanted money. My aunt bought red roses and white daisies, complained about the price, and once the bouquet was made changed her mind and obliged the flower seller to undo it and make two bunches. She said to me: I'll bring this one, you this one, he'll be pleased. She alluded naturally to her Enzo, and, from the moment we got in the car, despite the endless interruptions, she did nothing but talk about him with a sweetness that contrasted with her fierce manner of confronting the city. She continued to talk about him even as we went in among the burial niches and monumental tombs, old and new, along paths and stairs that always went down, as if we were in the upper-class neighborhoods of the dead and to find Enzo's tomb we had to descend. I was struck by the silence, by the gray of the rust-streaked niches, by the smell of rotting earth, by certain dark cross-shaped cracks in the marble that seemed to have been left for the breathing of those who no longer had breath.

Until that moment, I had never been in a cemetery. My father and mother had never taken me, nor did I know if they had ever been, certainly they didn't go on All Souls' Day. Vittoria realized this right away and took advantage of it to again fault my father. He's afraid, she said, he's always been like that, he's afraid of illness and death: all proud people, Giannì, all those who think they're something, pretend that death doesn't exist. Your father — when your grandmother may she rest in peace died — didn't even show up at the funeral. And he did the same with your grandfather, two minutes and he was gone, because he's a coward, he didn't want to see them dead so he wouldn't have to feel that he, too, would die.

I tried to respond, but prudently, that my father was very brave, and to defend him I recalled what he had once told me, and that is that the dead are objects that have broken, a television, the radio, the mixer, and the best thing is to remember them as they were when they were working, because the only acceptable tomb is memory. But she didn't like that answer, and since she didn't treat me like a child with whom words must be measured, she scolded me, said I was parroting my father's bullshit, your mother does that, too, and I, too, as a girl, did the same. But once she met Enzo, she had erased my father from her head. E-rased, she articulated and, finally stopping in front of a wall of niches, pointed to one low down that had a small fenced flower bed, a lighted lamp in the shape of a flame, and two pictures in oval frames. This is it, she said, we're here. Enzo is the one on the left, the other is his mother. But, instead of taking a solemn or remorseful attitude as I expected, she grew angry because some paper and dead flowers had been left a few steps away. She gave a long, unhappy sigh, handed me her flowers, said: wait here, don't move, in this shit place if you don't get mad nothing works, and left me.

I stood with the two bunches of flowers in my hand, staring at Enzo as he appeared in a black-and-white photo. He didn't look handsome and that disappointed me. He had a round face and was smiling, with white, wolf-like teeth. His nose was large, his eyes very lively, his forehead low and framed by wavy black hair. He must have been stupid, I thought, at my house a broad forehead — my mother, my father, I had one like that — was considered a sure sign of intelligence and noble sentiments, while a low forehead, my father said, was characteristic of imbeciles. But, I said to myself, eyes are meaningful, too (this my mother claimed): the more they sparkle, the smarter the person is. Enzo's eyes shot arrows of happiness, and so I was confused by a gaze that was in evident contradiction with the forehead.

In the silence of the cemetery, Vittoria's loud voice could be heard battling with someone, which worried me, I was afraid they would beat her or have her arrested, and on my own I wouldn't have known how to get out of that place, which all seemed the same, with its rustling sounds, small birds, rotting flowers. But she returned quickly with a mopey old man who opened up a metal-framed chair with striped fabric and right away started sweeping the path. She watched him with a hostile expression and asked me:

"What do you say about Enzo? He's handsome, isn't he handsome?"

"He's handsome," I lied.

"He's very handsome," she corrected me. And as soon as the old man left, she took the faded flowers out of the vases, threw them to one side along with the stagnant water, ordered me to go get fresh water at a fountain that I would find just around the corner. I was afraid of getting lost, so I hesitated, and she chased me away, waving her hand: go, go.

I went, I found the fountain, which had a feeble jet. With a shudder I imagined that Enzo's ghost was whispering affectionate words to Vittoria from the cross-shaped slits. How I liked that bond that had never been broken. The water gave a hiss, slowly lengthening its stream into the metal vases. If Enzo was an ugly man, well, his ugliness suddenly moved me, or rather the word lost meaning, dissolved in the gurgle of the water. What truly counted was the capacity to inspire love, even if one was ugly, even if spiteful, even if stupid. I felt there was some grandeur in that, and hoped that, whatever face was coming to me, I would have that capacity, as Enzo surely had, and Vittoria had. I went back to the tomb with the two vases full of water, hoping that my aunt would continue to talk to me as if I were a grownup and tell me in detail, in her brazen semi-dialect, about that supreme love.

But as soon as I turned onto the path I got scared. Vittoria was sitting, legs spread, on the folding chair the old man had brought and was bent over, her face in her hands, her elbows on her thighs. She was talking — she was talking to Enzo, it wasn't a fantasy, I heard her voice but not what she was saying. She really maintained relations with him, even after death, and that dialogue of theirs filled me with emotion. I advanced as slowly as possible, stamping on the dirt path with the soles of my feet so she'd hear me. But she didn't seem to notice me until I was beside her. At that point she took her hands away from her face, sliding them slowly over her skin: a painful movement that was intended to wipe away the tears and at the same time deliberately show me her grief, without embarrassment but, rather, as a medal. Eyes red and shining, wet at the corners. At my house, it was a duty to hide your feelings, not to seemed impolite. Whereas she, after seventeen years — what seemed an eternity to me — was still in despair, wept in front of the tomb, spoke to the marble, addressed bones she couldn't even see, a man who no longer existed. She took just one of the vases and said wearily: you arrange your flowers and I will do mine. I obeyed, placing my vase on the ground, unwrapping the flowers, while she, sniffling, unwrapped hers and grumbled:

"Did you tell your father I told you about Enzo? And did he talk to you about him? Did he tell you the truth? Did he tell you that first he acted like his friend — he wanted to know everything about Enzo, tell me, he would say to him — and then he made him suffer, ruined him? Did he tell you how we fought over the house, our parents' house, that pit of a house where I live now?"

I shook my head no, and would have liked to explain to her that I wasn't interested in their stories of fights, I just wanted her to tell me about love, I didn't know anyone who could talk to me about it the way she could. But Vittoria wanted above all to say bad things about my father, and insisted that I listen, she wanted me to understand clearly why she was angry with him. So — sitting on the chair arranging her flowers, I doing the same, squatting nearby — she started in on the story of the fight over the house, the only thing left by the parents to their five children.

It was a long story and was hurtful to me. Your father — she said — didn't want to give in. He was adamant: the house belongs to all of us, it's Papa and Mamma's house, they bought it with their money, and I'm the only one who helped them, and to help them I put my money into it. I answered: it's true, Andrea, but all of you are settled, one way or another you have jobs, but I have nothing, and the others agree about leaving it all to me. But he said that we had to sell the house and divide the proceeds among the five of us. If the others didn't want their share, fine, but he wanted his. There was an argument that went on for months: your father on one side and the three others and I on the other. Since no solution could be found, Enzo intervened — look at him, with that face, those eyes, that smile. At the time, no one knew about our great love story but your father, who was his friend, my brother, and our adviser. Enzo defended me, he said: Andrea, your sister can't compensate you, where would she get the money. And your father said to him: you shut up, you're nobody, you don't know how to put two words together, what do you have to do with my business and my sister. Enzo was too distressed, he said: all right, let's have the house appraised and I'll give you your share out of my own pocket. But your father started cursing, he yelled at him: how can you give me the money, you shit, you're just a cop, where would you find the money, and if you have it that means you're a thief, a thief in a uniform. And so on like that, you see? Your father went so far as to tell him — listen carefully, he seems like a refined man but he's crude — that he, Enzo, was not only screwing me but also wanted to screw

104

the rest of us out of our parents' house. So Enzo said if he kept on like that he'd take out his pistol and shoot him. He said "I'll shoot you" so convincingly that your father turned white with fear, he shut up and left. But now, Giannì — here my aunt blew her nose, dried her wet eyes, began to twist her mouth to contain passion and fury — you must listen well to what your father did: he went straight to Enzo's wife and in front of the three children said: Margherì, your husband is fucking my sister. He did that, he took that responsibility on himself, and he made a mess of my life, Enzo's, Margherita's, and the life of those three poor little kids.

Now the sun had reached the flower bed and the flowers shone in the vases much brighter than the lamp in the shape of a flame: the light of day made the colors so vivid that the light of the dead seemed useless, appeared spent. I felt sad, sad for Vittoria, for Enzo, for his wife, Margherita, for the three small children. Was it possible that my father had behaved like that? I couldn't believe it, he had always said: the worst thing, Giovanna, is to be a snitch. And yet, according to Vittoria, he had done that, and even though he must have had good reasons — I was sure — it wasn't like him, no, I ruled it out. But I didn't dare say so to Vittoria, it seemed offensive to claim that, on the seventeenth anniversary of their love, she was telling lies in front of Enzo's tomb. So I said nothing, though I was unhappy that once again I wasn't defending my father, and I looked at her uncertainly, while she, as if to soothe herself, cleaned with a tear-stained handkerchief the glass ovals that protected the photos. The silence weighed on me, and I asked her:

"How did Enzo die?"

"Of a terrible illness."

"When?"

"A few months after things ended between us."

"He died of grief?"

"Yes, of grief. Your father made him get sick, your father who was the cause of our separation. He killed him."

I said:

"And then why didn't you get sick and die? Didn't you feel the pain?"

She stared me straight in the eyes, so that I immediately lowered my gaze.

"I suffered, Giannì, I'm still suffering. But suffering didn't kill me, first so that I would go on always thinking of Enzo; second, out of love for his children and also Margherita, because I am a good woman and I felt a duty to help her bring up those three kids, for whom I worked and work as a maid in the houses of the wealthy of half of Naples, from morning to night; third, out of hate, hate for your father, hate that makes you go on even when you don't want to live any longer."

I pressed her:

"How was it that Margherita wasn't angry when you took her husband, but rather let you help her, you who'd stolen him from her?"

She lighted a cigarette, inhaled deeply. While my father and mother didn't blink in the face of my questions, but evaded them when they were embarrassed and sometimes consulted with each other before answering, Vittoria got irritated, cursed, displayed her impatience openly, but answered, explicitly, as no adult had ever done with me. You see I'm right, she said, you're intelligent, an intelligent little slut like me, but also a bitch, you act like a saint but you like turning the knife in the wound. Steal her husband, exactly, you're right, that's what I did. Enzo I stole, I took him away from Margherita and the children, and I would have died rather than give him back. That, she exclaimed, is a terrible thing, but if love is very strong, sometimes you have to do it.

You don't choose, you realize that without the ugly things the good ones don't exist, and you act that way because you can't help it. As for Margherita, yes, she was angry, she took her husband back, screaming and hitting, but later when she realized that Enzo was sick, sick with an illness that had erupted inside in a few weeks of rage, she became depressed, she said to him go, go back to Vittoria, I'm sorry, if I'd known you'd get sick I would have sent you back to her before. But now it was too late, and so we went through his illness together, she and I, up to the last minute. What a person Margherita is, a wonderful woman, sensible, I'd like you to meet her. As soon as she understood how much I loved her husband, and how much I was suffering, she said: all right, we loved the same man, and I understand you, how could one not love Enzo. So enough, I had these children with Enzo, if you want to love them, too, I have nothing against it. Understand? Do you understand the generosity? Your father, your mother, their friends, all those important people, do they have this greatness, do they have this generosity?

I didn't know what to say, I murmured only:

"I've ruined your anniversary, I'm sorry, I

shouldn't have asked you to tell the story."

"You haven't ruined anything, in fact you've made me happy. I've talked about Enzo, and whenever I talk about him I don't remember only the grief, but also how happy we were."

"That's what I want to know more about."

"The happiness?"

"Yes."

Her eyes became more inflamed.

"You know what happens between men and women?"

"Yes."

"You say yes but you know nothing. They fuck. You know that word?"

I was startled.

"Yes."

"Enzo and I did that thing eleven times altogether. Then he went back to his wife and I never did it again with anyone. Enzo kissed me and touched me and licked me all over, and I touched him and kissed him all the way to his toes and caressed him and licked and sucked. Then he put his dick inside me and held my ass with both hands, one here and one there, and he thrust it into me with such force that it made me cry out. If you, in all your life, don't do this thing as I did it, with the passion I did it with, the love I did it with, and I don't mean eleven times but at least once, it's pointless to live. Tell your father: Vittoria said that if I don't fuck the way she fucked with Enzo, it's pointless for me to live. You have to say it just like that. He thinks he deprived me of something, with what he did to me. But he didn't deprive me of anything, I've had everything, I *have* everything. It's your father who has nothing."

Those words of hers I've never been able to erase. They came unexpectedly, I would never have imagined that she could say them to me. Of course, she treated me like an adult, and I was glad that from the start she had abandoned the proper way to speak to a girl of thirteen. But still, what she said was so surprising that I was tempted to put my hands over my ears. I didn't, I didn't move, I couldn't even avoid her gaze, which sought in my face the effect of the words. It was, in short, physically — yes, physically — overwhelming, her speaking to me like that, there, in the cemetery, in front of the portrait of Enzo, without worrying that someone might hear her. Oh what a story, oh to learn to speak like that, outside of every convention of my house. Until that moment no one had displayed to me — just to me — an adherence to pleasure so desperately carnal, I was astounded. I had felt

110

a warmth in my stomach much stronger than what I felt when Vittoria had made me dance. Nor was there anything comparable in the warmth of certain secret conversations I had with Angela, in the languor that some of our recent hugs provoked in me, when we locked ourselves in the bathroom of her house or mine. Listening to Vittoria, I not only desired the pleasure she said she had felt; it seemed to me that that pleasure would be impossible if it weren't followed immediately by the grief that she still felt and by her unfailing fidelity. Since I said nothing, she gave me worried looks, muttered:

"Let's go, it's late. But remember these things: did you like them?"

"Yes."

"I knew it: you and I are alike."

She stood up, refreshed, folded the chair, then stared for a moment at the bracelet with the blue leaves.

"I gave you one," she said, "much more beautiful."

6.

Seeing Vittoria soon became a habit. My parents, surprising me — but maybe, if I think about it, completely consistent with their choices in life and the upbringing they had given me — didn't reproach me either together or separately. They refrained from saying: you should have told us you had an appointment with Aunt Vittoria. They refrained from saying: you plotted to skip school and keep it secret from us, that's bad, you behaved stupidly. They refrained from saying: the city is very dangerous, you can't go around like that, at your age anything could happen. Above all, they refrained from saying: forget about that woman, you know she hates us, you are not to see her anymore. Instead, they did the opposite, especially my mother. They wanted to know if the morning had been interesting. They asked me what impression the cemetery had made. They smiled, amused, as soon as I started describing how badly Vittoria drove. Even when my father asked me — but almost absently — what we had talked about and I mentioned — but almost without intention — the fight about the inheritance of the house and Enzo, he didn't get upset, he responded concisely: yes, we quarreled, I didn't share her choices, it was clear that this Enzo wanted to get possession of our parents' apartment, under the uniform he was a crook, he went so far as to threaten me with a pistol and then, to try to prevent my sister's ruin, I had to tell his wife everything. As for my mother, she added only that her sister-in-law, despite her nasty character, was a naïve woman and rather than get angry one should feel sorry for her, because her naïveté had ruined her life. Anyway, she said later, when we were alone, your father and I trust you and your good sense, don't disappoint me. And since I had just told her that I would like to know the other aunts and uncles Vittoria had mentioned, and possibly my cousins, who must be my age, my mother sat me on her lap, said she was glad I was curious, and concluded: if you want to see Vittoria again go ahead, the crucial thing is that you tell us.

We confronted the question of other possible meetings and I immediately assumed a cautious tone. I said that I had to study, that skipping school had been a mistake, that if I was really going to see my aunt, I would do it on Sundays. Naturally, I never mentioned how Vittoria had talked to me about her love for Enzo. I intuited that if I had reported just one of those words they would have gotten angry.

A less anxious period began. At school things had improved in the last part of the year, I was promoted with a respectable

113

average, and vacation began. In accordance with an old custom, we spent two weeks in July at the beach in Calabria with Mariano, Costanza, Angela, and Ida. And we also spent the first ten days of August with them at Villetta Barrea, in Abruzzo. The time flew by, and the new school year began. I was starting the first year of high school, not in the high school where my father taught or the one where my mother taught but at a school on the Vomero. Meanwhile my relationship with Vittoria didn't fade but, rather, solidified. Already before the summer vacation, I'd begun to telephone her: I felt the need for her rough tone, I liked being treated as if I were her age. During our stay at the beach and in the mountains, I'd start talking about her as soon as Angela and Ida boasted about their rich grandparents and other wealthy relatives. And in September, with permission from my mother and father, I saw her a couple of times. Then, during the fall, since there were no particular tensions at my house, our meetings became a routine.

At first, I thought that thanks to me there might be a rapprochement between the siblings, and I went so far as to convince myself that my task was to bring about a reconciliation. But that didn't happen.

Instead, a rite of extreme coldness was established. My mother drove me to her sister-in-law's house, but she brought something to read or to correct and waited in the car; or Vittoria came to get me at San Giacomo dei Capri, but she didn't knock at our door by surprise as she'd done the first time; I met her in the street. My aunt never said: ask your mother if she wants to come up, I'll make her a coffee. My father was careful not to say: have her come up, sit a while, we'll have a little chat and then you'll go. Their mutual hatred remained intact, and I soon gave up any attempt at mediation. I began instead to say to myself explicitly that that hatred was an advantage for me: if my father and his sister made peace, my encounters with Vittoria wouldn't be exclusive, I might be downgraded to niece, and certainly I would lose the role of friend, confidante, accomplice. Sometimes I felt that if they stopped hating each other I would do something to make them start again.

7.

Once, without any warning, my aunt brought me to meet her and my father's other siblings. We went to see Uncle Nicola, who worked on the railroad. Vittoria called him the eldest brother, as if my father, who was the firstborn, had never existed. We went to see Aunt Anna and Aunt Rosetta, housewives. Aunt Anna was married to a printer at the newspaper *Il Mattino,* Aunt Rosetta to a postal worker. It was a sort of exploration of blood relations, and Vittoria herself, in dialect, said of that journey: we're going to meet your blood. We traveled through Naples in the green Fiat 500, going first to Cavone, where Aunt Anna lived, then to the Campi Flegrei, where Uncle Nicola lived, then to Pozzuoli, to Aunt Rosetta.

I realized that I barely remembered these relatives, maybe I had never actually known their names. I tried to hide it, but Vittoria noticed and immediately started saying mean things about my father, who had deprived me of the affection of people certainly without education, not smooth talkers, but warm-hearted. How important to her the heart was, coinciding in her gestures with her large breasts, which she struck with her broad hand and gnarled fingers. It was in those situations that she began to suggest to me: look at what we're like and what your father and mother are like, then tell me. She insisted forcefully on that matter of looking. She said I had blinders like a horse, I looked but didn't see the things that could disturb me. Look, look, look, she hammered into me.

In fact, I let nothing escape me. Those relatives, their children a little older than me or my age, were a pleasant novelty. Vittoria flung me into their houses without warning, and yet aunts and uncles, nieces and nephews welcomed me with great familiarity, as if they knew me well and had been simply waiting, over the years, for my visit. The apartments were small, drab, furnished with objects that I had been brought up to judge crude if not vulgar. No books, only at Aunt Anna's house did I see some mysteries. They all spoke to me in a cordial dialect mixed with Italian, and I made an effort to do the same, or at least I made room in my hypercorrect Italian for some Neapolitan cadences. No one mentioned my father, no one asked how he was, no one charged me with saying hello to him, evident signs of hostility, but they tried in every way to make me understand that they weren't angry with me. They called me Giannina, as Vittoria did and as my parents never had. I loved them all, I had never felt so open to affection. And I was so relaxed and funny that I began to think that that name assigned to me by Vittoria — Giannina — had miraculously brought forth from my same body another person, more pleasant or anyway different from the Giovanna by which I was known to my parents, to Angela, to Ida, to my classmates. They were happy occasions for me, and I think also for Vittoria, who instead of displaying the aggressive sides of her character was, during those visits, good-natured. Above all, I noticed that brother, sisters, sister- and brothers-in-law, nieces and nephews treated her tenderly, as one does an unfortunate person one loves dearly. Uncle Nicola especially was kind to her, he remembered that she liked strawberry gelato and as soon as he discovered that I liked it, too, he sent one of his children to buy some for everyone. When we left, he kissed me on the forehead and said:

"Luckily you've got nothing of your father in you."

I was learning to hide from my parents what was happening to me. Or, rather, I perfected my method of lying by telling the truth. Naturally I didn't do it lightly, it pained me. When I was at home and heard them moving about the rooms with the familiar footsteps that I loved, when we had breakfast together, had lunch, dinner, my love for them prevailed, I was always on the point of crying: Papa, Mamma, you're right, Vittoria hates you, she's vengeful, she wants to take me away from you to hurt you, hold on to me, forbid me to see her. But as soon as they started with their hypercorrect sentences, with those controlled tones of theirs, as if truly every word concealed others, truer, from which they excluded me, I secretly called Vittoria, I made dates.

By now only my mother questioned me politely about what happened.

"Where did you go?"

"To Uncle Nicola's house, he says hello to you."

"How did he seem to you?"

"A little dumb."

"Don't talk like that about your uncle."

"He's always laughing for no reason."

"Yes, I remember he does that."

"He's not at all like Papa, not even a little."

"It's true."

I was soon involved in another important visit. My aunt took me — as usual without warning — to see Margherita, who lived not far from her house. That whole area revived the agonies of childhood. The peeling walls upset me, the abandoned-looking low buildings, the gray-blue or yellowish colors, the fierce dogs that would chase the 500 for a stretch, barking, the smell of gas. Vittoria parked, she headed toward a wide courtyard surrounded by pale-blue buildings, went through a door, and only when she set off up the stairs turned to tell me: this is where Enzo's wife and children live.

We reached the third floor and instead of ringing — first surprise — Vittoria opened the door with her own key. She said aloud: it's us, and there was immediately an enthusiastic shout in dialect — *oh, I'm so glad* — that announced the appearance of a small round woman, dressed all in black, with a beautiful face that, along with her blue eyes, seemed drowned in a circle of rosy fat. She welcomed us to the dark kitchen, introduced me to her children, two boys over twenty, Tonino and Corrado, and a girl, Giuliana, who could have been eighteen. She was slender, very beautiful, dark, wearing a lot of eye makeup, her mother must have looked like that as a young woman. Tonino, too, the oldest, was handsome, he had an air of strength but seemed very shy, he turned red just shaking my hand and barely spoke a word to me. Corrado, the only expansive one, seemed identical to the man I had seen in the photo at the cemetery: the same wavy hair, same low forehead, same lively eyes, same smile. When I saw on a kitchen wall a photo of Enzo in his police-man's uniform, his pistol at his side, a photo much bigger than the one in the cemetery — it was in an ornate frame and in front of it a red light was burning — and noticed that he had a long trunk and short legs, that son seemed to me a living ghost. I don't know how many silly things he said to me, in a relaxed, charming way, a burst of ironic compliments, and I was amused, I was pleased that he made me the center of at-tention. But Margherita found him impolite, she murmured several times: Currà, you're rude, leave the child alone, and ordered him in dialect to stop it. Corrado was silent, star-ing at me with bright eyes, while his mother fed me sweets, the lovely Giuliana, with her full figure and vivid colors, said a thousand flattering things in a shrill voice, and Tonino overwhelmed me with quiet courtesies.

During that visit both Margherita and Vit-toria often glanced at the man in the frame. Just as frequently they mentioned him, in partial phrases such as: you know how amused Enzo would be, you know how angry he'd be, you know how much he would have liked. Probably for nearly twenty years they'd acted like that, a couple of women recalling the same man. I looked at them, studied them. I imagined Margherita young, resembling Giuliana, and Enzo like Corrado, and Vittoria with my face, and my father — even my father — as he was in the photo that was locked in the metal box, the one where in the background you could read RIA. Certainly, on those streets there had been a *pasticceria,* a *salumeria,* a *sartoria* — pastry shop, grocery, dressmaker's, who knows — and they had been passed by and passed again and had even been photographed, maybe before the young predator Vittoria took away from the beautiful tender Margherita the husband with wolf-like teeth, or maybe even afterward, during their secret relationship, and then never again, when my father had been the informer, and there had been only pain and fury. But time had gone by. Now both my aunt and Margherita had a calm, quiet tone, and yet I couldn't help thinking that the man in the photo must have clutched Margherita's buttocks exactly as he had clutched my aunt's when she stole him, with the same skilled force. The thought made me blush to the point where Corrado said: are you thinking of something nice, and I almost shouted no, but I couldn't get rid of those visions, and I went on imagining that there, in the dark kitchen, the two women had told each other countless times, in detail, acts and words of the man they had shared, and that they must have struggled before finding a balance between good feelings and bad.

Also that sharing of the children couldn't have been entirely untroubled. Probably it wasn't even now. I quickly noticed, in fact, at least three things: first, Corrado was Vittoria's favorite and the other two were annoyed by that; second, Margherita was dominated by my aunt, she'd say something and then glance at her to see if she agreed, and if she didn't Margherita took back what she'd said; third, all three children loved their mother, sometimes they seemed to protect her from Vittoria, and yet they had toward my aunt a sort of wary devotion, they respected her as if she were the tutelary divinity of their existence and they feared her. The nature of their relations became completely clear when, I don't know how, it emerged that Tonino had a friend, Roberto, who had grown up there in Pascone and at around fifteen had moved to Milan with his family. But the young man would arrive this evening, and Tonino had invited him to sleep at their house. This made Margherita angry.

"What were you thinking, where can we put him."

"I couldn't say no."

"Why? Do you owe him something? What favor did he do you?"

"None."

"So?"

They argued for a while: Giuliana was on Tonino's side, Corrado on his mother's. All of them — I understood — had known Roberto for a long time; he and Tonino had been schoolmates, and Giuliana insisted passionately that he was a good, modest, very intelligent person. Only Corrado disliked him. He turned to me, correcting his sister:

"Don't believe it, he's a pain in the ass."

"Wash your mouth out, when you talk about him," Giuliana raged, while Tonino said aggressively:

"Better than your friends."

"My friends will beat the shit out of him if he says things like he said the other time," Corrado responded.

There was a moment of silence. Margherita, Tonino, and Giuliana turned toward Vittoria, and even Corrado broke off with the expression of one who would like to eat his words. My aunt took another moment, then she intervened in a tone that I didn't yet know, threatening and at the same time pained, as if her stomach hurt:

"Who are these friends of yours, let's hear."

"No one," Corrado said with a nervous laugh.

"Are you talking about the son of Sargente, the lawyer?"

"No."

"Are you talking about Rosario Sargente?"

"I said no, it's no one."

"Currà, you know I'll break every bone in your body if you so much as say hello to that 'no one.' "

The atmosphere became so tense that Margherita, Tonino, and Giuliana seemed on the point of minimizing the conflict with Corrado themselves, just to protect him from my aunt's anger. But Corrado wouldn't give in, he went back to disparaging Roberto.

"Anyway he's gone to Milan and has no right to tell us how we should behave here."

Since her brother wouldn't give in and so was being unfair to my aunt, too, Giuliana got angry again:

"You're the one who should shut up, I could listen to Roberto forever."

"Because you're an idiot."

"That's enough, Currà," his mother reproached him. "Roberto is good as gold. But, Tonì, why does he have to sleep here?"

"Because I invited him," said Tonino.

"So? Tell him you made a mistake, the house is small and there's no room."

"Rather, tell him," Corrado interrupted again, "that he shouldn't show his face in the neighborhood, it's better for him."

Tonino and Giuliana, exasperated, turned to Vittoria at the same time, as if it were up to her to settle the thing one way or another. And it struck me that Margherita herself turned to her as if to say: Vittò, what should I do? Vittoria said in a low tone: your mother is right, there's no room, let's say Corrado comes to sleep at my house. The eyes of Margherita, Tonino, Giuliana lighted up with gratitude. Corrado instead scowled, tried again to denigrate the guest, but my aunt hissed: quiet. The boy made a gesture of raising his arms in a sign of surrender, but reluctantly. Then, as if he knew he owed Vittoria a more palpable gesture of submission, he went up behind her and kissed her repeatedly, noisily, on the neck and on one cheek. She, sitting next to the kitchen table, acted annoyed, said in dialect: Holy Madonna, Currà, how clingy you are. Were those three young people in some way her blood, too, and therefore mine? I liked Tonino, Giuliana, Corrado, I also liked Margherita. What a pity to be the last to arrive, not to speak the language they spoke, not to have true intimacy.

8.

Vittoria, as if she had perceived that sense of estrangement, at times seemed to want to help me get over it, at others accentuated it purposely. Madonna, she'd exclaim, look, we have the same hands, and she'd put hers next to mine, and her thumb would bump against my thumb. That bump filled me with emotion, I would have liked to hug her tight, or stretch out next to her with my head on her shoulder, hear her breath, her rough voice. But, more often, as soon as I said something that seemed wrong to her, she chided me, saying, like father like daughter; or she made fun of the way my mother dressed me. You're grown up, feel those tits you have, you can't go out dressed like a little doll, you should rebel, Giannì, they're ruining you. Then she started up her refrain: look at them, your parents, look at them carefully, don't let them fool you.

This was very important to her, and every time we met she insisted that I report to her how I'd spent my days. But since I stuck to generic information, she soon got annoyed, teased me cruelly, or laughed noisily, throwing open her big mouth. She was exasperated that all I told her was how much my father studied, how respected he was, that an article of his had been published in a famous journal, and that my mother adored him because he was so handsome and intelligent, that they were both so smart, and that my mother proofread and often rewrote love stories written just for women, she knew everything, she was really nice. You love them, Vittoria said angrily, bitterly, because they're your parents, but if you can't understand that they're shitty people you'll become shit like them and I won't want to see you anymore.

To please her, I once told her that my father had many voices and that he modulated them according to circumstances. He had the voice of affection, the imperious voice, the cold voice, all of which spoke a beautiful Italian, but he also had the voice of contempt, which spoke Italian but sometimes dialect as well, and he used it with anyone who irritated him, especially dishonest shopkeepers, drivers who didn't know how to drive, people who were rude. As for my mother, I said that she was somewhat dominated by a friend named Costanza, and at times was annoyed by Costanza's husband, Mariano, a friend who was like a brother to my father but joked in a cruel way. Vittoria didn't appreciate even those more specific confidences, though; on the contrary, she said they were gossip without substance. I discovered that she remembered Mariano, she called him an imbecile, anything but a friend who was like a brother. That phrase made her angry. Andrea, she said in a very harsh tone, doesn't know the meaning of "brother." I remember that we were in her house, in the kitchen, and outside, on the dreary street, it was raining. I must have had a forlorn expression, my eyes teared, and this, to my surprise, to my pleasure, softened her in a way that nothing had before. She smiled at me, she pulled me to her, sat me on her lap and kissed me hard on one cheek, nibbling at it. Then she whispered in dialect: sorry, I'm not angry with you but with your father; then she stuck a hand under my skirt and patted me lightly, again and again, with the palm of her hand, between my thigh and my bottom. She said in my ear, yet again: look at them carefully, your parents, otherwise you're lost.

9.

The frequency of those sudden explosions of affection bursting out of a tonality that was almost always displeased increased and made her increasingly necessary to me. The dead time between our encounters passed unbearably slowly, and in the interval in which I didn't see her or couldn't telephone her I felt the need to talk about her. So I ended up by confiding even more in Angela and Ida, after demanding oaths of extreme secrecy. They were the only ones with whom I could boast of my relationship with my aunt, but at first they scarcely listened to me, they immediately wanted to tell me cute stories and anecdotes about their eccentric relatives. But they soon had to give in, there was no comparison between those relatives and Vittoria, who — as I told it — was completely outside their experience. Their aunts and cousins and grandmothers were wealthy ladies of the Vomero, Posillipo, Via Manzoni, Via Tasso. Whereas I placed my father's sister imaginatively in a neighborhood of cemeteries, wastelands, fierce dogs, gas flares, skeletons of abandoned buildings, and I said: she had an unhappy and unique love, he died of grief, but she'll love him forever.

Once I confided to them in a very low voice: when Aunt Vittoria talks about how they loved each other, she uses "fuck," she told me how much and how she and Enzo fucked. Angela was struck above all by that last point, she questioned me at length, and maybe I exaggerated my answers, I had Vittoria say things I'd fantasized myself for a long time. But I didn't feel guilty, the substance was true, my aunt had talked to me like that. You don't know — I said, becoming emotional — what a great friendship she and I have: we're really close, she hugs me, kisses me, she's always telling me we're alike. I said nothing, naturally, about the fights she had had with my father, the arguments about the inheritance of a miserable apartment, about the betrayal that had come out of it — that all seemed too degrading. Instead, I told them about how after Enzo's death, Margherita and Vittoria had lived in a spirit of admirable cooperation and had taken care of the children as if they had taken turns giving birth to them, first one, then the other. That image, I have to say, came to me by chance, but I expressed it even better in the later stories, to the point where I believed myself that both of them had made Tonino, Giuliana, and Corrado. Especially with Ida, almost without realizing it, I came close to giving the two women the capacity to fly through night skies or invent magic potions as they gathered enchanted herbs in the Capodimonte woods. Certainly, I told her that Vittoria talked to Enzo at the cemetery, and he gave her advice.

"Do they talk the way you and I are talking?" Ida asked.

"Yes."

"So he's the one who wanted your aunt to be a second mamma to his children."

"For sure. He was a policeman, he could do what he wanted, he even had a pistol."

"It's like my mamma and your mamma were mammas of all three of us?"

"Yes."

Ida was distressed, but Angela was excited. The more I told and retold these stories, elaborating them, the more they exclaimed: how wonderful, they make me cry. Their interest increased in a particular way when I began to talk about how entertaining Corrado was, how beautiful Giuliana, the fascination of Tonino. I myself was amazed at the warmth with which I described Tonino. That I liked him was a discovery for me, too: at the time, he hadn't made a great impression, in fact he had seemed to me the least substantial of the three. But I talked so much about him, I invented so well, that when Ida, the expert in novels, said to me: you're in love, I admitted — mainly to see how Angela would react — that it was true, I loved him.

So a situation was created in which my friends continuously asked me for new details about Vittoria, Tonino, Corrado, Giuliana, and their mother, and I didn't have to be asked twice to provide them. Up to a certain point, everything went well. Then they started asking if they could meet at least Aunt Vittoria and Tonino. I immediately said no, it was something of mine, my invention, that as long as it lasted made me feel good: I had gone too far, the reality would be poor in comparison. And then I intuited that my parents' approval was fake, already I was making a huge effort to keep things in balance. A wrong move would be enough — Mamma, Papa, can I take Angela and Ida to see Aunt Vittoria? — and in a flash bad feelings would ignite. But Angela and Ida were curious, they insisted. I was disoriented during that autumn, squeezed between the pressures of my friends and Vittoria's. The former wanted to verify that the world I was entering really was more exciting than the one we lived in; the second seemed close to pushing me away from that world, from her, unless I admitted that I was on her side and not my father and mother's. So I now felt colorless to my parents, colorless to Vittoria, not showing a truthful face to my friends. It was in that atmosphere that, almost without realizing it, I began seriously to spy on my parents.

10.

What I found out about my father was an unsuspected attachment to money. I caught him several times accusing my mother, in a low but insistent voice, of spending too much and on useless things. Otherwise, his life was the same as ever: school in the morning, study in the afternoon, meetings at night at our house or someone else's. As for my mother, when it came to money I often heard her reply, also in a low voice: it's money that I earn, I can spend some of it on myself. But the new fact was that although she had always had a blandly ironic attitude toward my father's meetings, which, especially to tease Mariano, she called "plots to straighten out the world," she suddenly began to take part in them, not only when they were held at our house but also, to the explicit annoyance of my father, when they were held at other people's houses. So I often spent the evenings on the telephone with Angela or Vittoria.

From Angela I learned that Costanza didn't have the same curiosity as my mother about the meetings, and that even if they were at her house she preferred to go out or watch television or read. I ended up reporting to Vittoria — although with some uncertainty — both those fights about money and my mother's sudden interest in my father's evening activities. She unexpectedly praised me:

"You finally realized how attached your father is to money."

"Yes."

"It was for money that he ruined my life."

I didn't respond, I was just glad I'd finally found some information that satisfied her. She pressed me:

"What does your mother buy?"

"Clothes, underwear. And a lot of lotions."

"A real bitch," she exclaimed, pleased.

I understood that Vittoria required events and behaviors of that type, not only to confirm the fact that she was right and my father and mother wrong but also as a sign that I was learning to look beyond appearances, to understand.

That she was pleased by spying of that type basically encouraged me. I didn't want to stop being their daughter, as she seemed to demand, the bond with my parents was strong and I dismissed the idea that my father's attention to money or my mother's small extravagances could make me not love them. The risk was rather that, wanting to gratify Vittoria and solidify the intimacy between us, and having nothing to recount, I would begin almost inadvertently to invent. But, luckily, the lies that came to mind were exaggerated, I attributed crimes so novelistic to my family that I restrained myself, I was afraid that Vittoria would say: you're a liar. So I ended up looking for small real anomalies and inflating them slightly. But even then I was uneasy. I wasn't a truly affectionate daughter and I wasn't a truly loyal spy.

One night we went to dinner at Mariano and Costanza's house. As we drove down Via Cimarosa a mass of black clouds that extended fringelike fingers struck me as a bad omen. In my friends' big apartment, I was immediately cold; the radiators weren't working yet, and I kept on a wool jacket that my mother considered very elegant. Although at our hosts' house there were always good things to eat — they had a silent maid who cooked very well, I looked at her and thought of Vittoria, who worked in apartments like this — I barely tasted the food because I was worried about getting the jacket dirty: my mother had told me to take it off. Ida, Angela, and I were bored; it took an eternity filled with Mariano's chatter to get to dessert. Finally, the moment arrived to ask if we could leave the table, and Costanza allowed us to go. We went into the hall and sat on the floor. Ida began throwing a red rubber ball to annoy Angela and me, while Angela was asking me when I would let her meet my aunt. She was especially insistent, and said:

"You want to know something?"

"What?"

"In my opinion your aunt doesn't exist."

"Of course she exists."

"Then if she exists she's not the way you say. That's why you won't let us meet her."

"She's even better than what I tell you about her."

"Then take us to see her," said Ida, and threw the ball hard at me. To avoid getting hit I flung myself backward on the floor and found myself stretched out between the wall and the open door of the dining room. The table our parents still lingered at was rectangular, set in the middle of the room. From where I was, I saw all four of them in profile. My mother was sitting opposite

Mariano, Costanza opposite my father, I don't know what they were talking about. My father said something, Costanza laughed, Mariano replied. I was lying on the floor and I could see not so much their faces as the outlines of their legs, their feet. Mariano had stretched his under the table, he was talking to my father and at the same time he was squeezing one of my mother's ankles between his.

I sat up in a hurry with an obscure sense of shame and threw the ball hard at Ida. But I resisted only a few minutes, and lay down on the floor again. Mariano kept his legs stretched out under the table, but now my mother had pulled hers away and turned with her whole body toward my father. She was saying: it's November but it's still warm.

What are you doing, Angela asked, and she lay down cautiously, gently, on top of me, saying: until a little while ago we fit perfectly and now, look, you're longer than me.

11.

For the rest of the evening I never lost sight of my mother and Mariano. She barely took part in the conversation, exchanged not even a glance with him, stared at Costanza or my father, but as if she had urgent thoughts and didn't see them. Whereas Mariano couldn't take his eyes off her. He looked at her feet, at a knee, at an ear with a sullen, melancholy gaze that contrasted with the usual tone of his aggressive chatter. The rare times that they exchanged a word, my mother answered in monosyllables, Mariano spoke to her for no reason in a low voice and in a caressing way I had never heard in him. After a while, Angela began to insist that I spend the night with them. She always did that on these occasions, and in general my mother agreed after a few remarks on the bother I might cause, while my father was always implicitly favorable. But this time the request wasn't immediately agreed to, my mother hesitated. Then Mariano intervened and, after pointing out that the next day was Sunday, and there was no school, assured her that he would bring me himself to San Giacomo dei Capri before lunch. I heard them negotiating pointlessly, it was taken for granted that I would stay, and I suspected that in that exchange — in my mother's words there was a feeble resistance, in Mariano's an urgent request — they were saying something else that to them was clear and escaped the rest of us. When my mother agreed that I would sleep with Angela, Mariano had a serious, almost emotional expression, as if on my staying overnight depended, I don't know, his university career or the solution of the serious problems that he and my father had been engaged with for decades.

Shortly before eleven, after much hesitation, my parents decided to go.

"You don't have any pajamas," my mother said.

"She can wear a pair of mine," said Angela.

"And a toothbrush?"

"She has hers, she left it the last time and I put it away."

Costanza intervened with a hint of sarcasm at that anomalous resistance in the face of something completely normal. When Angela stays at your house, she said, doesn't she wear a pair of Giovanna's pajamas, doesn't she have her toothbrush? Yes, of course, my mother gave in uneasily and said: Andrea, let's go, it's late. My father got up from the couch with a slightly annoyed expression, he wanted a good-night kiss from me. My mother was distracted and didn't ask me, she kissed Costanza, instead, on both cheeks, with smacks that she never made and that seemed to me dictated by the need to underline their old pact of friendship. Her eyes were agitated, I thought: what's wrong, she doesn't feel well. She was about to head toward the door but, as if she suddenly remembered that she had Mariano right behind her and hadn't said goodbye, she almost fell back against his chest as if she were fainting, and in that position — while my father was saying goodbye to Costanza, praising the dinner yet again — she turned her head and offered him her mouth. It was an instant, with my heart in my throat I thought they would kiss as in the movies. But he touched her cheek with his lips and she did the same.

As soon as my parents left the apartment, Mariano and Costanza began to clear the table and ordered us to get ready for bed. But I couldn't concentrate. What had happened before my eyes, what had I seen: innocent playfulness on Mariano's part, a premeditated illicit act of his, an illicit act of both? My mother was always so transparent: how could she tolerate that contact under the table, and with a man much less attractive than my father? She had no liking for Mariano — how stupid he is, I'd heard her say a couple of times — and even with Costanza she couldn't contain herself, she had often asked her, in the tone of a feeble

141

joke, how she could stand a person who could never be quiet. And so what was the meaning of her ankle between his ankles? How long had they been in that position? For a few seconds, a minute, ten minutes? Why hadn't my mother immediately pulled her leg away? And the distractedness that followed? I was confused.

I brushed my teeth for too long, so that Ida said in a hostile way: that's enough, you'll wear them out. It was always like that, as soon as we were in their room she became aggressive. In reality, she was afraid that we two older ones would leave her out, and so she sulked preventively. For the same reason she immediately announced, combatively, that she, too, wanted to sleep in Angela's bed and not by herself in hers. The two sisters argued for a while — we're too cramped, go away, no, we're fine — but Ida wouldn't give in, she never did. So Angela winked at me, and said to her: as soon as you fall asleep *I'm* going to sleep in your bed. Fine, Ida exulted, and, satisfied not so much because she would sleep with me all night as because her sister wouldn't, she tried to start a pillow fight. We counterattacked listlessly, she stopped, settled herself between us, and turned off the light. In the dark she said happily: it's raining, I love that we're together, I'm not sleepy, please let's talk all night. But Angela shushed her, said that she, on the other hand, was sleepy, and after a few laughs there was only the sound of the rain against the windows.

Immediately my mother's ankle between Mariano's came to mind. I tried to take the sheen off the image, I wanted to convince myself that it meant nothing, that it was only something playful between friends. I didn't succeed. If it means nothing, I said to myself, tell Vittoria. My aunt would surely be able to tell me what weight I should give that scene, hadn't she urged me to spy on my parents? Look, look carefully, she had said. Now I had looked, and I had seen something. I had only to obey her with greater diligence to find out if it was nonsense or not. But I realized right away that never ever would I report to her what I had seen. Even if there was nothing bad, Vittoria would find the bad. I had seen in action — she would explain to me — the desire to fuck, and not the desire to fuck of the educational books that my parents had given me, with bright-colored figures and tidy, elementary captions, but something revolting and at the same time ridiculous, like gargling when you have a sore throat. That I wouldn't be able to tolerate. But I had only to evoke my aunt, and she was already invading my head with her exciting, repulsive lexicon, and I saw clearly, in the dark, Mariano and my mother entwined in the ways that her vocabulary suggested. Was it possible that the two of them were able to feel that same extraordinary pleasure that Vittoria said she had known and that she hoped for me as the only true gift that life could give me? The mere idea that, if I were to act as an informer, she would use the words she had for herself and Enzo, but degrading them in order to degrade my mother and, through her, my father, convinced me further that the best thing was never to talk to her about that scene.

"She's sleeping," Angela whispered.

"Let's us sleep, too."

"Yes, but in her bed."

I heard her moving cautiously in the dark. She appeared at my side, took my hand, I slipped away carefully, followed her to the other bed. We pulled up the covers, it was cold. I thought of Mariano and my mother, I thought of my father when he discovered their secret. I knew clearly that at my house everything would change for the worse, soon. I said to myself: even if I don't tell her, Vittoria will find out; or maybe she already knows and has just been pushing me to see it with my own eyes. Angela whispered:

"Talk to me about Tonino."

"He's tall."

"Go on."

"He has deep black eyes."

"Does he really want to be your boyfriend?"

"Yes."

"If you're boyfriend and girlfriend will you kiss?"

"Yes."

"With your tongue?"

"Yes."

She hugged me tight, and I hugged her as we did when we slept together. We stayed like that, trying to cling as closely as possible to each other, I with my arms around her neck, she with hers around my hips. Slowly an odor of hers arrived that I knew well, it was intense and also sweet, it gave off warmth. You're squeezing me too tight, I murmured, and she, suffocating a giggle against my chest, called me Tonino. I sighed, I said: Angela. She repeated, this time without laughing, Tonino, Tonino, Tonino, and she added: swear you'll let me meet him, otherwise we're not friends anymore. I swore, and we kissed each other with long kisses, caressing each other. Although we were sleepy, we couldn't stop. It was a serene pleasure, it banished distress, and so to give it up seemed pointless.

III

III

1.

I watched my mother for days. If the telephone rang and she hurried to answer in too much of a rush and her voice, at first loud, soon became a whisper, I suspected that the caller was Mariano. If she spent too much time attending to how she looked and discarded one dress and then another and still another, and even went so far as to call me to get my opinion on what looked best, I was sure she must be going to a secret tryst with her lover, terminology I had learned by occasionally skimming the proofs of her romance novels.

I discovered then that I could become incurably jealous. Until that moment I had been sure that my mother belonged to me and that my right to have her always available was indisputable. In the puppet theater of my mind my father was mine and legitimately also hers. They slept together, they kissed, they had conceived me according to the ways that had been explained to me around the age of six. Their relationship was for me a given, and just for that reason had never consciously disturbed me. But, incongruously, I felt that outside of that relationship my mother was indivisible and inviolable, she belonged to me alone. Her body I considered mine, mine her perfume, mine even her thoughts, which — I had been sure of it as far back as I could remember — could be occupied only by me. Now, instead, it had become plausible — and here again I used formulas learned from the novels she worked on — that my mother was giving herself to someone outside the family accords, secretly. That other man considered himself authorized to hold her ankle between his under the table, and in unknown places he put his saliva in her mouth, sucked the nipples that I had sucked and — as Vittoria said with a dialectal cadence that I didn't have but that now more than ever, out of desperation, I would have liked to have — grabbed one buttock, grabbed the other. When she came home breathless because countless duties, work and domestic, harassed her, I saw her eyes full of light, I sensed under her clothes the signs of Mariano's hands, I perceived all over her, who didn't smoke, the smoke smell from his fingers, yellow with nicotine. Just touching her soon began to repulse me, and yet I couldn't bear to lose the pleasure of sitting on her lap, of playing with her earlobes to annoy her and hearing her say stop it, you're making my ears purple, of laughing together. Why is she doing this: I racked my brains. I didn't see a single good reason that would justify her betrayal, and so I tried to figure out how I could transport her back to the time before that contact under the dinner table and have her again the way she was when I didn't even realize how much I cared about her, when, rather, it seemed obvious that she was there, ready for my needs, and that she would always be there.

2.

In that phase I avoided calling Vittoria, or seeing her. I justified it by thinking: this way it's easier to say to Angela and Ida that she's busy and doesn't have time even to see me. But the reason was different. I felt like crying all the time, and I knew by now that only with my aunt would I be able to weep in complete freedom, screaming, sobbing. Oh yes, I wanted a moment of release, no words, no confidences, only an expulsion of suffering. But who would assure me that, just as I erupted into tears, I wouldn't fling in her face her responsibility, wouldn't yell with all the fury I was capable of that, yes, I had done as she told me, I had looked exactly as she had told me to look, and now I knew that I shouldn't have, I shouldn't have under any circumstances, because I had discovered that my father's best friend — in essence a repulsive man — was squeezing my mother's ankle between his while they were having dinner, and that my mother didn't jump up indignantly, didn't cry, how dare you, but let him squeeze it? I was afraid, in other words, that, once I started crying, my decision to remain silent would suddenly collapse, and that I absolutely didn't want. I knew very well that as soon as I told Vittoria she would pick up the telephone and tell my father everything for the joy of hurting him.

Then what? Gradually I calmed down. I examined yet again what I had really seen, I got rid of the fantasies by force, day by day I tried to drive out the impression that something very serious was about to happen to my family. I felt the need for company, I wanted to distract myself. So I spent even more time with Angela and Ida, and that intensified their demands to meet my

152

aunt. In the end I thought: what will it cost me, what's the harm? So one afternoon I decided to ask my mother: some Sunday could I bring Angela and Ida to meet Aunt Vittoria?

My obsessions aside, at that time she was objectively overloaded with work. She raced to school, came home, went out again, came home, shut herself in her room to work until late at night. I took it for granted that she would absently say: all right. Instead, she didn't seem pleased.

"What do Angela and Ida have to do with Aunt Vittoria?"

"They're my friends, they want to meet her."

"You know that Aunt Vittoria won't make a good impression."

"Why?"

"Because she's not a presentable woman."

"What do you mean?"

"That's enough, I don't have time now to discuss it. In my opinion you should stop seeing her as well."

I was angry, I said I wanted to talk about it with my father. My head was bursting, against my will: *you* aren't presentable, not Aunt Vittoria; I'll tell Papa what you do with Mariano and you'll pay. Then, without waiting for her usual work of mediation, I ran to my father's study, feeling — I was surprised at myself, frightened, I couldn't restrain myself — that I was truly capable of dumping on him what I had seen together with what I had intuited. But when I went into the room and almost shouted, as if it were a question of life and death, that I wanted Angela and Ida to meet Vittoria, he looked up from his papers and said affectionately: there's no need to shout, what's going on?

I immediately felt relieved. I repressed the information I had on the tip of my tongue, I kissed him hard on one cheek, I told him about Angela and Ida's request, I complained about my mother's rigid position. He maintained his conciliatory tone and didn't rule out the initiative, but he repeated his aversion toward his sister. He said: Vittoria is your problem, your private curiosity, and I don't want to comment on it, but you'll see that Angela and Ida won't like her.

Surprisingly Costanza, who had never in her life met my aunt, manifested the same hostility, as if she had consulted with my mother. Her daughters had to battle for a long time to get permission, they reported to me what she had proposed: invite her here, or meet her, I don't know, in a café in Piazza Vanvitelli, long enough to satisfy Giovanna and be done. As for Mariano, he was no less against it: what's the point of spending a Sunday with that woman, and then, good God, to go down there, a terrible place, there's nothing interesting to see. But in my eyes he didn't even have the right to breathe, and so I explained to Angela, lying, that my aunt had said we had to go to her, to her house, or nothing doing. In the end, Costanza and Mariano capitulated, but together with my parents they organized everything in detail. Vittoria would pick me up at nine-thirty; then we would go together to get Angela and Ida; finally, coming home, my friends would be dropped off at their house at two and I at my house at two-thirty.

Then I telephoned Vittoria, with trepidation: until that moment I hadn't even consulted her. She was brusque as usual, she scolded me because she hadn't heard from me for a long time, but in essence she seemed glad that I wanted to bring my friends with me. She said: everything that pleases you pleases me, and she accepted the finicky schedule that had been imposed, even if in the tone of someone who's thinking: sure, why not, I'll do what I feel like.

3.

So it was that one Sunday, when Christmas decorations were already appearing in the shop windows, Vittoria arrived punctually at my house. I had been waiting for her apprehensively at the front door for a quarter of an hour. She seemed cheerful, she descended to Via Cimarosa in the Fiat 500 at high speed, singing and making me sing, too. We found Costanza waiting with her daughters, all three pretty and tidy, as if in a television ad. When I suddenly realized that my aunt hadn't even brought the car to the curb and already, a cigarette between her lips, was registering Costanza's extreme elegance with a mocking look, I said anxiously:

"Don't get out, I'll let my friends in and we'll go."

But she didn't even hear me, she laughed, she muttered in dialect:

"Did she sleep like that or is she going to an early-morning reception?"

Then she got out of the car and greeted Costanza with a cordiality so exaggerated that it seemed clearly fake. I tried to get out, but the door was defective, and while I was struggling with it I observed in great agitation Costanza smiling politely, with

Angela on one side and Ida on the other, while Vittoria was saying something, cutting the air with broad gestures. I hoped she wasn't using curse words, and meanwhile I managed to open the door. I rushed out in time to hear my aunt, half in Italian, half in dialect, complimenting my friends:

"Pretty, pretty, pretty. Like their mother."

"Thank you," said Costanza.

"And these earrings?"

She began to praise Costanza's earrings — she touched them with her finger — then moved on to her necklace, her dress, she touched everything for a few seconds, as if she were standing before a decorated mannequin. I was afraid, at one point, that she would pull up the hem of Costanza's dress to examine her stockings more closely, to look at her underpants, she would have been capable of it. But suddenly she calmed down, as if an invisible noose had tightened around her throat to remind her to compose herself, and she paused with a serious expression on the bracelet Costanza had on her wrist, a bracelet I knew well, it was the one that Angela and Ida's mother especially liked. It was of white gold, with a flower whose petals were diamonds and rubies, splendid precisely in the sense that it gave off light; even my mother envied it.

"It's really beautiful," Vittoria said, holding Costanza's hand and touching the bracelet with her fingertips with what seemed to me sincere admiration.

"Yes, I like it, too."

"You're very attached to it?"

"I'm fond of it, I've had it for years."

"Well, watch out, it's so pretty some thug'll pass by and grab it off you."

Then she let go of her hand as if a sudden impulse of disgust had replaced the praise and returned to Angela and Ida. She said in a false tone that they were much more precious than all the bracelets in the world, and she got in the car while Costanza ordered: girls, be good, don't make me worry, I'll be waiting for you here at two, and, since my aunt didn't answer, and in fact had got in the driver's seat without saying goodbye, and with one of her most glowering looks, I shouted with feigned cheer from the window, yes, Costanza, at two, don't worry.

4.

We drove off, and Vittoria, with her usual inexpert yet reckless driving, took us on the ring road and then all the way down to Pascone. She wasn't kind to my friends; during the journey she kept reprimanding them because their voices were too loud. I yelled, too, the engine made a racket and it was natural to raise your voice, but she took it out only on them. We tried to control ourselves, she got angry just the same, she said that her head hurt, she ordered us not to even breathe. I guessed that something had irked her, maybe she didn't like the two girls, it was hard to say. We went much of the way without saying a word, I beside her, Angela and Ida on the very uncomfortable back seat. Until, out of the blue, my aunt herself broke the silence, but a hoarse, mean voice came out, as she asked my friends:

"You're not baptized, either?"

"No," Ida said readily.

"But," Angela added, "Papa said if we want to we can be baptized when we grow up."

"What if you die in the meantime? You know you'll go to limbo?"

"Limbo doesn't exist," said Ida.

"Nor Paradise, purgatory, or hell," Angela added.

"Who told you that?"

"Papa."

"And where does he think God puts those who sin and those who don't sin?"

"God doesn't exist, either," said Ida.

159

"And sin doesn't exist," Angela explained.

"That's what Papa told you?"

"Yes."

"Papa is a shit."

"You shouldn't say bad words," Ida admonished her.

I intervened so that Vittoria wouldn't lose patience for good.

"Sin exists: it's when there's no friendship, there's no love, and you waste something good."

"You see?" said Vittoria. "Giannina understands and you don't."

"It's not true, I understand, too," Ida said nervously. "Sin is a bitterness. We say 'What a sin' when something we like falls on the floor and breaks."

She waited to be praised, but the praise didn't arrive, my aunt said only: a bitterness, eh? I thought it was unfair to behave like that with my friend, she was younger but very smart, she devoured difficult books, and I liked the observation. So I repeated "What a sin" once or twice, I wanted Vittoria to hear it clearly, what a sin, what a sin. My anguish increased, but without a precise cause. Maybe I was thinking of how everything had turned brittle, right before that terrible remark of my father's about my face, when I'd gotten my period, when my chest had swelled, who knows. What to do. I'd given too much importance to the words that wounded me, too much weight to this aunt, oh to be a little child again, six, seven, maybe eight, or even younger, and erase all the steps that had led me to the ankles of Mariano and my mother, to being shut up now in this ramshackle car, constantly at risk of hitting other cars, of going off the road, so that maybe in a few minutes I'd be dead, or gravely injured, and would lose an arm, a leg, or be blind for the rest of my life.

"Where are we going?" I asked, and I knew it was an infraction, in the past I had ventured only once to ask a question like that and Vittoria had replied irritably: where I want to go. In this situation, though, she seemed to respond willingly. She didn't look at me, she looked at Angela and Ida in the rearview mirror and said:

"To church."

"We don't know any prayers," I warned her.

"That's bad, you have to learn them, they're useful."

"But for now we don't know them."

"Now it doesn't matter. Now we're not going to say prayers, we're going to the parish flea market. If you don't know how

161

to pray, surely you know how to help sell."

"Yes," Ida exclaimed happily, "I'm good at it."

I felt relieved.

"Did you organize it?" I asked Vittoria.

"The whole parish but mainly my children."

For the first time in my presence, she defined as *hers* Margherita's three children, and she did it with pride.

"Corrado, too?" I asked.

"Corrado is a piece of shit, but he does what I say, otherwise I'll break his legs."

"And Tonino?"

"Tonino is good."

Angela couldn't contain herself and let out a shout of enthusiasm.

5.

I had rarely entered a church and only when my father wanted to show me one that in his opinion was particularly beautiful. According to him the churches of Naples were elegant structures, richly endowed with works of art, and shouldn't be left in the state of neglect they were in. On one occasion — I think we were in San Lorenzo but I wouldn't swear to it — he reprimanded me because I had started running up and

162

down the naves and then, when I couldn't find him, had called him with a terrified shout. He said that people who don't believe in God, as, in fact, he and I didn't, should nevertheless, out of respect for believers, behave politely: you don't have to wet your fingers in the holy water font, you don't have to make the sign of the cross, but you should take off your hat even if the weather is cold, not speak in a loud voice, not light a cigarette or go in smoking. Vittoria, on the other hand, lighted cigarette in her mouth, dragged us into a church that was gray-white outside, shadowy inside, saying in a loud voice: make the sign of the cross. We didn't, she noticed, and, one after the other — Ida first, me last — she took our hand and guided it to forehead, chest, and shoulders, saying with irritation: in the name of the Father, the Son, and the Holy Ghost. Then, as her bad mood got worse, she dragged us down a dimly lit nave, grumbling: you've made me late. Coming to a door with an excessively shiny doorknob, she opened it without knocking and closed it behind her, leaving us alone.

"Your aunt is mean and she's very ugly," Ida whispered.

"That's not true."

"Yes, it is," Angela said in a serious tone.

I felt the tears coming, I struggled to hold them back.

"She says she and I are identical."

"Really," said Angela, "you're not ugly and you're not mean."

Ida specified:

"You're only that way sometimes, but hardly ever."

Vittoria reappeared with a short young man who had a handsome, cordial face. He wore a black pullover, gray pants, and, around his neck on a leather cord, a wooden cross without the body of Jesus.

"This is Giannina, and these are her two friends," said my aunt.

"Giacomo," the young man introduced himself; he had a refined voice, without dialect.

"Don Giacomo," Vittoria corrected him, annoyed.

"Are you the priest?" Ida asked.

"Yes."

"We don't say prayers."

"Doesn't matter. You can pray even without saying prayers."

I was curious.

"How?"

"You just have to be sincere. Join your hands and say: my God, please, protect me, help me, et cetera."

"Do you pray only in church?"

"Everywhere."

"And God hears you even if you don't know anything about him and you don't even believe he exists?"

"God listens to everyone," the priest answered kindly.

"Impossible," said Ida, "there'd be such a racket he wouldn't understand a thing."

My aunt gave her a slap with the tips of her fingers and scolded her, because you can't say to God: it's impossible — for him everything is possible. Don Giacomo caught the unhappiness in Ida's eyes and caressed her in the exact spot where Vittoria had hit her, while in a near whisper he said that children can say and do what they like, since they're still innocent anyway. Then, to my surprise, he mentioned a Roberto who — I quickly understood — was the one who'd been talked about some time ago at Margherita's house, that is, the young man from that area who now lived and studied in Milan, the friend of Tonino and Giuliana. Don Giacomo called him *our Roberto* and cited him with affection, because it was he who had pointed out to him that hostility toward children isn't rare, that even the holy apostles had shown it, not understanding that you have to become a child to enter the kingdom of Heaven. Jesus, in fact, reproaches them, he says: what are you doing, don't send away the little children, let them come to me. Here the priest turned meaningfully to my aunt — our discontent should never touch children, he said, and I thought that he, too, must have noted in Vittoria an unusual distress — while he kept one hand on Ida's head. Then he continued with a few heartfelt phrases about childhood, innocence, youth, the dangers of the streets.

"You don't agree?" he asked my aunt, soothing, and she turned purple as if he had caught her not listening.

"With whom?"

"With Roberto."

"He spoke well but without thinking of the consequences."

"One speaks well precisely when one doesn't think of the consequences."

Angela, curious, whispered to me:

"Who is this Roberto?"

I knew nothing about Roberto. I would have liked to say: I know him very well, he's great; or, using Corrado's words, no, he's a pain in the ass. Instead, I signaled her to be quiet, annoyed as I always was when my belonging to the world of my aunt was revealed as superficial. Angela was obediently silent, but not Ida, she asked the priest: "What's Roberto like?"

Don Giacomo laughed, he said that Roberto had the beauty and intelligence of those who have faith. Next time he comes — he promised us — I'll have you meet him, but now let's go sell, come on, otherwise the poor will complain. So we passed through a doorway into a kind of courtyard where, under an L-shaped portico decorated with gilded festoons and multicolor Christmas lights, there were stands crammed with used objects. Margherita, Giuliana, Corrado, Tonino, and others I didn't know were decorating and arranging things, and welcoming with ostentatious gaiety the possible buyers for charity, people who — to look at them — appeared only slightly less poor than how I imagined the poor.

6.

Margherita praised my friends, called them pretty little ladies, and introduced them to her children, who welcomed them cordially. Giuliana chose Ida as her helper, Tonino wanted Angela, I stood listening to Corrado, who was chatting, trying to joke with Vittoria, but she was treating him badly. I couldn't bear it for long, and my mind wandered, so with the excuse that I wanted to see what was for sale I walked among the stands, absently touching this or that. There were many homemade sweets, but mainly eyeglasses, bundles of papers, an old telephone, glasses, cups, books, a coffeepot, all well-worn objects, touched over the years by hands that by now were probably hands of the dead, poverty being sold to poverty.

People were arriving now, and I heard someone say to the priest the word "widow" — there's the widow, too, they said — and since they were looking toward the stalls supervised by Margherita, her children, and my aunt, I thought for a while that they were referring to Margherita. But gradually I realized that they meant Vittoria. There's the widow, they said, today we'll have music and dancing. And I didn't understand if they uttered widow with scorn or with respect: certainly it surprised me that they associated my aunt, who was unmarried, with both widowhood and entertainment.

I looked at her carefully, from a distance. She was standing erect behind one of the stalls, and her narrow chest with the large breasts seemed to jump out from the piles of dusty objects. She didn't seem ugly, I didn't want her to be, and yet Angela and Ida had said she was. Maybe it's because today something has gone wrong, I thought. Her eyes were troubled, she gestured in her aggressive way or, unexpectedly, let out a shout and moved for a few moments to the rhythm of the music that came from an old record player. I said to myself: yes, she's angry because of some business of her own that I don't know about, or she's worried about Corrado. We two are made like that, when we have good thoughts we're pretty, but we turn ugly with mean ones, we have to get them out of our heads.

I wandered idly through the courtyard. I had wanted that morning to drive out the anguish, but it wasn't working. My mother and Mariano were too big a weight, it hurt my bones as if I had the flu. I could see that Angela was happy and light-hearted, she was pretty, she was laughing with Tonino. Everyone at that moment appeared to me handsome and good and just, especially Don Giacomo, who, with the sun on him, welcomed the parishioners kindly, shaking hands, not avoiding hugs. Was it possible that only Vittoria and I were grim, tense? My eyes were burning, my mouth was very bitter, I was afraid that Corrado — I was standing beside him again, partly to help him sell, partly to look for relief — would smell my heavy breath. Maybe the acid yet sweetish taste came not from the back of my throat but from the objects on the tables. I felt very sad. And the whole time the Christmas market went on it was depressing to see myself reflected in my aunt, who sometimes greeted the parishioners with an artificial brightness, sometimes stared into space, eyes wide. Yes, she was feeling at least as badly as I was. Corrado said to her: what's wrong, Vittò, you're sick, you've got an ugly face, and she answered: yes, I'm sick at heart, I'm sick in my chest, I'm sick to my stomach, I have a terrible face. And she tried to smile with her wide mouth, but she couldn't, so, turning very pale, she said to him: go get me a glass of water.

While Corrado went to get the water I thought: she's sick inside and I'm exactly like her, she's the person I feel closest to. The morning was passing, I would return to my mother and father, and I didn't know how long I could stand the disorder at home. So, just as when my mother opposed me and I ran to my father to tell on her, so an urgent need to vent suddenly rose up in my breast. It was intolerable that Mariano should hug my mother, hold her tight, while she had on the clothes I knew, while she put on the earrings and other jewelry I had played with as a child and that I sometimes wore myself. The jealousy increased, creating hideous images. I couldn't bear the intrusion of that malicious stranger, and finally, unable to resist, I made a decision without realizing I'd made it, and said impulsively, in a voice that arrived like shattering glass: aunt (even though she had ordered me never to call her that), aunt, I have to tell you something, but it's a secret that you mustn't tell anyone, swear you won't. She replied weakly that she would never swear, never, the only oath she had taken was the oath to love Enzo forever, and that she would maintain until death. I was desperate, I told her that if she didn't swear I couldn't talk. Screw you then, she muttered, the nasty things you don't say to anyone become dogs that eat your head at night while you're sleeping. And so, frightened by that image, needing consolation, a moment later I pulled her aside and told her about Mariano, my mother, what I had seen mixed with what I had imagined. Then I begged her:

"Please, don't tell Papa."

She stared at me for a long moment, then replied in dialect, mean, incomprehensibly mocking:

"Papa? You think Papa gives a fuck about

the ankles of Mariano and Nella under the table?"

7.

The time passed very slowly, I kept checking the clock. Ida was having fun with Giuliana, Tonino seemed completely at ease with Angela, I felt like a failure, like a cake made with the wrong ingredients. What had I done. What would happen now. Corrado returned with the water for Vittoria, in no hurry, idly. I found him boring, but at that moment I felt lost and hoped that he would pay even a little attention to me. He didn't, in fact, he didn't even wait for my aunt to finish drinking, he vanished among the parishioners. Vittoria followed him with her gaze, she was forgetting that I was there next to her waiting for explanations, advice. Was it possible that she had judged insignificant even that grievous fact I had told her? I watched her closely, she was gruffly demanding from a fat woman in her fifties an excessive amount for a pair of sunglasses, but she didn't lose sight of Corrado: there was something about his behavior that — it appeared to me — seemed to her more serious than what I had revealed to her. Look at him, she said to me, he's too sociable, just like his father. And suddenly she called him: Currà. And when he didn't hear or pretended not to, she abandoned the fat woman whose glasses she was wrapping and, clutching the scissors she used to cut the ribbon for tying up packages and grabbing me with her left hand, dragged me with her through the courtyard.

Corrado was talking to three or four young men, one of whom was tall and thin and had buck teeth that gave the impression that he was laughing even when there was nothing to laugh at. My aunt, apparently calm, ordered her godson — today that seems to me the right definition for the three children — to return immediately to the stand. He answered playfully: two minutes and I'll be there, while the boy with the buck teeth seemed to laugh. My aunt turned to him abruptly and said she would cut off his *pesce* — she used precisely that dialect word, *pesce, fish,* in a calm voice, brandishing the scissors — if he kept laughing. But the kid didn't seem to want to stop, and I sensed all Vittoria's fury, on the verge of exploding. I was worried, she didn't seem to understand that his buck teeth prevented him from keeping his mouth closed, she didn't seem to understand that he would laugh even during an earthquake. In fact, suddenly she yelled at him:

"You're laughing, Rosà, you dare to laugh?"

"No."

"Yes, you're laughing because you think your father will protect you, but you're wrong, no one protects you from me. You leave Corrado alone, understand?"

"Yes."

"No, you don't understand, you're convinced I can't do anything to you, but watch out."

She pointed the scissors at him and, right before my eyes, and in front of some parishioners who were starting to wonder about that unexpectedly loud tone of voice, pricked the boy in one leg, so that he jumped back, the terrified astonishment of his eyes spoiling the fixed mask of his laugh.

My aunt pressed him, threatened to prick him again.

"Get it now, Rosà," she said, "or do I have to keep going? I don't give a fuck if you're the son of attorney Sargente."

The young man, whose name was Rosario, and who was evidently the son of that lawyer I didn't know, raised one hand in a sign of surrender, retreated, went off with his friends.

Corrado, indignant, started to follow

174

them, but Vittoria stood in front of him with the scissors saying:

"Don't you move, because if you make me mad I'll use these with you, too."

I pulled her by the arm.

"That guy," I said, frightened, "can't close his mouth."

"He dared to laugh in my face," Vittoria replied, panting, "and no one laughs in my face."

"He was laughing but not on purpose."

"On purpose or not, he was laughing."

Corrado scowled, he said:

"Forget it, Giannì, it's pointless to talk to her."

But my aunt gave a cry, she yelled at him, gasping:

"You shut up, I don't want to hear a word."

She was clutching the scissors, I realized that she was having a hard time controlling herself. Her capacity for affection must long ago have been used up, probably with the death of Enzo, but her capacity for hatred — it seemed to me — had no limit. I had just seen how she behaved with poor Rosario Sargente, and she would have been capable of hurting even Corrado: imagine then what she would do to my mother and especially my father, now that I had told

175

her about Mariano. The idea of it made me feel like crying again. I'd been reckless, the words had spilled out unintentionally. Or maybe not, maybe in some part of me I had long ago decided to tell Vittoria what I had seen, I had already decided when I gave in to the pressure of my friends and arranged that meeting. I could no longer be innocent, behind my thoughts there were other thoughts, childhood was over. I strained, and yet innocence eluded me, the tears that I felt continuously in my eyes hardly proved that I wasn't guilty. Luckily, Don Giacomo arrived, soothing, and that kept me from crying. Come, come, he said to Corrado, putting an arm around his shoulders, let's not make Vittoria mad, she's not well today, help her carry the pastries. My aunt sighed bitterly, placed the scissors on the edge of one of the stands, glanced at the street beyond the courtyard, perhaps to see if Rosario and the others were still there, then said firmly: I don't want help, and disappeared through the doorway that led to the church.

8.

She returned soon afterward carrying two large trays of almond pastries, each with

176

blue and pink icing stripes and a small sugared almond on top. The parishioners fought over them; eating even one was enough to disgust me, my stomach was contracted, my heart pounding in my throat. Don Giacomo brought over an accordion, holding it in both arms as if it were a red-and-white child. I thought he knew how to play, but he delivered it a little awkwardly to Vittoria, who took it without protest — was it the same one I'd seen in the corner at her house? — sat down on a chair, sullenly, and played with her eyes closed, grimacing.

Angela came up behind me and said cheerfully: your aunt — you see her — is really ugly. At that moment it was very true: Vittoria contorted her face like a devil while she played, and even though she was good and the parishioners applauded, she made a repellent spectacle. She tossed her shoulders, curled her lips, wrinkled her forehead, stretched her trunk backward so far that it seemed to be much longer than her legs, which were spread indecorously. It was a blessing when a white-haired man took over and began to play. But my aunt still wouldn't calm down, she went to Tonino, grabbed him by one arm and forced him to dance, taking him away from Angela. Now she seemed happy, but maybe it was only the tremendous ferocity she had in her body and wanted to vent by dancing. Seeing her, others danced, too, old and young, even Don Giacomo. I closed my eyes to cancel out everything. I felt abandoned, and for the first time in my life, against everything my parents had taught me, I tried to pray. God, I said, God, please, if you truly can do everything, don't let my aunt say anything to my father, and I closed my eyes tight, as if squeezing my eyelids could concentrate in the prayer enough force to hurl it up to the Lord in the kingdom of Heaven. Afterward, I prayed that my aunt would stop dancing and return us to Costanza on time, a prayer that was miraculously answered. To my surprise, despite pastries, music, songs, interminable dances, we departed in time to leave behind the hazy Industrial Zone and arrive punctually on the Vomero, on Via Cimarosa, at Angela and Ida's house. Costanza, too, was punctual, she appeared in a dress even more beautiful than the one of the morning. Vittoria got out of the 500, delivered Angela and Ida, and praised her again, again admired all her things. She admired the dress, the hairstyle, the makeup, the earrings, the necklace, the bracelet, which she touched, almost caressed, asking me: do you like it, Giannì?

It seemed to me that she intended to mock her with all that praise, even more than in the morning. We must have grown so in tune that I imagined I could hear in my head, with a destructive energy, her traitorous voice, her vulgar words: what's the use, bitch, of getting all decked out like this, your husband is fucking the mamma of my niece Giannina, oh, oh, oh. So I prayed again to the Lord God, especially when Vittoria got in the car and we set off. I prayed all the way to San Giacomo dei Capri, an interminable journey during which Vittoria didn't say a word and I didn't dare ask her another time: don't say anything to my father, I beg you; if you want to do something for me, reprimand my mother but keep the secret from my father. I entreated God, even if he didn't exist: God, don't let Vittoria say I'm coming up with you, I have to speak to your father.

To my great astonishment, I was again miraculously heard. How wonderful miracles were and how decisive: Vittoria left me outside without even a mention of my mother, Mariano, my father. She said only, in dialect: Giannì, remember that you're my niece, that you and I are alike, and if you call me, if you say, Vittoria, come, I'll hurry

179

right away, I'll never leave you alone. Her face, after those words, seemed more serene, and I wanted to believe that if Angela had seen it now she would have found it beautiful, just as at that moment it seemed to me. But as soon as I was alone, at home — while, shut in my room, I looked at myself in the closet mirror and confirmed that no miracle would ever be able to erase the face that was coming to me — I gave in and finally wept. I resolved not to spy on my parents anymore, and never to see my aunt again.

9.

When I try to assign phases to the continuous flow of life that has passed through me up until today, I'm convinced that I permanently became someone else when, one afternoon, Costanza came to visit without her daughters. Overseen by my mother, who for days had had puffy eyes and a reddened face — due, she said, to the cold wind that blew from the sea and caused the windowpanes and the balcony railings to vibrate — Costanza, her face severe, sallow, gave me her white-gold bracelet.

"Why are you giving it to me?" I asked, bewildered.

"She's not giving it to you," my mother said, "she's returning it to you."

Costanza's beautiful mouth quavered for a long moment before she managed to say:

"I thought it was mine, but it was yours."

I didn't understand, I didn't want to understand. I preferred to thank her and try to put it on, but I couldn't manage. In absolute silence Costanza, fingers trembling, helped me.

"How does it look?" I asked my mother, pretending frivolity.

"Good," she said without even a smile and left the room, followed by Costanza, who never came to our house again.

Mariano, too, disappeared from Via San Giacomo dei Capri, and as a result I saw Angela and Ida less frequently. At first, we talked on the telephone: none of us three understood what was happening. A couple of days before Costanza's visit, Angela told me that my father and her father had had a fight in the apartment on Via Cimarosa. At the outset, the discussion had seemed very similar to the ones they had on the usual subjects, politics, Marxism, the end of history, economics, the state, but then it had turned surprisingly violent. Mariano had shouted: now get out of my house immediately, I don't want to see you ever

181

again; and my father, suddenly dissolving his image of the patient friend, had begun yelling the ugliest words in dialect. Angela and Ida were frightened, but no one paid any attention to them, not even Costanza, who at a certain point couldn't bear to listen to the shouting and said she was going to get some air. At which Mariano shouted, also in dialect: yes, get out, slut, don't come back, and Costanza slammed the door so hard that it reopened, Mariano had to kick it closed, my father opened it again and ran after Costanza.

In the following days, all we did was talk on the phone about that fight. Neither Angela nor Ida nor I could understand why Marxism and the other things our parents discussed passionately even before we were born had suddenly caused so many problems. In reality, for different reasons, both they and I understood much more of that scene than we admitted. We intuited, for example, that it had to do with sex, not Marxism, but not the sex that interested and amused us in every circumstance; we felt that, completely unexpectedly, a form of sex was erupting into our lives that wasn't attractive, that in fact disgusted us, because we dimly perceived that it had to do not with our bodies, or the bodies of our contemporaries, or actors and singers, but with the bodies of our parents. Sex — we imagined — had drawn them into something sticky and repulsive, utterly different from what they themselves had taught us. According to Ida, the words that Mariano and my father had shouted at each other gave the idea of feverish spitting, of threads of mucus that smeared everything, especially our most secret desires. It was for this reason, perhaps, that my friends — very inclined to talk about Tonino, Corrado, and how much they liked those two boys — became sad and began to turn away from that type of sex. As for me, I knew much more about the secret dealings in our families than Angela and Ida, so the effort to avoid understanding what was happening to my father, my mother, Mariano, Costanza was much greater and exhausted me. It was I, in fact, who in distress withdrew and abandoned the telephone confidences. Maybe, more than Angela, more than Ida, I felt that a single wrong word would open a dangerous passage to the reality of the facts.

In that phase, lies and prayers established themselves solidly in my daily life and again helped a lot. The lies, for the most part, I told myself. I was unhappy, and in school and at home pretended an extreme cheerfulness. I would see my mother's face in the morning on the verge of losing its features, red around the nose, disfigured by depression, and I would say in a tone of gay affirmation: how nice you look today. As for my father — who had all of a sudden stopped studying as soon as he opened his eyes, whom I found ready to go out early in the morning, or very pale, with dull eyes, in the evening — I constantly presented him with exercises that I had to do for school, even though they weren't complicated, as if it weren't obvious that his mind was elsewhere and he had no wish to help me.

At the same time, although I continued not to believe in God, I devoted myself to prayer as if I did. God — I entreated — let the fight between my father and Mariano be about Marxism and the end of history, let it not be because Vittoria telephoned my father and reported to him what I told her. At first, it seemed to me that the Lord was listening to me yet again. As far as I knew, it was Mariano who had attacked my father and not the opposite, as would surely have happened if Vittoria had used my information to be, in turn, an informer. But I quickly realized that something didn't add up. Why had my father railed against Mariano in a dialect he never used? Why had Costanza left the house slamming the door? Why had my father, not her husband, run after her?

Behind my casual lies, my prayers, I lived in apprehension. Vittoria must have told my father everything, and my father had rushed to Mariano's house to fight about it. Costanza, as a result of that fight, had discovered that her husband was holding my mother's ankles between his under the table and had in turn made a scene. It must have happened like that. But why had Mariano yelled at his wife, while she, desolate, left the apartment on Via Cimarosa: yes, get out, slut, don't come back? And why had my father run after her?

I felt that something was escaping me, something that at times I got a glimpse of and grasped its meaning, and then, as soon as the meaning tried to surface, I drew back. So I constantly returned to the more obscure facts: Costanza's visit, for example, which had followed the quarrel; my mother's face, so worn, and her violet eyes that cast suddenly imperious glances at an old friend by whom she had tended to be dominated; Costanza's remorseful look and the contrite gesture with which she seemed to want to give me a gift, while instead — my mother had explained — it was not a gift but a restitution; the trembling fingers with which Angela and Ida's mother had helped me put on my wrist the white-gold bracelet she was so fond of; the bracelet itself, which I now wore day and night. Oh, of those events that took place in my room, of that dense network of glances, gestures, words around a bracelet that without explanation had been given to me and described as mine, I certainly knew more than what I could tell myself. So I prayed, especially at night, when I woke up scared by what I was afraid was about to happen. God, I whispered, God, I know it's my fault, I shouldn't have insisted on meeting Vittoria, I shouldn't have gone against my parents' wishes; but now that it's happened put things back in order, please. I truly hoped that God would do that, because if he didn't, everything would collapse. San Giacomo dei Capri would tumble onto the Vomero and the Vomero onto the entire city, and the entire city would drown in the sea.

In the dark, I was dying of anguish. I felt such a weight crushing my stomach that I got up in the middle of the night to vomit. I made noise on purpose: sharp feelings in my chest, in my head had wounded me deeply, I hoped that my parents would appear and help me. But they didn't. And yet

186

they were awake; a strip of light scratched the darkness right outside their bedroom. I deduced from that that they no longer wished to concern themselves with me, and so they never, for any reason, interrupted their nighttime murmuring. At most, a sudden peak broke the monotony, a syllable, half a word that my mother uttered like the tip of a knife on a windowpane, my father like distant thunder. In the morning they were exhausted. We had breakfast in silence, eyes lowered, I couldn't stand it. I prayed, God, that's enough, make something happen, anything, good or bad doesn't matter: let me die, for example, that should shake them up, reconcile them, and afterward let me be resurrected into a family that's happy again.

One Sunday, at lunch, a violent internal energy suddenly incited my mind and my tongue. I said in a light tone, showing the bracelet:

"Papa, Aunt Vittoria gave me this, right?"

My mother took a sip of wine, my father didn't look up from his plate, he said:

"In a certain sense, yes."

"And why did you give it to Costanza?"

This time he raised his eyes, stared at me coldly, without saying anything.

"Answer her," my mother ordered him,

but he didn't obey. Then she almost shouted: "For fifteen years your father has had another wife."

Spots of red burned her face, her eyes were frantic. I realized that it must have seemed a terrible revelation to her, she already regretted having made it. But I wasn't surprised nor did it seem to me any sort of wrong, rather I had the impression of having always known it and for a moment I was sure that everything could be healed. If the thing had been going on for fifteen years it could go on forever, the three of us just had to say it's fine like that and peace would return, my mother in her room, my father in his study, the meetings, the books. And so, as if to help them move toward this reconciliation, I said to my mother:

"And you, too, you have another husband."

My mother turned pale, she murmured:

"Me no, I assure you, I don't."

She denied it with such desperation that, maybe because all that suffering hurt me too much, I felt like repeating, in falsetto: I assure you, I assure you, and I laughed. The laugh escaped against my will, I saw the rage in my father's eyes and I was afraid of it, I was ashamed. I would have liked to explain

188

to him: it wasn't a real laugh, Papa, but a contraction I couldn't help, it happens, I saw it recently on the face of a boy named Rosario Sargente. But the laugh wouldn't be erased, it changed into a frozen smile, I felt it on my face and couldn't get rid of it.

My father got up slowly, moved to leave the table.

"Where are you going?" my mother said alarmed.

"To sleep," he said.

It was two in the afternoon: usually at that hour, especially on Sunday or when he had the day off from school, he shut himself in to study and went on until dinnertime. Instead he yawned, to let us know that he really was sleepy. My mother said:

"I'm coming to sleep, too."

He shook his head, and we both read in his face that the usual lying down with her in the same bed had become intolerable to him. Before he left the kitchen, he said to me, in a tone of surrender that for him was very rare:

"There's nothing to be done about it, Giovanna, you really are like my sister."

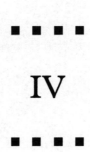

IV

VI

1.

It took my parents almost two years to decide to separate, even though during that time they lived under the same roof only for brief periods. My father disappeared for weeks without warning, leaving me with the fear that he had taken his life in some dark, squalid place in Naples. I discovered only later that he went to live happily in a beautiful house in Posillipo that Costanza's parents had given their daughter, who was now permanently fighting with Mariano. When my father reappeared he was affectionate and courteous, he seemed to want to return to my mother and me. But after a few days of reconciliation my parents began fighting about everything. There was one thing, however, about which they were always in agreement: for my own good I shouldn't ever see Vittoria again.

I didn't object, I was of the same opinion. And on the other hand, my aunt, from the moment the crisis exploded, hadn't been seen or heard from. I guessed that she was waiting for me to seek her out: she, the servant, believed that she had me forever in her service. But I had promised myself not to stand by her anymore. I was exhausted, she had unloaded on me all of herself, her hatreds, her need for revenge, her language, and I hoped that from the mixture of fear and fascination I'd felt toward her at least the fascination was fading.

But one afternoon Vittoria began tempting me again. The telephone rang, I answered and heard her at the other end saying: hello, is Giannina there, I want to talk to Giannina. I hung up, holding my breath. But she phoned again and again, every day at the same time, never on Sunday. I forced myself not to answer. I let the phone ring, and if my mother was home and she went to answer, I yelled: I'm not here for anyone, imitating the imperative tone in which she sometimes shouted the same formula from her room.

I'd hold my breath, pray with my eyes closed that it wasn't Vittoria. And, fortunately, it wasn't, or at least if it was my mother didn't tell me. Instead, the phone calls gradually became less frequent, until I thought she had given up and I began to answer the phone without anxiety. But, unexpectedly, Vittoria erupted again, shouting from the other end of the line: hello, you're Giannina, I want to talk to Giannina. But I didn't want to be Giannina anymore, and I always hung up. Of course, sometimes I heard suffering in her weary voice, I felt pity, and I became curious to see her, to question her, to provoke her. Sometimes when I was especially depressed I was tempted to cry: yes, it's me, explain to me what happened, what did you do to my father and mother. But I always kept silent, cutting off the call, and I got used to not naming her even to myself.

Eventually, I also decided to separate from her bracelet. I stopped wearing it, put it in a drawer in my bedside table. But, whenever I remembered it my stomach hurt, I broke into a sweat, I had thoughts that wouldn't go away. How was it possible that my father and Costanza had loved each other for so long — even before my birth — without either my mother or Mariano knowing? And how had my father fallen in love with the wife of his best friend not as the victim of a fleeting infatuation but — I said to myself — in a deliberate way, so that his love still endured? And Costanza, so refined, so well brought up, so affectionate, a visitor in our

195

house as long as I could remember, how had she been able to hold on to my mother's husband for fifteen years right before her eyes? And why had Mariano, who had known my mother forever, only in recent times squeezed her ankle between his under the table, and — as by now was clear, my mother swore to me over and over — without her consent? What happened, in other words, in the world of adults, in the heads of very reasonable people, in their bodies loaded with knowledge? What reduced them to the most untrustworthy animals, worse than reptiles?

The anxiety was so intense that to these and other questions I never sought true answers. I repressed them as soon as they surfaced, and even today I have a hard time returning to them. The problem, I began to suspect, was the bracelet. Evidently, it was as if impregnated with the moods of that affair, and though I was careful not to open the drawer I'd put it in, it imposed itself anyway, as if the glitter of its stones, its gold, scattered afflictions. How was it possible that my father, who seemed to love me without limits, had taken away my aunt's gift and given it to Costanza? If the bracelet originally belonged to Vittoria, and therefore was a sign of her taste, of her idea of beauty and elegance, how could Costanza like it so much that she had kept it and worn it for thirteen years? How, I thought, had my father, so hostile to his sister, so different from her in every way, convinced himself that a piece of jewelry belonging to her, an ornament meant for me, could be suitable not for my mother, for example, but for that very elegant second wife of his, the descendant of goldsmiths, so wealthy that she had no need for jewelry? Vittoria and Costanza were such dissimilar women, they diverged in every way. The first had no education, the second was extremely cultivated; the first was vulgar, the second refined; the first was poor, the second rich. And yet, for me, the bracelet pressed them into one another and confused them, confusing me.

Today I think it was thanks to this obsessive brooding that I slowly managed to remove myself from my parents' suffering, to convince myself that their reciprocal accusations, their pleading with each other, their mutual contempt left me completely indifferent. But it took months. At first I floundered as if I were drowning and, terrified, I looked for something to hold on to. Sometimes, especially at night, when I woke up feeling distraught, I thought that, even though my father was the declared enemy of every form of magic, he had feared that that object, given its source, could magically hurt me, and so he had removed it from the house for my well-being. That idea soothed me, it had the advantage of restoring a loving father who from my first months of life had tried to protect me from Aunt Vittoria's malice, that aunt-witch's desire to take possession of me and make me like her. But it didn't last long as, sooner or later, I ended up asking myself: if he loved Costanza to the point of betraying my mother, to the point of separating from her and me, why did he give her a maleficent bracelet? Maybe — I fantasized in my half sleep — because he liked the bracelet so much and giving it to her kept him from throwing it into the sea. Or because, bewitched by the object himself, before getting rid of it he had wanted to see it at least once on Costanza's wrist, and it was that desire that had lost him. Costanza had seemed to him still more beautiful than she already was, and the enchanted bracelet, binding him to her forever, prevented him from continuing to love only my mother. To protect me, in other words, my father had ended up subjecting himself to the evil magic of his sister (I often went so far as to imagine that Vittoria had foreseen every detail of that wrong move of his), and that had ruined the whole family.

The return to childish fairy tales just as I felt I was truly emerging from childhood had for a while the advantage of reducing to the minimum not only my father's responsibility but mine, too. If, in fact, Vittoria's magic arts were at the origin of all the wrongs, the current drama had begun when I was just born, and so *I* had no guilt, the obscure force that had led me to seek out and meet my aunt had been at work for some time, *I* had nothing to do with it, *I,* like the small children of Jesus, was innocent. But this picture faded, too, sooner or later. Curse or not, the fact was that thirteen years ago my father had judged beautiful the object that his sister had given me, and its beauty had been ratified by a refined woman like Costanza. As a result, an incongruous juxtaposition of vulgarity and refinement again became central, even in the fairy-tale world I was constructing; and that further absence of clear boundaries, at a moment when I was losing every old orientation, confused me even more. My aunt, who was vulgar, became a woman of taste. My father and Costanza, people of taste, became — as the wrongs they had done my mother and even the hateful

Mariano also demonstrated — vulgar. So sometimes before falling asleep I imagined an underground tunnel that put in communication my father, Costanza, and Vittoria, even against their will. Despite all their claims to being different, they seemed to be made of the same clay. My father, in my imagination, grasped Costanza's buttocks and pulled her toward himself just as Enzo had done in the past with my aunt and certainly with Margherita. So he had caused suffering for my mother, who wept as in the fairy tales, filling jars and jars with tears until she lost her reason. And I, who had stayed with her, would have a dull life, without the amusement that he could give me, without his intelligence about the things of the world, qualities that Costanza, Ida, and Angela would get the benefit of instead.

This was the atmosphere when, coming home from school one day, I discovered that the bracelet was painfully meaningful not only for me. I opened the door of the house with my keys, I found my mother in my room, standing in front of the night table, lost in thought. She had taken the bracelet out of the drawer and was holding it in her hand, staring at it, as if it were the necklace of Harmonia and she wanted to pierce the surface to arrive at its properties as a maleficent object. I noticed then that her shoulders were rounded, she had become thin and hunched.

"Don't you wear it anymore?" she asked noticing my presence but without turning.

"I don't like it."

"You know it wasn't Vittoria's but your grandmother's?"

"Who told you that?"

She said that she had telephoned Vittoria and had learned from her that her mother had left it to her when she was dying. I looked at her in bewilderment. I thought there was no reason ever to speak to Vittoria, because she was unreliable and dangerous, but evidently the ban concerned only me.

"Is it true?" I asked, showing skepticism.

"Who knows, almost everything that comes from your father's family, including your father, is false."

"Did you talk to him?"

"Yes."

To get to the bottom of the matter she had assailed my father — is it true the bracelet was your mother's, is it true she left it to your sister? — and he had stammered that he was very fond of that piece of jewelry, he remembered it on his mother's wrist, and so, when he found out that Vittoria wanted to sell it, he had given her some money and taken it.

"When did my grandmother die?" I asked.

"Before you were born."

"Then Aunt Vittoria told a lie, she didn't give me the bracelet."

"That's what your father says."

I sensed that she didn't believe him, and since I had believed Vittoria and still believed her, although unwillingly, I didn't believe him, either. But, against my will, here was the bracelet already following the path of a new story full of consequences. In my mind, the object in a few seconds became an essential part of the fights between brother and sister, a further fragment of their hatreds. I imagined my grandmother lying there gasping for breath, eyes wide, mouth open, and my father and Vittoria, on the edge of her death agony, fighting over the bracelet. He tore it off, took it away in a storm of insults and curses, throwing bills in the air. I asked:

"In your view, Papa, at least at first, took the bracelet from Vittoria to give to me when I grew up?"

"No."

That monosyllable, so sharp, hurt me, I said:

"But he didn't take it to give to you, either."

My mother nodded yes, she put the bracelet back in the drawer, and, as if her strength were about to fail, lay down on my bed sobbing. I felt uneasy, for months she who never cried had been crying all the time, and I would have liked to as well, but I restrained myself, why didn't she? I caressed her shoulder, I kissed her hair. It was very clear now that, however he had come into possession of that piece of jewelry, my father's objective had been to hook it around Costanza's slender wrist. The bracelet, however you looked at it, in whatever type of story you inserted it — a fairy tale, an interesting or boring story — showed only that our body, agitated by the life that writhes within, consuming it, does stupid things that it shouldn't do. And even if I could accept that in general — for Mariano, for example, and even for my mother and for me — I would never have imagined that stupidity could ruin even superior people like Costanza, like my father. I reflected for a long time on all that, I fantasized about it, at school, on the street, at lunch, at dinner, at night. I looked for meanings to get around that impression of scant intelligence in people who had so much of it.

2.

In that couple of years many significant things happened. When my father, after repeating that I really was like his sister, disappeared from home for the first time, I thought he had left because of the revulsion I inspired. Grieved, resentful, I decided that I wouldn't study. I didn't open a book, I stopped doing my homework, and as the winter passed I became more and more alien to myself. I eliminated any habits that he had imposed: reading the newspaper, watching the television news. I went from wearing white or pink to black, my eyes were black, my lips, every item of clothing was black. I was in a daze, indifferent to the teachers' reproaches, unmoved by my mother's complaints. Instead of studying I read novels, watched movies on TV, deafened myself with music. The main thing was, I lived mutely, a few words and that was all. I'd never had friends, apart from the long tradition with Angela and Ida. But from the moment they, too, were swallowed up by the tragedy of our families, I was completely alone, my voice whirling aimlessly in my head. I laughed to myself, I made faces, I spent a lot of time on the steps behind the high school or at the Floridiana, on the

paths bordered by trees and hedges that I
had once walked with my mother, with
Costanza, with Angela, with Ida still in her
carriage. I liked plunging stupefied into that
long-ago happy time as if I were already old,
staring beyond the low wall, without seeing
it, into the gardens of Villa Santarella, or
sitting on a bench in the Floridiana looking
out at the sea and the whole city.

Angela and Ida reappeared late and only
on the telephone. It was Angela who called
me, very excited, saying she wanted to show
me the new house in Posillipo as soon as
possible.

"When are you coming?" she asked.

"I don't know."

"Your father said you'll stay with us a lot."

"I have to keep my mother company."

"Are you mad at me?"

"No."

Having confirmed that I still loved her,
she changed her tone, became more anxious, and confided to me some secrets of
her own, even though she must have understood that I didn't want to hear them. She
said that my father would become a kind of
father to them, because after the divorce he
would marry Costanza. She said that
Mariano not only didn't want to see Costanza anymore but not them, either, and

that was because — he had yelled it one night and she and Ida had heard — he had no doubt that their real father was mine. Finally, she revealed that she had a boyfriend but I shouldn't tell anyone: the boyfriend was Tonino. He called her often, they met in Posillipo, had taken a lot of walks to Mergellina, and less than a week ago had declared their love for each other.

Even though the phone call was long, I said almost nothing. I didn't even utter a word when she whispered ironically that, since perhaps we were sisters, I would become Tonino's sister-in-law. Only when Ida, who must have been there beside her, cried to me, forlornly, it's not true that we're sisters, your father is nice but I want mine, I said softly: I agree with Ida, and even if your mother and my father get married, you'll still be Mariano's daughters and I'll be Andrea's. I kept to myself my irritation at her letting me know that she was going out with Tonino. I muttered only:

"I was joking when I said he liked me, Tonino never liked me."

"I know, I asked him before saying yes, and he swore that he never liked you. He loved me from the moment he saw me, all he thinks about is me."

Then, as if the distress behind the chatter

had built up pressure and broken through the dam, she burst into tears, said sorry, and hung up.

How much we all cried, I couldn't stand any more tears. In June my mother went to see what I had been up to in school and discovered that I hadn't been promoted. She knew, of course, that I was doing very poorly, but failure seemed extreme to her. She wanted to talk to the teachers, she wanted to talk to the principal, she dragged me with her as if I were the proof that an injustice had been done. It was torture for both of us. The teachers had a hard time remembering me, but they showed the records of bad grades, they proved to her that I had had an excessive number of absences. She was upset, especially about the absences. She murmured: where did you go, what did you do. I said: I was at the Floridiana. This girl, the literature professor interrupted at one point, evidently has no talent for classical studies. I didn't answer, but I would have liked to shout that, now that I was grown up, now that I was no longer a puppet, I didn't feel I had a talent for anything: I wasn't intelligent, I wasn't capable of good intentions, I wasn't pretty, I wasn't even nice. My mother — too much eye makeup, too much powder on her cheeks, the skin on her face drawn, like a veil — answered for me: she has talent, she's very talented, except this year she was a little lost.

As soon as we were outside she started blaming my father: it's his fault, he left, he's the one who should have been keeping an eye on you, helping and encouraging you. She continued at home, and since she didn't know how to track down her guilty husband, the next day she looked for him at school. I don't know what happened between them, but that night my mother said:

"We won't tell anyone."

"What?"

"That you weren't promoted."

I felt even more humiliated. I discovered that I wanted people to know, that failure, after all, was my only mark of distinction. I hoped that my mother would tell her colleagues at school, the people she corrected proofs and wrote for, and that my father — my father especially — would tell those who respected and loved him: Giovanna isn't like me and her mother, she doesn't learn, she doesn't work hard, she's ugly inside and out like her aunt, maybe she'll go and live with her, in the Macello neighborhood, in the Industrial Zone.

"Why not?" I asked.

"Because it's pointless to make a drama out of it, it's just a small setback. You'll repeat a year, you'll study and become the best in the class. Agreed?"

"Yes," I answered unwillingly and was about to go to my room, but she held me back.

"Wait, remember not to say anything, even to Angela and Ida."

"Were they promoted?"

"Yes."

"Did Papa ask you not to tell them?"

She didn't answer, she bent over her work, she looked even thinner to me. I understood that they were ashamed of my failure, maybe it was the only feeling they still had in common.

3.

There were no vacations that summer, my mother didn't take one, I don't know about my father, we didn't see him until the following year, in late winter, when she summoned him to ask him to make their separation legal. But that didn't bother me, I spent the entire summer pretending not to notice that my mother was in despair. I remained indifferent even as she and my father began to discuss dividing their things and quarreled furiously when he started in with: Nella, I urgently need the notes that are in the first drawer of the desk, and my mother yelled that she would prevent him — forever, in any way — from taking from the house a single book, a notebook, even just the pen he usually used and the typewriter. Whereas I was hurt, humiliated by that order: don't tell anyone you weren't promoted. For the first time my parents seemed petty, just as Vittoria had painted them, and so I avoided, any way I could, talking to Angela and Ida or seeing them: I was afraid they would ask how I'd done in school or, I don't know, how things were going in my second year of high school, when in reality I was repeating the first. I liked lying more and more, I felt now that praying and telling lies provided the same consolation. But having to resort to fabrication to keep my parents from being shamed, and to cover up the fact that I hadn't inherited their abilities, wounded me, depressed me.

One time when Ida called I made my mother say I wasn't there, even though in that phase of a lot of reading and even more movies I would have been happier to talk to her than to Angela. I preferred absolute isolation: if it had been possible, I wouldn't have spoken even to my mother. At school now, I dressed and made myself up to look like a dissolute woman among respectable kids, and I kept everyone at a distance, even the teachers, who tolerated my sullen behavior only because my mother had found a way of letting them know that she, too, was a teacher. At home, when she wasn't there, I played loud music and sometimes danced furiously. The neighbors frequently came to protest, but when they rang I didn't open the door.

One afternoon when I was alone and letting loose, the doorbell rang. I looked through the peephole, sure that it was angry neighbors, and saw Corrado on the landing. I decided not to open the door even then, but I realized that he must have heard my footsteps in the hall. He stared into the eye of the peephole with his usual boldness, maybe he even heard my breath on the other side of the door, and his serious expression turned into a broad, reassuring smile. I remembered the photograph of his father I had seen at the cemetery, the one in which Vittoria's lover was laughing with satisfaction, and I thought that they shouldn't put pictures of the dead laughing in cemeteries, luckily Corrado's smile was on a living person. I let him in mainly because my parents had always ordered me not to let anyone in in their absence, and I didn't regret it. He stayed for an hour, and for the first time since that long crisis began a lightheartedness came over me that I'd thought was no longer possible.

When I met Margherita's children, I had appreciated Tonino's self-possession, the beautiful Giuliana's lively responses, but Corrado's somewhat spiteful talk annoyed me, the way he ridiculed everyone, even Aunt Vittoria, with cracks that weren't funny. That afternoon, instead, no matter what came out of his mouth — in general unquestionably stupid — I bent over laughing, with tears in my eyes. It was something new that later became a characteristic of mine: I begin with a laugh made out of nothing and then I can't stop, laughter turns into giggles. That afternoon the culmination was the word "dimwit." I had never heard the word and when he said it I thought it was funny and burst out laughing. Corrado realized it and with his Italianized dialect began saying it continuously — that *dimwit,* this *dimwit* — to denigrate sometimes his brother Tonino, sometimes his sister Giuliana, while my laughter satisfied and incited him. Tonino, in his view, was a *dimwit* because he was going out with my friend Angela who was even more of a *dimwit.* He asked his brother: have you kissed her? Sometimes. And do you feel her up? No, because I respect her. You respect her? So you're a *dimwit,* only a dimwit gets a girlfriend and then respects her, why the fuck do you have a girlfriend if you're gonna respect her? You'll see, if Angela's not a dimmer dimwit than you, she'll say: Tonì, please, don't respect me anymore or I'll leave you. Ha ha ha.

I had so much fun that afternoon. I liked the casual way Corrado talked about sex, I liked the way he mocked the relationship between his brother and Angela. He seemed to know a lot, through direct experience, of what goes on between boyfriend and girlfriend, and every so often he'd mention the dialect word for some sexual practice and in dialect explain to me what it meant. Even if I didn't understand very well because I hadn't really mastered that vocabulary, I let out prudent, constricted little laughs, to then laugh wholeheartedly only when, one way or other, he went back to saying dimwit again.

He was incapable of distinguishing between serious and facetious, everything about sex seemed comic to him. I understood that for him kissing was funny but also not kissing, touching but also not

213

touching. Funniest of all, according to him, were his sister Giuliana and Roberto, Tonino's very intelligent friend. Those two, who had loved each other since they were little without telling each other, had finally got engaged. Giuliana was madly in love with Roberto, for her he was the handsomest, most intelligent, most courageous, most just, and furthermore he believed in God much more than Jesus Christ did, even though Jesus was God's son. All the sanctimonious types of Pascone not to mention the ones in Milan, the city where Roberto had studied, were of the same opinion as Giuliana, but, Corrado told me, there were also many other people with a head on their shoulders who didn't share all that enthusiasm. Among those, he and his friends had to be included, for example Rosario, the guy with the buck teeth.

"Maybe you're all wrong, maybe Giuliana's right," I said.

He took a serious tone, but I immediately realized it was fake.

"You don't know Roberto, but you know Giuliana, you were at the parish church and you saw the dances they do, Vittoria playing the accordion, the sort of people who are there. So you tell me: do you trust what they think or what I think?"

214

I was already laughing, I said:

"What you think."

"And so in your opinion, objectively, what is Roberto?"

"A dimwit," I almost shouted, and laughed uncontrollably, by now the muscles of my face hurt from laughing.

The more we talked that way, the more intense became a pleasant sense of breaking the rules. *I* had let into the empty house that kid who had to be at least six or seven years older than me, *I* had agreed to joke around with him, for almost an hour, about sexual things. Gradually, I felt ready for every other possible transgression, and he guessed it, his eyes sparkled, he said: you want to see something. I shook my head no, but laughing, and Corrado laughed, too, pulled down his zipper, murmured, give me your hand and I'll let you touch it. But since I was laughing and didn't give him my hand, he took it, politely. Squeeze, he said, no, that's too hard, good, like that, you've never touched the dimwit, right. He said it just to make me giggle again, and I laughed, I whispered, That's enough, my mother might come back, and he replied: We'll let her touch it, too, the dimwit. Oh how we laughed, it seemed to me so ridiculous to hold that thick, rigid thingy in my hand, I pulled it out myself, I thought, he hasn't even kissed me. I thought it while he said to me: put it in your mouth, and I would even have done that, just then I would have done anything he asked me merely to laugh, but from his pants came a strong toilet odor that disgusted me, and at the same time he said suddenly, that's enough, took it out of my hand, and stuck it back in his underpants, with a hoarse groan that unnerved me. I saw him sink back against the chair for a few seconds, eyes closed, then he shook himself, pulled up his zipper, jumped to his feet, looked at the clock, and said:

"I have to run, Gianni, but we had so much fun we have to see each other again."

"My mother doesn't let me go out, I have to study."

"It's pointless for you to study, you're already smart."

"I'm not smart, I failed, I'm repeating the year."

He looked at me in disbelief.

"Come on, that's impossible. I never flunked and they flunk you? That's not fair, you should rebel. You know, I really wasn't cut out for school. They gave me a machinist's diploma because I'm a nice guy."

"You're not a nice guy, you're an idiot."

"You're saying you had fun with an idiot?"

216

"Yes."

"Then you're an idiot, too?"

"Yes."

Only when he was already on the landing did Corrado tap himself on the forehead and exclaim: I was about to forget something important, and he pulled out of his pants pocket a worn envelope. He said that was what he had come for, Vittoria sent it to me. Luckily, he had remembered, if he had forgotten it my aunt would have shrieked like a frog. He said *frog* to make me laugh at a senseless comparison, but this time I didn't. As soon as he gave me the envelope and disappeared down the stairs, my anguish returned.

The envelope, all creased and dirty, was sealed. I opened it in a hurry, before my mother came home. It was only a few lines, and still there were a lot of spelling mistakes. Vittoria said that since I had not kept in touch with her, since I didn't answer the phone, I had proved that, exactly like my father and mother, I was incapable of feeling affection for my relatives, and therefore I should give back the bracelet. She would send Corrado to get it.

217

4.

I began to wear the bracelet again for two reasons: first, since Vittoria wanted it back, I wanted to show it off in class at least for a while and let it be understood that my situation as a repeater said nothing about the girl I was; second, because my father, as the separation approached, was trying to reestablish contact with me, and when he appeared at school I wanted him to see it on my wrist to let him understand that, if he ever invited me to Costanza's house, I would certainly wear it. But neither my classmates nor my father seemed to notice, the first out of envy, the second because simply mentioning it probably embarrassed him.

My father generally showed up outside school with a friendly manner, and we went together to eat *panzarotti* and *pastacresciuta* in a shop not far from the funicular. He asked me about my teachers, my classes, my grades, but I had the impression that the answers didn't interest him, even if he put on an attentive expression. Besides, that subject was quickly exhausted, he didn't go on to anything else, I didn't venture questions about his new life, and we ended up in silence.

The silence saddened me, irritated me; I felt that my father was giving up on being my father. He looked at me when he thought I was distracted and didn't notice, but I did notice and felt that his gaze was bewildered, as if he had trouble recognizing me, all in black from head to toe, with heavy makeup; or maybe as if I had become too well known to him, better known than when I had been his beloved daughter — he knew that I was two-faced and devious. When we got to the house, he became cordial again, kissed me on the forehead, said: say hello to Mamma. I waved goodbye again and, as soon as the door closed behind me, imagined despondently that he was relieved, accelerating noisily as he departed.

Often, on the stairs or in the elevator, I started singing to myself some Neapolitan songs that I hated. I pretended to be a singer, I bared my neck and shoulders slightly and halfheartedly repeated lines that seemed especially absurd to me. On the landing, I would compose myself, open the door with the key, and, going in, find my mother, who, in turn, had just come home from school.

"Papa says hello."

"Good for him. Have you eaten?"

"Yes."

"What?"

"Panzarotti and *pastacresciuta."*

"Tell him, please, that you can't always eat *panzarotti* and *pastacresciuta.* Apart from anything else, they're bad for him, too."

The sincere tone of that last phrase and similar ones that occasionally escaped her surprised me. After the long period of despair something in her was changing, maybe the substance itself of the despair. By now she was skin and bones, she smoked more than Vittoria, her shoulders were increasingly rounded, and when she sat at her work she looked like a hook cast to catch some sort of elusive fish. And yet, for some time now, instead of worrying about herself she'd seemed worried about her ex-husband. Sometimes I was convinced that she considered him near death or even already dead, though no one realized it yet. Not that she had stopped blaming him in every possible way, but she mixed bitterness with apprehension, she hated him and yet seemed to fear that outside her guardianship he would soon lose his health and his life. I didn't know what to do. Her physical appearance concerned me, but the progressive loss of any other interest that wasn't the time spent with her husband made me angry. When I skimmed the stories she corrected and often rewrote there was always an extraordinary man who for one reason or another had died. And if a friend came by the house — in general teachers from the high school where she taught — I often heard her say things like: my ex-husband has many faults, but on this matter he is absolutely right, he says that, he thinks this. She quoted him frequently and with respect. But not only that. When she discovered that my father had begun to write with some frequency for *Unità,* she who generally bought the *Repubblica* went to buy that paper, too, and showed me the byline, marked certain sentences, cut out the articles. I thought that if a man had done to me what he had done to her, I would bash in his chest and tear out his heart, and I was sure that she, too, in all that time, must have dreamed of such destruction. But now, increasingly, a bitter sarcasm alternated with a quiet cult of memory. One evening I found her putting the family photos in order, including the ones she kept shut in the metal box. She said:

"Come look at this, look how handsome your father is here."

She showed me a black-and-white snapshot I'd never seen, although earlier I had rummaged everywhere. She had pulled it out of the Italian dictionary she'd had since high school, a place where it would never have occurred to me to look for pictures. My father must not have known about it, either, since in it, not blotted out, was Vittoria when she was still a girl and who else but — I recognized him immediately — Enzo. There was more: between my father and my aunt on one side, and Enzo on the other, a tiny woman was sitting in a chair, not yet old but not young, with an expression that to me looked harsh. I murmured:

"Here Papa and Aunt Vittoria look happy, look how she's smiling at him."

"Yes."

"And this is Enzo, the criminal cop."

"Yes."

"And here he and Papa aren't mad at each other."

"No, at first they were friends, Enzo used to visit the family."

"Who's that lady?"

"Your grandmother."

"What was she like?"

"Odious."

"Why?"

"She didn't love your father, so she didn't like me, either. She never even wanted to speak to me, or see me, I was always the

222

one who wasn't part of the family, a stranger. Imagine, she preferred Enzo to your father."

I examined the picture attentively, I felt a pang. I grabbed a magnifying glass from the pen holder and used it to enlarge the right wrist of my father and Vittoria's mother.

"Look," I said, offering her the lens, "grandmother is wearing my bracelet."

She didn't take the lens, she bent over the picture in her fishhook-like pose, shook her head, muttered:

"I never noticed."

"I saw it right away."

She grimaced with irritation.

"Yes, you saw it right away. While I showed you your father and you didn't even look at him."

"I looked and he doesn't seem so handsome as you say."

"He's very handsome, you're still young and you don't understand how handsome a very intelligent man can be."

"I understand perfectly well. But here he looks like Aunt Vittoria's twin brother."

My mother accentuated her weary tone.

"Look, he left me, not you."

"He left both of us, I hate him."

She shook her head.

"It's up to me to hate him."

"Me, too."

"No, you're angry now and you're saying things you don't think. But in essence he's a good man. He seems like a lying traitor, but he's honest and in a certain sense even faithful. His true great love is Costanza, he has stayed with her all these years, and he'll stay with her until death. The point is, she's the one he wanted to give his mother's bracelet to."

5.

My discovery hurt us both, but we reacted in different ways. Who knows how many times my mother had leafed through that dictionary, how many times she had looked at that image, and yet had never noticed that the bracelet that Mariano's wife had shown off for years, that she had for years considered a refined object she would have liked to possess, was the same that showed up on the arm of her mother-in-law in that photo. In the image fixed in black and white she had seen only my father when he was a young man. There she had recognized the reasons she loved him and so had kept the photo in the dictionary like a flower that, even when it dries, reminds us of the moment it was given to us. She had never paid attention to the rest and so, when I showed her the bracelet, she must have suffered terribly. But she suffered without letting me see it, controlling her reactions and trying to blur my inopportune gaze with sentimental or nostalgic little speeches. My father good, honest, faithful? Costanza the great love, the true wife? My grandmother who preferred Enzo, the seducer of Vittoria, to her own son? She improvised many stories of that type and jumping from one to the next slowly returned to take shelter in the cult of her ex-husband. Of course, today I can say that if she hadn't in some way filled the void he left she would have fallen into it and died. But in my eyes the way she had chosen was the more offensive one.

As for me, the picture gave me the audacity to think that I wouldn't return the bracelet to Vittoria for any reason. The rationales I proposed were very messy. It's mine, I said to myself, because it was my grandmother's. It's mine, I said to myself, because Vittoria appropriated it for herself against my father's will, because my father appropriated it for himself against Vittoria's will. It's mine, I said to myself, because it's owed to me, it's owed to me whether Vittoria really gave it to me or whether that's a lie and my father took it to give to a stranger.

It's mine, I said to myself, because that stranger, Costanza, gave it back to me, and so it's not right for my aunt to claim it. It's mine, I concluded, because I recognized it in the picture and my mother didn't, because I can look pain in the face and endure it and also cause it, while she can't. I feel sorry for her, she's not even able to become Mariano's lover, she doesn't know how to have fun, she wastes her energy on stupid pages in books for people like her.

I wasn't like her. I was like Vittoria and my father, who in that picture were physically very similar. So I wrote a letter to my aunt. It came out much longer than the one she had written me, I listed the entire jumble of reasons that I wanted to keep the bracelet. Then I put the letter in the backpack where I carried my schoolbooks and waited for the day when Corrado or Vittoria would reappear.

6.

To my surprise, however, it was Costanza who showed up outside school. I hadn't seen her since the morning when, compelled by my mother, she had brought me the bracelet. She looked even more beautiful than before, even more elegant, with a faint perfume that my mother had used for years but no longer did. The only detail I didn't like: her eyes were swollen. She said to me in her husky, seductive voice that she wanted to take me to a little family party, her daughters and I: my father was busy at school for most of the afternoon, but he had called my mother, and she had given her consent.

"Where?" I asked.

"At my house."

"Why?"

"You don't remember? It's Ida's birthday."

"I have a lot of homework."

"Tomorrow is Sunday."

"I hate studying on Sunday."

"You're not willing to make a small sacrifice? Ida always talks about you, she really loves you."

I gave in, I got in the car, perfumed as much as she was, and we drove toward Posillipo. She asked me about school, and I was very careful not to say that I was still in the first year of high school, even though I didn't know what they studied in the second, and since she was a teacher I was afraid of making a mistake with every answer. I avoided asking her about Angela, and Costanza right away began to tell me how sorry her daughters were that we didn't see one another anymore. She said that Angela had dreamed about me recently, a dream in which she lost a shoe and I found it for her or something like that. While she talked I fiddled with the bracelet, I wanted her to notice that I was wearing it. Then I said: it's not our fault if we don't see each other anymore. As soon as I said those words, Costanza lost her cordial tone, she muttered: you're right, it's not your fault, and stopped talking, as if she had decided that because of the traffic she had to concentrate on driving. But she couldn't contain herself and added suddenly: don't think that it's your father's fault, there's no fault in what happened, one does harm without wanting to. And she slowed down, pulled over, said: I'm sorry and — good Lord, I couldn't bear any more crying — burst into tears.

"You don't know," she sobbed, "how badly your father feels, how he worries about you, he doesn't sleep, he misses you, and Angela and Ida and I also miss you."

"I miss him, too," I said uneasily, "I miss all of you, even Mariano. And I know there's no fault, it happened, no one can do anything about it."

She dried her eyes with her fingertips, every gesture of hers was light, decorous.

"How wise you are," she said, "you always

228

had a good influence on my daughters."

"I'm not wise, but I read a lot of novels."

"Good, you're growing up, you have witty answers."

"No, I'm serious: instead of my own words, phrases from books come to mind."

"Angela doesn't read anymore. You know she has a boyfriend?"

"Yes."

"Do you have one?"

"No."

"Love is complicated, Angela's starting too soon."

She made up her reddened eyes, asked me if she looked all right, started off again. She went on, hinting discreetly, to talk about her daughter, she wanted to know, without asking explicit questions, if I was more informed than she was. I got nervous, I didn't want to say the wrong thing. I quickly realized that she didn't know anything about Tonino, not his age, or what he did, not even his name, and for my part I avoided connecting him to Vittoria, Margherita, Enzo, I didn't even say that he was almost ten years older than Angela. I muttered only that he was very serious, and in order not to say anything else I was on the verge of pretending that I didn't feel well and wanted to go home. But by now we had arrived, the car was gliding along a tree-lined street, Costanza parked. I was captivated by the light that radiated from the sea and by the splendor of the garden: how much of Naples you could see, how much sky, how much of Vesuvius. So here was where my father lived. Leaving Via San Giacomo dei Capri he hadn't lost much in altitude and had certainly gained in beauty. Costanza asked me:

"Would you do me a very small favor?"

"Yes."

"Would you take off the bracelet? The girls don't know I gave it to you."

"Maybe everything would be less complicated if you told the truth."

She said haltingly:

"The truth is difficult, growing up you'll understand that, novels aren't sufficient for it. So will you do me that favor?"

Lies, lies, adults forbid them and yet they tell so many. I nodded, unhooked the bracelet, put it in my pocket. She thanked me, we went into the house. I saw Angela again after such a long time, I saw Ida, we quickly found a semblance of friendship, even if all three of us were very changed. You're so thin, Ida said, your feet are so long, and what big breasts you have, yes, they're very big, and why are you all dressed

230

in black?

We ate in a sun-filled kitchen, with sparkling furniture and appliances. We three girls began to joke, I got the giggles, and Costanza, seeing us, seemed relieved. Every trace of her tears had disappeared, she was so nice that she concerned herself more with me than with her daughters. At one point, she chided them because they were excitedly telling me in minute detail about a trip to London with their grandparents and wouldn't let me get a word in. The whole time she looked at me kindly, twice she whispered in my ear: I'm so happy you're here, what a pretty girl you've become. What does she want, I wondered. Maybe she wants to take me away from my mother, too, wants me to come and live in this house. Would I mind? No, maybe not. It was big, very light, full of luxuries. Almost certainly I would be comfortable, if my father didn't sleep, eat, go to the bathroom in that space exactly as he had done when he lived with us on San Giacomo dei Capri. But that was precisely the obstacle. He lived there, and his presence made it inconceivable that I should live there, resume my friendship with Angela and Ida, eat the food cooked by Costanza's silent, industrious maid. What I most dreaded — I realized —

231

was the moment my father returned with his bag full of books and kissed that wife on the lips as he had always done with the other and said that he was very tired and yet would joke around with the three of us, would pretend to love us, would take Ida on his lap and help her blow out the candles and sing happy birthday and then, suddenly cool, as he knew how to be, would withdraw into another room, into his new study, whose function was the same as the one on Via San Giacomo dei Capri, and shut himself in, and Costanza would say, just as my mother always had, keep your voices down, please, don't disturb Andrea, he has to work.

"What's wrong?" Costanza asked me. "You've turned pale, is something wrong?"

"Mamma," Angela grumbled, "will you leave us alone for a while?"

7.

The three of us spent the afternoon by ourselves and for a good part of the time Angela talked about Tonino. She did her best to convince me that she was really fond of that guy. Tonino didn't talk much, and he talked sluggishly, but what he said was always important. He let her order him

232

around because he loved her, but he could assert himself with anyone who wanted to put a foot on his head. Tonino came to meet her at school every day — tall, curly-haired, he was so handsome she spotted him in the crowd, he had broad shoulders, his muscles were visible even when he was wearing a jacket. Tonino had a surveyor's diploma and was already working a little, but he had great aspirations and in secret, without even telling his mother and siblings, he was studying architecture. Tonino was a good friend of Roberto, Giuliana's fiancé, even though they were very different: she had met him because they had all four of them gone to have a pizza, and what a disappointment, Roberto was so ordinary, even a little boring, it was hard to understand why Giuliana, such a pretty girl, felt so strongly about him, and why Tonino, who was much better-looking and more intelligent than Roberto, had so much respect for him.

I listened, but Angela couldn't convince me, in fact it seemed to me that she was using her boyfriend to let me know that, in spite of her parents' separation, she was happy. I asked her:

"Why haven't you told your mother about him?"

"What does my mother have to do with it?"

"She wanted information from me."

She was alarmed:

"Did you tell her who he is, did you tell her where I met him?"

"No."

"I don't want her to know anything."

"And Mariano?"

"Even worse."

"You know that if my father sees him, he'll make you leave him immediately?"

"Your father is nobody, he can't say anything, he has no right to tell me what I have to do."

Ida made ostentatious nods of agreement, she emphasized:

"Our father is Mariano, that's clear. But my sister and I decided that we aren't anyone's daughters: we don't even consider our mother our mother anymore."

Angela lowered her voice as we traditionally did when we talked about sex with a rude vocabulary:

"She's a whore, she's your father's whore."

I said:

"I'm reading a book where a girl spits on a picture of her father and makes her friend do it, too."

Angela asked:

"Would you spit on a picture of your father?"

"Would you?" I asked in turn.

"On a picture of my mother, yes."

"Not me," said Ida.

I thought a moment and said:

"I would pee on a picture of my father."

This hypothesis excited Angela.

"We can do it together."

"If you do it," said Ida, "I'll watch and I'll write you."

"What does it mean that you'll write us?" I asked.

"I'll write about you that you pee on a photo of Andrea."

"A story?"

"Yes."

I was glad. The two sisters exiling themselves in their own house, that cutting of blood ties, just as I would have wanted to cut them, I liked that, and I also liked their foul language.

"If you like writing stories like that, I can tell you some true things I've done," I said.

"What things?" Angela asked.

I lowered my voice:

"I'm more of a whore than your mother."

They were extremely interested in my revelation; they insisted that I tell them everything.

235

"Do you have a boyfriend?" Ida asked.

"You don't need a boyfriend to be a whore. You can be a whore with whoever comes along."

"And are you a whore with whoever comes along?" Angela asked.

I said yes. I said that I talked to boys about sex in the bad words of dialect, and I laughed a lot, really a lot, and when I had laughed enough the boys pulled it out and wanted me to hold it or put it in my mouth.

"How disgusting," Ida said.

"Yes," I admitted, "it's all kind of disgusting."

"All what?" Angela asked.

"Boys, it's like being in the toilet of a train."

"But kisses are lovely," said Ida.

I shook my head hard.

"Boys get fed up with kissing, they don't even touch you, they go right ahead and unzip their pants, they're only interested in you touching them."

"Not true," Angela huffed, "Tonino kisses me."

I was offended that she doubted what I was saying.

"Tonino kisses you, but he doesn't do anything else."

"That's not true."

"Let's hear it then: what do you do with Tonino?"

Angela murmured:

"He's very religious and he respects me."

"You see? What do you have a boyfriend for if he respects you?"

Angela was silent, she shook her head, she had a flash of impatience.

"I have him because he loves me. Maybe nobody loves you. They even flunked you."

"Is that true?" asked Ida.

"Who told you?"

Angela hesitated, she already seemed sorry for having given in to the impulse to humiliate me. She muttered:

"You told Corrado and Corrado told Tonino."

Ida wanted to console me.

"But we didn't tell anyone," she said and tried to caress me on the cheek. I pulled away, hissed:

"Only bitches like you study like parrots, get promoted, and are respected by their boyfriends. I don't study, I get flunked, and I'm a whore."

8.

It was dark when my father arrived. Costanza seemed irritated, she said to him:

why are you so late, you knew Giovanna was here. We had dinner, and he pretended he was happy. I knew him well, he was pretending a cheerfulness he didn't feel. I hoped that in the past, when he lived with my mother and me, he had never faked it as he was obviously faking it that evening.

I did nothing to hide the fact that I was angry, that Costanza annoyed me with her sweet attentions, that Angela had insulted me and I didn't want to have anything to do with her, that I couldn't stand the many displays of affection with which Ida tried to placate me. I felt a meanness inside that needed to be expressed at all costs: surely it's in my eyes and my whole face, I thought, alarmed at myself. I went so far as to whisper to Ida: it's your birthday and Mariano's not here, there must be a reason, maybe you're too whiny, maybe you're too clingy. Ida stopped speaking to me, her lower lip trembled, as if I had slapped her.

This couldn't go unnoticed. My father realized that I had said something mean to Ida and, interrupting some polite chat with Angela, he turned to me, reproachful: please, Giovanna, don't be rude, stop it. I said nothing, I smiled in a way that irritated him even more, so that he added forcefully: do we understand each other? I nodded yes, careful not to laugh. I waited a while and said, my face burning red: I'm going to the bathroom.

I locked myself in, and washed my face in a frenzy to remove that burning anger. He thinks he can hurt me, but I can do that, too. Before I went back to the dining room, I made up my eyes again as Costanza had done after her tears, I fished the bracelet out of my pocket and put it on my wrist, and returned to the table. Angela widened her eyes in wonder, she said:

"Why do you have Mamma's bracelet?"

"She gave it to me."

She turned to Costanza:

"Why did you give it to her, I wanted it."

"I liked it, too," Ida murmured.

My father intervened, ashen:

"Giovanna, give back the bracelet."

Costanza shook her head, she, too, seemed suddenly drained.

"No, the bracelet is Giovanna's, I gave it to her."

"Why?" Ida asked.

"Because she's a good, studious girl."

I looked at Angela and Ida, they were unhappy. My sense of revenge faded, their unhappiness made me unhappy. Everything was sad and bleak, there was nothing, nothing at all that I could be pleased about, the way I'd been as a child, when they, too, were children. But now — I gave a start — they're so wounded, so distressed, that to make themselves feel better they'll say they know a secret of mine, they'll say that I was held back, that I don't learn, that I'm stupid by nature, I have only bad qualities, I don't deserve the bracelet. I said to Costanza, in a rush:

"I'm not good or studious. Last year I was failed, now I'm repeating."

Costanza looked uncertainly at my father, he coughed faintly, said reluctantly but making light of it, as if to curb an exaggeration:

"It's true, but this year she's doing really well and she'll probably do two years in one. Come on, Giovanna, give the bracelet to Angela and Ida."

I said:

"The bracelet is my grandmother's, I can't give it to strangers."

My father then dug up from the depths of his throat his terrible voice, the one full of ice and disdain:

"I know damn well who that bracelet belongs to, take it off immediately."

I tore it off my wrist and hurled it at one of the kitchen cabinets.

240

9.

My father drove me home. I left the Posillipo apartment unexpectedly victorious, but exhausted by tension. In my backpack I carried the bracelet and a piece of cake for my mother. Costanza got angry with my father, she had gone to pick the bracelet up off the floor. After making sure that it wasn't broken, she repeated, articulating her words, without taking her eyes off his, that the bracelet was irrevocably mine and she didn't want any more discussion. So in an atmosphere where it was no longer possible even to feign good cheer, Ida had blown out her candles, the party had ended, Costanza had ordered me to take some cake to her former friend — this is for Nella — and Angela, depressed, had cut a big piece and diligently wrapped it. Now my father was driving to the Vomero, but he was upset, I'd never seen him like that. His features were very different from the ones I was used to, his eyes were very clear, the skin of his face stretched over the bones, and he uttered a confusion of words, twisting his mouth as if he couldn't articulate them except with extreme effort.

He began with phrases of this type: I understand, you think I destroyed your mother's life and now you want to get revenge by destroying mine, Costanza's, Angela's, and Ida's. The tone appeared good-natured, but I felt all his tension and was frightened, I was afraid that at any moment he would hit me, that we would end up crashing into a wall or another car. He noticed, he muttered: you're afraid of me, I lied, I said no, I exclaimed that it wasn't true, I didn't want to ruin him, I loved him. But he insisted, he poured out a river of words, dumped them on me. You're afraid of me, he said, I don't seem what I was, and maybe you're right, maybe every so often I become the person I never wanted to be, I'm sorry if I frighten you, give me time, you'll see, I'll go back to being the way you know me, this is a difficult period, everything's falling apart, I had an idea that it would turn out this way, and you mustn't apologize if you have bad feelings, it's normal, but don't forget that you're my only daughter, you'll always be my only daughter, and your mother, I'll always love her, you can't understand now, but you will, it's hard, I was faithful to your mother for a long time, but I've loved Costanza since before you were born, and yet between us there was never anything, I thought of her as the sister I would have liked to have, the opposite of your aunt, the exact opposite, intelligent, cultured, sensitive, for me she was my sister the way Mariano was my brother, a brother to study with, talk to, confide in, and I knew everything about Mariano, he has always betrayed Costanza, now you're old enough, I can tell you these things, Mariano had other women and he liked telling me all his affairs, and I thought poor Costanza, I felt sorry for her, I would have liked to protect her from her own fiancé, from her own husband, I thought my involvement came from being like brother and sister, but instead once, by chance, yes, by chance, we went on a trip together, a work trip, a teacher thing, it was very important to her, it was important to me, too, but innocent, I swear to you I had never betrayed your mother — I've loved your mother since our school days and I love her now, too, I love you and her — but we had dinner, Costanza and I and a lot of other people, and we talked a lot, we talked in the restaurant, then on the street, then all night in my room, lying on the bed as we also used to do when Mariano and your mother were there, then we were four young people, we cuddled with each other and talked, you can understand, can't you, the way you and Ida and Angela talk about everything, but now in the room it was only Costanza and me, and we discovered that ours wasn't the love of brother and sister, it was another type of love, we were amazed ourselves, it's impossible to know how and why these things happen, what the deep reasons are and the superficial ones, but don't believe that we continued afterward, no, it was only an intense and inescapable feeling, I'm so sad, Giovanna, I'm sorry, I'm sorry also about the bracelet, I always considered it Costanza's, I saw it and said to myself: you know how she'd like it, you know how beautiful it would look, that was why when my mother died I wanted it no matter what, I hit Vittoria because of her insistence that it was hers, and when you were born I said to her: give it to the child, and for once she listened to me, but I gave it right away to Costanza, the bracelet belonging to my mother who never loved me, never, maybe the good I wanted to do her did harm, I don't know, we perform acts that seem like acts but in fact they're symbols, you know what symbols are, that's something I should explain to you, good becomes evil without your realizing it, you understand, I didn't wrong you, you were a newborn, I would have wronged Costanza, in my mind I had already given her the bracelet long before.

He went on like that the whole way, even more chaotically than in this summary of mine. I never understood how a man so devoted to reflection and study, capable of conceiving the most gleaming sentences, could at times, when he was overwhelmed by emotions, make such muddled speeches. I tried to interrupt him several times. I said: I understand Papa. I said: this doesn't concern me, it's between you and Mamma, it's between you and Costanza, I don't want to know. I said: I'm sorry you feel bad, I feel bad, too, Mamma feels bad, and doesn't it seem a little ridiculous that all this feeling bad means you love us.

I didn't intend to be sarcastic. Part of me really wished, at that point, to discuss with him the bad that, while you seem to be good, gradually or suddenly spreads through your mind, your stomach, your whole body. Where does it come from, Papa — I wanted to say to him — how do you control it, and why does it not sweep away the good but, rather, coexists with it. At that moment it seemed to me that, although he was talking mainly about love, he knew the bad better than Aunt Vittoria, and since I felt bad in myself, too, felt that it kept advancing, I would have liked to talk about it. But it was impossible, he noticed only the sarcastic edge of my words and continued anxiously to pile up justifications, accusations, a frenzy of self-denigration and a frenzy to redeem himself by listing his grand reasons, his pain and suffering. When we got home I kissed him on the side of his mouth and ran away, he had an acid smell that disgusted me.

My mother asked without interest:

"How did it go?"

"Fine. Costanza sent you a piece of cake."

"You eat it."

"I don't feel like it."

"Not even for breakfast tomorrow?"

"No."

"Then throw it away."

10.

Some time passed, and Corrado showed up again. I was just outside school, about to go in, I heard someone call me, but even before I heard his voice, before I turned and saw him in the crowd of students, I'd known that I would meet him that morning. I was glad, it seemed a presentiment, but I have to admit that I'd been thinking of him for a while, especially during the boring after-noons of studying, when my mother went out and I was alone in the house and hoped he'd show up suddenly like the other time. I never believed it was a question of love, I had something else in mind. I was worried because if Corrado didn't come that might mean that my aunt would appear in person to demand the bracelet, and the letter I had composed would be useless, I would have to deal with her directly, which terrified me.

But there was something else. A very violent need for degradation was growing inside me — a fearless degradation, a yearning to feel heroically vile — and it seemed to me that Corrado had sensed that need and was ready to support it without a fuss. So I was waiting for him, I wanted him to appear, and there he was, finally. He asked me, in that way of his that hovered between serious and humorous, not to go to school, and I immediately agreed, in fact I pulled him away from the entrance for fear that the teachers would see him, and I proposed going to the Floridiana, I dragged him there happily.

He started joking to make me laugh, but I stopped him, I took out the letter.

"You'll give it to Vittoria?"

"And the bracelet?"

"It's mine, I'm not giving it to her."

"Look, she'll be angry, she's harassing me, you don't know how important it is to her."

"And you don't know how important it is to me."

"You had a mean look. It was nice, I really liked it."

"It's not just a look, I'm all mean, by nature."

"All?"

We had moved off the paths, and were hidden among trees and bushes that gave off the sweet scent of living leaves. This time he kissed me, but I didn't like his tongue, it was gross, rough, he seemed to want to thrust mine into the back of my throat. He kissed me and touched my breasts, but roughly, he squeezed them too hard, first on top of the shirt, then he tried to stick his hand in one of the cups of my bra, but without real interest, and he quickly got tired of it. He abandoned my breasts but went on kissing me, he pulled up my skirt and with the palm of his hand pushed violently against the crotch of my underpants and rubbed me for a few seconds. Laughing, I muttered: enough, and I didn't have to insist, he seemed glad to be spared that duty. He looked around, unzipped his fly, pulled my hand inside his pants. I assessed the situation. If he touched me, he hurt me, he bothered me; I started feeling like I wanted to go home and go to sleep. I decided to act myself, as a way of keeping him from acting. I took it out cautiously, I asked him in a whisper: can I give you a blow job. I knew only the word, nothing else, I pronounced it in an unnatural dialect. I imagined that you had to suck hard, as if you were attached greedily to a large nipple, or maybe lick. I hoped he would explain what to do, and, whatever it was, it would be better than the contact with his raspy tongue. I felt lost, why am I here, why do I want this thing. I felt no desire, it didn't seem like a fun game, I wasn't even curious, the smell that came from that large, tense, compact excrescence was unpleasant. Anxious, I hoped that someone — a mother taking her children out for a walk — would see us from the path and shout reproaches and insults. But there was no one, and since he didn't say anything, in fact to me he seemed in a daze, I decided on a light kiss, a light touch of the lips. Luckily, it was enough. He immediately put his thing back into his pants and let out a short, hoarse cry. Afterward we walked through the Floridiana, but I was bored. Corrado had lost the desire to make me laugh, and was talking now in a serious, affected tone, making an effort to use Italian while I would have preferred dialect. Before we separated he asked me:

"You remember Rosario, my friend?"

"The one with the buck teeth?"

"Yes, he's sort of ugly but nice."

"He's not ugly, he's so-so."

"Anyway I'm better-looking."

"Well."

"He has a car. Wanna come for a ride with us?"

"It depends."

"On what?"

"On whether you show me a good time or not."

"We'll show you a good time."

"We'll see," I said.

11.

Corrado called me a few days later to tell me about my aunt. Vittoria had ordered him to report to me word for word that if I dared to act the teacher as I had done with that letter, she would come to the house and hit me in front of that bitch my mother. For that reason — he urged me — take her the bracelet, please, she wants it absolutely next Sunday, she needs it, she has to show it off at some church event.

He didn't merely summarize the message, he also told me how we were to organize ourselves for the occasion. He and his friend would come and pick me up in the car and drive me to Pascone. I would give back the bracelet — but listen to me, we'll drop you off in the square: you can't tell Vittoria that I came to get you in my friend's car, remember, that'll make her mad, you have to say you got there on the bus — and afterward we'll go and have fun. O.K.?

In those days I was particularly restless; I didn't feel well, I had a cough. I thought I was hideous and wanted to be more hideous. Before going to school, I'd stand in front of the mirror doing my best to look like a crazy person — my clothes, my hair. I wanted people not to want to be with me, exactly as I tried to let them know that I didn't want to be with them. Everyone irritated me, neighbors, people on the street, classmates, teachers. My mother especially annoyed me, smoking continuously, drinking gin before going to bed, complaining lethargically about everything, assuming an expression both worried and disgusted as soon as I said I needed a notebook or a book. But mostly I couldn't stand her because of the increasingly conspicuous devotion she now displayed toward everything my father did or said, as if he hadn't betrayed her for at least fifteen years with a woman who was her friend, who was the wife of his best friend. In other words, she exasperated me. I'd recently gotten into the habit of erasing my expression of indifference and shouting at her in my improvised Neapolitan, purposely, that she had to stop it, that she had to not care — go to the movies, Ma, go dancing, he's not your husband anymore, consider him dead, he went to live in Costanza's house, is it possible that he's still all you're concerned with, that he's still all you think about? I wanted to let her know that I felt contempt for her, that I wasn't like her and would never be like her. So once when my father telephoned and she started off in her docile fashion with phrases like "Don't worry, I'll take care of it," I began repeating her slavish locutions in a loud voice but mixing in insults and obscenities in a dialect I didn't know well, didn't pronounce well. She hung up immediately, so as to spare her ex-husband my vulgar voice, stared at me for a few seconds, then went into her study, obviously to cry. I'd had enough, I accepted Corrado's proposal immediately. Better to confront my aunt and give blow jobs to the two of them than stay shut up here in San Giacomo dei Capri, in this shit life.

I told my mother I was going on a trip to

252

Caserta with my classmates. I put on makeup, I wore the shortest skirt I had, I chose a tight, low-cut shirt, I stuck the bracelet in my purse in case I found myself in a situation where I was forced to give it back, and I hurried downstairs at nine in the morning, the time I had agreed on with Corrado. To my surprise I found waiting for me a yellow car of I don't know what make — my father had no interest in cars and so I was completely ignorant — but to me it seemed so grand that I was sorry not to be more in touch with Angela and Ida, it would have been satisfying to boast about it. At the wheel was Rosario, in the back seat Corrado, and both were exposed to the air and the sun, because the car had no roof — it was a convertible.

When Corrado saw me come out the front door, he waved with exaggerated joviality, but when I started to get in next to Rosario he said assertively:

"No, sweetheart, you sit next to me."

I was disappointed, I wanted to show off on the seat beside the driver, who was wearing a blue jacket with gold buttons, a blue shirt, and a red tie, and had combed his hair back, which gave him the profile of a strong, dangerous man — plus he had fangs. I insisted with a conciliatory smile:

"I'll sit here, thanks."

But Corrado said, in an unexpectedly mean voice:

"Giannì, are you deaf, I told you come here this second."

I wasn't used to that tone, it intimidated me, but I still felt like replying:

"I'm keeping Rosario company, he's not your chauffeur."

"What does a chauffeur have to do with it, you belong to me, you have to sit where I am."

"I don't belong to anyone, Corrà, and anyway it's Rosario's car and I'll sit where he says."

Rosario said nothing, he simply turned to me with his laughing boy's face, stared at my breasts for a long second, and ran the knuckles of his right hand over the seat next to him. I got in and sat down, closed the door, and he set off with a calculated screeching of the tires. Oh, I had done it, hair in the wind, beautiful Sunday sun in my face, I relaxed. And Rosario was such a good driver, he darted here and there, with the confidence of a racecar champion, and I wasn't afraid.

"Is the car yours?"

"Yes."

"Are you rich?"

"Yes."

"Afterward can we go to the Parco della Rimembranza?"

"We can go wherever you want."

Corrado cut in right away, reaching one hand out onto my shoulder and squeezing it:

"But you'll do what I tell you to do."

Rosario looked in the rearview mirror.

"Currà, cool it, Giannina does what she likes."

"You cool it, I brought her."

"So what?" I interjected pushing away his hand.

"Shut up, this is a conversation between me and Rosario."

I said that I would speak how and when I liked, and the whole way I devoted myself to Rosario. I realized that he was proud of his car, and I told him that he drove much better than my father. I goaded him to brag, I took an interest in everything he knew about engines, I went so far as to ask him if in some near future he would teach me to drive the way he did. Finally, taking advantage of the fact that he had his hand on the knob of the gear shift, I placed mine on his, saying: so I'll help you shift, and on to laughter, I was laughing because I had the giggles, he was laughing because of the shape of his mouth. He was excited by the contact with my hand, I realized. How is it possible, I said to myself, that boys are so stupid, how is it possible that those two, if I merely touch them, if I simply let them touch me, go blind, they don't see and don't feel the disgust I feel for myself. Corrado was upset because I wasn't sitting next to him, Rosario was happy because I was next to him with my hand on his. With a little shrewdness could one make them submit to anything? Were bare thighs, an exposed breast sufficient? Was it enough merely to touch them? Had my mother taken my father like this, as a girl? Had Costanza taken him away from her like this? Had Vittoria also done this with Enzo, taking him away from Margherita? When Corrado, unhappy, touched my neck with his fingers and then caressed the edge of the material beyond which rose the curve of my breast, I let him do it. At the same time I squeezed Rosario's hand hard for a few seconds. I'm not even pretty, I thought, in amazement, while amid caresses, giggles, allusive if not obscene words, wind and cloud-streaked sky, the car flew, along with the time, and the walls of tufa topped with barbed wire, the abandoned warehouses, the low pale-blue buildings at the end of Via Pascone came into view.

As soon as I recognized them I felt sick to my stomach, the impression of power vanished: now I had to reckon with my aunt. Corrado, reasserting, mainly to himself, that it was he who commanded me, said:

"We'll leave you here."

"O.K."

"We'll go to the square, don't make us wait. And remember you got here by public transit."

"How?"

"Bus, funicular, metro. What you must never say is that we brought you."

"O.K."

"Listen, be quick about it."

I nodded, got out of the car.

12.

I walked for a short stretch with my heart racing. I reached Vittoria's house, rang the bell, and she opened the door. At first I didn't understand. I had prepared a short speech to deliver firmly, centered on the feelings that had collected around the bracelet and made it absolutely mine. As soon as she saw me, she hit me with a long, aggressive, sorrowful, maudlin monologue that disoriented and intimidated me. The more she talked, the more clearly I realized that giving back the bracelet was nothing more than an excuse. Vittoria was fond of me, she thought I loved her, too, and above all she wanted to chastise me for having disappointed her.

I hoped — she said in a loud voice, in a dialect that I struggled to understand in spite of my recent efforts to learn it — that you were now on my side, that seeing what sort of people your father and mother really are would allow you to understand who I am, what sort of life I've had because of my brother. But no, I waited in vain for you every Sunday. A phone call would have been enough, but no, you didn't understand, you thought it's my fault if your family turned out to be shit, and in the end what do you do, look at this, you write me this letter — this letter, to me — to underscore the fact that I didn't go to school, to underscore the fact that you can write and I can't. Oh, you really are like your father, no, worse, you don't respect me, you can't see what sort of person I am, you don't have feelings. So give me back the bracelet, it was my dearly beloved mother's and you don't deserve it. I was wrong, you don't have my blood, you're a stranger.

So I gathered that if in that endless family

quarrel I had chosen the right side, if I had treated her as the only support remaining to me, my only guide for life, if I had welcomed the parish church, Margherita, her children as a sort of permanent Sunday refuge, giving back the piece of jewelry would have been unnecessary. While she was yelling, her eyes were fierce and yet sorrowful, I saw white saliva in her mouth that from time to time stained her lips. Vittoria simply wanted me to admit that I loved her, that I was grateful to her for showing me how mediocre my father was, and so I would love her forever, that out of gratitude I would be her support in old age, and other such things. And I, on the spot, decided to tell her just that. In a brief series of statements I went so far as to pretend that my parents had kept me from calling her, then I added that the letter told the truth: the bracelet was a very dear memory of how she had helped me, saved me, put me on the right path. I said it like that, in an emotional voice, and I was amazed at how good I was at speaking to her in a falsely heartfelt way, at how carefully and effectively I chose words, at how I wasn't like her, but worse.

Slowly Vittoria calmed down, and I was relieved. Now I had to find a way of leaving and getting back to the two waiting boys; I hoped she would forget about the bracelet.

She didn't say anything else about it, in fact, but insisted that I should go with her to hear Roberto, who was speaking in church. Now I was really in a fix: it was very important to her. She praised Tonino's friend, I guessed he'd become her pet after he got engaged to Giuliana. You can't imagine what a good boy he is, she said, intelligent, sensible: afterward we'll all eat at Margherita's house, you'll stay, too. Politely I said that I really couldn't, I had to go home, and I hugged her as if I really did love her, and who knows, maybe I did, I no longer understood anything about my feelings. I muttered:

"I'm going, Mamma's expecting me, but I'll be back soon."

She gave in:

"All right, I'll go with you."

"No, no, no, there's no need."

"I'll take you to the bus stop."

"No, I know where the stop is, thanks."

There was no way out, she wanted to come with me. I didn't have the slightest idea where the stop was, I hoped it was someplace far from where Rosario and Corrado were waiting for me. Yet it seemed that we were going precisely in that direction, and the whole way I kept repeating, anxiously: all right, thanks, I can go by myself. But my aunt wouldn't stop, in fact the more I tried to get away, the more intensely did she look like one who feels that something isn't right. We turned the corner, finally, and, as I feared, the bus stop was right in the square where Corrado and Rosario were sitting, clearly visible in the car with the top down.

Vittoria saw the car immediately, a patch of yellow steel sparkling in the sun.

"You came with Corrado and that shithead?"

"No."

"Swear."

"I swear, no."

She pushed me backward with a hand to the chest and headed toward the car shouting insults in dialect. But Rosario took off immediately, tires screeching, and she ran after him for a few meters, yelling fiercely, then she took off a shoe and threw it in the direction of the convertible. The car disappeared, leaving her furious, bent double, on the edge of the street.

"You're a liar," she said when, recovering her shoe, she returned to me, still panting.

"I swear I didn't."

"Now I'll telephone your mother and we'll see."

"Please don't do that. I didn't come with them, but don't call my mother."

I told her that, since my mother didn't want me to see her but it was very important to me, I had told her I was going to Caserta with my classmates. I was convincing: the fact that I had deceived my mother, just to see her, cheered her.

"All day?"

"I have to be back in the afternoon."

She searched my eyes with a bewildered expression.

"So come with me to hear Roberto and then you'll go."

"I'll risk being late."

"You'll risk getting slapped by me if I find out you're lying to me and you want to go with those two."

I followed her unhappily, praying: God, please, I don't feel like going to church, let Corrado and Rosario not leave, let them be waiting for me somewhere, get rid of my aunt, I'll die of boredom in church. The way there was familiar to me by now: empty streets, weeds and garbage, graffiti-covered walls, crumbling apartment buildings. The whole time Vittoria kept an arm around my shoulders, sometimes she pressed me tight against her. She spoke mainly about Giuliana — Corrado worried her, while she had a high regard for that girl and for Tonino — and how sensible she had become. Love — she said, in an inspired tone and using a formula that didn't belong to her, that in fact baffled and irritated me — is a ray of sun that warms the soul. I was disappointed. Maybe I should have observed my aunt with the same attention with which she had urged me to spy on my parents. Maybe I would have discovered that behind the harshness that had charmed me there was a soft, foolish little woman, tough on the surface, tender underneath. If Vittoria really is that, I thought, discouraged, then she is ugly, she has the ugliness of banality.

Every time I heard the rumble of a car I looked sidewards, hoping that Rosario and Corrado would reappear and seize me, but also fearing that she would start shouting again and get mad at me. We reached the church, which was surprisingly crowded. I went straight to the holy water font, wet my fingers, crossed myself before Vittoria could make me. There was an odor of breath and of flowers, a polite din, a child's shrill voice immediately shushed with muffled tones. Behind a table placed at the end of the central nave, I saw the figure of Don Giacomo, standing with his back to the altar, he was saying something emphatically. He seemed pleased by our entrance, gave a sign of greeting without breaking off. I would have happily sat in the back pews, which were empty, but my aunt grabbed my arm and led me along the right nave. We sat in the first rows, next to Margherita, who had saved us a place, and who when she saw me turned red with pleasure. I sat squeezed between her and Vittoria, the one large, soft, the other tense, thin. Don Giacomo was silent, the hum rose in pitch, I was just in time to look around, to recognize Giuliana, surprisingly demure in the front row, and, on her right, Tonino, broad-shouldered, his torso erect. Then the priest said: come, Roberto, what are you doing there, sit beside me, and an impressive silence fell, as if suddenly no one in that space could breathe.

But maybe that's not how it went, probably it was I who cancelled out every sound when a tall but stooping young man, thin as a shadow, stood up. It seemed to me that a long gold chain visible only to me was attached to his back, holding him, and he swayed lightly as if he were hanging from the cupola, the tips of his shoes barely grazing the floor. When he reached the table and turned, I had the impression that he had more eyes than face: they were blue, blue in a dark, bony, unharmonious face locked between a great mass of rebellious hair and a thick beard that looked blue.

I was almost fifteen and until that moment no boy had truly attracted me, least of all Corrado, least of all Rosario. But as soon as I saw Roberto — even before he opened his mouth, even before he was ignited by any feeling, even before he uttered a word — I felt a violent pain in my chest and knew that everything in my life was about to change, that I wanted him, that I would necessarily have to have him, that even if I didn't believe in God I would pray every day and every night that that would happen, and that only that wish, only that hope, only that prayer could keep me from immediately, now, falling down dead on the ground.

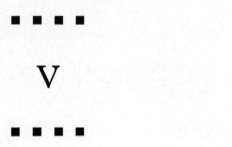

V

1.

Don Giacomo sat at the shabby table at the
end of the nave and watched Roberto the
whole time with an attitude of concentrated
listening, his cheek resting on the palm of
his hand. Roberto spoke standing up, in a
brusque yet attractive tone, his back to the
altar and a large crucifixion with a dark
cross and a yellow Christ. I remember
almost nothing of what he said, maybe
because he was expressing himself from
within a culture that was alien to me, maybe
because emotion kept me from listening. I
have in mind many phrases that are surely
his, but I don't know how to place them in
time, I confuse the words of then with those
which followed. Yet some are more likely to
have been uttered that Sunday. Sometimes,
for instance, I'm sure that in the church he
discussed the parable of the good trees that
bear good fruit, and the bad trees that bear
bad fruit and so end up as wood to be

burned. Or more often I feel certain that he insisted on the exact calculation of our resources when we plunge into a great undertaking, because it's wrong to start, let's say, building a tower if you don't have the money to build it up to the last stone. Or I think he urged us all to have courage, reminding us that the only way not to waste our life is to lose it through saving others. Or I imagine that he reasoned about the need to be truly fair, merciful, and faithful, without concealing unfairness, a hard heart, infidelity behind respect for conventions. But really I don't know, time has passed and I can't decide. For me his talk, from beginning to end, was a flow of enchanting sounds that came from his beautiful mouth, his throat. I stared at his prominent Adam's apple as if behind that knob vibrated the breath of the first human being of the male sex to come into the world and not, instead, one of the infinite reproductions that crowd the planet. How beautiful and terrible were his pale-blue eyes carved into his dark face, his long fingers, his shining lips. About one of his words I have no doubt, he uttered it often on that occasion, plucking its petals like a daisy. I refer to "compunction," I understood that he was using it in an anomalous way. He said that it should be cleansed of the ugly uses that had been made of it, he spoke of it as of a needle that had to pull the thread through the scattered fragments of our existence. He gave it the meaning of an extreme vigilance over oneself, it was the knife that would prick conscience to keep it from going to sleep.

2.

As soon as Roberto stopped speaking, my aunt dragged me over to Giuliana. I was struck by how she had changed; her beauty seemed infantile to me. She has no makeup, I thought, she's not wearing a woman's colors, and I felt uneasy about my short skirt, my lipstick and heavy eye makeup, my low neckline. I'm out of place, I said to myself, while Giuliana whispered: I'm so happy to see you, did you like him? I murmured a few confused words of compliments for her, enthusiasm for her boyfriend's words. Let's introduce her to him, Vittoria interrupted, and Giuliana led us to Roberto.

"This is my niece," my aunt said with a pride that increased my embarrassment, "a really smart girl."

"I'm not smart," I almost shouted and held out my hand, hoping that he would at

271

least touch it.

He took it in his without squeezing it, he said what a pleasure with an affectionate look, while my aunt reproached me: she's too modest, the opposite of my brother who was always presumptuous. Roberto asked me about school, what I was studying, what I was reading. A few seconds passed, I had the impression his questions weren't just something to say, I froze. I stammered something about the boredom of classes, about a difficult book I'd been reading for months, it would never end, it was about the search for lost time. Giuliana said to him in a whisper: they're calling you, but he kept his eyes on mine, he was amazed that I was reading a book both beautiful and complicated, he turned to his fiancée: you said she was smart, but she's really smart. My aunt was filled with pride, she repeated that I was her niece, and meanwhile a couple of smiling parishioners gestured, pointing to the priest. I wanted to find some words that would strike Roberto to his depths, but my head was empty, I couldn't find anything. And he was already being dragged away by the very warmth he had inspired, he said goodbye to me with a gesture of regret, and ended up in a large group with Don Giacomo.

I didn't dare follow him even with my eyes, I stayed beside Giuliana, who seemed radiant. I thought again of the framed picture of her father in Margherita's kitchen, the flame of the small flashing light that illuminated his pupils, and I found it disorienting that a young woman could carry in herself the features of that man and yet be beautiful. I envied her: her slim body in a beige dress and her clear face radiated a joyous strength. But when I first met her that energy had been expressed in a loud voice and exaggerated gestures; now instead Giuliana was serene, as if the pride of loving and being loved had tied up with invisible threads her exuberant manner. She said in a forced Italian: I know what happened to you, I'm very sorry, I feel for you. And she took my hand in hers as her boyfriend had just done. But I wasn't annoyed, I talked to her sincerely about my mother's suffering, even if my most vigilant self never lost sight of Roberto, I was hoping he would look for me with his gaze. He didn't, and I realized that he spoke to everyone with the same cordial curiosity he had shown toward me. He didn't hurry, but detained his interlocutors and behaved in a way that caused those who crowded around just to talk to him — to draw on the kindness of his smile, on the beauty of his face nourished by its lack of harmony — to gradually start talking to others as well. If I went over to him, I thought, he would surely give me room, too, he would lead me into some discussion. But then I would be forced to express myself more articulately, and he would right away realize that it wasn't true, I'm not smart, I don't know anything about the things he cares about. So I was gripped by unease, to insist on talking to him would humiliate me, he would say: how ignorant that girl is. And suddenly, while Giuliana was still talking to me, I said to her that I had to go. She insisted that I should come and have lunch at her house: Roberto is staying, *too,* she said. But now I was frightened, I wanted literally to escape. I left the church quickly.

Once I was outside, in the square, the fresh air made me dizzy. I looked around as if I had come out of a theater after a powerfully absorbing movie. Not only did I not know how to get home but I didn't care about getting there. I would have stayed here forever: slept under the portico, neither eating nor drinking, letting myself die thinking of Roberto. At that moment, no other affection or desire mattered to me in the least.

But I heard someone calling my name: it was Vittoria, and she joined me. She used her most cloying tones to try to keep me, until she gave up and explained what I had to do to get back to San Giacomo dei Capri: the metro takes you to Piazza Amedeo and there you get the funicular, then once you're at Piazza Vanvitelli you know how to go. When she saw me in a daze — what is it, you didn't understand? — she offered to take me home in the 500, even though she had to go to lunch at Margherita's. I politely refused, she started talking to me in exaggeratedly sentimental dialect, smoothing my hair, holding my arm, kissing me on the cheek a couple of times with wet lips, and I was even more convinced that she wasn't a vengeful gorgon but a poor, lonely woman who wanted affection and who at that moment loved me especially because I had made her look good in Roberto's eyes. You were great, she said, I'm studying this, I'm reading this other thing, great, great great. I felt guilty toward her, at least as much as my father surely did, and I wanted to make up for it, I reached into the pocket where I had the bracelet and offered it to her.

"I didn't want to give it to you," I said, "it seemed to me that it was mine, but it belongs to you and no one but you should have it."

She wasn't expecting my gesture, she looked at the bracelet with evident annoyance, as if it were a little snake or a bad omen. She said:

"No, I gave it to you, for me it's enough if you love me."

"Take it."

In the end, she accepted it, unwillingly, but she didn't put it on her wrist. She stuck it in her purse and stood at the bus stop holding me tight, laughing, singing, until the bus arrived. I went up the steps as if each one were conclusive and I were about to make a surprise entrance into another story of mine and another life.

I'd been on the bus for a few minutes, sitting next to the window, when I heard insistent honking. I saw that Rosario's convertible had pulled up beside the bus in the passing lane. Corrado was waving, shouting, get off, Giannì, come on. They had been waiting for me, patiently hiding somewhere or other, all the time imagining that I would satisfy their every desire. I looked at them with sympathy, they seemed tenderly insignificant as they went by in the wind. Rosario, driving, gestured to me slowly to get off, Corrado continued to shout: we'll wait for you at the next stop, we'll have fun, and meanwhile he cast commanding glances at me, hoping that I would obey him. When I smiled absently and didn't respond, Rosario, too, looked up to figure out what I meant to do. I shook my head no only to him, told him, moving my lips: I can't.

The convertible accelerated, leaving the bus behind.

3.

My mother was surprised that the trip to Caserta had lasted such a short time. What in the world, she asked idly, you're already back, did something bad happen, did you fight? I could have not answered, gone to shut myself in my room as usual, put on some loud music, read and read and read about lost time or anything, but I didn't. I confessed to her right away that I hadn't gone to Caserta but to see Vittoria, and when I saw that she turned yellow with disappointment, I did something I hadn't done for several years: I sat on her lap with my arms around her neck and kissed her lightly on her eyes. She resisted. She murmured that I was grown up and was heavy, she chastised me for the lie I'd told, for how I was dressed, the vulgar makeup, holding me tight around the waist with her thin arms. After a while, she asked me about Vittoria.

"Did she do something that scared you?"

"No."

"You seem upset."

"I'm fine."

"But your hands are cold, you're sweaty. Are you sure nothing happened?"

"Very sure."

She was surprised, she was alarmed, she was pleased, or maybe it was I who was mixing happiness, bewilderment, and worry thinking that they were her reactions. I never mentioned Roberto, I didn't think I'd find the right words, and then I'd hate myself. Instead I explained to her that I'd heard some talks in the church that I'd liked.

"Every Sunday," I told her, "the priest invites this really smart friend of his, they set up a table at the end of the central nave, and he talks."

"About what?"

"I can't repeat it now."

"You see, you're upset?"

I wasn't upset, or rather I was in a state of happy agitation, and that condition didn't go away even when she said uneasily that a few days earlier, completely by chance, she had met Mariano and, knowing I was on an

278

outing to Caserta, had invited him for coffee that afternoon.

Not even that news could change my mood, I asked:

"Do you want to be with Mariano?"

"Of course not."

"Why is it that you all can never tell the truth?"

"Giovanna, I swear to you, it is the truth: there is nothing and never was anything between me and him. But since your father has started to see him again, why shouldn't I?"

That last bit of information upset me. My mother told me briefly that it was a recent change, the two former friends had met once when Mariano came to see his daughters and, for love of the children, they had spoken politely. I burst out:

"If my father has re-established relations with a friend he betrayed, why doesn't he examine his conscience and re-establish relations with his sister?"

"Because Mariano is a civilized person and Vittoria isn't."

"That's ridiculous. It's because Mariano teaches at the university, makes him feel good, gives him a certain status, while Vittoria makes him feel like what he is."

"You realize how you're speaking of your father?"

"Yes."

"Then stop it."

"I'm saying what I think."

I went to my room, taking refuge in the thought of Roberto. It was Vittoria who had introduced me to him. He was part of my aunt's world, not my parents'. Vittoria spent time with him, appreciated him, had approved, if not encouraged, his engagement to Giuliana. In my eyes that made her more sensitive, more intelligent than the people my parents had spent their lives with, Mariano and Costanza at the top of the list. I shut myself in the bathroom in a state of nervous tension, I carefully took off my makeup, I put on a pair of jeans and a white shirt. What would Roberto say, if I told him what had happened in my house, my parents' behavior, that recomposition in the midst of the rot of an old friendship. The violent buzz of the intercom startled me. A few minutes passed, I heard Mariano's voice, my mother's, I hoped she wouldn't assert herself and summon me. She didn't, I started studying, but there was no escape, I heard her call: Giovanna, come and say hello to Mariano. I huffed, closed the book, went.

I was struck by how thin Angela and Ida's father was, he was a match for my mother. Seeing him I felt sorry for him, but it didn't last. I was irritated that his excited gaze fell immediately on my breasts, just like Corrado and Rosario, even if this time my chest was completely covered by the shirt.

"You've grown so much," he exclaimed, with emotion, and wanted to hug me, kiss me on the cheeks.

"Want a chocolate? Mariano brought them."

I refused, I said I had to study.

"I know you're busy making up for your lost year," he said.

I nodded yes, I muttered: I'm going. Before leaving I felt his gaze on me again and I was ashamed. I thought how Roberto had looked only at my eyes.

4.

I soon understood what had happened: I had fallen in love at first sight. I had read enough about that type of love, but, I don't know why, I never used that expression to myself. I preferred to consider Roberto — his face, his voice, his hands around mine — a sort of miraculous consolation for my agitated days and nights. Naturally, I wanted

281

to see him again, but after the first upheaval
— that unforgettable moment when seeing
him had coincided with a violent need for
him — a sort of calm realism had taken
over. Roberto was a man, I a girl. Roberto
loved someone else, who was very beautiful
and good. Roberto was inaccessible, he lived
in Milan, I didn't know anything about what
was important to him. The only possible
contact was Vittoria, and Vittoria was a
complicated person, apart from the fact that
every attempt to see her would be painful
to my mother. So I let the days pass, uncertain what to do. Then I thought that I surely
had the right to a life of my own without
having to constantly worry about my parents' reactions, especially since they weren't
worrying at all about mine. And I couldn't
resist, one afternoon when I was alone in
the house I called my aunt. I regretted not
having accepted her invitation to lunch, I
seemed to have wasted an important opportunity, and I wanted to cautiously find
out when I could go and visit her with some
certainty of seeing Roberto. I was sure I
would be warmly welcomed, after giving
back the bracelet, but Vittoria wouldn't let
me get a word in. I learned from her that
the day after the lie about Caserta my
mother had called her to say, in her feeble

way, that she was to leave me alone, that she wasn't ever to see me again. In light of which she was now furious. She insulted her sister-in-law, shouted that she would wait outside the house to stab her. She yelled: how could she dare to say that *I* am doing all I can to steal you from her when it's all of *you* taking away from me every reason for living, *you,* your father, your mother, and you, too, you thought that all you had to do was give me back the bracelet and everything would be fine. She shouted: if you're on your parents' side don't call me ever again, get it? And, breathless, she went on to gasp a series of obscenities about her brother and sister-in-law, after which she hung up.

I tried to call her back to tell her that I was on her side, that in fact I was extremely angry about that phone call of my mother's, but she didn't answer. I felt depressed, just then I needed her affection, I was afraid that without her I would never have the chance to see Roberto. And meanwhile time slipped away, days of grim unhappiness, then of bitter reflection. I began to think of him as of the silhouette of a very distant mountain, a bluish substance contained within heavy lines. Probably — I said to myself — no one in Pascone has ever seen him with the clarity I was capable of there in the church. He was born in that area, grew up there, is a childhood friend of Tonino. They all appreciate him as a particularly luminous fragment of that bleak background, and Giuliana herself must be in love with him not for what he really is but for their common origins and the aura of someone who, though he came from the foul-smelling Industrial Zone, went to school in Milan and has managed to distinguish himself. Except that — I persuaded myself — precisely the aspects of him that they're able to love prevent them from seeing him seriously and recognizing his uniqueness. Roberto mustn't be treated like an ordinary person with special abilities, Roberto must be protected. For example, if I were Giuliana, I would fight with all my strength to keep him from coming to lunch at my house, I would prevent Vittoria, Margherita, Corrado from spoiling him for me and spoiling the reasons he chose me. I would keep him outside that world, I would say to him: let's run away, I'll come to you in Milan. But Giuliana, in my view, isn't truly aware of her good fortune. As far as I'm concerned, if I succeeded even just in becoming his friend, I would never make him waste his time with my mother, who is surely much more presentable than Vittoria and Margherita. And I would especially avoid any possible encounter with my father. The energy that Roberto gives off needs care in order not to be dissipated, and I feel that I would be able to assure him that care. Oh yes, become his friend, only that, and show him that, somewhere inside me unknown even to myself, I possess the qualities he needs.

5.

Around that time I began to think that if I wasn't beautiful physically maybe I could be beautiful spiritually. But how? I had by now discovered that I didn't have a good character, I inclined to malicious words and actions. If I had good qualities, I was suppressing them, deliberately, in order not to feel that I was a pathetic girl from a good family. Now I had the impression that I had found the path to my salvation but didn't know how to take it and maybe didn't deserve it.

I was in that state when, one afternoon, completely by chance, I ran into Don Giacomo, the priest from Pascone. I was in Piazza Vanvitelli, I no longer remember why, I was walking along, thinking of my own affairs, and almost bumped into him. Giannina, he exclaimed. Finding him there cancelled out for a few seconds the square, the buildings, and threw me again into the church, sitting beside Vittoria, Roberto standing behind the table. When everything returned to its place, I was glad that the priest had recognized me and remembered my name. It made me so happy that I hugged him as if he were a friend from elementary school. Then I started to feel intimidated, I began to stammer and addressed him with the formal *lei,* but he insisted on the informal *tu.* He was going to take the Montesanto funicular, I offered to walk with him and immediately went on, too gaily, to declare my enthusiasm for the experience I'd had in the church.

"When will Roberto come back to speak?" I asked.

"Did you like his talk?"

"Yes."

"Did you notice how much he manages to pull out from the Gospel?"

I didn't remember anything — what did I know about the Gospels — only Roberto had remained stamped in my mind. But I nodded just the same, I said:

"No teacher in school is absorbing the way he is, I'd come to hear him again."

The priest darkened, and only at that

point I realized that, although he was the same person, something in his aspect had changed: he had a yellowish complexion, his eyes had reddened.

"Roberto won't be back," he said, "and in church there won't be any more initiatives of that type."

I was really upset.

"Didn't people like them?"

"My superiors and some of the parishioners didn't."

Now I was disappointed and angry, I said:

"Isn't your superior God?"

"Yes, but it's his lieutenants who call the shots."

"So you address him directly."

Don Giacomo made a gesture with his hand as if to signal an indeterminate distance, and I realized that on his fingers, on the back of his hand, and even on his wrist he had broad violet stains.

"God is outside," he said smiling.

"And prayer?"

"I'm worn out, apparently by now prayer is my trade. What about you? Have you been praying, even if you don't believe in it?"

"Yes."

"And did it help?"

"No, it's a magic that ultimately isn't successful."

287

Don Giacomo was silent. I realized I had said something wrong, I wanted to apologize.

"Sometimes I say everything that goes through my head," I muttered. "I'm sorry."

"For what? You've brightened my day, lucky I ran into you."

He looked at his right hand as if it hid a secret.

"Are you ill?" I asked.

"I've just been to a doctor friend here on Via Kerbaker, it's only a rash."

"What causes it?"

"When you're made to do things you don't want to and you obey, it works on your mind, it works on everything."

"Obedience is a skin disease?"

He looked at me for a moment in bewilderment, he smiled.

"Good for you, it's exactly that, a skin disease. And you are a good cure, don't change, always say what comes to your mind. A little more conversation with you and I bet I'll improve."

I said impulsively:

"I want to improve, too. What should I do?"

The priest answered:

"Drive out pride, which is always lurking."

"And then?"

"Treat others with kindness and a sense of fairness."

"And then?"

"Then the thing that at your age is most difficult: honor your father and mother. But you have to try, Giannì, it's important."

"My father and mother I don't understand anymore."

"When you grow up you'll understand them."

They all said I would understand when I grew up. I answered:

"Then I won't grow up."

We said goodbye at the funicular, and I haven't seen him since. I didn't dare ask about Roberto, I didn't ask if Vittoria had talked about me, if she had told him what had happened in my house. I said only, ashamed of myself:

"I feel ugly, like I'm a bad person, and yet I'd like to be loved."

But I said it too late, in a whisper, when he had already turned away.

6.

That encounter helped me, and I tried first of all to change my relationship with my parents. Honoring them was out of the question, but maybe, yes, I could at least look for ways to get a little closer to them.

With my mother things started out pretty well, even though it wasn't easy to get my aggressive tone under control. I never talked to her about the phone call she had made to Vittoria, but every so often I'd yell orders, rebukes, recriminations, betrayals. As usual, she didn't react, she remained impassive, as if she had the ability to become deaf on command. But slowly I modified my attitude. I observed her from the hall, carefully dressed, with her hair combed, even when she didn't have to go out and no one was coming, and the sight of her bony back, of a person consumed by suffering, bent for hours over her work, softened me. One night, spying on her, I likened her to my aunt. No question they were enemies, no question in terms of upbringing and cultivation there was no comparison. But hadn't Vittoria remained bound to Enzo even though he'd been dead for so long? And hadn't her faithfulness seemed to me a mark of greatness? I was suddenly surprised to think that my mother was showing an even nobler soul, and I reflected on that idea for hours.

Vittoria's love had been returned, her lover had loved her always. My mother instead had been betrayed in the vilest way, and yet she had managed to hold on to her feeling intact. She was neither able nor willing to think of herself without her ex-husband, in fact it seemed to her that her life still had meaning only if my father deigned to be in touch by phone and bestow it. Her acquiescence suddenly began to appeal to me. How could I attack and insult her for that dependency? Was it possible that I had taken for weakness the strength — yes, the strength — of her way of loving absolutely?

Once I said to her in a matter-of-fact tone: "Since you like Mariano, take him."

"How many times do I have to tell you? Mariano is repulsive to me."

"And Papa?"

"Papa is Papa."

"Why don't you ever say anything bad about him?"

"What I say is one thing and what I think is another."

"You let yourself go in your thoughts?"

"A little, but then I end up going back to all the years when we were happy, and I forget I hate him."

It seemed to me that that phrase — *I forget I hate him* — captured something true and alive, and that was precisely the way I tried to reconsider my father. I hardly ever saw him now, I didn't go to the house in Posillipo, I had eliminated Angela and Ida from my life. And, however much I tried to understand why he had left my mother and me and had gone to live with Costanza and her daughters, I couldn't. In the past I had considered him far superior to my mother, but now I felt he had no greatness of soul, even in a negative sense. The rare times he came by to take me to school I was very attentive to the way he complained, but only to repeat to myself that those complaints were false. He wanted to make me believe that he wasn't happy or anyway that he was just slightly less unhappy than when he lived in the apartment on Via San Giacomo dei Capri. I didn't believe him, naturally, but I studied him and thought: I have to put aside my feelings of the present, I have to think of when I was a child and adored him; because if Mamma continues to be attached to him in spite of everything, if she can reach the point where she forgets she hates him, maybe his exceptionality wasn't only an effect of childhood. So I made a considerable effort to give him back some virtues. But not out of affection: it seemed to me that I had no feelings for him. I tried only to convince myself that my mother had loved a person of some substance, and so, when I saw him, I tried to be cordial. I talked to him about school, about some silliness involving the teachers, and even complimented him sometimes, on his explanation of a difficult passage from a Latin writer, say, or on his haircut.

"Luckily, this time they didn't cut it too short. Did you change barbers?"

"No, there's one near the house, it's not worth it. And then what do I care about my hair, it's already white, yours that's young and beautiful is what counts."

I ignored the allusion to the beauty of my hair, I found it out of place. I said:

"It's not white, you just have a little gray at the temples."

"I'm getting old."

"When I was little you were much older, you've gotten young again."

"Suffering doesn't make you younger."

"You obviously haven't felt enough of it. I know you're back in touch with Mariano."

"Who told you that?"

"Mamma."

"It's not true, but we meet sometimes, when he comes to see his daughters."

"Do you fight?"

"No."

"Then what's not right?"

There wasn't anything that wasn't right, he just wanted me to understand that he missed me, and that my absence was painful to him. Sometimes he acted the part so well that I forgot I didn't believe him. He was still handsome, he hadn't gotten thin like my mother, he didn't have rashes on his skin: falling into the net of his loving voice, sliding again into childhood, confiding in him was easy. One day, while as usual we were eating *panzarotti* and *pastacresciuta* after school, I said impulsively that I wanted to read the Gospels.

"Why?"

"Is that bad?"

"It's very good."

"What if I become a Christian?"

"I don't see anything wrong with that."

"What if I get baptized?"

"The important thing is that it not be a whim. If you have faith, it's fine."

No opposition, then, but I immediately repented that I had told him of my intention. To think of him as an authoritative person, worthy of love, now, after Roberto, seemed intolerable. What did he have to do with my life anymore? I didn't want in any way to restore to him authority and affection. If I ever read the Gospels, I would do it for the young man who had spoken in church.

7.

That attempt — failed from the start — to get close to my father again intensified my desire to see Roberto. I couldn't resist and decided to phone Vittoria. She answered in a voice that was depressed, hoarse from cigarettes, and this time she didn't attack or insult me, but she wasn't affectionate, either.

"What do you want?"

"I want to know how you're doing."

"I'm fine."

"Can I come see you one Sunday?"

"To do what?"

"To say hello. Plus I was glad to meet Giuliana's fiancé: if he's back in this area, I'd happily come and see him."

"They're not doing anything in church anymore, they want to get rid of the priest."

She didn't give me time to tell her I'd run into Don Giacomo and knew all about it. She switched into very heavy dialect, she was mad at everyone, the parishioners, the bishops, the cardinals, the Pope, but also at Don Giacomo and even Roberto.

"The priest overdid it," she said. "He was like medicine: first he cured us, then came the side effects, and now we feel much worse than before."

"And Roberto?"

"Roberto takes the easy way out. He comes, throws things into disarray, and leaves, you don't see him for months. Either he's in Milan or he's here, and that's not something that's good for Giuliana."

"Love, yes," I said, "love does no harm."

"What do you know?"

"Love is good, it overcomes even long absences, it stands up to everything."

"You don't know anything, Gianni, you speak in Italian but you don't know anything. Love is opaque like the glass in the bathroom window."

That image struck me, I immediately had the impression that it contradicted the way she had recounted her romance with Enzo. I praised her, I said I wanted to talk to her more, I asked:

"Sometime when you all have lunch together — you, Margherita, Giuliana, Corrado, Tonino, Roberto — can I come, too?"

She was irritated, she turned aggressive.

"Better for you to stay home: that, according to your mother, is the place for you."

"But I'd like to see all of you. Is Giuliana there? I'll make arrangements with her."

"Giuliana is at her house."

"And Tonino?"

"You think Tonino eats, sleeps, and shits here?"

She hung up abruptly, rude, vulgar as usual. I would have liked an invitation, a definite date, the certainty that even in six months, in a year, I would see Roberto again. That hadn't happened, and yet I felt pleasantly agitated. Vittoria had said nothing clear about the relationship between Giuliana and Roberto, but I had understood that there were some stumbling blocks. Of course, one couldn't depend on my aunt's assessment, in all likelihood what disturbed her was exactly what made the couple happy. Yet I fantasized that with perseverance, with patience, with the best intentions, I could become a kind of mediator between them and my aunt: that is, a person who could speak everybody's language. I looked for a copy of the Gospels.

8.

I didn't find one at home, but I hadn't reckoned with the fact that with my father it was enough to mention a book, because he immediately got it for me. A few days after our conversation, he appeared outside school with an edition of the Gospels with commentary.

"Reading isn't enough," he said. "Texts like these have to be studied."

His eyes lit up as he uttered that statement. His true existential condition was revealed as soon as he was dealing with books, ideas, lofty questions. At that moment, it became clear that he was unhappy only when his head was empty and he couldn't hide from himself what he had done to my mother and me. When, instead, he devoted himself to great thoughts supported by meticulously annotated books, he was happy, he lacked nothing. He had transferred his life to Costanza's house and lived there in comfort. His new study was a large luminous room with a window overlooking the sea. He had resumed the meetings with all the people I remembered from childhood, apart from Mariano, naturally, but the fiction of a return to order was now solidified, and you could predict that soon Mariano, too, would return to the debates. So the only thing that spoiled my father's days was the empty moments when he found himself face to face with his offenses. But it didn't take much to sneak away, and that request of mine was surely a good opportunity, it must have given him the impression that things were returning to normal even with me.

In fact, he promptly followed the commented edition with an old volume of the Gospels in Greek — the translations are good but the original text is crucial — and then, without a break, he pressed me to ask my mother to help him resolve some very boring matters of certificates or some such thing. I took the book, I promised to talk to her. When I did she got huffy, grumpy, sarcastic, but gave in. And although she spent the days in school or correcting homework and proofs, she found the time to wait in long lines at the windows of various agencies, fighting with lazy bureaucrats.

It was then that I noticed how I myself had changed. I was barely indignant at my mother's subservience when from my room I heard her announce to him on the phone that she had done it. I wasn't furious when, her voice burned by too many cigarettes, by drinking gin at night, she softened and invited him to come by and get the documents that she had tracked down at the registry office, the copies she had had made at the national library, the certificates she had obtained for him from the university. I wasn't even too hostile when, one night, my father showed up, looking discouraged, and they talked in the living room. I heard my mother laugh once or twice, then that was it, she must have realized that it was a laugh from the past. In other words, I didn't think: if she's stupid so much the worse for her; now I seemed to understand her feelings. My attitude toward my father fluctuated more. I hated his opportunism. And I darkened when he called to me to say hello, and casually asked:

"So? Are you studying the Gospels?"

"Yes," I said, "but I don't like the story."

He gave me an ironic smile:

"That's interesting, you don't like the story."

He kissed me on the forehead and in the doorway said:

"We'll talk about it later."

Talk about it with him, never, ever. What could I say to him. I had begun to read with the idea that these were fables that would lead me to a love of God like Roberto's. I felt a need for it, my body was so tense that the nerves sometimes seemed like high-tension wires. But those texts didn't follow the course of a fable, they unfolded in real places, the people had real jobs, they were people who had really existed. And ferocity stood out more than any other feeling. Finishing one gospel, I began the next, and the story seemed even more terrible. Yes, it

300

was a disturbing story. I read and became agitated. We were all serving a Lord who kept us under surveillance to see what we chose, good or evil. What an absurdity, how could one accept such a servile condition? I hated the idea that there was a Father in Heaven and we children were below, in the mud, in the blood. What sort of father was God, what sort of family that of his creatures: it frightened and at the same time infuriated me. I hated that Father who had created such frail beings, continuously exposed to suffering, so easily perishing. I hated the fact that he was watching how we puppets dealt with hunger, thirst, illness, terror, cruelty, pride, even the good sentiments that, always at risk of bad faith, concealed betrayal. I hated the fact that he had a son born of a virgin mother and subjected him to the worst, like the unhappiest of his creatures. I hated that the son, although he had the power to work miracles, used that power for games that were scarcely effective, not for anything that really improved the human condition. I hated that the son tended to mistreat his mother and didn't have the courage to stand up to his father. I hated that the Lord God let his son die, suffering atrocious torture, and didn't deign to respond to his cry for help. Yes, it was a story that depressed me. And the final resurrection? A horribly mutilated body that returned to life? I had a horror of the resurrected, I couldn't sleep at night. Why have the experience of death if you are going to return to life for eternity? And what was the sense of eternal life in a crowd of resuscitated dead people? Was it really a reward, or was it a condition of intolerable horror? No, no, the Father who lived in Heaven was exactly like the unloving father of the chapters in Matthew and Luke, the one who gives stones, snakes, and scorpions to the son who is hungry and asks for bread. If I were to talk about it with my father, I would be at risk of coming out with: this Father, Papa, is worse than you. So I found myself justifying all of his creatures, even the worst. Their condition was harsh, and when they nevertheless succeeded in expressing, from within their sludge, truly great sentiments I was on their side. On my mother's side, for example, not her ex-husband's. He used her and then thanked her with mawkish flattery, taking advantage of her capacity for sublime feeling.

One night my mother said to me:

"Your father is younger than you. You're growing up and he's still a child. He'll remain a child forever, an extraordinarily intelligent child hypnotized by his games. If you don't keep an eye on him, he gets hurt. I should have understood him as a girl, but then he seemed to me a grown man."

She'd been mistaken and yet she held tight to her love. I looked at her with affection. I wanted to love like that, too, but not a man who didn't deserve it. She asked me:

"What are you reading?"

"The Gospels."

"Why?"

"Because there's a guy I like, and he knows them really well."

"Are you in love?"

"No, are you crazy, he has a girlfriend: I just want to be his friend."

"Don't tell Papa, he'll want to start discussing it and he'll ruin the reading for you."

But I didn't run that risk, I'd already read it all, down to the last line, and if my father interrogated me, I would respond with generic phrases. I hoped, one day, to talk about it in depth with Roberto, and to make appropriate observations. In church I'd thought I couldn't live without him, but time was passing, I continued to live. That impression of indispensability was changing. Indispensable now seemed to me not his physical presence — I imagined him far away, in Milan, happy, engaged in countless fine and useful things, recognized by every-one for his merits — but reorganizing myself around a goal: becoming a person who could earn his respect. I now felt him as an authority equally indeterminate — would he approve if I acted in such and such a way, or would he be opposed — and indis-putable.

Also around then I gave up caressing myself every night before going to sleep as a reward for the unbearable effort of existing. It seemed to me that the desolate creatures destined for death had a single small bit of luck: alleviate the suffering, forget it for a moment, setting off between their legs the device that leads to a little pleasure. But I was convinced that, if Roberto knew, he would regret having tolerated beside him, even just for a few minutes, a person who was in the habit of giving herself pleasure on her own.

9.

At that time, without deciding to — on the contrary, as though I were resuming an old routine — I went back to studying, even though school seemed to me even more than before a place of crude banter. I started getting good grades and at the same time forced myself to be friendlier toward my classmates, and I began going out with them on Saturday nights, though I avoided establishing friendships. Naturally, I could never completely eliminate my sharp tones, aggressive outbursts, hostile silences. And yet it seemed to me that I could become better. Sometimes I stared at a pot, a glass, a spoon, or even a stone on the sidewalk, a dry leaf, and marveled at its shape, whether it was crafted or appeared in its natural state. Streets in Rione Alto that I had known since childhood I now examined as if I were seeing them for the first time, stores, passersby, eight-story buildings, balconies that were white stripes against ochre or green or blue walls. The black lava paving stones of Via San Giacomo dei Capri on which I had walked countless times, the old gray-pink or rust-colored structures, the gardens. The same thing happened with people: teachers, neighbors, shopkeepers, passersby on the streets of the Vomero. I was amazed by a gesture, a look, the expression on a face. These were moments when everything seemed to have a secret depth and it was up to me to discover it. But it didn't last. Although I tried to resist, what prevailed was a sense of annoyance at everything, a tendency to scathing judgments, an urge to quarrel. I don't want to be like that, I said to myself, especially in a state of half sleep, and yet I was that, and realizing that it was the only way I could express myself — harsh, mean — sometimes pushed me not to rectify things but, with a treacherous pleasure, to do worse. I thought: if I'm not lovable, fine, let them not love me; nobody knows what I carry inside me day and night, and I took refuge in the thought of Roberto.

And yet, with pleasure, with surprise, I realized that, in spite of my outbursts, my classmates, both girls and boys, sought me out, invited me to parties, seemed to appreciate even my abusiveness. It was thanks to this new climate, I think, that I managed to keep Corrado and Rosario at bay. Of the two, the first to show up again was Corrado. He appeared outside school, he said:

"Let's take a walk in the Floridiana."

I wanted to refuse, but to interest the girls who were looking on I nodded agreement, though when he put his arm around my shoulders I slipped out. At first, he tried to make me laugh, and I laughed out of politeness, but when he tried to draw me off the paths, in among the bushes, I said no, first nicely, then decisively.

"Aren't we going together?" he asked, sincerely surprised.

"No."

"What do you mean no? What about the things we did?"

"What things?"

He was embarrassed.

"You know."

"I don't remember."

"You said they were fun."

"I was lying."

To my surprise, he seemed intimidated. He kept insisting, trying, bewildered, to kiss me. Then he gave up, turned mopey, muttered: I don't understand you, you're insulting me. We went to sit on a white step, facing a Naples that seemed beautiful under a transparent dome, outside was the blue sky and inside were vapors, as if all the stones in the city were breathing.

"You're making a mistake," he said.

"What mistake?"

"You think you're better than me, you don't understand who I am."

"Who are you?"

"Wait and see."

"I'll wait."

"The one who won't wait, Giannì, is Rosario."

"What does Rosario have to do with it?"

"He's in love with you."

"Come on."

"It's true. You led him on and now he's sure you love him — he talks all the time about your boobs."

"He's wrong, tell him I love somebody else."

"Who?"

"I can't tell you."

He insisted, I tried to change the subject, and he put an arm around my shoulders again.

"Am I the other guy?"

"No."

"You wouldn't have done all those nice things if you didn't love me."

"I'm telling you it's true."

"Then you're a slut."

"If I want, sure."

I thought of asking about Roberto, but I knew Corrado hated him, that he would cut the conversation short with a few offensive remarks, so I held off and tried to get there through Giuliana.

"She's so beautiful," I said praising his sister.

"Are you kidding, she's getting so skinny she looks like a hollowed-out corpse, you've never seen her when she wakes up in the morning."

He tossed out a lot of vulgar remarks, he said that Giuliana was now acting like a goody-goody, to hold on to her fiancé with his university degree, but there was nothing goody about her. If a person has a sister, he concluded, he loses the desire for women, because he knows you females are in every way worse than us males.

"Then take your hands off me and don't try to kiss me again."

"What does that have to do with it, I'm in love."

"And if you're in love, you don't see me?"

"I see you but I forget you're like my sister."

"It's the same for Roberto: he doesn't see Giuliana the way you see her, he sees her the way you see me."

He was annoyed, the subject irked him.

"What do you care what Roberto sees, he's blind, he doesn't understand anything about women."

"Maybe, but when he talks everybody listens to him."

"You, too?"

"Come on."

"Only people who are stupid like him."

"So your sister is stupid?"

"Yes."

"Only you are intelligent?"

"Me, you, and Rosario. He wants to see you."

I thought for a moment then said:

"I have a ton of homework."

"He'll get mad, he's the son of Sargente the lawyer."

"He's important?"

"Important and dangerous."

"I don't have time, Corrà, you two don't study, I do."

"You only want to be with people who study?"

"No, but there's a real difference between you and — just for example — Roberto. Imagine if he has time to spare, he's always got his head in a book."

"Again? Are you in love?"

"Are you kidding."

"If Rosario starts thinking you're in love with Roberto, he'll either kill him or have him killed."

I said I absolutely had to go. I didn't mention Roberto again.

10.

Not long afterward Rosario showed up outside school. I saw him right away, leaning on his convertible, tall, thin, with his forced smile, dressed with a display of wealth that among my classmates was considered vulgar. He didn't signal his presence, it was as if he believed that if not him, certainly his yellow car couldn't go unnoticed. And he was right, everyone looked at it admiringly. And naturally noticed me when, unwillingly but as if following a distant order, I went over to him. Rosario sat at the wheel with ostentatious cool, with equal cool I got in next to him.

"You have to take me home immediately," I said.

"You're the boss and I'm the slave," he said.

He started the engine and set off nervously, honking to make a path through the crowd of students.

"You remember where I live?" I asked, suddenly alarmed because he was going up the street leading to San Martino.

"On San Giacomo dei Capri."

"But this isn't the way to San Giacomo dei Capri."

"We'll go later."

He stopped on a narrow street near Sant'Elmo, turned and looked at me, his face still cheerful.

"Giannì," he said seriously, "I liked you as soon as I saw you. I wanted to tell you in person, in a quiet place."

"I'm ugly, go find a pretty girl."

"You're not ugly, you're a certain type."

"A certain type means I'm ugly."

"Come on, not even statues have boobs like yours."

He leaned over to kiss me on the mouth, I pulled back, avoiding his face.

"We can't kiss," I said, "you've got buck teeth and your lips are too thin."

"So why have plenty of other girls kissed me?"

"Obviously they didn't have teeth, go get kissed by them."

"Don't play at insulting me, Giannì, that's not fair."

"I'm not the one who's playing, it's you. You're always laughing and then I feel like joking."

"You know it's the shape of my mouth. Inside I'm very serious."

"So am I. You tell me I'm ugly, and I say you have buck teeth. Now we're even, take me home because my mother gets worried."

But he didn't retreat, he stayed very close to me. He repeated that I was a type, the type he liked, and he complained in a low voice that I hadn't understood how serious his intentions were. Then suddenly he raised his voice and said anxiously:

"Corrado is a liar, he says you did certain things with him but I don't believe it."

I tried to open the car door, I said angrily:

312

"I have to go."

"Wait: if you did them with him, why not with me?"

I lost my patience:

"You're really bugging me, Rosà, I don't do anything with anyone."

"You're in love with someone else."

"I'm not in love with anyone."

"Corrado says that since you saw Roberto Matese, you've turned stupid."

"I don't even know who Roberto Matese is."

"I'm telling you: he's someone who thinks he's a big deal."

"Then it's not the same Roberto I know."

"Trust me, it's him. And if you don't believe it, I'll bring him right to you and we'll see."

"You'll bring him to me? You?"

"Just say the word."

"And he'd come?"

"No, not spontaneously. I'd have to force him."

"You're ridiculous. No one forces the Roberto I know to do anything."

"Depends on the force. With the right force everybody does what they have to."

I looked at him, worried. He laughed, but his eyes were serious.

"I don't care about any Roberto or about

Corrado or you," I said.

He looked intensely at my breasts, as if I were hiding something in my bra, then muttered:

"Give me a kiss and I'll take you home."

At that moment I was sure he would hurt me and yet, incongruously, I thought that, even if he was ugly, I liked him more than Corrado. For a second I saw him as a very bright demon who would grab my head in both hands and first forcibly kiss me, then beat me against the window until I was dead.

"I'm not giving you anything," I said. "Either you take me home or I get out and go."

He stared into my eyes for a very long time, then started the engine.

"You're the boss."

11.

I discovered that the boys in my class also talked with interest about my large breasts. My deskmate, Mirella, told me, adding that a friend of hers who was a year ahead of us — his name was Silvestro, I remember, and he had a certain renown because he came to school on a motorbike that made everyone envious — had said in the courtyard, in a loud voice: her ass isn't bad, either, just put a pillow over her face and you'd have a great fuck.

I didn't sleep that night, I wept in humiliation and rage. I felt like telling my father, an irritating thought left over from childhood, as a child I had imagined that he would confront any problem I had and solve it. But right afterward I thought of my mother, who had almost no bosom, and of Costanza, who had a round, full one, and said to myself that surely my father liked women's breasts even more than Silvestro, Corrado, Rosario. He was like all men, and if I hadn't been his daughter he would undoubtedly have talked about Vittoria in my presence with exactly the same contempt with which Silvestro had talked about me, he would have said she was ugly but had an enormous bosom, a firm ass, and Enzo must have put a pillow over her face. Poor Vittoria, to have my father for a brother: how rough men were, how brutal in every word they dedicated to love. They liked humiliating us, dragging us along their lewd path. I was discouraged, and in lightning flashes — even today, in moments of suffering I feel as if I had an electrical storm in my head — I went so far as to ask myself if Roberto was like that, if he expressed himself that way. It didn't seem possible, and the mere fact that I had posed the question made me feel even worse. Surely, I thought, he speaks to Giuliana with gentle words and of course he desires her, but he desires her sweetly. I finally calmed down by imagining how gracious their relationship must be and vowing to find a way to love them both and all my life be the person to whom they would confide everything. Enough of bosom, ass, pillow. Who in the world was Silvestro, what did he know about me, he wasn't even a brother who'd seen me as a child and knew the dailiness of my body, luckily I had no brothers. How could he have dared to talk like that, in front of everyone.

I calmed down, but it took days for Mirella's revelation to fade. One morning I was in class with my mind free of troubles. While I was sharpening a pencil, the bell for recess rang. I went into the hall and found myself facing Silvestro. He was a large kid, a lot taller than me, with very pale freckled skin. It was hot, he was wearing a short-sleeved yellow shirt. Without thinking I struck his arm with the point of my pencil, launching it with all my strength. And he screamed, a long scream like a seagull's, and staring at his arm said: the point's still in there. He started crying, I exclaimed, I was pushed, sorry, I didn't do it on purpose. I looked at the pencil: I muttered, the point really broke, let me see.

I was amazed. If I'd had a knife in my hands, what would I have done, would I have stuck it in his arm, or where? Silvestro, supported by his friends, dragged me to the principal, and I continued to defend myself even to her, swearing that someone had shoved me during the scuffle at recess. It seemed too humiliating to tell the story of the large bosom and the pillow, I couldn't bear to seem like a girl who's ugly and won't admit it. When it was clear that Mirella wouldn't speak up to explain my reasons I was really relieved. It was an accident, I repeated endlessly. The principal gradually got Silvestro to calm down, and summoned my parents.

12.

My mother took it in the worst way. She knew I had started studying again, and the decision I'd made to take the exam to make up my repeated year was important to her. This stupid matter seemed to her yet another betrayal, maybe it confirmed for her that, since my father's departure, neither of us had been able to live with dignity. She murmured that we had to protect what we were, we had to be aware of ourselves. And she got angry, angry in a way she never was, but not with me, now she obsessively traced every trouble of mine back to Vittoria. She said that in this way I was supporting her, that my aunt wanted to make me like her in my behavior, in my words, in everything. Her small eyes sank further into her face, her bones seemed to be nearly breaking the skin. She said slowly: she wants to use you to prove that your father and I are all appearance, that while we have risen a little, you will plummet, and everything will even out. She then went to the telephone and reported everything to her ex-husband, but while with me she had lost her calm, with him she regained it. She spoke to him in a very low voice, as if between them there were agreements from which the more I threatened to violate them with my bad behavior, the more forcefully I was excluded. I thought, with a sense of desolation: everything is so disconnected, I try to hold the pieces together and I can't, there's something about me that doesn't work, we've all got something in us that doesn't work, except Roberto and Giuliana. Meanwhile my mother was saying on the phone: please, you go. And she repeated it several times: all right, you're right, I know you're busy, but please, go. When she hung up I said bitterly:

"I don't want Papa to go to the principal."

She answered:

"Quiet, you want what we want."

It was known that the principal, while she was indulgent toward those who listened to her little speeches in silence and said a few words of reproach to their offspring, became harsh with parents who defended their children. I was sure that I could trust my mother, she had always managed very well with the principal. But my father had stated on several occasions, sometimes even light-heartedly, that anything that had to do with the scholastic world irritated him — colleagues put him in a bad mood, he despised hierarchies, the rites of collegial bodies — and so he was always wary of setting foot in my school in the guise of parent, he knew that he would surely be harmful to me. But this time he was punctual, at the end of the school day. I saw him in the hall and joined him reluctantly. I muttered anxiously, with a deliberately Neapolitan cadence: Papa, I really didn't do it on purpose, but it's better if you put the blame on me, otherwise it will go badly. He told me not to worry and, once in the presence of the principal, he was very cordial. He listened to her attentively when she told him in detail how difficult it was to run a high school, he told her in turn a little story about the ignorance of the local superintendent, he complimented her out of the blue on how nice her earrings looked. The principal narrowed her eyes, pleased, struck the air lightly with her hand as if to chase him away, laughed, and with that same hand covered her mouth. Only when it seemed as if they would never stop the chitchat, my father returned abruptly to my bad behavior. To my astonishment, he said that certainly I had hit Silvestro on purpose, he knew me well, and if I had reacted like that I had a good reason for it, he didn't know what that good reason was and didn't want to know, but he had learned long ago that in the scuffles between boys and girls boys are always wrong and girls always right, and that even if that wasn't the case this time, boys should still be brought up to assume their responsibilities, even when they appeared to have none. Naturally, this is an approximate summary, my father spoke at length and his phrases were fascinating and finely honed, the sort of discourse that is so elegantly formulated it amazes you, and at the same time it's pronounced with unquestionable authority, and you understand that it admits no objections.

I waited anxiously for the principal to respond. She did so in a devout voice, she called him professor, she was so enthralled that I was ashamed to have been born female, to be destined to be treated like that by a man even if I was well educated, even if I occupied an important position. Yet instead of screaming with rage, I felt very pleased. The principal didn't want to let my father go, and it was clear that she kept asking him questions just to hear his tone of voice again and, who knows, maybe hoping for further compliments or the start of a friendship with a courteous and refined person who had considered her worthy of his brilliant reflections.

Even before she made up her mind to let us go, I was sure that as soon as we were in the courtyard my father would make me laugh, mimicking the tone of her voice, the way she made sure her hair was in order, the expression with which she reacted to his compliments. That is exactly what happened.

"Did you see how she batted her eyelashes? And the move with her hand, to smooth her hair? And her voice? Oh yes, uh-huh, professor, of course."

I laughed, really like a child, my old child-ish admiration for that man was returning. I laughed loudly, but in embarrassment. I didn't know whether to let go or remind myself that he didn't deserve that admira-tion and scold him: you told her that men are always wrong and should assume their responsibilities, but you have never done that with Mamma, or with me. You're a liar, Papa, a liar who frightens me just because of that good will you can draw out when you want to.

13.

His overexcitement at the success of his mission lasted until we were in the car. While he was still settling himself behind the wheel, my father rolled out pompous remarks one after another.

"Take this as a lesson. Anyone can be made to behave properly. You can be sure that for the rest of your high-school years that woman will be on your side."

I couldn't restrain myself and I said:

"Not on mine, on yours."

He noticed the animosity, he seemed ashamed of his self-praise. He didn't start the car, he ran both hands over his face, from the forehead to the chin, as if to erase what he had been until a moment earlier.

"Would you prefer to face everything by yourself?"

"Yes."

"You didn't like the way I behaved?"

"You were great. If you asked her to be your girlfriend, she'd say yes."

"What should I have done, in your view?"

"Nothing, mind your own business. You left, you have another wife and other daughters, forget Mamma and me."

"Your mother and I love each other. And you are my only, beloved daughter."

"That's a lie."

My father had a flash of rage in his eyes, he seemed offended. I thought, here's where I got the energy to hit Silvestro. But the rush of blood lasted an instant, he said gently:

"I'll take you home."

"Mine or yours?"

"Wherever you want."

"I don't want anything. Everyone always does what you want, Papa, you know how to get inside people's heads."

"What do you mean?"

Here again the surge of blood, I saw it in his pupils: I really could, if I wanted, make him lose his calm. But he'll never go so far as to hit me, I thought, he doesn't need to. He could annihilate me with words, he knows how to do it, he's been trained since he was a boy, that's how he destroyed Vittoria and Enzo's love. And surely he's trained me, too, he wanted me to be like him, until I disappointed him. But he won't attack me even with words, he thinks he loves me and he's afraid of hurting me. I changed my tone.

"I'm sorry," I said, "I don't want you to worry about me, I don't want you to waste time doing things you don't want to do because of me."

"Then behave yourself. Why in the world did you hit that boy? It's not done, it's not right. That's the way my sister acted and she didn't get past fifth grade."

"I've decided to make up my lost year."

"That's good news."

"And I've decided not to see Aunt Vittoria anymore."

"If it's your decision, I'm glad."

"But I'll still see Margherita's children."

He looked at me in bewilderment.

"Who's Margherita?"

For a few seconds I thought he was pretending, then I changed my mind. While his sister knew obsessively even his most secret decisions, after the break he hadn't wanted to know anything more about her. He had fought with Vittoria for decades, but of her life he was ignorant, with a proud indifference that was an important element of his hatred. I explained to him:

"Margherita is a friend of Aunt Vittoria's."

He made a gesture of irritation.

"Oh, that's right, I didn't remember her name."

"She has three children: Tonino, Giuliana, and Corrado. Giuliana is the best of all. I'm very fond of her, she's five years older than me and she's really intelligent. Her fiancé studies in Milan, he graduated there. I met him and he's really smart."

"What's his name?"

"Roberto Matese."

He looked at me uncertainly.

"Roberto Matese?"

When my father used that tone of voice there was no doubt: someone had come to mind for whom he had genuine admiration and a barely perceptible envy. In fact, his curiosity increased, he wanted to know in what circumstances I'd met him, and was immediately sure that my Roberto was the same as a young scholar who wrote very remarkable essays in an important journal published by the Catholic University. I felt my face burning with pride, with a sense of revenge. I thought: you read, you study, you write, but he's much better than you, you also know it, right now you're admitting it. He asked, in amazement:

"You met in Pascone?"

"Yes, at the church, he was born there, but then he moved to Milan. Aunt Vittoria introduced me to him."

He seemed confused, as if in the space of a few sentences geography had become muddled and he had trouble keeping together Milan, the Vomero, Pascone, the house where he was born. But he quickly regained his usual understanding tone, part paternal, part professorial:

"Good, I'm glad. You have the right and the duty to deepen your acquaintance with anyone who interests you. That's how one grows. It's too bad you've nearly cut off your relationship with Angela and Ida. You all have so many things in common. You should go back to being friends the way you used to be. You know Angela also has friends in Pascone?"

It seemed that that name, in general uttered with annoyance, with bitterness, with contempt not only in my presence but probably also in Angela's, to bring shame on his stepdaughter's friendships, was pronounced this time in a much less resentful way. But maybe I exaggerated, I couldn't control the impulse, which also hurt me, to cheapen it.

I stared at the delicate hand that turned the key to start the car, I decided:

"O.K., I'll come to your house for a little while."

"No long face?"

"No."

He cheered up, set off.

"But it's not my house, it's also yours."

"I know," I said.

As we drove toward Posillipo, I asked him, after a long silence:

"Do you talk to Angela and Ida a lot, do you have a good relationship?"

"Fairly good."

"Better than their relationship with Mariano?"

"Maybe."

"Do you love them more than me?"

"What are you talking about? I love you much more."

14.

It was a lovely afternoon. Ida wanted to read me some of her poems, which I found very beautiful. She hugged me tight when I responded enthusiastically; she complained about school, which was boring and oppressive, the biggest obstacle to the free expression of her literary vocation; she promised she would let me read a long novel inspired by the three of us, if only she could find time to finish it. Angela couldn't stop touching me, hugging me, as if she'd gotten unused to my presence and wanted to make sure I was really there. Out of the blue, she started talking about episodes of our childhood with great intimacy, sometimes laughing, sometimes with her eyes full of tears. I recalled almost nothing of what she evoked, but I didn't tell her. I nodded yes, I laughed, and occasionally, hearing her so happy, I was seized by real nostalgia for a time that I nevertheless considered past forever and that had been imperfectly revived by her over-affectionate imagination.

You speak so well, she said as soon as Ida went off unwillingly to study. I discovered that I wanted to tell her the same thing. I had moved into Vittoria's territory, not to mention Corrado and Rosario's, and had deliberately filled my speech with dialect and dialectal cadences. But here was our jargon again, coming mainly from bits of childhood reading that we didn't even remember anymore. You left me alone — she complained but without reproach — and confessed, laughing, that she had almost always felt out of place, her normality was me. So in the end we became pleasantly reacquainted, and she seemed glad. I asked about Tonino, she answered:

"I'm trying to stop seeing him."

"Why?"

"I don't like him."

"He's handsome."

"If you want I'll give him to you."

"No, thanks."

"You see? Even you don't like him. I only liked him because I thought you liked him."

"Not true."

"Very true. If you like something, I always make myself like it."

I spent some words in favor of Tonino and his siblings, I praised him because he was a good young man and had proper ambitions. But Angela replied that he was always so serious, so pathetic with those short sentences that sounded like prophecies. A young man born old, she described him, too tied to the priests. The rare times they saw each other, all Tonino did was complain that Don Giacomo had been sent away from the parish because of the debates he organized, he'd been sent to Colombia. It was his only subject of conversation, he didn't know anything about movies, television, books, singers. At most he sometimes talked about houses, he said human beings are snails that have lost their shells, but they can't live long without a roof over their heads. His sister wasn't like him, Giuliana had more character, and even though she was losing weight, she was beautiful.

"She's twenty," she said, "but she seems young. She pays attention to whatever comes out of my mouth, as if I were really something. Sometimes she seems to be in awe of me. And you know what she said about you? She said you're extraordinary."

"Me?"

"Yes."

"I don't believe it."

"It's true. She told me her fiancé said so, too."

Those remarks agitated me, but I didn't let her see. Should I believe it? Giuliana considered me extraordinary, and so did Roberto? Or was it a way of being nice to make me happy and reinforce our relationship? I said to Angela that I felt like a rock with an elemental life hidden under it, anything but extraordinary, but if she went out with Tonino and Giuliana and even Roberto, I'd happily go for a walk with them.

She seemed enthusiastic, and the following Saturday she called me. Giuliana wasn't there, and naturally not her fiancé, but she had a date with Tonino and going out by herself with him bored her, she asked me to come along. I was happy to go, and we walked along the sea from Mergellina to the Palazzo Reale, Tonino in the middle, between Angela and me.

How many times had I met him? Once, twice? I remembered him as awkward but pleasant, and in fact he was a tall young man, all sinews and muscles, with black hair, regular features, a timidity that caused him to measure out his words, his gestures. But soon I thought I could understand the reason for Angela's impatience. Tonino seemed to weigh the consequences of every word, which made you want to finish his sentences for him or eliminate the useless ones, to yell at him: I get it, go on. I was patient. Unlike Angela, whose attention wandered — she looked at the sea, the buildings — I questioned him at length and found everything he said interesting. First, he talked about his secret studies, to be an architect, and he told me exhaustively, detail after detail, how he had taken a difficult exam and had passed brilliantly. Then he told me that, ever since Don Giacomo had had to leave the parish, Vittoria had become more unbearable than usual and made life difficult for everyone. Finally, at my cautious urging, he talked a lot about Roberto with great affection and a respect so boundless that Angela said: your sister shouldn't be engaged to him, you should. But I liked that devotion that had not a hint of envy or malice. Tonino said things that moved me. Roberto was destined to a brilliant university career. Roberto had recently published an essay in a prestigious international journal. Roberto was good, he was modest, he had an energy that animated even the most disheartened people. Roberto inspired the best feelings. I listened without interrupting, I would have let that very slow accumulation of details go on into eternity. But Angela gave more and more signs of annoyance, and so the evening came to an end with just a little more conversation.

"Are he and your sister going to live in Milan?" I asked.

"Yes."

"After they get married."

"Giuliana would like to join him right away."

"Why doesn't she?"

"You know Vittoria, she has set our mother against it. And now they both want them to get married first."

"If Roberto comes to Naples, I'd love to talk to him."

"Of course."

"With him and Giuliana."

"Give me your number, I'll have them call you."

When we parted, he said to me gratefully: "It was a lovely evening, thank you, I hope we'll see each other soon."

"We have a lot of studying to do," Angela cut him off.

"Yes," I said, "but we'll find the time."

"You don't come to Pascone anymore?"

"You know what my aunt's like, one time she's loving, the next she'd like to kill me."

He shook his head, desolate.

"She's not a bad person, but if she goes on the way she is she'll be alone. Not even Giuliana can stand her anymore."

He wanted to start talking about the cross — that was how he described Vittoria — that he and his siblings had had to bear since childhood, but Angela stopped him abruptly. He tried to kiss her, she avoided him. That's enough — she almost shouted when we left him behind — did you see how exasperating he is, he always says the same thing in the same exact words, never a joke, never a laugh, he's so lame.

I let her vent, in fact I said several times that she was right. He's a wet blanket, I said, but then I added: and yet he's unusual, boys are all ugly and aggressive and stinking, instead he's just a little too restrained, and even if talking to him is like watching paint dry don't leave him, poor guy, where would you find another one like him.

We laughed continuously. We laughed at words like lame, wet blanket, and especially that expression we'd heard as children, maybe from Mariano: watch the paint dry. We laughed because Tonino never looked a person in the eye, not Angela or anyone else, as if he had something to hide. We laughed, finally, because she told me that even though as soon as he embraced her his pants swelled up and she immediately moved her belly away in disgust, he never took the initiative, he had never even put a hand in her bra.

15.

The next day Giuliana called. She was cordial and yet very serious, as if she had an important purpose that wouldn't allow a playful tone or frivolity. She said she had heard from Tonino my intention to call her and so she had gone ahead and called me, with joy. She wanted to see me, and so did Roberto. He was coming to Naples the following week for a conference, and they would both be really happy to get together.

"See me?"

"Yes."

"No, I'd love to see you, but him no, I'd be embarrassed."

"Why? Roberto is really friendly."

I agreed, naturally, I had waited a long time for such an opportunity. But to keep my agitation under control, maybe even to try to establish a good relationship with her beforehand, I proposed that we meet for a walk. She was glad, she said: even today. She was a secretary in a dentist's office in Via Foria, and we met in the late afternoon, at the metro stop in Piazza Cavour, an area that I liked because it reminded me of the Museo grandparents, the genteel relatives of childhood.

Just seeing Giuliana from a distance depressed me, though. She was tall, harmonious in her movements, she came toward me radiating confidence and pride. It was as if the composure I'd noticed earlier in church had spread into her clothes, her shoes, her gait, and now seemed innate. She greeted me with a cheerful chattiness to put me at my ease, and we walked without a destination. We passed the museum, and turned uphill onto Via Santa Teresa; I was at a loss for words, overwhelmed by how her extreme thinness, her light makeup, gave her a sort of ascetic beauty that instilled respect.

Here, I thought, is what Roberto has done: he has transformed a girl from a poor neighborhood into a young woman you'd find in a poem. At one point, I exclaimed:

"You've really changed, you look even more beautiful than when I saw you in church."

"Thank you."

"It must be love," I ventured, it was a phrase I'd often heard from Costanza, from my mother.

She laughed, denied it, said:

"If by love you mean Roberto, no, it's not about Roberto."

She herself had felt the need to change and had made a great effort that was ongoing. First, she tried to explain in general terms the urge to please those we respect, those we love, but then, step by step, the attempt to express herself in the abstract got tangled up, and she went on to tell me that Roberto liked everything about her, whether she stayed the same as she had always been since childhood, or whether she changed. He imposed nothing, hair like this, dress like that, nothing.

"You," she said, "I feel you're worried, you think he's one of those types who are always at their books and intimidate you and lay down the law. He's not like that, I remember him as a child, he wasn't someone who studied a lot, in fact he never studied the way those scholars study. You always saw him on the street playing ball, he learns distractedly, he's always done ten things at once. He's like an animal that can't distinguish between good things and poisonous ones, everything is fine with him, because — I've seen it — he transforms every element just by touching it and in a way that leaves you amazed."

"Maybe he also does that with people."

She laughed, a nervous laugh.

"Yes, good for you, also with people. Let's say that, being near him, I felt and feel the need to change. Naturally, the first to notice that I was changing was Vittoria, she can't bear it if we don't depend on her in every way, and she got angry, she said I was getting foolish, I wasn't eating and was turning into a broomstick. But my mother's glad, she'd like me to change even more and Tonino to change, and Corrado. One night she said to me secretly, so Vittoria wouldn't hear: when you go to Milan with Roberto, take your brothers, don't stay here, no good can come of it. But nothing escapes Vittoria, Gianni, she hears even what's said in a low voice or isn't even said. So instead of getting mad at my mother, the last time Roberto came to Pascone she confronted him and said: you were born in these houses, you grew up on these streets, Milan came later, it's here you have to return. He listened to her, as always — he's the kind of person who listens even to leaves in the wind — and then he said something tactful about accounts that should never be left open, and added that in the meantime, however, he had some to close in Milan. He's like that: he listens to you, and then he goes his own way, or anyway all the ways that interest him, maybe even including the path that you suggest to him."

"So you'll get married and live in Milan?"

"Yes."

"And then Roberto will quarrel with Vittoria?"

"No: I will break with Vittoria, Tonino will break with her, Corrado will break with her. But not Roberto, Roberto does what he has to do and doesn't break with anyone."

She admired him, what she most liked about him was his benevolent determination. I felt that she relied on him completely, considered him her savior, who would get her away from her place of birth, her insufficient schooling, the frailty of her mother, the power of my aunt. I asked her if she went to Milan to see Roberto often and she darkened, she said it was complicated, Vittoria didn't want her to. She'd been three or four times and only because Tonino had gone with her, those few stays had been enough to make her love the city. Roberto had lots of friends, some very important. He insisted on introducing her to all of them and took her everywhere, to this one's house, to an appointment with that one. It was all wonderful, but she also felt very anxious. After those experiences, her heart wouldn't stop racing. On every occasion she wondered why Roberto had chosen her, who was stupid and ignorant, and didn't know how to dress, when Milan had the cream of the crop of extraordinary young women. And also in Naples, she said, you, you're a proper girl. Not to mention Angela, she expresses herself so well, she's pretty, she's elegant. But me? what am I, what do I have to do with him?

I felt pleasure in the superiority she was attributing to me, yet I told her it was nonsense. Angela and I talked the way our parents had brought us up, and our mothers chose our clothes, or anyway we chose them according to their taste, which we thought was ours. The fact was, rather, that

Roberto had wanted her and only her, because he was in love with what she was, so he would never trade her for other women. You're so pretty, so vivacious, I exclaimed, the rest can be learned, you're already learning it: I'll help you if you want, so will Angela, we'll help you.

We turned back, I walked with her to the metro at Piazza Cavour.

"You mustn't feel embarrassed with Roberto," she repeated, "really, he's very down to earth, you'll see."

We embraced, I was glad about the friendship that was starting. But I also discovered that I was on Vittoria's side. I wanted Roberto to leave Milan, to settle in Naples. I wanted my aunt to prevail and compel the future spouses to live in, I don't know, Pascone, so that I could weld my life to theirs and see them when I wanted, even every day.

16.

I made a mistake: I told Angela that I had seen Giuliana and was going to see Roberto soon, too. She didn't like that. She who had spoken ill of Tonino and well of Giuliana abruptly changed her mind: she said that Tonino was a good guy and that his sister was a harpy and tormented him. It didn't take much to figure out that she was jealous: she couldn't bear that Giuliana had talked to me without going through her.

"Better not to see her anymore," she said one evening when we went out for a walk. "She's grown up and treats us like little girls."

"That's not true."

"Yes, it is. At first, with me, she pretended that I was the teacher and she the student. She clung to me, she said: how nice, if you marry Tonino we'll be related. But she's a phony. She ingratiates her way in, she acts like a friend, and instead she's looking after her own interests. Now she's focused on you, I'm not enough for her anymore. She's used me and thrown me aside."

"Don't exaggerate. She's a nice girl, she can be your friend as much as mine."

I had to work hard to soothe her, and I didn't completely succeed. As we talked I realized she wanted many things at the same time, and that kept her in a permanent state of dissatisfaction. She wanted to end it with Tonino but not with Giuliana, whom she was fond of; she didn't want Giuliana to be attached to me, excluding her; she didn't want Roberto to disturb, even as a ghost, our eventual close trio; she wanted me, even as part of that eventual trio, to have her at the front of my mind and not the other. Finally, since I wouldn't agree, she stopped being malicious about Giuliana and began to talk about her as a victim of her fiancé.

"Everything Giuliana does she does for him," she said.

"And isn't that lovely?"

"You think it's lovely to be a slave?"

"I think it's lovely to love."

"Even if he doesn't love her?"

"How do you know he doesn't love her?"

"She says so, she says it can't be that he loves her."

"Everyone who loves is afraid of not being loved."

"If someone makes you live in anguish the way Giuliana lives, what pleasure is there in loving?"

"How do you know she's anguished?"

"I saw them together once, with Tonino."

"So?"

"Giuliana can't bear the idea of him not liking her anymore."

"It must be the same for him."

"He's in Milan, you know how many women he has."

That last remark was particularly upsetting to me. I didn't even want to think of the possibility that Roberto had other women. I preferred him devoted to Giuliana and faithful until death. I asked her:

"Is Giuliana afraid of being cheated on?"

"She never said so but I think she is."

"The time I saw him he didn't seem the type who cheats."

"Did your father seem like someone who would cheat? And yet he did: he cheated on your mother with my mother."

I reacted harshly.

"My father and your mother are liars."

She had a bewildered expression.

"You don't like what I'm saying?"

"No. It's a pointless comparison."

"Maybe. But I'd like to test this Roberto."

"How?"

Her eyes lighted up, she half closed her mouth, arched her back, thrusting her chest forward. Like this, she said. She wanted to talk to him with that expression on her face and in that provocative pose. In fact, she would wear something very low-cut and a miniskirt and would nudge Roberto often with her shoulder and lean her bosom against his arm and put a hand on his thigh and take his arm when they walked. Oh, she said, visibly disgusted, what shits men are, you do just a couple of those things and whatever age they are they go mad, whether you're skin and bones or fat or have pimples and fleas.

This rant made me mad. She had begun with our girlish talk and now suddenly was speaking with a grown woman's vulgarity. I said, struggling to restrain a threatening tone:

"Don't you dare do those things with Roberto."

"Why?" She was surprised. "It's for Giuliana. If he's a good guy, fine, but if not that's how we'll save her."

"In her place I wouldn't want to be saved."

She looked at me as if she couldn't understand. She said:

"I was joking. Promise me one thing?"

"What?"

"If Giuliana calls you, call me right away, I want to be at this get-together with Roberto, too."

"O.K. But if she says that'll make her fiancé uncomfortable, I can't do anything."

She went silent, she lowered her gaze, and when, a fraction of a second later, she raised it again, her eyes held a painful request for clarity.

"It's all over between us, you don't love me anymore."

"No, I love you and will until I die."

"Then give me a kiss."

I kissed her on the cheek. She wanted my

344

mouth, I avoided her.

"We're not children anymore," I said.

She went unhappily toward Mergellina.

17.

Giuliana called one afternoon to make a date for the following Sunday in Piazza Amedeo; Roberto would be there, too. I felt that the moment so longed for, so intensely imagined, had truly arrived, and again, even more violently, I was afraid. I stammered, I talked about all the homework I had, she said laughing: Giannì, calm down, Roberto won't eat you, I want him to see that I have friends who study, who speak well, do me this favor.

I retreated, confused, and, just to find something that would complicate things to the point of preventing the meeting, I brought up Angela. I had already decided almost without admitting it that, if Giuliana really intended to have me meet her fiancé, I wouldn't say anything to Angela, I wanted to avert more annoyance and tension. But sometimes thoughts release a latent force, seize on images against your will, thrust them before your eyes for a fraction of a second. I thought surely that the figure of Angela, once evoked, would not be welcomed by Giuliana and would lead her to say: all right, let's put it off to another time. But in my mind there was more: I imagined my friend in her low-cut blouse, batting her eyelashes, opening her lips into an O, arching her back; and suddenly it seemed that setting her beside Roberto, leaving her free to disrupt and disconnect that couple, could become a tidal wave. I said:

"There's a problem: I told Angela we were going to see each other and probably Roberto as well."

"So?"

"She wants to come."

Giuliana was silent for a long moment, then said:

"Giannì, I love Angela, but she's not an easy type, she always wants to be in the middle."

"I know."

"What if you didn't say anything about this date?"

"Impossible. One way or another she'll find out that I met your fiancé and she won't speak to me anymore. Better to forget it."

More seconds of silence, then she agreed:

"O.K., have her come, too."

From that point on my heart raced. The fear that I might seem ignorant and unintelligent to Roberto kept me from sleeping and brought me within a step of calling my father to ask him questions about life, death, God, Christianity, Communism, so that I could use his answers, which were always crammed with knowledge, in a possible conversation. But I resisted, I didn't want to contaminate Giuliana's fiancé, of whom I preserved an image as of a heavenly apparition, with my father's earthly small-mindedness. And then my obsession with my appearance intensified. How would I dress? Was there some way of improving myself at least a little?

Unlike Angela, who since she was a child had cared a lot about clothes, I, during that long period of crisis, had provocatively abandoned the desire to make myself pretty. You're ugly — I had concluded — and an ugly person is ridiculous if she tries to beautify herself. So my only mania remained cleanliness, and I washed constantly. Otherwise I bundled myself in black, hiding, or, contrarily, put on heavy makeup, wore bright colors, made myself vulgar on purpose. But for that occasion I tried and tried to see if I could find a middle ground that would make me acceptable. Since I was never happy with myself, in the end all I cared about was that the colors I chose wouldn't clash, and, after yelling to my mother that I was going out with Angela, I went through the door, hurried down along San Giacomo dei Capri.

I'll be sick from the tension, I thought as the funicular descended at its usual jangling slow pace toward Piazza Amedeo, I'll stumble, I'll hit my head, I'll die. Or I'll get mad and rip someone's eyes out. I was late, sweaty, kept straightening my hair with my fingers in fear that it was pasted to my skull the way Vittoria's sometimes was. When I reached the piazza, I immediately saw Angela, who beckoned me, she was sitting outside a café, already sipping something. I went over and sat down with her; there was a tepid sun. There they are, the couple, she said in a low voice, and I understood that the couple were behind me. I not only forced myself not to turn, but, instead of getting up, as Angela was already doing, I stayed seated. I felt Giuliana's hand resting lightly on my shoulder — hi, Gianni — I looked out of the corner of my eye at her manicured fingers, the sleeve of her brown jacket, a bracelet just sticking out. Angela was already uttering the first cordial remarks, now I, too, would have liked to say something, respond to the greeting. But the bracelet half covered by the sleeve of the jacket was the one I had given back to my aunt and I was so surprised I didn't even say hi. Vittoria, Vittoria, I didn't know what to think, she really was the way my parents had described her. She had taken it from me, her niece, and now, even though it seemed that she couldn't do without it, she had given it to her goddaughter. How brightly the bracelet shone on Giuliana's wrist, how it gained value.

18.

That second encounter with Roberto confirmed to me that I remembered almost nothing of the first. I finally stood up, he was several steps behind Giuliana. He seemed very tall, over six feet, but when he sat down he folded himself in as if he were piling up all his limbs and compressing them on the chair so as not to seem hulking. I had in mind a man of average height and yet here he was, powerful yet small, a person who could expand or shrink at will. He certainly was handsome, much more than I remembered: black hair, broad forehead, sparkling eyes, high cheekbones, chiseled nose, and the mouth, oh the mouth, with regular white teeth that were like a patch of light on his dark skin. But his behavior disoriented me. For most of the time we spent at that table he exhibited not a single one of the gifts as a speaker that he had displayed in church and that had made such a deep impression on me. He resorted to brief remarks, to barely communicative gestures. Only his eyes were those of his talk before the altar, attentive to every detail, slightly ironic. Otherwise I got the idea of one of those shy teachers who emanate good humor and sympathy, don't make you anxious, and not only ask their little questions politely, with clarity and precision, but, after listening to the answers without interrupting you, without commenting, say with a kind smile: you can go.

Unlike Roberto, Giuliana was nervously talkative. Introducing us to her fiancé, she bestowed on each of us an abundance of wonderful qualities, and, although she was sitting in the shade, seemed luminous as she spoke. I forced myself to ignore the bracelet, even though I couldn't help every so often seeing it sparkle on her slender wrist and thinking: maybe that's the magic source of her light. Not her words, they were opaque. Why is she talking so much, I wondered, what's worrying her, certainly not our beauty. Contrary to my predictions, Angela, while she was certainly as pretty as usual, hadn't overdone it with her clothes: her skirt was short but not too short, she wore a tight shirt but not low cut, and though she flashed smiles, and appeared self-assured, she did nothing especially seductive. As for me, I was a sack of potatoes — I felt I was, *I wanted to be,* a sack of potatoes — gray, compact, the protrusion of my bosom buried under a jacket, and I managed very well. It surely wasn't our physical aspect that worried her, since there was no competition between her and us. I was convinced instead that what made her anxious was the possibility that we wouldn't be up to it. Her declared intention was to show us off to her fiancé as her friends from good families. She wanted him to like us because we were girls from the Vomero, high-school students, decent people. In other words she had summoned us there to bear witness to the fact that she was eliminating Pascone from herself, she was preparing to live respectably with him in Milan. And I think it was that — not the bracelet — that intensified my irritation. I didn't like being put on display, I didn't want to feel the way I did when my parents would make me show their friends how good I was at doing this, at saying that, and, as soon as I saw that I was obliged to be at my best, I

351

became obtuse. I sat silently, my head empty, I even looked ostentatiously at my watch a couple of times. The result was that Roberto, after a few polite remarks, ended up concentrating on Angela in classic professorial tones. He asked her: how is your school, what condition is it in, do you have gym, how old are your teachers, how are their classes, what do you do in your free time, and she talked, on and on, in her confident little student's voice, and smiled, and laughed, saying amusing things about her classmates, her teachers.

Giuliana not only listened with a smile but often intervened in the conversation. She had moved her chair close to her fiancé's, occasionally she rested her head on his shoulder, laughing loudly when he laughed softly at Angela's witty remarks. She seemed more serene, Angela was doing well, Roberto didn't appear to be bored. After a while he said:

"Where do you find the time to read?"

"I don't," Angela answered. "I used to read when I was a child but not anymore, school eats me alive. My sister reads a lot. And she does, too, she reads."

She indicated me with a gracious gesture and a look of affection.

"Giannina," said Roberto.

I corrected him scowling:

"Giovanna."

"Giovanna," said Roberto, "I remember you well."

"It's easy, I'm just like Aunt Vittoria."

"No, that's not why."

"Then why?"

"I don't know, but if I think of it I'll tell you."

"There's no need."

And yet there was a need, I didn't want to be remembered because I was slovenly, ugly, grim, locked in a presumptuous silence. I fixed my eyes on his, and since he looked at me with friendliness and that encouraged me — it was an inane friendliness, gently ironic — I forced myself not to look away, I wanted to see if the kindness gave way to annoyance. I did it with a persistence that until a moment earlier I didn't know I was capable of, even blinking would have seemed like giving in.

He continued in the tone of a good-humored professor, he asked how school left me time to read and not Angela: did my teachers not give much homework? I said darkly that my teachers were trained beasts, they recited their lessons mechanically and equally mechanically gave such a quantity of homework that if we students had given

353

it to them, they would never have gotten it done. But I didn't worry about homework, I read when I felt like it, if a book gripped me I would read day and night, I didn't care about school. What do you read, he asked, and since I answered vaguely — at my house there's nothing but books, my father used to make suggestions, but then he left and I choose myself, every so often I pull one out, essays, novels, what I feel like — he insisted that I name at least a few titles, the most recent I had read. So I answered: the Gospels, lying to make an impression, that reading had been several months earlier, now I was reading something else. But I had so much hoped that that moment would arrive and in case it did I had written down all my impressions in a notebook just so I'd be able to list them for him. Now it was happening, and suddenly, with no hesitation, I went on talking, continuing to look him in the face with feigned calm. In reality I was furious inside, furious for no reason, or worse, as if it were precisely the texts of Mark, Matthew, Luke, and John that were making me angry, and the anger erased everything around me, the square, the newspaper stand, the entrance to the metro, the bright green of the park, Angela and Giuliana, everything except Roberto. Finally, I

354

stopped and looked down. I had a headache, I tried to control my breath so he wouldn't notice that I was panting.

There was a long silence. Only then I realized that Angela was looking at me with pride in her eyes — I was her childhood friend, she was proud of me, she was saying it without words — and I drew strength from it. Giuliana, on the other hand, clung to her fiancé, staring at me in bewilderment, as if there were something unseemly about me and she wanted to warn me with a look. Roberto asked me:

"So you think the Gospels tell a terrible story?"

"Yes."

"Why?"

"It doesn't work. Jesus is the son of God, but he performs pointless miracles, he lets himself be betrayed and ends up on the cross. Not only: he asks his father to spare him the cross, but his father doesn't lift a finger and doesn't spare him any torment at all. Why didn't God come himself to suffer? Why did he dump the poor performance of his own creation on his son? What is doing the will of the father — draining the cup of torments to the dregs?"

Roberto shook his head slightly, the irony disappeared.

He said — but here I'm summarizing, I was agitated, I can't remember clearly:

"God isn't easy."

"He should think about becoming easy, if he wants me to understand anything."

"An easy God isn't God. He is other from us. We don't communicate with God, he's so beyond our level that he can't be questioned, only invoked. If he manifests himself, he does it in silence, through small precious mute signs that go by completely common names. Doing his will is bowing your head and obligating yourself to believe in him."

"I already have too many obligations."

The irony reappeared in his eyes, I sensed with pleasure that my roughness interested him.

"Obligation to God is worth the trouble. Do you like poetry?"

"Yes."

"Do you read it?"

"When I can."

"Poetry is made up of words, exactly like the conversation we're having. If the poet takes our banal words and frees them from the bounds of our talk, you see that from within their banality they manifest an unexpected energy. God manifests himself in the same way."

356

"The poet isn't God, he's simply someone like us who also knows how to create poems."

"But that creation opens your eyes, amazes you."

"When the poet is good, yes."

"And it surprises you, gives you a jolt."

"Sometimes."

"God is that: a jolt in a dark room where you can no longer find the floor, the walls, the ceiling. There's no way to reason about it, to discuss it. It's a matter of faith. If you believe, it works. Otherwise, no."

"Why should I believe in a jolt?"

"Because of religious spirit."

"I don't know what that is."

"Think of an investigation like one in a murder mystery, except that the mystery remains a mystery. Religious spirit is just that: a propulsion onward, always onward, to expose what lies hidden."

"I don't understand you."

"Mysteries can't be understood."

"Unsolved mysteries scare me. I identified with the three women who go to the grave, can't find the body of Jesus, and run away."

"Life should make you run away when it's dull."

"Life makes me run away when it's suffering."

"You're saying that you're not content with things as they are?"

"I'm saying that no one should be put on the cross, especially by the will of his father. But that's not how things are."

"If you don't like the way things are, you have to change them."

"I should change even creation?"

"Of course, we are made for that."

"And God?"

"God, too, if necessary."

"Careful, you're blaspheming."

For a second I had the impression that Roberto was so struck by my effort to stand up to him that his eyes were wet with emotion. He said:

"If blasphemy allows me even just a small step forward, I blaspheme."

"Seriously?"

"Yes. I like God, and I would do anything, even what offends him, to be closer to him. For that reason I advise you not to be in a hurry to throw everything up in the air: wait a little, the story of the Gospels says more than what you find in it now."

"There are so many other books. I read the Gospels only because you talked about them that time in church and I got curious."

"Reread them. They tell about passion and

the cross, that is, suffering, the thing that disorients you most."

"Silence disorients me."

"You, too, were silent for a good half hour. But then, you see, you spoke."

Angela exclaimed, amused:

"Maybe she's God."

Roberto didn't laugh, and I managed to restrain a nervous giggle in time. He said:

"Now I know why I remembered you."

"What did I do?"

"You put a lot of force into your words."

"You put even more."

"I don't do it on purpose."

"I do. I'm proud, I'm not good, I'm often unjust."

This time he laughed, but not the three of us. Giuliana in a low voice reminded him that he had an appointment and they couldn't be late. She said it in the tone of regret of someone who is sorry to leave such nice company; then she got up, hugged Angela, gave me a polite nod. Roberto, too, said goodbye, I felt a shudder when he leaned over and kissed my cheeks. As soon as the fiancés went off on Via Crispi, Angela pulled on my arm.

"You made an impression," she exclaimed with enthusiasm.

"He said I read the wrong way."

"It's not true. He not only listened to you, he argued with you."

"Of course, he argues with anybody. But you, you just talked, weren't you supposed to cling to him?"

"You said I shouldn't. And anyway I couldn't. The time I saw him with Tonino he seemed like an idiot, now he seems magic."

"He's like all of them."

I held onto that disdainful tone, even though Angela kept refuting me with phrases like: compare how he treated me and how he treated you, you were like two professors. And she imitated our voices, mocked some moments of the dialogue. I made faces, giggled, but in reality I was pleased with myself. Angela was right, Roberto had talked to me. But not enough, I wanted to talk to him again and again, now, in the afternoon, tomorrow, forever. But that was impossible, and already the gratification was passing, a bitterness returned that made me weary.

19.

I quickly got worse. The encounter with Roberto seemed to have served only to demonstrate that the one person I cared about

— the one person who in a very brief exchange had made me feel a pleasantly exciting steam inside — had his world elsewhere, could grant me just a few minutes.

When I got home, I found the apartment on Via San Giacomo dei Capri empty, only the rumbling of the city could be heard, my mother had gone out with one of her most boring friends. I felt alone and, worse, that I had no prospect of redemption. I lay down on the bed to calm myself and tried to sleep. I woke with a start, in my mind the bracelet on Giuliana's wrist. I was agitated, maybe I'd had a bad dream, I dialed Vittoria's number. She answered right away but with a hello that seemed to come from the middle of a fight, evidently shouted at the end of a sentence that had been shouted even louder right before the phone rang.

"It's Giovanna," I almost whispered.

"Fine. And what the fuck do you want?"

"I wanted to ask you about my bracelet."

She interrupted me.

"Yours? Aha, we're at that point, you call to tell me it's yours? Gianni, I've been too nice to you, but now I'm done, you stay in your place, get it? The bracelet belongs to someone who loves me, I don't know if I've made myself clear."

No, she hadn't, or at least I didn't understand. I was frightened, I couldn't even
remember why I'd called, certainly it was
the wrong moment. But I heard Giuliana
yelling:

"It's Giannina? Give me the phone. Be
quiet, Vittò, quiet, don't say another word."

Right afterward came the voice of Margherita, mother and daughter were evidently at
my aunt's house. Margherita said something
like:

"Vittò, please, forget it, the child has nothing to do with it."

But Vittoria shouted:

"Did you hear, Giannì, here they call you
a child. But are you a child? Yes? Then why
do you put yourself between Giuliana and
her fiancé? Answer me, instead of being a
pain in the ass about the bracelet. Are you
worse than my brother? Tell me, I'm listening: are you more arrogant than your father?"

There was immediately a new cry from
Giuliana. She yelled:

"That's enough, you're crazy. Cut out
your tongue, you don't know what you're
talking about."

Then she hung up. I stood with the receiver in my hand, incredulous. What was
happening. And why had my aunt attacked

me in that way. Maybe I had been wrong to say "my bracelet," I had been out of line. And yet it was the right formulation, she had given it to me. But I had certainly not called her to get it back, I only wanted her to explain why she hadn't kept it. Why if she loved that bracelet so much did she keep getting rid of it?

I hung up, went to lie down again. I must have had a really bad dream, which had to do with the picture of Enzo on his grave: I was overcome by anguish. And now there was that pile-up of voices on the phone, I heard them again in my mind, and only then did I understand that Vittoria was angry with me because of the meeting that morning. Evidently, Giuliana had just told her about it, but what had Vittoria seen in that story that made her so furious? Now I would like to have been present and heard word for word what Giuliana said. Maybe, if I, too, had heard her account, I would have understood what really happened in Piazza Amedeo.

The phone rang again, I started, I was afraid to answer. Then I thought it might be my mother, and I went back to the hall, cautiously picked up the receiver. Giuliana murmured: hello. She apologized for Vittoria, she sniffled, maybe she was crying. I asked:

"Did I do something wrong this morning?"

"No, Gianni, Roberto is enthusiastic about you."

"Really?"

"I swear."

"I'm glad, tell him that talking to him was really good for me."

"No need for me to tell him, you'll tell him. He wants to get together again tomorrow afternoon, if you can. We'll go and have coffee, the three of us."

The painful grip of my headache became tighter. I muttered:

"O.K. Is Vittoria still angry?"

"No, don't worry."

"Will you let me talk to her?"

"Better not to, she's a little upset."

"Why is she angry with me?"

"Because she's crazy, she's always been crazy, and she's ruined the lives of all of us."

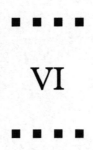

VI

IV

1.

The time of my adolescence is slow, made up of large gray blocks and sudden humps of color, green or red or purple. The blocks don't have hours, days, months, years, and the seasons are indefinite, it's hot or cold, rainy or sunny. Even the bulges don't have a definite time, the color counts more than any date. The hue itself, moreover, that certain emotions take on is of unimportant duration, the one who is writing knows. As soon as you look for words, the slowness becomes a whirlwind and the colors get mixed together like the colors of different fruits in a blender. Not only does "time passed" become an empty formula but also "one afternoon," "one morning," "one evening" become merely markers of convenience. All I can say is that I really did manage to make up the lost year and without a great effort. I had a good memory — I realized — and learned from books more than from school. Even if I read absentmindedly, I remembered everything.

That small success improved relations with my parents, who became proud of me again, especially my father. But I got no satisfaction out of it; their shadows were like an irritating pain that wouldn't go away, an unseemly part of me that had to be cut out. I decided — at first just to distance them ironically and then as a deliberate rejection of the parental bond — to call them by their names. Nella, increasingly malnourished and whiny, was now my father's widow, even though he was still living, in excellent health and surrounded by comforts. She continued to safeguard for him with care the things she had stubbornly prevented him from taking away. She was always available for visits from his ghost, for the phone calls he made from beyond the grave of their married life. And I was convinced that she saw Mariano from time to time only to find out what great matters her ex-husband was occupying himself with. Otherwise, clenching her teeth, she disciplined herself to a long series of daily duties, me among them. But she no longer concentrated on me — and it was a relief — with the determination she put into correcting piles and piles of homework or making love stories hang together. You're grown up, she said more and more often, you take care of it.

I was glad to be able to come and go, finally, without too much control. The less she and my father concerned themselves with me, the better I felt. Andrea especially, ah, let him be silent. I was increasingly less able to endure the wise instructions for life that my father felt it his duty to concoct for me when we saw each other in Posillipo, if I was visiting Angela and Ida, or near my school, to eat *panzarotti* and *pastacresciuta* together. The wish that there could be a friendship between Roberto and me was miraculously coming true, so that I seemed to be guided and instructed by him, in a way that my father, too absorbed in himself and his misdeeds, had never known how to do. One night, now long ago, in the dim apartment on Via San Giacomo dci Capri, Andrea, speaking rashly, had stripped me of my confidence; Giuliana's fiancé was kindly, affectionately restoring it. I was so proud of that relationship with Roberto that I occasionally mentioned him to my father, just for the fun of seeing how serious and attentive he became. He asked about him, he wanted to know what sort of person he was, what we talked about, if I had ever told Roberto about him and his work. I don't know if he really respected Roberto, hard to say, I had long considered Andrea's words unreliable. Once, I remember, he said earnestly that he was a lucky young man, who had been able to get away in time from a shit city like Naples and construct for himself a prestigious university career in Milan. On another occasion he said to me: it's good you're spending time with people who are better than you, it's the only way to go up and not down. A couple of times, finally, he went so far as to ask me if I could introduce him, he felt the need to get out of the quarrelsome, petty-minded group he'd been stuck in since he was a boy. He seemed to me a small, frail man.

2.

It happened just like that, Roberto and I became friends. I don't want to exaggerate, he didn't come to Naples often; the occasions for meeting were rare. But bit by bit we established a little routine that, without becoming really regular, resulted in our finding a way of talking even just for a few minutes, when the opportunity arose, and always in the company of Giuliana.

At first, I have to admit, I was very anxious. Every time we met I thought I'd overdone it, that trying to keep up with him — he was ten years older than me, I was a high-school student, he taught at the university — was a presumption, that surely I had made myself ridiculous. I went over in my mind, countless times, what he had said, what I had answered, and was ashamed of every word. I heard the frivolity with which I had dismissed complicated questions and in my breast grew a sense of unease very similar to what I'd felt as a child when I did something impulsively that would certainly displease my parents. I doubted that I could have inspired any fondness on his part. In my memory, his ironic tone spilled over into explicit mockery. I recalled a contemptuous attitude I'd taken, certain parts of the conversation where I had tried to impress, and I felt cold, nauseated, I wanted to expel myself from myself as if I were about to vomit myself.

In fact, however, it wasn't like that. Each of those encounters improved me, Roberto's words immediately set off a need for reading and information. The days became a race to arrive at a future meeting more prepared, with complex questions on the tip of my tongue. I began to look through the books my father had left at home to find some that might be helpful for understanding. But understanding what, or whom? The Gospels, the Father, the Son, the Holy Spirit, transcendence and silence, the tangle of faith and the absence of faith, the radical nature of Christ, the horrors of inequality, violence, always carried out against the weakest, the savage, boundless world of the capitalist system, the advent of robots, the urgent need for Communism? Though his perspective was broad, Roberto was constantly moving beyond it. He held together heaven and earth, he knew everything, he blended together minor examples, stories, quotations, theories, and I tried to keep up, alternating between the certainty that I'd sounded like a girl who talks pretending to know and the hope that I'd soon have another chance to prove I was better than that.

3.

During that time, I often turned to either Giuliana or Angela to settle myself. Giuliana seemed for obvious reasons closer, more comforting. There was the thought of Roberto that gave us a reason to spend time together and, during his long absences, we wandered around the Vomero talking about him. I observed her: she radiated a charming freshness, she always wore my aunt's bracelet on her wrist, men rested their eyes on her and turned for a last look as if they couldn't bear to deprive themselves of her image. I didn't exist, beside her, and yet a knowing tone on my part or an arcane word was enough to sap her energy, so that she seemed without vitality. Once she said to me:

"You read so many books."

"I like that better than homework."

"I get tired right away."

"It's a matter of habit."

I admitted that the passion for reading wasn't my thing, that it came from my father: it was he who had convinced me as a child of the importance of books and the enormous value of intellectual activity.

"Once that idea gets in your mind," I said, "you can't free yourself from it."

"Thank goodness. Intellectuals are good people."

"My father isn't good."

"But Roberto is, and you, too."

"I'm not an intellectual."

"You are. You study, you know how to talk about everything, and you're open with everyone, even Vittoria. I'm not up to it and I lose patience right away."

I was pleased — I have to admit — with those declarations of respect. Since that was how she imagined intellectuals, I tried to live up to her expectations, partly because she didn't like it if I merely chatted casually, as if with her fiancé I gave the best of myself and with her I limited myself to ordinary things. In fact, she urged me to speak on complex subjects, she wanted me to talk about books I had enjoyed or was enjoying. She said: tell me about them. And she showed the same anxious curiosity about films, music. Not even Angela and Ida, until then, had let me talk so much about what I loved, what to me was not an obligation but a pastime. School had never taken notice of the disorderly jumble of interests that came from reading, and none of my classmates had ever wanted me to recount — just to give an example — the plot of *Tom Jones.* So we got along well, in that phase. We met often, I waited for her at the exit of the Montesanto funicular, she came up to the Vomero as if it were a foreign country where she was happily on vacation. We went from Piazza Vanvitelli to Piazza degli Artisti and back, paying no attention to the people on the street, the traffic, the shops, because I became absorbed in the pleasure of beguiling her with names, titles, stories, and she seemed to see only what I had seen, reading or at the movies or listening to music.

In Roberto's absence, and in the company of his fiancée, I played at being the custodian of vast learning, and Giuliana hung on my words as if she asked nothing more than to recognize how superior I was, in spite of the difference in our ages, in spite of her beauty. But at times I felt that something wasn't quite right for her, there was an uneasiness that she forcibly repressed. And I was alarmed, I remembered the quarrelsome voice of Vittoria on the phone: "Why do you put yourself between Giuliana and her fiancé? Are you worse than my brother? Tell me, I'm listening: are you more arrogant than your father?" I just wanted to be a good friend, and I was afraid that, thanks to Vittoria's terrible arts, Giuliana would be persuaded of the contrary and push me away.

4.

Angela often joined us — she was offended if we excluded her. But the two didn't get on well, and Giuliana's uneasiness became more obvious. Angela, who was very chatty, tended to make fun of me and also of her, to provocatively say mean things about Tonino, to dismantle with her sarcasm every attempt at serious conversation. I didn't get mad, but Giuliana darkened, she defended her brother and sooner or later responded to Angela's facetious remarks with bursts of aggressive dialect.

In other words, what with me was latent with Angela became open, and there was always the risk of a serious break. When it was just Angela and me, Angela showed that she knew a lot about Giuliana and Roberto, even though, after the meeting in Piazza Amedeo, she had completely given up poking her nose in their business. When she backed off, I was both relieved and irritated. Once when she came to my house I asked:

"You don't like Roberto?"

"Sure, I like him."

"Then what is it that bothers you."

"Nothing. But if you and he are talking to each other there's no space for anyone else."

"There's Giuliana."

"Poor Giuliana."

"What do you mean."

"You know how bored she is in the midst of you professors."

"She's not at all bored."

"She's bored, but she pretends, to hold on to her position."

"What position?"

"Of fiancée. Does it seem to you that someone like Giuliana, secretary in a dentist's office, listens to you two talk about reason and faith, and really isn't bored?"

I burst out:

"You think the only fun thing is talking about necklaces and bracelets and underpants and bras?"

She was offended:

"That's not all I talk about."

"Not before, but lately it is."

"That's not true."

I apologized, she replied: all right, but you've been devious. And naturally she started up again with intensified malice:

"Luckily she goes to see him now and then in Milan."

"What do you mean?"

"That finally they're going to bed and doing what they should."

"Tonino always goes to Milan with Giuliana."

"You think Tonino keeps watch day and night?"

I grumbled:

"You think if two people love each other they have to sleep together?"

"Yes."

"Ask Tonino if they sleep together, and

377

we'll see."

"I already have, but Tonino says nothing about these things."

"It means that he has nothing to say."

"It means that he also thinks love can do without sex."

"Who else thinks that?"

She answered with a small, unexpectedly sad smile:

"You."

5.

According to Angela, I had nothing amusing to say anymore on that subject. Now, it was true that I had cut out the vulgar stories, but only because it had seemed to me childish to exaggerate my few experiences and I didn't have any more substantial material. Since my relationship with Roberto and Giuliana had solidified, I had been fending off my schoolmate Silvestro, who after the episode of the pencil had become fond of me and had several times proposed that we go out secretly. But I had been very harsh with Corrado, who continued his propositions, and cautious but firm with Rosario, who at fixed intervals appeared outside school suggesting that I go with him to an attic apartment he had on

378

Via Manzoni. Now those three suitors of mine seemed to belong to a debased humanity that I had unfortunately been part of. Angela, on the other hand, seemed to have become someone else: she cheated on Tonino and didn't spare Ida and me any detail of the occasional relations she had with classmates and even with a teacher over fifty; she herself had a grimace of disgust when she talked about him.

That disgust struck me, it was genuine. I knew it and wanted to say: I see it in your face, let's talk about it. But we never did, it seemed that sex had to be exciting by definition. I didn't want to admit, to Angela or even to Ida, that I would prefer to be a nun rather than smell Corrado's toilet stink again. I also didn't like Angela's interpretation of my lack of enthusiasm as an act of devotion toward Roberto. And then, of course, the truth was difficult. Disgust had its ambiguities, difficult to put into words. What disgusted me about Corrado might not have disgusted me if it had been Roberto. So I confined myself to pointing out contradictions, I'd say:

"Why do you stay with Tonino, if you do those things with other guys?"

"Because Tonino is a good guy and the others are pigs."

"And you do it with pigs?"

"Yes."

"Why?"

"Because I like the way they look at me."

"Make Tonino look at you the same way."

"He doesn't do that."

"Maybe he's not a man," Ida said once.

"Oh no, he's very much a man."

"So?"

"He's not a pig, that's all."

"I don't believe it," said Ida. "There are no men who aren't pigs."

"Yes, there are," I said thinking of Roberto.

"Yes, there are," said Angela, citing with inventive expressions Tonino's erections when he touched her.

I think it was then, as she was talking, enjoying herself, that I felt the lack of a serious discussion on the subject, not with them but with Roberto and Giuliana. Would Roberto avoid it? No, I was sure he would answer me and would find a way even in this case to make very articulate arguments. The problem was the risk of seeming inappropriate in Giuliana's eyes. Why bring up that subject in the presence of her fiancé? Altogether we had seen each other six times, apart from the meeting in Piazza Amedeo, and almost never for very long. Objectively, then, we weren't that intimate. Although he always tended to use very concrete examples when he was discussing big questions, I wouldn't have had the courage to ask: why, if you dig even a little, do you find sex in all things, even the most elevated; why, to describe sex, is a single adjective not sufficient, why does it take many — embarrassing, bland, tragic, happy, pleasant, repulsive — and never one at a time but all together; is it possible that a great love can exist without sex, is it possible that sexual practices between male and female don't spoil the need to love and be loved in return? I imagined these and other questions, in a detached tone, maybe slightly solemn, so that he and Giuliana wouldn't think I wanted to spy on their private life. But I knew I would never do it. Instead I persevered with Ida.

"Why do you think there aren't any men who aren't pigs?"

"I don't think, I know."

"So even Mariano is a pig?"

"Of course, he goes to bed with your mother."

I started, I said coldly:

"They see each other sometimes, but it's friendship."

"I think they're just friends, too," Angela

intervened.

Ida shook her head energetically, repeated decisively: they're not just friends. And she exclaimed:

"I won't kiss a man, it's disgusting."

"Not even a nice one like Tonino?" asked Angela.

"No, I'll only kiss women. You want to hear a story I wrote?"

"No," said Angela.

I stared in silence at Ida's shoes, which were green. I remembered that her father had looked at my cleavage.

6.

We often returned to the subject of Roberto and Giuliana; Angela extracted information from Tonino just for the fun of reporting it to me. One day she called because she found out that there had been yet another argument, this time between Vittoria and Margherita. They had quarreled because Margherita didn't share Vittoria's idea that Roberto should marry Giuliana right away and come to live in Naples. My aunt as usual made a lot of noise, Margherita as usual objected calmly, and Giuliana was quiet as if the matter didn't concern her. Then suddenly Giuliana had started shouting, she began breaking plates, soup bowls, glasses, and not even Vittoria, who was very strong, was able to stop her. She cried: I'm leaving immediately, I'm going to live with him, I can't stand all of you anymore. Tonino and Corrado had to intervene.

That story confused me. I said:

"It's Vittoria's fault, she never minds her own business."

"It's the fault of them all, apparently Giuliana is very jealous. Tonino says he'd bet his life on Roberto, he's a fair and faithful person. But when Tonino goes to Milan with her, she makes scenes, because she can't bear, I don't know, that some girl student is too friendly, some colleague is too flirtatious, and so on and so on."

"I don't believe it."

"You're wrong. Giuliana seems serene, but Tonino told me she has nervous exhaustion."

"Meaning?"

"When she feels bad, she doesn't eat, she cries and screams."

"Now how is she?"

"Fine. Tonight she's coming to the movies with Tonino and me, why don't you come, too?"

"If I come I'm sitting with Giuliana, don't leave me with Tonino."

Angela laughed.

"I'm inviting you just so you can free me from Tonino, I can't take it anymore."

I went, but the day didn't go well: first the afternoon and then the evening were particularly distressing. The four of us met in Piazza del Plebiscito, in front of Caffè Gambrinus, and we set off on Via Toledo toward the Modernissimo cinema. I wasn't able to exchange even a word with Giuliana, I noticed only her agitated gaze, her bloodshot eyes, and the bracelet on her wrist. Angela immediately took her by the arm, I was a few paces back with Tonino. I asked him:

"Everything O.K.?"

"O.K."

"I know you often take your sister to see Roberto."

"No, not often."

"Sometimes we get together."

"Yes, Giuliana told me."

"They're a handsome couple."

"They are."

"I hear that when they get married they're going to move to Naples."

"Doesn't look like it."

I couldn't get anything else out of him: he was a polite young man and wanted to entertain me, but not on that subject. So after a while I let him talk to me about a friend of his in Venice, he was planning to visit him and figure out if he could move there.

"What about Angela?"

"Angela isn't happy with me."

"That's not true."

"Yes, it is."

We got to the Modernissimo, I don't remember what movie was showing — maybe it will come to me later. Tonino paid for all the tickets and bought candy, ice cream. We went in eating, the lights were still on. We sat down, first Tonino, then Angela, Giuliana, and me. At first we paid no attention to three boys sitting right behind us, high-school kids like Angela's and my classmates, sixteen at most. We just heard them talking, laughing, while we girls were already cutting out Tonino, chatting without paying attention to anything.

It was precisely our ignoring them that caused the three boys to get restless. I really became aware of them only when the one who was maybe the boldest said in a loud voice: come and sit here next to us, we'll show you the film. Angela burst out laughing and turned around, maybe she was nervous, and the boys laughed, too, the bold one made some more inviting remarks. I

385

turned around and changed my mind about them, they weren't like our classmates, they reminded me of Corrado or Rosario, slightly improved by school. I turned to Giuliana: she was older, I was expecting a sympathetic smile. Instead she was serious, rigid, her eyes fixed on Tonino, who seemed deaf, staring, impassive, at the blank screen.

The ads began, the bold kid caressed Giuliana's hair and whispered, how nice, and one of the others shook Angela's seat. She tugged Tonino's arm and said: these guys are bothering me, make them stop. Giuliana murmured: forget it, I don't know if she was talking to Angela or directly to her brother. Anyway, Angela ignored her and said to Tonino, peeved: I'm not going out with you anymore, I'm fed up, I'm pissed. The bold kid exclaimed instantly: good for you, we told you so, come on over, plenty of room here. Someone else in the audience went *sssh.* Tonino said slowly, drawing out the words: let's sit a little farther down, we're not comfortable here. He got up, and his sister did the same so promptly that I did, too. Angela remained seated for a few more seconds, then she got up and said to Tonino: you're ridiculous.

We settled ourselves in the same order a few rows ahead, Angela started whispering in Tonino's ear: she was angry, I realized that she was taking advantage of the moment to get rid of him. The innumerable ads were finally over, the lights went on again. The three kids were having fun, I heard them laughing, I turned. They had stood up and were climbing noisily over one two three rows, and in an instant they were sitting behind us again. Their spokesman said: you let that shit order you around, we're insulted, we can't stand to be treated like that, we want to watch the movie with you.

Then it was a matter of seconds. The lights went out, the film began clamorously. The boy's voice was drowned out by the music, we were all reduced to flashes of light. Angela said to Tonino in a loud voice: did you hear, he called you a shit? Laughter from the boys, *sssh* from the audience, Tonino jumped up unexpectedly, Giuliana said: no, Tonì. But he slapped Angela so violently that her head banged against my cheekbone, it hurt. The boys shut up, disoriented, Tonino twisted around like an open door banging in a gust of wind, and unrepeatable obscenities came out of his mouth in a sustained rhythm. Angela burst into tears, Giuliana grabbed my hand, she said: we have to go, let's get him out of here.

Get her brother out of there by force, she meant, as if the person in danger weren't Angela or the two of us but him. By now the boys' spokesman had recovered from his surprise, and said: oh, I'm real scared, we're shaking, you clown, you only know how to fight with girls, come on. Giuliana seemed to want to erase his voice as she cried, Tonì, they're kids. The seconds passed, with one hand Tonino grabbed the boy by the head — maybe by an ear, I wouldn't swear — grabbed it and pulled it toward him as if to detach it. Instead he hit him under the chin with the other hand closed in a fist, and the boy flew backward, he sat in his seat again with his mouth bleeding. The other two wanted to help their friend, but when they saw that Tonino meant to climb over the seats, they looked frantically for the exit. Giuliana grabbed her brother to keep him from going after them, the music of the film's opening was blaring, the audience was shouting, Angela weeping, the wounded kid shrieking. Tonino shoved his sister aside, started taking it out again on the kid, who had fallen in tears and groans and curses on the seat. He slapped and punched him, insulting him in a dialect incomprehensible to me it was so fast and loaded with fury, one word exploding inside the next. Now everyone in the theater was shouting, turn on the lights, call the police, and Giuliana and I, and Angela, too, grabbed hold of Tonino's arms yelling: let's go, that's enough, let's go. Finally, we managed to pull him away and get to the exit. Go, Tonì, run, Giuliana shouted, hitting him on the back, and he repeated twice, in dialect: it's not possible that, in this city, a respectable person can't watch a film in peace. He spoke mainly to me, to see if I agreed. To calm him down I agreed, and he ran away toward Piazza Dante, handsome in spite of his wild eyes, his blue lips.

7.

We got out of there fast, too, heading toward the basilica of the Spirito Santo, and slowed down only when we felt protected by the crowd in the Pignasecca market. Then I became aware of my fear. Angela, too, was terrified, and so was Giuliana, who seemed to have taken part in the brawl herself, her hair was disheveled, the collar of her jacket half torn. I looked to see if she still had the bracelet on her wrist, and it was there, but it wasn't shining.

"I have to get home right away," Giuliana said, speaking to me.

"Go, and call me, let me know how Tonino is."

"Were you scared?"

"Yes."

"I'm sorry, Tonino usually controls himself, but sometimes he just can't see straight."

Angela interrupted, her eyes filled with tears:

"I was scared, too."

Giuliana turned pale with rage, she almost yelled:

"Shut up, you better just shut up."

I had never seen her so furious. She kissed me on the cheeks and left.

Angela and I reached the funicular. I was confused, the phrase was impressed on me: sometimes he just can't see straight anymore. All the way home, I listened distractedly to my friend's complaints. She was in despair: I was stupid, she said. But then she touched her red, swollen cheek, her neck hurt, she cried: how could he dare, he slapped me, me, not even my father and mother ever slap me, I don't want to see him ever ever again. She wept, then started in with another grievance: Giuliana hadn't said goodbye to her, she had said goodbye only to me. It's not right to put all the blame on me, she muttered, how was I sup-

390

posed to know that Tonino was a beast. When I left her at her house, she admitted: all right, it's my fault, but Tonino and Giuliana aren't well brought up, I never would have expected it, his hitting me, he could have killed me, he could have killed those boys, too, I was wrong to love an animal like that. I said: you're wrong, Tonino and Giuliana are very well brought up, but there can be times when you really can't see straight anymore.

I walked back home, slowly. I couldn't get that expression — unable to see straight — out of my mind. Everything seems in order, hello, see you soon, make yourself at home, what can I give you to drink, could you lower the volume a little, thank you, you're welcome. But there's a black veil that can drop at any moment. It's a sudden blindness, you don't know how to keep your distance, you crash into things. Does it happen only to some people or to everybody that, once a certain level is passed, they can't see straight anymore? And was it truer when you saw everything clearly or when the strongest and deepest feelings — hatred, love — blinded you? Had Enzo, blinded by Vittoria, been unable to see Margherita? Had my father, blinded by Costanza, been unable to see my mother? Had I, blinded by the insult of my classmate Silvestro, been unable to see straight? Was Roberto also someone who could be blinded? Or was he always able — in every circumstance, under the pressure of whatever emotional impulse — to remain clear and serene?

The apartment was dark, very silent. My mother must have decided to spend Saturday evening out. The phone rang, I answered it immediately, sure that it would be Giuliana. It was Tonino, who said slowly, with a calm that I liked because now it seemed to be his own rich invention:

"I wanted to apologize and say goodbye to you."

"Where are you going?"

"Venice."

"When are you leaving?"

"Tonight."

"Why did you decide that."

"Because otherwise I'll throw my life away."

"What does Giuliana say."

"Nothing, she doesn't know, nobody knows."

"Not even Roberto?"

"No, if he knew what I did tonight he'd never speak to me again."

"Giuliana will tell him."

"I won't."

"Send me your address?"

"As soon as I have one, I'll write to you."

"Why are you calling me?"

"Because you're someone who understands."

I hung up, I felt sad. I went into the kitchen, got some water, went back out to the hall. But the day wasn't over. The door of the bedroom that once had been my parents' opened and my mother appeared. She wasn't wearing her usual clothes, but was dressed up. She said in a natural tone:

"Weren't you supposed to go to the movies?"

"We didn't go."

"Now we're going: how is it outside, do I need a coat?"

From the same room — he, too, nicely dressed — Mariano appeared.

8.

That was the last stage of the long crisis in my house and, at the same time, an important moment in my arduous approach to the adult world. I learned — just at that moment, when I decided to appear cordial, and reply to my mother that the evening was warm, and accept Mariano's habitual kiss on the cheeks as well as the usual glance at my breasts — that it was impossible to stop growing up. When the two closed the door behind them, I went to the bathroom and took a long shower as if to wash them off me.

As I dried my hair in front of the mirror, I felt like laughing. I had been deceived in everything, not even my hair was beautiful, it was pasted to my skull and I couldn't give it volume and splendor. As for my face, it had no harmony, just like Vittoria's. But the mistake had been to make it a tragedy. If you looked even just for a moment at those who had the privilege of a beautiful, refined face, you discovered that it hid infernos no different from those expressed by coarse, ugly faces. The splendor of a face, enhanced even by kindness, harbored and promised suffering still more than a dull face.

Angela, for example, after the episode of the movie and the disappearance of Tonino from her life, grew sad, became mean. She talked to me at length on the phone, accusing me of not being on her side, of having let a man hit her, of having supported Giuliana. I tried to deny it, but it was useless. She said she had told the story to Costanza, and even to my father. Costanza had sided with her, but Andrea had done more: once he understood who Tonino was, whose son he was, where he was born and grew up, he had become very angry, not so much with her as with me. She reported that my father had said literally: Giovanna knows very well what sort of people they are, she should have protected you. But you didn't protect me, she cried, and I imagined that her sweet harmonious seductive face, there in the house in Posillipo, as she held the white receiver to her ear, had become at that moment uglier than mine. I said to her: please, from now on leave me alone — confide in Andrea and Costanza, they understand you better. And I hung up.

Right afterward I intensified my relations with Giuliana. Angela tried often to make up, she'd say to me: let's go out together. I always answered, even if it wasn't true: I have a date, I'm seeing Giuliana. And I let her understand or said explicitly: you can't come with me, she can't stand you.

I also reduced to a minimum my relations with my mother. I was curt, saying things like: I won't be here today, I'm going to Pascone, and when she asked why, I answered, because I feel like it. I behaved like that certainly to feel free from all the old bonds, to make it clear that I didn't care anymore about the judgment of relatives and friends, their values, their wanting me to be consistent with what they imagined themselves to be.

9.

Undoubtedly, I became closer to Giuliana in order to cultivate my friendship with Roberto, I won't deny it. But it also seemed to me that Giuliana really needed me, now that Tonino had left without explanation, leaving her alone to fight with Vittoria and her bullying. One afternoon she called me, extremely upset, to tell me that her mother — egged on by my aunt, naturally — wanted her to tell Roberto: either you marry me immediately and we come and live in Naples or the engagement is off.

"But I can't," she said desperately, "he's really busy, he's doing some work that's important for his career. I would be crazy to say to him: marry me immediately. And anyway I want to get away from this city, forever."

She was sick of everything. I advised her to explain Roberto's problems to Margherita and Vittoria and, after much hesitation, she did that, but the two women weren't convinced and went on to corrode her brain with countless insinuations. They are ignorant people, she said desperately, and want to persuade me that if Roberto puts his problems as a professor first and our wedding second it means he doesn't love me enough and is only wasting my time.

That hammering wasn't without effect; I soon realized that sometimes even Giuliana doubted Roberto. Of course, in general she reacted angrily and got mad at Vittoria, who put terrible ideas in her mother's head, but, repeated over and over, the terrible ideas were making progress even in her and saddening her.

"You see where I live?" she said one afternoon when I had gone to see her and we were taking a walk on the bleak streets of her neighborhood. "While Roberto is in Milan, he's always busy, he meets so many intelligent people, and sometimes he has so much to do I can't even get him on the phone."

"That's what his life is."

"I should be his life."

"I don't know."

She got irritated.

"No? So what is it: studying, talking to women colleagues and women students? Maybe Vittoria is right: he marries me or that's it."

Things became more problematic when Roberto told her he had to go to London for ten days for work. Giuliana was more upset than usual, and gradually it became clear that the problem wasn't so much the sojourn abroad — I knew he had gone away other times, although only for two or three days — as the fact that he wasn't going by himself. Then I also became alarmed.

"Who's he going with?"

"With Michela and two other professors."

"Who's Michela?"

"Someone who can't leave him alone."

"You go, too."

"Where, Gianni? Where? Don't think of how you grew up, think of how I grew up, think of Vittoria, think of my mother, think of this shitty place. It's all easy for you, for me no."

It seemed unfair: if I made an effort to understand her problems, she had no idea of mine. But I pretended nothing was wrong, I let her vent, I devoted myself to calming her. At the center of my arguments was as usual the rare quality of her fiancé. Roberto wasn't an ordinary person but a man of great spiritual force, very cultured, faithful. Even if that Michela had designs, he wouldn't give in. He loves you, I said, and he'll behave in an honest way.

She burst out laughing, became bitter. The change was so sudden that I thought of

Tonino and what had happened in the movie theater. She planted her anxious eyes in mine, abruptly stopped speaking her half-dialectal Italian, moved on to dialect alone.

"How do you know he loves me?"

"It's not just me who knows it, everyone knows it, surely even this Michela."

"Men, good or not, you brush against them and they want to fuck."

"Vittoria told you that, but it's nonsense."

"Vittoria says terrible things, but not nonsense."

"Anyway you have to trust Roberto, otherwise you'll feel terrible."

"I already feel really terrible, Giannì."

At that point, I realized that Giuliana attributed to Michela not only the desire to go to bed with Roberto but the intention of taking him away from her and marrying him. It occurred to me that he, absorbed in his studies, probably didn't even suspect that she could have those anxieties. And I thought maybe it would be enough to tell him: Giuliana is afraid of losing you, she's very agitated, reassure her. Or anyway that was the reason I gave myself when I asked for the phone number of her fiancé.

"If you want," I said, "I'll talk to him and try to find out how things are with this Michela."

"You'd do that?"

"Of course."

"But he mustn't think you're calling on my account."

"Don't be silly."

"And you have to report to me everything you say and everything he says."

"Of course."

10.

I wrote down the number in one of my notebooks, drawing a rectangle around it with a red crayon. One afternoon, feeling very nervous, I called, taking advantage of the fact that my mother wasn't home. Roberto seemed surprised, even apprehensive. He must have thought that something had happened to Giuliana, it was his first question. I said she was fine, uttered a jumble of words, and then, suddenly discarding all the preambles I had thought of to give formality to the phone call, I said in an almost threatening tone:

"If you promised to marry Giuliana and you don't marry her, you're irresponsible."

He was silent for a moment, then I heard him laugh.

"I always keep my promises. Did your aunt tell you to call me?"

"No, I do what I feel like doing."

From there we started a conversation that unsettled me because it demonstrated his willingness to talk to me about personal matters. He said that he loved Giuliana, that the only thing that could keep him from marrying her would be that she didn't want to marry him. I assured him that Giuliana wanted it more than anything, but I added that she was insecure, she was afraid of losing him, afraid that he would fall in love with someone else. He answered that he knew that and did everything possible to reassure her. I believe you, I said, but now you're going abroad, you might meet another girl: if you discover that Giuliana doesn't understand anything about you and your work, while that other person does, what will you do? He gave me a long answer. He began with Naples, Pascone, his childhood there. He talked about them as of marvelous places, very different from the way I saw them. He said that he had contracted a debt there and had to repay it. He tried to explain to me that his love for Giuliana, born on those streets, was like a reminder, the constant memory of that debt. And when I asked him what he meant by debt he explained that he owed a spiritual compensation to the place where he was born, and a lifetime wouldn't be sufficient to restore the balance. So I replied: you want to marry her as if you were marrying Pascone? He seemed embarrassed, he said that he was grateful to me because I was forcing him to reflect, and he struggled to articulate his thoughts: I want to marry her because she is the very incarnation of my debt. He maintained a low tone, although occasionally he uttered a solemn phrase like "we can't be saved by ourselves alone." Sometimes I seemed to be talking to one of my classmates: he chose elementary constructions, and that made me feel at ease, but also upset me. At times I suspected he was mimicking behavior suitable to what I was, a girl, and for a moment I thought that maybe with that Michela he would have talked with greater richness and complexity. On the other hand what claim did I have? I thanked him for the conversation, he thanked me for letting him talk about Giuliana and for the friendship I had demonstrated for both of them. I said without thinking:

"Tonino left, she's suffering a lot, she's alone."

"I know and I'll try to remedy that. It was a real pleasure to talk to you."

"For me, too."

I reported every word to Giuliana, she regained some color, and she needed it. It didn't seem to me that things got noticeably worse when Roberto left for London. She said that he called her, had written her a wonderful letter, and she never mentioned Michela. She cheered up when he told her he'd just had a new article published in an important review. She seemed proud of him, she was happy, as if she had written the article. But she complained, laughing, that she could boast about it only to me: Vittoria, her mother, Corrado couldn't appreciate it; and Tonino, the only one who would have understood, was far away, working as a waiter, who knew if he was still studying.

"Will you let me read it?" I asked.

"I don't have the review."

"But you read it?"

She realized I took it for granted that he had her read everything he wrote, and I did: my father had had my mother read everything, sometimes he had even made me read pages that he liked. She darkened, I saw in her eyes that she would have liked to answer yes, I've read them, she automatically gave a nod of assent. But then she looked down, looked up again angrily, said:

"No, I haven't read them, and I don't want to."

"Why."

"I'm afraid I won't understand."

"Maybe you should try anyway, it must be important to him."

"If it was important, he would give them to me. But he hasn't, and so he's sure I can't understand."

I remember we were out walking on Toledo, it was hot. The schools were closing, soon the grades would be coming out. The street was crowded with kids, boys and girls, it was nice not to have homework, to be outside. Giuliana looked at them as if she didn't understand the reason for all that energy. She ran her fingers over her forehead, I sensed she was getting depressed, I said quickly:

"It's because you live apart, but when you're married, you'll see, he'll want you to read everything."

"He has Michela read everything."

The news hurt me, too, but I didn't have time to react. Right at the end of that sentence a powerful male voice called us, I heard first Giuliana's name, then mine. We turned at the same time and saw Rosario in the doorway of a café across the street. Giuliana made a gesture of irritation, she hit the air with her hand, she wanted to keep going as if she hadn't heard. But I had already nodded in greeting, and he was crossing the street to join us.

"Do you know the lawyer Sargente's son?" Giuliana said.

"Corrado introduced me."

"Corrado's an idiot."

Meanwhile Rosario was crossing the street and, naturally, laughing; he seemed very happy to have met us.

"It's fate," he said, "to run into you so far from Pascone. Come on, let me get you something."

Giuliana replied stiffly:

"We're in a hurry."

He had an expression of exaggerated worry.

"What's the matter, you don't feel well today, you're nervous?"

"I'm very well."

"Your fiancé is jealous? He said you shouldn't talk to me?"

"My fiancé doesn't even know you exist."

"But you know, right? You know, and you're always thinking of me, but you don't tell your fiancé. And yet you should tell him, you should tell him everything. Between fiancés there shouldn't be secrets, otherwise the relationship doesn't work and you suffer. I see you're suffering, I look at you and I think: she's so skinny, what a pity. You were so round and soft, and you're turning into a broomstick."

"You're the good-looking one."

"Better than your fiancé. Giannì, come on, you want a sfogliatella?"

I answered:

"It's late, we have to go."

"I'll drive you in the car. First we'll take Giuliana to Pascone and then we'll go up to Rione Alto."

He dragged us to the bar, but once there he completely ignored Giuliana, who sat in a corner near the door staring at the street and the passersby. He talked continuously while I ate the sfogliatella, standing so close to me that every so often I had to move a little. He whispered racy compliments in my ear and aloud praised, I don't know, my eyes, my hair. He went so far as to ask in a whisper if I was still a virgin and I laughed nervously, I said yes.

"I'm going," Giuliana grumbled, and left the bar.

Rosario mentioned his house on Via Manzoni, the number, the floor, he said it had a view of the sea. Finally, he said:

"You're always welcome, you want to come over?"

"Now?" I said, pretending to be amused.

"Whenever you want."

"Not now," I said seriously, I thanked him for the sfogliatella and joined Giuliana in the street. She exclaimed angrily:

"Don't give that shit any leeway."

"I didn't, he took it."

"If your aunt sees you together she'll kill you and him."

"I know."

"Did he tell you about Via Manzoni?"

"Yes, what do you know about it?"

Giuliana shook her head hard, as if she wanted with that gesture of negation to get rid of the images that came to mind.

"I've been there."

"With Rosario?"

"Who else?"

"Now?"

"What do you mean, I was younger than you."

"Why?"

"Because I was even more of an idiot than I am now."

I would have liked her to tell me about it, but she said there was nothing to tell. Rosario was a nobody, but because of the father he had — the ugly Naples, Gianni, the terrible Italy that no one can change, least of all Roberto with the fine words he speaks and writes — he thought he was hot shit. He was so stupid he thought that since they had sometimes been together he had the right to remind her of it on every occasion. Her eyes became wet with tears:

"I have to get out of Pascone, Giannì, I have to get out of Naples. Vittoria wants to keep me here, she likes being at war all the time. And Roberto deep down sees it the way she does, he told you he has a debt. But what debt? I want to get married and live in Milan in a nice house of my own, in peace."

I looked at her in bewilderment.

"Even if for him it's important to come back here?"

She shook her head hard, began to cry. We stopped in Piazza Dante. I said:

"Why are you acting like this?"

She dried her eyes with her fingertips, murmured:

"Would you go with me to see Roberto?"

I answered immediately:

"Yes."

12.

Margherita summoned me Sunday morning, but I didn't go directly to her house, I went first to Vittoria's. I was sure she was

408

behind the decision to ask me to take Giuliana to see Roberto and I imagined that she would cancel the assignment if I didn't show myself affectionately subordinate. During that entire time, I had barely glimpsed her when I went to see Giuliana, and she had been ambivalent as usual. I'd become convinced over time that when she recognized herself in me she was overwhelmed with affection, while if she perceived something of my father she suspected that I might do to her and the people she was attached to what her brother had done to her in the past. Besides, I was the same. I found her extraordinary when I imagined myself becoming a combative adult, and repulsive when I recognized in her traits of my father's. That morning something suddenly occurred to me that seemed intolerable and yet funny: neither Vittoria nor my father nor I could cut out our common roots, and so, depending on the situation, it was always ourselves we ended up loving or hating.

It turned out to be a lucky day, Vittoria seemed happy to see me. I let her hug and kiss me with her usual clingy intensity. I love you so much, she said, and we left quickly for Margherita's. On the way, she revealed to me what I already knew but pretended not to, that the very rare times when Giuliana had been allowed to see Roberto in Milan, Tonino had gone with her. But now he had left for Venice, abandoning the family — Vittoria's eyes filled with tears in a mixture of suffering and contempt — and since Corrado absolutely couldn't be trusted, they had thought of me.

"I'll do it happily," I said.

"But you have to do it right."

I decided to duel a little, when she was in a good mood she liked it. I asked:

"In what sense?"

"Gianni, Margherita is timid but not me, and so I will tell you straight: you must assure me that Giuliana will always be with you, night and day. You understand what that means?"

"Yes."

"Good for you. Men — keep it in mind — want one thing only. But Giuliana mustn't give him that thing before she gets married, otherwise he won't marry her."

"I don't think Roberto is that type of man."

"They're all that type of man."

"I'm not sure."

"If I say all, Gianni, it's all."

"Even Enzo?"

"Enzo more than others."

"Why did you give him that thing?"

Vittoria looked at me with pleased surprise. She burst out laughing, she clasped me around the shoulders hard, gave me a kiss on the cheek.

"You're like me, Gianni, and even worse, that's why I like you. I gave it to him because he was already married, he had three children, and if I didn't give it to him I would have to give him up. But I couldn't, because I loved him too much."

I pretended to be satisfied with that answer, even if I would have liked to show her that she was a twisted person, that the thing that is most important to males you don't grant on the basis of opportunistic evaluations, that Giuliana was a grownup and could do what she liked, that she and Margherita, in short, had no right to keep a young woman of twenty under surveillance. But I was silent because my only desire was to go to Milan and see Roberto, see with my own eyes where and how he lived. And then I knew that I shouldn't take things too far with Vittoria, while I'd made her laugh now, a small affront would be enough for her to throw me out. So I chose the path of consent and we reached Margherita's house. There I assured Giuliana's mother that I would diligently watch over the fiancés, and

411

Vittoria, while I spoke in a good Italian to give myself authority, whispered often to her goddaughter: get it, you and Giannina have to be together at all times, the main thing is you have to sleep together, and Giuliana nodded distractedly, and the only one who annoyed me with his teasing looks was Corrado. He offered several times to take me to the bus, and when all the pacts with Vittoria were ratified — we were to return Sunday night, absolutely, Roberto would pay for the train tickets — I left and he came with me. On the street and while we were waiting at the bus stop, all he did was mock me, making offensive remarks as if he were joking. Mostly he kept asking me explicitly to do again the things I had done in the past.

"A blow job," he said to me in dialect, "and then that's all: there's an old abandoned building near here."

"No, you make me sick."

"If I find out you did it with Rosario, I'll tell Vittoria."

"I don't give a fuck," I answered, in a dialect that made him laugh hard, it was so badly pronounced.

I felt like laughing, too. I didn't want to fight even with Corrado, I was too glad to be going away. On the way home I concen-

trated on what lie I would have to tell my
mother to explain a trip to Milan. But soon
I convinced myself that I didn't owe her
even the effort of lying, and at dinner I said
to her, in the tone of one who considers the
thing irrefutable, that Giuliana, Vittoria's
goddaughter, was going to visit her fiancé in
Milan and I had promised to go with her.

"This weekend?"

"Yes."

"But Saturday is your birthday, I've organized a party, your father is coming, Angela
and Ida are coming."

For a few seconds my chest felt empty.
How attached I'd been to my birthday as a
child, and yet this time it had gone right
out of my mind. I had the impression that I
had wronged myself even more than my
mother. I couldn't assign myself value, I was
becoming a background figure, a shadow
beside Giuliana, the ugly chaperone of the
princess who goes to the prince. For that
role was I willing to give up a long, pleasant
family tradition, candles to blow out, surprising presents? Yes, I admitted, and proposed to Nella:

"Let's celebrate when I get back."

"You're upsetting me."

"Mamma, don't make a big deal out of
nothing."

"Your father will be hurt, too."

"You'll see, he'll be glad: Giuliana's fiancé is someone really smart, Papa respects him."

She made a grimace of displeasure, as if he were responsible for my inadequate emotions.

"Are you going to be promoted?"

"Mamma, that's my thing, don't interfere."

She muttered:

"We don't count for you at all anymore."

I said that wasn't true and yet I thought: Roberto counts more.

13.

On Friday night began one of the most senseless enterprises of my adolescence.

The night journey to Milan was very boring. I tried to make conversation with Giuliana, but, especially after I told her that I would be sixteen the next day, she seemed embarrassed, an embarrassment she'd displayed the moment she arrived at the station with an enormous red suitcase and overstuffed purse, and realized that I had only a small suitcase with a few essentials. I'm sorry she said, to drag you with me and ruin the day, and that brief exchange was it, we couldn't find the right tone or the ease

414

that leads to intimacy. At one point, I announced that I was hungry and wanted to explore the train to find something to eat. Giuliana listlessly took out of her bag some good things her mother had prepared, but she ate only a few mouthfuls of *frittata di pasta;* I ate the rest. The compartment was crowded, we settled ourselves uncomfortably in the berths. She seemed dulled by anguish, I heard her tossing and turning, she never went to the bathroom.

But at least an hour before we arrived she shut herself in for a long time and returned with her hair fixed and light makeup put on; she had even changed her clothes. We stood in the corridor, outside a pale day was dawning. She asked if anything was excessive or out of place. I reassured her, and at that point she seemed to relax a little, and spoke to me with an affectionate candor.

"I envy you," she said.

"Why."

"You don't fix yourself up, you're happy the way you are."

"That's not true."

"Yes, it is. You have something inside that's only yours and it's enough for you."

"I don't have anything, you have everything."

415

She shook her head, murmured:

"Roberto says you're really intelligent, that you have a great sensibility."

My face was burning.

"He's wrong."

"It's true. When Vittoria didn't want to let me go, he's the one who suggested that I ask you to come with me."

"I thought my aunt had decided."

She smiled. Of course, she'd made the decision, nothing was done without Vittoria's consent. But the idea had come from Roberto; Giuliana without mentioning her fiancé had talked to her mother, and Margherita had consulted with Vittoria. I was overwhelmed — so it was he who wanted me in Milan — and I answered Giuliana, who now wanted to talk, in monosyllables, I couldn't calm down. Soon I would see him again and the whole day I would be with him, in his house, at lunch, at dinner, sleeping. Gradually, I became less agitated, I said:

"Do you know how to get to Roberto's house?"

"Yes, but he's coming to meet us."

Giuliana checked her face again, then took out of her purse a leather pouch, shook it, my aunt's bracelet slid out onto the palm of her hand.

"Shall I wear it?" she asked.

416

"Why not?"

"I'm always worried. Vittoria gets angry if she doesn't see it on my wrist. But then she's afraid I'll lose it, she harasses me and I get scared."

"Be careful. Do you like it?"

"No."

"Why?"

There was a long, embarrassed pause.

"You don't know?"

"No."

"Not even Tonino told you?"

"No."

"My father stole it from my grandmother, my mother's mother, who at the time was very sick, to give to Vittoria's mother."

"Stole it? Your father, Enzo?"

"Yes, he took it secretly."

"And Vittoria knows?"

"Of course she knows."

"And your mother?"

"She told me."

I thought of the photo of Enzo in the kitchen, the one in the policeman's uniform. He watched over the two women even in death, armed with his pistol. He kept them together in the cult of his image, wife and lover. What power men have, even the most small-minded, even over courageous and violent women like my aunt. I said, unable

417

to contain my sarcasm:

"Your father stole the bracelet from his dying mother-in-law to give it as a present to the healthy mother of his lover."

"You got it, that's right. There's never been money in my house, and he was a man who liked to make a good impression on those he still didn't know, but he didn't hesitate to harm those whose affection he'd already won. My mother suffered a lot because of him."

I said without thinking:

"Vittoria, too."

But right afterward I felt the full truth, the full weight of those two words, and it seemed to me that I understood why Vittoria had that ambiguous attitude toward the bracelet. Formally she wanted it, but in substance she tended to get rid of it. Formally, it was her mother's, but in substance it wasn't. Formally, it was supposed to be a present for some celebration or other for his new mother-in-law, but in substance Enzo had stolen it from his old mother-in-law, who was dying. Ultimately, that piece of jewelry was the proof that my father wasn't all wrong about his sister's lover. And, more generally, it was evidence that the incomparable idyll recounted by my aunt must have been anything but an idyll.

Giuliana said with scorn:

"Vittoria doesn't suffer, Giannì, Vittoria makes people suffer. For me this bracelet is a permanent sign of bad times and pain. It makes me anxious, it brings bad luck."

"Objects aren't guilty, I like it."

Giuliana assumed an expression of ironic unease:

"I would have bet on it, Roberto likes it, too."

I helped her hook it on her wrist, the train was coming into the station.

14.

I recognized Roberto even before Giuliana did, he was standing in the crowd on the platform. I raised a hand so that he would pick us out in the parade of travelers, and he immediately raised his. Giuliana hurried, dragging her suitcase, Roberto went toward her. They embraced as if they wanted to crush each other, mixing fragments of their bodies, but they exchanged only a light kiss on the mouth. Afterward he took my hand in his and thanked me for coming with Giuliana: without you, he said, who knows when we would have seen each other again. Then he took from his fiancée the big suitcase and the bag, I followed a few steps

419

behind with my paltry suitcase.

He's a normal person, I thought, or maybe one of his many good qualities is that he knows how to be normal. In the bar in Piazza Amedeo, and the other times I'd met him, I'd felt I was dealing with a professor of great depth who was concerned with I wasn't sure what, exactly, but certainly complex branches of knowledge. Now I saw his hip pressed to Giuliana's, the way he kept leaning over to kiss her, and he was an ordinary fiancé of twenty-five such as you'd see on the street, in a movie, on television.

As we were about to descend a grand pale yellow staircase he wanted to take my suitcase, too, but I prevented him with determination, and so he continued to concern himself affectionately with Giuliana. I didn't know anything about Milan. We rode the metro for at least twenty minutes, and then it was a quarter of an hour's walk to the house. We climbed old dark stone stairs to the fifth floor. I felt proudly silent, alone with my bag, while Giuliana was free of burdens, talkative, and finally happy in every movement.

We came to a landing where there were three doors. Roberto opened the first and led us into an apartment that I liked immediately, despite a faint odor of gas. Unlike the apartment on San Giacomo dei Capri, tidy and chained to my mother's sense of order, here there was an impression of clean disorder. We crossed a hall with piles of books on the floor and entered a large room with unusual old furniture, a desk covered with folders, a table, a faded red couch, overflowing bookshelves, a television set sitting on a plastic cube.

Roberto, speaking mainly to me, apologized, said that even though the concierge tidied up every day, the house was structurally not very welcoming. I tried to say something ironic, I wanted to continue in the bold tone that — I was now sure — he liked. But Giuliana wouldn't let me speak, she said: forget the concierge, I'll take care of it, you'll see how nice it will be, and she threw her arms around his neck, clinging to him with the same energy she had put into the meeting at the station, this time giving him a long kiss. I immediately turned away, as if looking for a place to put my suitcase; a moment later she gave me precise instructions with a proprietary air.

She knew everything about the apartment, she dragged me into a kitchen whose dull colors seemed even duller in the low-watt electric light, checking to see if there was this, or that, criticizing the concierge for some sloppiness that she quickly began to remedy. At the same time, she never stopped talking to Roberto, she talked and talked, asking him about people she called by name — Gigi, Sandro, Nina — each of whom was associated with some problem regarding university life, about which she seemed to be well informed. Once or twice Roberto said: maybe Giovanna is getting bored, I exclaimed no, and she went on talking confidently.

It was a Giuliana different from the one who until that moment I'd thought I knew. She spoke decisively, sometimes even in a peremptory tone, and from everything she said — or alluded to — it was clear that not only did he tell her in detail about his life, about his problems at work, with his research, but he attributed to her the capacity to look after him and sustain him and guide him, as if she really had the necessary skills and wisdom. In other words, Roberto gave her credit and from that credit — I seemed to understand — Giuliana surprisingly, fearlessly, drew the strength to play that part. But then a couple of times he gently, kindly objected, said to her: no, it's not really like that. Then Giuliana broke off, blushed, became aggressive, quickly changed her opinion, trying to show him that she thought exactly as he did. At those moments I recognized her, I felt the suffering in those snags, I thought that if Roberto had abruptly let her know that she was saying one foolish thing after another, that her voice for him was like a nail scratching metal, she would fall down dead on the floor.

Naturally, I wasn't the only one who realized that the situation was fragile. Roberto, when those little cracks appeared, pulled her to him, spoke to her sweetly, kissed her, and I again got absorbed in something that momentarily blotted them out. It was my embarrassment, I think, that made him exclaim: I bet you're hungry, let's go to the café downstairs, they make really good pastries. Ten minutes later, I was eating sweets, drinking coffee, beginning to feel curious about the unknown city. I said so, and Roberto took us on a tour through the center. He knew everything about Milan and made an effort to show us the important monuments, recounting their history a little pedantically. We walked from a church to a courtyard to a square to a museum, without stopping, as if it were our last occasion to see the city before its destruction. Although Giuliana often mentioned that she hadn't slept a wink on the train and was tired, she appeared very interested, and I don't think she was pretending. She had a real desire to learn, added to a sort of sense of duty, as if her role as fiancée of a young professor imposed on her an always attentive gaze, an always receptive ear. I, however, felt divided. I discovered that day the pleasure of converting an unknown place to a precisely known place by adding the name and the history of that street to the name and history of that square, that building. But at the same time I recoiled in irritation. I thought back to instructive walks through Naples with my father, to his permanent display of knowledge and my role of adoring daughter. I wondered, is Roberto nothing but my father as a young man, that is, a trap? I looked at him as we ate a sandwich and drank a beer and he joked and planned a new itinerary. I looked at him as he stood apart with Giuliana, outside, under a big tree and talked about their affairs, she tense, he serene, she weeping a little, he with red ears. I looked at him as he came cheerfully toward me, his long arms raised, he had just heard about my birthday. I dismissed the thought that he was like my father, there was an enormous distance. It was I, rather, who felt I was playing the role of listening daughter, and I didn't like that feeling, I wanted to be a woman, a beloved woman.

Our tour continued. I listened to Roberto and wondered why am I here, tailing him and Giuliana, what am I doing with them. Sometimes I lingered purposely on details of a fresco to which he hadn't, I don't know, given the right importance. I did it as if to upset that walk, and Giuliana turned and whispered: Giannì, what are you doing, come on, you'll get lost. Oh, if I really could get lost, I thought at one point, leave myself somewhere, like an umbrella, and never have anything more to do with me. But if Roberto called to me, waited for me, repeated to me what he had already told Giuliana, praised two or three of my observations with remarks like: yes, it's true, I hadn't thought of that, then immediately I was fine and got excited. How wonderful to travel, how wonderful to know someone who knows everything, whose intelligence and looks and kindness are extraordinary, and who explains to you the value of what by yourself you wouldn't be able to appreciate.

15.

Things became complicated when we got home in the late afternoon. Roberto found a message on the answering machine in which a cheerful female voice reminded him of an obligation he had that evening. Giuliana was tired, she heard that voice, I saw that she was really annoyed. Roberto instead reproached himself for having forgotten the date, it was a dinner fixed long ago with what he called his work group, all people Giuliana already knew. In fact, she immediately remembered them, erased disappointment from her face, and displayed great enthusiasm. But now I knew her a little, I could tell when something made her happy and when it made her anxious. That dinner was ruining her day.

"I'll take a walk around," I said.

"Why," said Roberto, "you should come with us, they're nice people, you'll like them."

I resisted, I really didn't want to go. I knew that I would either be sullenly silent or become aggressive. Unexpectedly Giuliana intervened supporting me.

"She's right," she said, "she doesn't know anyone, she'll be bored."

But he looked at me insistently, as if I were a written page whose meaning wouldn't reveal itself. He said:

"You seem like a person who always thinks she'll be bored but then never is."

It was a remark whose quality surprised

me. He didn't say it casually but in the tone I had heard only once, in church: the warm, full tone of conviction that dazzled me, as if he knew more of me than I did. The equilibrium that had somehow or other lasted until that moment exploded. I really do get bored — I thought angrily — you don't know how bored I get, you don't know how bored I've been, how bored I am now. I was wrong to come here for you, I've only piled disorder on disorder, in spite of your kindness, your openness. And yet, just as that rage was ransacking me inside, everything changed. I wanted him to make no mistake. In some corner of my brain the idea was taking shape that Roberto had the power to clarify, and I wished that from that moment he — only he — would point out to me what I wasn't and what I was. Giuliana almost whispered:

"She's been too nice, let's not make her do things she doesn't want to."

But I interrupted her.

"No, no, it's O.K., I'll come," I said, but unenthusiastically, doing nothing to diminish the impression that I was going with them just so as not to create difficulties.

She looked bewildered and hurried off to wash her hair. While she was drying it, unhappy with the way it was turning out, while she was putting on her makeup, while she was wavering between a red dress or a brown skirt with a green shirt, while she was undecided between earrings and necklace or the bracelet, too, and questioned me, in search of reassurance, she said repeatedly: you don't have to go, stay here since you can, I have to go, but I'd gladly stay with you, it's all people from the university who talk, talk, talk, and you can't imagine how full of themselves they are. That's how she summed up what was scaring her just then, and she thought it scared me, too. But I had known that self-important babble of the cultivated since I was a child, that was all Mariano and my father and their friends ever did. Now, of course, I hated it, but it wasn't the talk in itself that intimidated me. So I said to her: don't worry, I'm coming as your friend, I'll keep you company.

We were in a small restaurant where the owner, gray-haired, tall, very thin, welcomed Roberto with respectful amiability. It's all ready, he said, indicating in a complicit tone a small room where a long table could be glimpsed, with a number of guests sitting and talking animatedly. So many people, I thought, and my shabby appearance made me uneasy; I didn't think of myself as having charms that would smooth relationships with strangers. Also, at first glance the girls all seemed young, pretty, cultured feminine types like Angela, who knew how to shine with soft poses, silky voices. The men were a minority, two or three, contemporaries of Roberto's or slightly older. Their gazes focused on Giuliana, beautiful, cordial, and when Roberto introduced me, their attention lasted only a few seconds, I was too frumpy.

We sat down, and I ended up a long way from Roberto and Giuliana, who had found seats next to each other. I perceived immediately that none of those young people were there for the pleasure of being together. Behind the good manners were tensions, enmities, and if they could have they would surely have spent the evening in another way. But already while Roberto was exchanging the first remarks, an atmosphere was created similar to what I had seen among the parishioners in the church in Pascone. Roberto's body — voice, gestures, gaze — began to act as a glue, and, seeing him among those people who loved him as I did, and loved each other only because they loved him, I, too, suddenly felt part of an inevitable bonding. What a voice he had, what eyes: Roberto, now, among a lot of people, seemed much more than what he had been with Giuliana, with me, in the hours of touring Milan. He became what he had been when he addressed that remark to me ("You seem like a person who always thinks she'll be bored but then never is"), and I had to admit that it hadn't been a privilege of mine, he had the gift of showing others more than they were able to see.

People ate, laughed, discussed, interrupted one another. They had grand themes at heart, of which I understood very little. Today I can say only that they talked about injustice, hunger, poverty, what to do in the face of the ferocity of the unjust person who takes for himself, taking away from others, what is the right way to behave. I could sum up more or less like this the discussion that rebounded in a lightly serious way from one end of the table to the other. Does one resort to the law? And if the law fosters injustice? And if the law itself is injustice, if the violence of the state safeguards it? Eyes shone with tension, the always erudite words sounded sincerely passionate. They debated a lot, knowledgeably, eating and drinking, and it struck me that the girls were even more passionate than the boys. I was familiar with the argumentative voices that came from my father's study, my sarcastic discussions with Angela, the fake passion that I sometimes displayed at school to please the teachers when they advocated sentiments that they themselves didn't feel. Whereas those girls, who probably taught or would teach at the university, were true and combative and compassionate. They cited groups or associations that I had never heard of, some had just returned from distant countries and recounted horrors they knew through direct experience. A dark-haired young woman named Michela immediately stood out for her vibrant words, she sat right opposite Roberto, and was naturally the Michela who obsessed Giuliana. She brought up an episode of abuse that had happened maybe before her eyes, I don't remember where, or maybe I don't feel like remembering. It was an episode so terrible that at one point she had to stop speaking to keep from crying. Giuliana up till then had been silent, she ate listlessly, her face dulled by the weariness of the evening and the day of touring. But when Michela's long tirade began, she dropped her fork on the plate and stared at her.

The girl — a coarse face, a bright gaze behind large eyeglasses with thin frames, very red, full lips — had begun speaking to the table but now was addressing only Roberto. It wasn't an anomaly, they all tended to do that, they unconsciously recognized in him the role of collector of individual speeches that, synthesized by his voice, became the conviction of all. But while the others every so often remembered the listeners, Michela appeared to care only about his attention, and the more she talked, the more Giuliana — I saw — withered. It was as if her face were wasting away until it was only transparent skin, displaying in advance what it would become when illness and old age arrived to ruin it. What was crippling her at that moment? Jealousy probably. Or maybe not, Michela wasn't doing anything that could make her jealous, no gesture, such as Angela had laid out for me, illustrating the strategy of seduction. Probably Giuliana was simply disfigured by the suffering caused by the quality of Michela's voice, the efficacy of her phrases, the ability with which she could pose questions alternating examples with generalizations. When her face seemed to be utterly drained of life, a harsh, aggressive voice came out, with a strong dialectal coloring:

"If you stabbed him, you'd resolve everything."

I knew right away that the words were out

of place in that climate and I'm sure Giuliana knew it, too. But I'm equally certain
that she said those words because they were
the only ones that came to mind to cleanly
cut the long thread of Michela's words.
There was silence, Giuliana realized she'd
said the wrong thing, and her eyes turned
glassy, as if she were about to faint. She
tried to take her distance from herself by
laughing nervously, she said to Roberto,
now in a more controlled Italian:

"Or at least that's what they'd do where
you and I come from, no?"

Roberto pulled her to him, circling her
shoulders, kissed her on the forehead, and
began a speech that step by step erased the
trivializing effect of his fiancée's words.
They'd do that not only where we come
from, he said, but everywhere, because it's
the easiest answer. But naturally he wasn't
in favor of easy answers, none of the young
people at that table were. And Giuliana, too,
was quick to say, again almost in dialect,
that she was against a violent response to
violence, but she got all tangled up — I felt
great pity for her — and immediately
stopped talking, they were all listening to
Roberto. To injustice, he said, you must give
a firm, stubborn response: you do this to
your neighbor and I tell you you mustn't do

it and if you continue to do it I will continue to oppose it, and if you crush me with your force I will rise up again, or if I can't rise up anymore others will, and still others. He stared at the table as he spoke, and then suddenly he looked up, he looked them in the face one by one with enchanting eyes.

In the end everyone was convinced that that was the right reaction, Giuliana herself, me. But Michela — and I perceived the surprise among the group — flared up, exasperated, she exclaimed that you can't respond to an unjust force with weakness. Silence: exasperation, even slight exasperation, was not envisaged at that table. I looked at Giuliana, she was staring angrily at Michela, I was afraid she would lash out at her again, even though the few words of her presumed rival seemed close to her thesis of stabbing. But Roberto was already responding: the just can only be weak, they have courage without force. And suddenly a few lines I'd read recently came to mind, I mixed them up with others, I said softly, almost without intending to: they have the weakness of the fool who stops offering meat and fat to God, who is more than sated, and gives it to his neighbor, to the widow, the orphan, the stranger. That's all that came out of my mouth, in a calm, even slightly ironic tone. And since my words were immediately taken up approvingly by Roberto, using and developing the metaphor of foolishness, everyone liked them, except perhaps Michela. She gave me an interested glance, and then for no reason Giuliana laughed, a noisy laugh.

"What is there to laugh about?" Michela asked coldly.

"I can't laugh?"

"Yes, let's laugh," Roberto interrupted, using the first person plural even though he hadn't laughed, "because today we have something to celebrate, Giovanna is sixteen."

At that moment the lights went out in the room, and a waiter appeared carrying a big cake with sixteen little candle flames wavering on the whiteness of the icing.

16.

It was a wonderful birthday, I felt surrounded by kindness and cordiality. But after a while Giuliana said she was very tired, and we went home. It struck me that, once in the apartment, she didn't go back to the proprietary tones of the morning, she was spellbound, looking at the darkness outside the living-room window, and let Roberto do everything. He was very thoughtful, gave us clean towels, made a funny speech about how uncomfortable the sofa was and how hard to open. The concierge is the only person who can do it easily, he said, and he had trouble himself, he tried and tried until a double bed all made, with white sheets, spilled out into the middle of the room. I touched the sheets, said: it's cool, do you have a blanket? He nodded yes, disappeared into the bedroom.

I said to Giuliana:

"Which side do you sleep on?"

Giuliana left the darkness outside the window and said:

"I'll sleep with Roberto, so you'll be comfortable."

I was sure that would happen, but just the same I insisted:

"Vittoria made me swear we'd sleep together."

"She made Tonino swear, too, but he didn't keep the oath. You want to keep it?"

"No."

"I love you," she said kissing me on the cheek without enthusiasm, while Roberto returned with a blanket and a pillow. Then it was Giuliana who disappeared into the bedroom, and, in case I woke up first and wanted to make breakfast, he showed me where the coffee, biscotti, cups were. The boiler gave off a violent odor of gas, I said:

"There's a leak, will we die?"

"No, I don't think so, the window frames are terrible."

"I'd be sorry to die at sixteen."

"I've lived here for seven years and I'm not dead."

"Who can assure me of that?"

He smiled, and said:

"No one. I'm glad you're here. Good night."

Those were the only words we exchanged by ourselves. He joined Giuliana in the bedroom, closed the door.

I opened my suitcase to get my pajamas, I heard Giuliana crying, he whispered something, she whispered. Then they began to laugh, first Giuliana, then Roberto. I went to the bathroom hoping they would go to sleep right away, I got undressed, brushed my teeth. Door opening, door closing, footsteps. Giuliana knocked, asked: can I come in. I let her in, she had over her arm a blue nightgown with white lace, she asked if I liked it, I praised it. She ran water in the bidet and began to undress. I left in a hurry (how stupid could I be, why did I get myself into this situation), the couch squeaked when I got under the covers. Giuliana crossed the room again in the nightgown that clung to her graceful body. She had nothing on underneath, her breasts were small but firm, shapely. Good night, she said, I answered good night. I turned out the light, put my head under the pillow, pressed it against my ears. What do I know about sex, everything and nothing: what I've read in books, the pleasure of masturbation, Angela's mouth and body, Corrado's genitals. For the first time, I felt my virginity as a humiliation. What I don't want is to imagine Giuliana's pleasure, feel myself in her place. I'm not her. I'm here and not in that room, I don't want him to kiss me and touch me and penetrate me as Vittoria told me Enzo did, I'm a friend of them both. Yet I was sweating under the covers, my hair was wet, I couldn't breathe, I pushed the pillow off my head. How yielding and sticky the flesh is, I tried to feel myself as just a skeleton, one by one I classified the noises in the house: wood creaking, refrigerator humming, small clicks perhaps from the boiler, woodworms in the desk. Not a sound came from the bedroom, not a squeaking of springs, not a sigh. Maybe they had confessed to being tired and were already asleep. Maybe they had decided by gestures not to use the bed, in order to avoid any noise. Maybe they were standing up. Maybe they didn't sigh, didn't groan, out of discretion. I imagined the joining of their bodies in positions that I had seen only drawn or painted, but as soon as I became aware of those images I banished them. Maybe they didn't really desire each other, they had wasted the whole day on tourist outings and chat. That was it, no passion, I doubted that one could make love in a silence so absolute: I would have laughed, would have uttered intense words. The bedroom door opened cautiously, I saw Giuliana's dark silhouette cross the room on tiptoe, heard her shut herself in the bathroom again. The water was running. I cried for a while, I fell asleep.

17.

An ambulance siren woke me. It was four in the morning, I struggled to remember where I was, and when I did I immediately thought: I'll be unhappy my whole life. I lay in bed awake until daylight, organizing in detail the unhappiness that awaited me. I had to stay near Roberto discreetly, I had to make myself loved. I had to learn more and more of the things that were important to him. I had to get a job that wasn't too distant from his, teach in the university,

439

maybe in Milan if Giuliana won, in Naples if my aunt won. I had to act so that the relationship of that couple lasted forever, patch up the holes myself, help them bring up their children. In other words I decided conclusively that I would live on their periphery, content with their crumbs. Then, without intending to, I fell asleep again.

I jumped up at nine, the house was still silent. I went to the bathroom, avoided looking at myself in the mirror, washed, hid myself in the shirt I'd worn the day before. Since muffled voices seemed to be coming from the bedroom, I explored the kitchen, set the table for three, got the moka ready. But the level of the sound coming from the other room didn't rise, the door didn't open, neither of the two peeked out. Only, after a while, I thought I heard Giuliana repress a laugh or maybe a sigh. That caused me such suffering that I decided — and maybe it wasn't a decision but, rather, an act of impatience — to knock on the door, with my knuckles, without hesitation.

Absolute silence. I knocked again, a demanding rap.

"Yes?" said Roberto.

I asked in a jolly tone:

"Shall I bring you coffee? It's ready."

"We're coming," said Roberto, but Giuliana exclaimed, at the same time:

"How nice, yes, thank you."

I heard them laughing because of that divergent simultaneous answer, and even more gaily I promised:

"Five minutes."

I found a tray, arranged on it cups, plates, silverware, bread, biscotti, butter, some strawberry jam that I scraped whitish traces of mold off, and the steaming moka. I did it with a sudden contentment, as if my sole possibility for survival were about to take shape at that moment. And the only thing that scared me was the abrupt tilt of the tray as with my free hand I turned the door handle. I was afraid that the moka, everything, would land on the floor, and though that didn't happen my contentment vanished, the tray's precarious equilibrium was transmitted to me. I advanced as if not the tray but I were in danger of landing on the floor.

The room wasn't dark, as I expected. There was light, the blind was rolled up, the window half open. The two were in bed, under a light white blanket. But Roberto had his head against the headboard and an expression of embarrassment — an ordinary male, shoulders too broad, narrow chest — while Giuliana, her shoulders bare, her cheek against his chest with its black hairs, one hand that touched his face as if for a just interrupted caress, was joyful. Seeing her like that swept away all my plans. Being near them didn't ease my unhappy situation but transformed me into the audience of their happiness: something that — it seemed to me at that moment — Giuliana in particular was hoping for. In the few minutes I had taken to get the tray ready they could have dressed, but she must have prevented him, she had slipped away naked, opened the window to change the air, and gone back to bed to assume the pose of the young woman after a night of love, close to him under the sheets, one leg over his two. No, no, my idea of becoming a sort of aunt always ready to rush in, give a hand, wasn't the worst of poisons. The spectacle of them — for Giuliana it must have been just that: a displaying of herself as if in a movie, a way, probably not at all malicious, of giving a form to her well-being, capitalizing on my entrance, so that I would see her and, seeing her, fix what was momentary, become its witness — that spectacle felt unbearably cruel. And yet I stayed there, sitting on the edge of the bed, prudently on Giuliana's side, thanking them yet again for the party of the day before, sipping coffee with the two of them, who had released themselves from their embrace, she barely covering herself with the sheet, he finally putting on a shirt, which I myself, at Giuliana's request, had handed him.

"How nice you are, Giannì, I won't ever forget this morning," she exclaimed and wanted to give me a hug, dangerously unsettling the tray that was resting on a pillow. Roberto, instead, said with detachment, after a sip of coffee, looking at me as if I were a painting he'd been summoned to give an opinion of:

"You're very beautiful."

18.

On the way home Giuliana did what she hadn't done on the way there. While the train moved at a wearyingly slow speed, she kept me in the corridor, between the compartment and the window, talking incessantly.

Roberto had come with us to the station, and the farewell between them had been painful; they had kissed and kissed some more and clung tightly to each other. I'd been unable to avoid looking at them, they were a couple pleasing to the eye, without a doubt he loved her and she couldn't do

443

without that love. But the phrase — *you're very beautiful* — wouldn't leave my mind: what a jolt to the heart it had been. My response had been rude, discordant, emotion mangling the vowels: don't make fun of me. And Giuliana had immediately added, serious: it's true, Giannì, you're really beautiful. I muttered: I'm like Vittoria, but they both exclaimed indignantly, he laughing, she striking the air with her hand: Vittoria, what are you talking about, are you crazy? Then, stupidly, I burst into tears. A brief cry, a few seconds, like a cough immediately choked off, which had, however, upset them. He said softly: what's the matter, calm down, what did we do wrong? And I recovered instantly, ashamed of myself, but that compliment remained intact in my mind, and was still there, in the station, at the track, while I settled the bags in the compartment and they talked through the window up to the last minute.

The train left, we stayed in the corridor. I said, to set a tone, to drive out Roberto's voice (you're very beautiful), to console Giuliana: how he loves you, it must be wonderful to be loved like that. And she, suddenly gripped by despair, began to vent, half in Italian, half in dialect, and never stopped. We were very close — hips touch-

444

ing, she often took my arm, my hand — but in reality separate: I who continued to hear Roberto as he said those three words to me (and I took pleasure in them, they seemed to me the secret magic formula of a resurrection), she who needed to relate in detail what made her suffer. She went on and on, grimacing with anger, with anguish, and I listened to her attentively, I encouraged her to keep talking. But while she suffered, widening her eyes, touching her hair obsessively, wrapping a lock around index and middle fingers and then abruptly freeing the fingers as if they were snakes, I was happy, and always on the point of interrupting her to ask abruptly: do you think Roberto was serious when he said I'm very beautiful?

Giuliana's monologue was long. Yes, she said, he loves me, but I love him much much more, because he changed my life, he unexpectedly took me away from the place where I was fated to stay and put me at his side, and now that's the only place I can be, you understand, if he changes his mind and sends me away, I wouldn't know how to be me anymore, I don't even know who I am; while he — he's always known who he is, he knew it as a child, I remember, you can't imagine what would happen if he just opened his mouth, you've seen the lawyer

Sargente's son, Rosario is mean, no one can touch Rosario, and Roberto, instead, charmed him, the way you do with snakes, and pacified him, if you've never seen these things you don't know what Roberto is, I've seen a lot of them, and not only with someone like Rosario, who's a jerk, think of last night, last night they were all professors, they were the absolute best, and yet you saw, they're there for him, they're so intelligent, so polite only to please him, because if he weren't there they'd tear each other apart, you should hear them as soon as Roberto looks away, jealousy, malice, bad words, obscenities; so, Giannì, there's no equality between him and me, if I were to die now, on this train, oh yes, Roberto surely would be sorry, Roberto would suffer, but then he'd go on being what he is, while I, I won't say if he dies — I can't even think of that — but if he leaves me — you saw how all the women look at him, you saw how pretty, intelligent they are, how much they know — if he leaves me because one of them takes him — Michela, for example, who's there only to talk to him, she doesn't give a damn about the others, she's someone important, who knows what she'll become, and just for that she wants him, because with him she could even become, I don't know, president of the republic — if Michela takes the place I have now, Gianni, I'll kill myself, I'd have to kill myself, because even if I went on living, my life would be nothing.

She talked like this more or less for hours, obsessively, opening her eyes wide, twisting her mouth. I listened to the unending murmur in the deserted corridor of the train for that whole time, and, I have to admit, I felt increasingly sorry for her but also a certain admiration. I considered her an adult, I was a girl. Certainly I wouldn't have been capable of such ruthless lucidity, at the most critical moments I knew how to hide from myself. But she didn't close her eyes, she didn't stop up her ears, she outlined her situation with precision. Still, I didn't do much to console her, I merely repeated every so often a concept that I wanted to acknowledge myself. Roberto, I said, has lived in Milan for a long time, he's met countless girls like that Michela, and you're right, it's obvious that they're all charmed by him, but it's with you he wants to live, because you're absolutely different from the others, so you shouldn't change, you should stay what you are, that's the only way he'll love you forever.

That was it, a little speech uttered with

slightly artificial distress. Otherwise, I slipped into a silent monologue of my own that developed parallel to hers. I'm not, I thought, beautiful, I never will be. Roberto perceived that I felt ugly and lost, and he wanted to console me with a comforting lie, that's probably the reason he said that. But what if he had really seen some beauty in me that I don't know how to see, if he really liked me? Of course, he said you're very beautiful in Giuliana's presence, so without innuendo. And Giuliana agreed, she didn't see any innuendo, either. But if on the other hand the innuendo were well hidden in the words, escaping even him? And if now, at this moment, it emerged, and Roberto, thinking back, were asking himself: why did I say that, what was my intention? Yes, what was his intention? I have to get to the bottom of this, it's important. I have his number, I'll call him, I'll say: do you really think I'm very beautiful? Be careful what you say: my face has already changed, and because of my father I turned ugly; don't you, too, play with changing me, making me become beautiful. I'm tired of being exposed to other people's words. I need to know what I really am and what sort of person I can be, help me. There, that's the sort of speech he should like. But what's

448

the purpose of it? What do I really want from him, just now, while this girl is showering me with her suffering? Do I want him to assure me that I'm pretty, prettier than anyone, even his fiancée? Do I want that? Or more, still more?

Giuliana was grateful for my patient listening. She took my hand, she was moved, she praised me — oh how smart you were, you gave Michela a punch in the face with half a sentence, Giannì, you have to help me, you have to help me always, if I have a daughter I'll name her for you, she has to be intelligent like you — and she wanted me to swear to support her in every way. I swore, but it wasn't enough, she imposed a real pact: at least until she was married and had gone to live in Milan, I had to make sure that she didn't lose her head and convince herself of things that weren't true.

I agreed, and she seemed calmer; we decided to stretch out in the berths. I fell asleep right away, but a few kilometers from Naples, when it was day, I felt someone shaking me. I came out of my half sleep and saw her holding out her wrist with frightened eyes:

"My God, Giannì, I don't have the bracelet."

19.

I got out of the berth:

"How is that possible?"

"I don't know, I don't know where I put it."

She dug in her purse, in her suitcase, and couldn't find it. I tried to calm her:

"You must have left it at Roberto's house."

"No, I had it here, in the pocket of my purse."

"Sure?"

"I'm not sure of anything."

"Did you have it in the pizzeria?"

"I remember that I wanted to put it on but maybe I didn't."

"I think you had it."

We went on like that until the train entered the station. Her nervousness infected me. I began to be afraid that the clasp had broken and she had lost it, or that it had been stolen in the metro or even that it had been taken off her while she was sleeping by one of the other passengers in the compartment. We both knew Vittoria's fury and took it for granted that if we returned without the bracelet she would give us a bad time.

Once we got off the train, Giuliana went to a telephone, dialed Roberto's number. While the phone rang she combed her hair with her fingers, muttering under her breath: he's not answering. She stared at me, she repeated: he's not answering. After a few seconds, she said in dialect, with her frenzy of self-destruction breaking down the wall between suitable and unsuitable words: he must be fucking Michela and doesn't want to interrupt. But finally Roberto answered, and she switched right away to an affectionate tone of voice, muffling her anguish but continuing to twirl her hair. She told him about the bracelet, she was silent for a moment, murmured docilely: O.K., I'll call you in five minutes. She hung up, she said in a rage: he has to finish fucking. Stop it, I said, irritated, calm down. She nodded, ashamed of herself, she apologized, saying Roberto didn't know anything about the bracelet, now he was going to look. I stayed with the bags, she began walking back and forth, still nervous, aggressive with the men who looked at her or made obscene remarks.

"Is it five minutes?" she almost yelled at me.

"It's ten."

"Couldn't you have told me?"

She hurried to put the token in the phone. Roberto answered right away, she listened, exclaimed: thank goodness. Roberto's voice even reached me, but indistinct. While he talked, Giuliana whispered to me in relief: he found it, I left it in the kitchen. She turned her back to say some words of love, but I heard them just the same. She hung up, seemed pleased, but it didn't last, she muttered: how can I know for sure that as soon as I leave Michela doesn't jump in his bed? She stopped beside the stairs that led to the metro, we would say goodbye there, we were going in opposite directions, but she said:

"Wait a minute, I don't want to go home, I don't want to hear Vittoria's interrogation."

"Don't answer."

"She'll torment me anyway because I don't have that fucking bracelet."

"You're too anxious, you can't live like that."

"I'm always anxious about something. You want to know what occurred to me now, just while I'm talking to you?"

"Tell me."

"If Michela goes to Roberto's house? If she sees the bracelet? If she takes it?"

"Apart from the fact that Roberto wouldn't let her, you know how many bracelets Michela can afford? What do you think she cares about yours, you don't even like it."

She stared at me, twisted a lock of hair around her fingers, and said:

"But Roberto likes it, and everything Roberto likes she likes."

She was about to let go of the hair with that mechanical gesture she'd been performing for hours, but there was no need, the hair was still around her fingers. She looked at it with an expression of horror. She murmured:

"What's happening?"

"You're so agitated you tore your hair out."

She looked at the lock, she had turned all red.

"I didn't tear it out, it came out by itself."

She grabbed another lock, she said:

"Look."

"Don't pull."

She pulled and another lock of long hair remained between her fingers, the blood that had rushed to her face drained and she became extremely pale.

"Am I dying, Giannì, am I dying?"

"You don't die if some hair falls out."

I tried to soothe her, but she was as if overwhelmed by all the anguish she'd felt from childhood till now: father, mother, Vittoria, the incomprehensible shouting of the adults around her, and now Roberto and that anguish of not deserving him and losing him. She wanted to show me her head, she said: move my hair aside, look. I did, there was a small patch of white scalp, an insignificant empty spot in the middle of her head. I went down with her, to her track.

"Don't say anything to Vittoria about the bracelet," I advised her, "just tell her about our tour of Milan."

"And if she asks me?"

"Stall for time."

"And if she wants to see it right away?"

"Tell her you lent it to me. Meanwhile get some rest."

I managed to persuade her to get on the train for Gianturco.

20.

I'm still fascinated by how our brain elaborates strategies and carries them out without revealing them. To say that it's a matter of the unconscious seems to me approximate, maybe even hypocritical. I knew clearly that I wanted to go back to Milan immediately, at all costs, I knew it with my whole self, but I didn't say it to myself. And without ever confessing the purpose of my new, tiring journey I feigned its necessity, its urgency, I claimed noble reasons for departing an hour after I arrived: to relieve Giuliana's state of anguish by recovering the bracelet; to say to her fiancé what she was silent about, which was that right away, before it was too late, he had to marry her and take her away from Pascone, without bothering about moral or social debts or other nonsense; to protect my adult friend, deflecting my aunt's angers onto me, still a girl.

So it was that I bought a new ticket and called my mother, informing her, without acknowledging her complaint in response, that I would be staying another day in Milan. The train was about to leave when I realized that I hadn't told Roberto. I called him as if what, with another convenient expression, we call fate were being fulfilled. He answered right away, and frankly I don't know what we said, but I'd like to report that it went like this:

"Giuliana urgently needs the bracelet, I'm about to leave."

"I'm sorry, you must be tired."

"It doesn't matter, I'm glad to come back."

"What time do you arrive?"

"At 22:08."

"I'll come to meet you."

"I'll wait for you."

But it's a pretend dialogue, meant to crudely outline a sort of tacit accord between Roberto and me: you told me I'm very beautiful, and so, as soon as I got off one train, look, though I'm dead tired, I'm returning on another, with the excuse of that magic bracelet, which — you know better than I do — is magic only because of the chance it offers us to sleep together tonight, in the same bed I saw you in yesterday morning with Giuliana. I suspect, however, that there was no real dialogue, but only a blunt statement of the sort I was in the habit of making at the time.

"Giuliana needs the bracelet urgently. I'm about to get on the train, I'll be arriving in Milan tonight."

Maybe he said something, maybe not.

21.

I was so tired that in spite of the crowded compartment, the chatter, the slammed doors, the loudspeaker announcements, the long whistles, the jangling, I slept for hours. The problems began when I woke up. I immediately touched my head, convinced that I was bald, I must have had a bad dream.

But whatever I had dreamed had vanished, leaving only the impression that my hair was coming out in clumps, more than Giuliana's, not my real hair but the hair my father had praised when I was a child.

I kept my eyes closed, half asleep. Giuliana's extreme physical closeness seemed to have infected me. Her desperation was now mine, too, she must have transmitted it to me, my body was wearing out the way hers had. Frightened, I forced myself to wake up completely, but Giuliana with her torments stayed fixed in my mind just as I was traveling toward her fiancé.

I was irritated, I couldn't bear my fellow passengers, I went out into the corridor. I tried to console myself with quotations on the power of love, which, even if you wanted to, are impossible to avoid. They were lines of poetry, sentences from novels, words read in books I had liked and transcribed in my notebooks. But Giuliana wouldn't fade, especially that gesture that left locks of hair in her hand, a part of herself that came off almost gently. Without any obvious connection I said to myself: even if I don't have the face of Vittoria yet, soon that face will lay itself on my bones and never go away.

It was an ugly moment, maybe the worst of those ugly years. I was standing in a cor-

457

ridor identical to the one where I had spent much of the previous night listening to Giuliana, who, to be sure of my attention, took my hand, pulled my arm, continuously jostled my body with hers. The sun was setting, the bluish countryside was pierced by the rumble of the moving train, another night was descending. Suddenly I was able to say to myself clearly that I didn't have noble intentions, I wasn't making that new journey to recover the bracelet, I didn't intend to help Giuliana. I was going to betray her, I was going to take the man she loved. I, much sneakier than Michela, intended to drive her out of the place that Roberto had offered her at his side and destroy her life. I felt authorized to do it because a young man who seemed to me extraordinary, more extraordinary than I considered my father when he had let slip that I was starting to get Vittoria's face, had said, on the contrary, that I was beautiful. But now — as the train was about to enter Milan — I had to admit that, just because, proud of that praise, I was going to do what I had in mind, and just because I had no intention of being stopped by anyone, my face could only be a copy of Vittoria's. Betraying Giuliana's trust, I would in fact become like my aunt when she destroyed

Margherita's life, and, why not, like her brother, my father, when he destroyed my mother's. I felt guilty. I was a virgin and that night I wanted to lose my virginity with the only person who had given me, thanks to his enormous authority as a male, a new beauty. It seemed my right, that was how I would enter adulthood. But as I got off the train I was scared, that wasn't the way I wanted to grow up. The beauty that Roberto had recognized in me too closely resembled the beauty of someone who hurts people.

22.

I thought I had understood, on the phone, that he would meet me on the platform as he had Giuliana and me, but I didn't find him there. I waited a little, I phoned. He was sorry, he was convinced that I was coming to his house, he was working on an essay that he had to deliver the next day. I was depressed, but I didn't say anything. I followed his directions, took the metro, got to his house. He greeted me cordially. I hoped he would kiss me on the mouth, he kissed me on the cheeks. He had set the table for dinner, made by the helpful concierge, and we ate. He didn't mention the bracelet, he didn't mention Giuliana, nor did I. He talked as if he needed me to clarify his ideas on the subject he was working on, and I had taken the train again purposely to listen to him. The essay was about compunction. He kept calling it training to prick your conscience, traversing it with needle and thread as if it were a piece of fabric out of which you're making a garment. I listened, he used the voice that had enchanted me. And I was again seduced — I'm in his house, among his books, that is his desk, we're eating together, he's talking to me about his work — I felt I was she who was necessary to him, exactly what I wanted to be.

After dinner he gave me the bracelet, but he did it as if it were toothpaste, a towel, and still made no reference to Giuliana: as if he'd eliminated her from his life. I tried to conduct myself the way he did, but I couldn't do it, I was overwhelmed by the thought of Vittoria's goddaughter. I knew much better than he did what physical and mental condition she was in, far from that beautiful city, far from that apartment, down, down, down on the edge of Naples, in the dreary house with the big photograph of Enzo in uniform. And yet we had been together in that room a few hours before, I had seen her in the bathroom while she dried her hair and masked her distress in the mirror, while she sat beside him in the restaurant, while she clung to him in the bed. Was it possible that now she seemed dead, I was there and she wasn't? Is it so easy — I thought — to die in the life of the people we can't live without? And on the thread of those thoughts, while he was talking about something or other in a sweetly ironic way — I was no longer listening, I caught only some words: sleep, sofa bed, the crushing darkness, staying awake until dawn, and at times Roberto's voice seemed the most beautiful among my father's voices — I said discouraged:

"I'm really tired and scared."

He said:

"You can sleep with me."

My words and his couldn't fit together, they seemed to be two consecutive remarks but they weren't. Spilling out into mine was the madness of that exhausting journey, Giuliana's despair, the fear of making an unforgivable mistake. In his was the end point of an allusive walk around the difficulty of opening the sofa bed. As soon as I realized it, I answered:

"No, I'll be fine here."

And, in demonstration, I curled up on the couch.

"Sure?"

"Yes."

He said:

"Why did you come back?"

"I don't know anymore."

A few seconds passed, he was standing, looking at me from above, sympathetically, I was on the couch, staring at him from below, confused. He didn't lean over me, he didn't caress me, he said nothing but good night and withdrew into his room.

I settled myself on the couch without getting undressed, I didn't want to deprive myself of the armor of my clothes. But soon I had a desire to wait for him to fall asleep, to go and get in his bed with my clothes on, just to be near him. Until I met Roberto I had never felt a need to be penetrated, at most I had felt some curiosity, immediately distanced by the fear of pain in a part of the body so delicate I was afraid that, touching it, I would scratch myself. After seeing him in the church I had been overwhelmed by a desire as violent as it was confused, an excitement that resembled a joyful tension, and that, while it certainly hit my genitals, as if swelling them, then spread out through my whole body. Nor, after we met at Piazza Amedeo and the occasional brief encounters that followed, had I ever imagined that he could enter me; rather, if I reflected on it, the rare times I'd had fantasies of that sort it had seemed to me a vulgar act. Only in Milan, when, the morning before, I had seen him in bed with Giuliana, I had had to admit that, like every man, he, too, had a penis, limp or erect, he put it inside Giuliana like a piston and would have been willing to put it inside me. But even that affirmation hadn't been decisive. Certainly, I had made the new journey with the idea that there would be that penetration, that the erotic scenario vividly drawn by my aunt long ago would concern me. Yet the need that impelled me required something different, and now, in my half sleep, I realized it. In the bed, next to him, I wanted to enjoy his respect, I wanted to discuss compunction, God who is sated while so many of his creatures are dying of hunger and thirst; I wanted to feel that I was much more than a cute or even very beautiful small animal with whom a brilliant male can play a little and distract himself. I fell asleep thinking sorrowfully that that, precisely that, would never happen. Having him inside me would have been easy, he would have penetrated me even now, in sleep, without surprise. He was convinced that I had returned for that type of betrayal and not for betrayals that were much more ferocious.

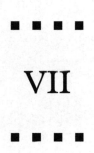

VII

1.

My mother wasn't home when I got there. I didn't eat anything, I got in bed and fell asleep right away. The house in the morning hours seemed empty and silent, I went to the bathroom, went back to bed and fell asleep again. But after a while I woke up with a start, Nella was sitting on the edge of the bed and shaking me.

"Everything all right?"

"Yes."

"That's enough sleeping."

"What time is it?"

"One-twenty."

"I'm really hungry."

She asked me distractedly about Milan, I told her just as distractedly about the places I'd seen, the Duomo, La Scala, the Galleria, the Navigli. Then she said she had good news: the principal had called my father and told him I had been promoted with excellent grades, including a nine in Greek.

"The principal called Papa?"

"Yes."

"The principal is stupid."

My mother smiled, she said:

"Get dressed, Mariano's in the other room."

I went into the kitchen barefoot, disheveled, in my pajamas. Mariano, who was already sitting at the table, jumped up, he wanted to congratulate me on my promotion, hugging and kissing me. He confirmed that I was now grown up, more grown up than the last time he'd seen me, and he said: how pretty you've gotten, Giovanna, one of these nights we'll go to dinner just you and me and have a nice chat. Then he turned to my mother in a tone of fake regret and exclaimed: how can it be that this young lady is a friend of Roberto Matese, one of our most promising young men, and talks to him about who knows how many interesting things, while I who've known her since she was a child can't even have a conversation with her. My mother nodded with an expression of pride, but it was clear that she knew nothing about Roberto, so I deduced it was my father who had spoken to Mariano of Roberto as a good friend of mine.

"I barely know him," I said.

"Is he nice?"

"Very."

"Is it true he's Neapolitan?"

"Yes, but not from the Vomero, he's from down below."

"Still, he's Neapolitan."

"Yes."

"What's he working on?"

"On compunction."

He looked at me in bewilderment.

"Compunction?"

He seemed disappointed and yet curious. Already a remote area of his brain was thinking that perhaps compunction was a subject it was urgent to reflect on.

"Compunction," I confirmed.

Mariano turned to my mother, laughing:

"You understand, Nella? Your daughter says she barely knows Roberto Matese and then we discover that he has talked to her about compunction."

I ate a lot; every so often I touched my hair to see if it was solidly planted in my scalp, I caressed it with my fingers, I pulled it a little. At the end of the meal, I jumped up and said I had to go and wash. Mariano, who until that moment had been stringing together sentence after sentence in the conviction that he was entertaining both me and Nella, assumed a worried expression, he said:

"Do you know about Ida?"

I shook my head no, my mother spoke: "She was failed."

"If you have time," said Mariano, "see her. Angela was promoted and yesterday morning left for Greece with a boyfriend of hers. Ida needs company and comfort, all she does is read and write. That's why she failed: she reads and writes and doesn't study."

I couldn't bear their grieved faces. I said:

"Comfort for what? If you don't turn it into a calamity, you'll see that Ida won't need comfort."

I shut myself in the bathroom, and when I came out the house was absolutely silent. I put my ear to my mother's door, not even a sigh. I opened it a little way, nothing. Nella and Mariano had evidently considered me rude and had gone out without even a cry of bye, Giovanna. So I called Ida, my father answered.

"Good for you," he exclaimed happily, as soon as he heard my voice.

"Good for you: the principal is a spy in your service."

He laughed with satisfaction.

"She's a fine person."

"Of course."

"I heard you were in Milan, a guest of Matese's."

"Who told you?"

He took some time to answer.

"Vittoria."

I exclaimed, in disbelief:

"You phone each other?"

"More: yesterday she came here. Costanza has a friend who needs care night and day and we thought of her."

I murmured:

"You've made peace."

"No, peace with Vittoria is impossible. But the years pass, we get older. And then you, slowly, shrewdly, acted as a bridge, good for you. You're clever, you're like me."

"I'll seduce principals, too?"

"That and much else. How did it go with Matese?"

"Get Mariano to tell you, I already told him."

"Vittoria gave me his address, I want to write to him. These are disastrous times, right-thinking people have to stay in touch. Do you have his phone number?"

"No. Let me talk to Ida."

"Not even a goodbye?"

"Bye, Andrea."

He was silent for a long second.

"Bye."

I heard him call Ida in the same tone of voice in which years before, when I was wanted on the phone, he called me. Ida arrived right away, she said, despondent, almost in a whisper:

"Give me a reason to get out of this house."

"Let's meet in an hour in the Floridiana."

2.

I waited for Ida at the park entrance. She arrived all sweaty, her brown hair tied in a ponytail, much taller than a few months earlier and thin and frail as a blade of grass. She carried a big, overstuffed black bag and was wearing a miniskirt, also black, and a black-and-white striped T-shirt. She had a very pale face that was leaving childhood behind, a full mouth, large round cheekbones. We looked for a bench in the shade. She said she was happy she'd been failed, she wanted to leave school and only write. I reminded her that I had also been failed, but I hadn't been happy about it, I had suffered. She responded, eyes defiant:

"You were ashamed, I'm not ashamed."

I said:

"I was ashamed because my parents were ashamed."

"I don't give a damn about my parents' shame, they have plenty of other things to be ashamed of."

"They're scared. They're afraid we won't be worthy of them."

"I don't want to be worthy, I want to be unworthy, I want to turn out badly."

She told me that to be as unworthy as possible she had overcome her disgust and had met with a man who for a while had worked in the garden of the house in Posillipo, married, with three children.

"How was it?" I asked.

"Horrible. His saliva was like sewer water and he was constantly saying bad words."

"But at least you got it over with."

"Yes, that."

"But now calm down and try to feel good."

"How?"

I proposed that we go to Venice to see Tonino. She replied that she would prefer another place, Rome. I insisted on Venice, I understood that it wasn't the city that was the problem but Tonino. In effect it emerged that Angela had told her about the slap, the rage that had seized that young man and caused him to lose control. He hurt my sister, she said. Yes, I admitted, but I like the effort he makes to behave well.

"He didn't manage with my sister."

"But he was much more committed than she was."

"You want to lose your virginity to Tonino?"

"No."

"Can I think about it and let you know?"

"Yes."

"I'd like to go someplace where I'm comfortable and can write."

"You want to write the story of the gardener?"

"I already did, but I won't read it to you because you're still a virgin and it would stifle any desire."

"Then read me something else."

"Really?"

"Yes."

"There's one I've wanted to read to you for a long time."

She dug in her bag, she pulled out notebooks and loose pages. She chose a notebook with a red cover, found what she was looking for. It was just a few pages, the story of a long unfulfilled desire. Two sisters had a friend who often slept at their house. The friend was more the friend of the older sister than of the younger. The older waited for the younger to fall asleep to switch to the guest's bed and sleep with her. The younger

474

tried to fight off sleep, pained by the idea that the two excluded her, but in the end she gave in. One time, though, she had pretended to be asleep, and so, in silence, in solitude, she had listened to their whispers and their kisses. From then on, she had kept on faking it so she could spy on them, and when, finally, the two older girls fell asleep she always wept a little, because it seemed that nobody loved her.

Ida read without emotion, quickly but pronouncing the words precisely. She never looked up from her notebook, she didn't look me in the face. At the end, she burst out crying, just like the suffering little girl of the story. I looked for a handkerchief, I dried her tears. I kissed her on the mouth even though two mothers were passing nearby, pushing baby carriages and chatting.

3.

The next morning, without even trying to call first, I went straight to Margherita's with the bracelet. I carefully avoided Vittoria's house, first because I wanted to see Giuliana in private and second because, after her sudden and surely temporary reconciliation with my father, I seemed to have no more curiosity about her. But it was a pointless tactic, my aunt opened the door, as if Margherita's house were hers. She greeted me with desolate good humor. Giuliana wasn't there, Margherita had taken her to the doctor, she was tidying the kitchen.

"But come, come in," she said, "how pretty you look, keep me company."

"How's Giuliana?"

"She's got a problem with her hair."

"I know."

"I know you know, and I also know how you helped her and how you were careful about everything. Good, good, good. Both Giuliana and Roberto love you a lot. I also love you. If your father made you like that, it means he's not completely the piece of shit he seems."

"Papa told me you have a new job."

She was standing beside the sink, behind her was the photo of Enzo with the small lighted lamp. For the first time since I'd been seeing her I perceived a slight embarrassment pass through her eyes.

"A very good one, yes."

"Are you going to move to Posillipo."

"Ah, yes."

"I'm glad."

"I'm a little sorry. I have to separate from

Margherita, Corrado, Giuliana, and I've already lost Tonino. Sometimes I think your father did it on purpose, finding me this job. He wants to make me suffer."

I burst out laughing, but immediately recovered myself.

"Maybe," I said.

"You don't believe it?"

"I believe it: you can expect anything from my father."

She gave me a nasty look.

"Don't talk like that about your father or I'll hit you."

"Sorry."

"I'm the one who has to speak badly of him, not you, you're his daughter."

"All right."

"Come here, give me a kiss. I love you, even if sometimes you make me mad."

I kissed her on the cheek, I dug in my purse.

"I brought the bracelet back to Giuliana, it somehow ended up in my purse."

She blocked my hand.

"What do you mean, somehow. Take it, I know you like it."

"Now it's Giuliana's."

"Giuliana doesn't like it, and you do."

"Why did you give it to her, if she doesn't like it?"

She looked at me nervously, she seemed uncertain about the sense of my question.

"Are you jealous?"

"No."

"I gave it to her because I saw that she was anxious. But the bracelet has been yours since you were born."

"But it wasn't a bracelet for a small child. Why didn't you keep it? You could have worn it on Sunday to Mass."

She gave me a mean look, and exclaimed:

"So now you're the one who's supposed to tell me what to do with my mother's bracelet? Keep it and shut up. Giuliana, if you want to know the truth, doesn't need it. She's so full of light that the bracelet or any other piece of jewelry for her is too much. Now she has this problem with her hair, but it's not serious, the doctor will give her a restorative treatment and it will pass. But you don't know how to fix yourself up, Giannì, come here."

She was agitated, as if the kitchen were a close, airless space. She dragged me into Margherita's bedroom, opened the doors of the wardrobe, I appeared in a long mirror. Vittoria ordered me: look at yourself. I looked, but mainly I saw her behind me. She said: you don't dress, my dear, you hide yourself in your clothes. She pulled my skirt

478

up around my waist, she exclaimed: look at those thighs, Heavenly Father, and turn around, yes, now that's an ass. She forced me to turn around, she gave me a violent clap on the underpants, then she made me turn again toward the mirror. Madonna, what a figure — she exclaimed, caressing my hips — you've got to get to know yourself, you've got to make the most of yourself, your beautiful parts you need to let them be seen. Especially your bosom, oh what a bosom, you don't know what a girl would do for a bosom like that. You punish it, you're ashamed of your tits, you lock them up. Look how you should do. And at that point, while I pulled my skirt down, she stuck her hand in the neck of my shirt, first in one cup of my bra, then in the other, and arranged my bosom so that it became a swelling wave, high above the neckline. She was excited: see? We're beautiful, Giannì, beautiful and smart. We were born well made and we shouldn't waste ourselves. I want to see you settled even better than Giuliana, you deserve to rise up to the paradise in the heavens, not like that shit your father who's remained on the earth but acts like he's so important. But remember: this here — she touched me delicately for a fraction of a second between my legs

— this here, I've told you countless times, hold it dear. Weigh the pros and cons before you give it, otherwise you'll go nowhere. Rather, listen to me: if I find out you've wasted it, I'll tell your father, and we'll beat you to death. Now stop — this time she dug in my purse, took the bracelet, clasped it on my wrist — see how nice you look, see what it does for you?

At that moment, in the background of the mirror, Corrado appeared.

"Hi," he said.

Vittoria turned, I did, too. She asked him, fanning herself with one hand because of the heat:

"Giannina's beautiful, isn't she?"

"Very beautiful."

4.

I urged Vittoria over and over to say hello to Giuliana for me, to tell her I loved her and she shouldn't worry about anything, everything would be for the best. Then I started toward the door, expecting Corrado to say: I'll walk a ways with you. But he was silent, dawdling idly. It was I who said to him:

"Corrà, will you walk me to the bus stop?"

"Yes, go with her," Vittoria ordered him,

and he followed me reluctantly down the stairs, along the street, in the blinding sun.

"What's wrong?" I asked.

He shrugged, muttered something I didn't understand, said more clearly that he felt lonely. Tonino had left, Giuliana would get married soon, and Vittoria was about to move to Posillipo, which was another city.

"I'm the idiot of the house, and I have to stay with my mother, who is more of an idiot than me," he said.

"You leave, too."

"Where to? To do what? And anyway I don't want to go. I was born here and I want to stay here."

"So?"

He tried to explain. He said he had always felt protected by Tonino's presence, by Giuliana's, and mainly by Vittoria's. He muttered: Gianni, I'm like my mother, we're two people who put up with everything because they don't know how to do anything and don't count for anything. But — you want to know something? — as soon as Vittoria goes, I'm taking down that photo of Papa in the kitchen, I've never been able to stand it, it scares me, and I already know that my mother will agree."

I encouraged him to do it, but I also told him that he shouldn't kid himself, Vittoria would never leave for good, she would return and return and return, ever more aggrieved and ever more unbearable.

"You should go live with Tonino," I advised him.

"We don't get along."

"Tonino is someone who knows how to deal with life."

"I'm not."

"Maybe I'll go to Venice and say hello."

"Good for you, say hello for me as well and tell him that he thought only of himself and didn't give a fuck about Mamma, Giuliana, or me."

I asked for his brother's address, but he had only the name of the restaurant where he worked. Now that he'd let off some steam he tried to return to his usual mask. He joked, mixing sweet talk with obscene proposals, so that I said laughing: get it through your head, Corrà, nothing else is going to happen between you and me. Then I turned serious and asked for Rosario's phone number. He looked surprised, he wanted to know if I had decided to fuck his friend. I answered that I didn't know and since he would have liked a decisive no, he was concerned, he took the tone of an older brother who wanted to protect me from dangerous choices. He went on like that for a while, and I realized that he really didn't intend to give me the number. Then I threatened him: all right, I'll find it myself, but I'll tell Rosario that you're jealous and wouldn't give it to me. He capitulated immediately, continuing to mutter: I'll tell Vittoria and she'll tell your father, and some nasty things will happen. I smiled, I wanted to give him a kiss on the cheek, I said, as seriously as I could, Corrà, you'd only be doing me a favor, I'm the first to want Vittoria and my father to know, in fact I want you to swear to me that if it happens you'll certainly tell them. Meanwhile the bus had arrived, and I left him there on the sidewalk, confused.

5.

In the hours that followed I realized I had no urgent need to lose my virginity. Sure, Rosario, for some obscure reasons, sort of attracted me, but I didn't call him. Instead, I called Ida to see if she had made up her mind to come to Venice with me, and she said she was ready, she had just told Costanza: her mother was happy not to have her around for a while and had given her a lot of money.

Right afterward I called Tonino at the

number of the restaurant where he worked. At first, he seemed happy about my plan, but when he found out that Ida was coming he let a few seconds pass, then he said he lived in a small room in Mestre, three of us couldn't stay there. I replied: Tonì, we're coming anyway to say hello; then if you want to get together good and if not we'll survive. He changed his tone, swore he was glad, he'd be expecting us.

Since I had already spent on trains all the money my mother had given me for my birthday when I left for Milan, I bugged her until she gave me some more, this time for my promotion. Now we were all ready to go when, on a morning of light rain and pleasant coolness, Rosario called at nine on the dot. Corrado must have talked to him, because the first thing he said was:

"Giannì, they tell me you've finally made up your mind."

"Where are you."

"In the bar down below."

"Down below where?"

"Down below your house. Come down, I'll wait with the umbrella."

I wasn't irritated. Instead, I sensed that everything was getting under way and that ending up pressed against another person on a cool day was better than on a hot day.

"I don't need your umbrella," I answered.

"You mean I should go?"

"No."

"Then come on."

"Where are you taking me?"

"To Via Manzoni."

I didn't comb my hair, didn't put on makeup, did nothing of what Vittoria had advised, except put on her bracelet. I found Rosario in the entranceway with the usual apparent cheerfulness stamped on his face, but when we ended up in the rainy-day traffic, the worst, he threatened and insulted most of the other drivers, who he claimed were incompetent. I was worried, I said:

"If it's not the day, Rosà, take me home again."

"Don't worry, it's the day, but look how this shit drives."

"Calm down."

"What's wrong, I'm too crude for you?"

"No."

"You want to know why I'm nervous?"

"No."

"Giannì, I'm nervous because I've wanted you from the first time I saw you, but I can't figure out if you want me. What do you say, you want me?"

"Yes. But don't hurt me."

"Hurt you? I'll make you feel good."

485

"And you mustn't take too long, I have things to do."

"It'll take the time it takes."

He found a parking spot right in front of his building, which was at least five stories tall.

"What luck," I said while, without even locking the car, he set off quickly toward the entrance.

"It's not luck," he said, "it's that they know this is my place and no one better take it."

"Otherwise?"

"Otherwise I shoot."

"So you're a gangster?"

"So you're a respectable girl who goes to high school?"

I didn't answer, we climbed the stairs in silence to the fifth floor. I thought that in fifty years, if Roberto and I were much closer friends than now, I would tell him about that afternoon so that he could explain it to me. He knew how to find meaning in everything we do, it was his work, and to hear my father and Mariano he was good at it.

Rosario opened the door, the apartment was completely dark. Wait, he said. He didn't turn on the light; moving with assurance, he pulled up the shades one after another. The gray light of the rainy day spread through a big empty room, there wasn't even a chair. I went in and closed the door behind me; I could hear the lashing of rain against the windows and the howling of the wind.

"You can't see anything," I said, looking out the windows.

"We chose a bad day."

"No, it seems like the right day to me."

He came toward me swiftly, grabbed my neck with one hand, and kissed me, pressing hard on my mouth and trying to open it with his tongue. With the other hand he squeezed one of my breasts. I pushed him back with a slight pressure against his chest, he giggled nervously and snorted through his nose. He retreated, leaving only his hand on my breast.

"What's wrong?" he asked.

"Do you have to kiss me?"

"You don't like it?"

"No."

"All girls like it."

"Not me, and I'd also prefer you not to touch my breasts. But if you need to, O.K."

He let go of my breast, muttered:

"I don't need anything."

He lowered his fly, pulled out his penis to show me. I was afraid he'd have something enormous in his pants, but I saw with relief that it wasn't very different from Corrado's, and besides it seemed to have a more elegant shape. He took my hand and said:

"Touch it."

I touched it, it was hot as if he had a fever there. Since all in all it was pleasant to squeeze it, I didn't take my hand away.

"That O.K. with you?"

"Yes."

"Then tell me what you want to do, I don't want to make you unhappy."

"Can I stay dressed?"

"Girls take their clothes off."

"If we can do it without my taking my clothes off you'd do me a favor."

"At least your underpants you'll have to take off."

I let go of his penis, I took off my jeans and underpants.

"O.K.?"

"O.K., but it's not done like that."

"I know, but I'm asking you as a favor."

"Can I at least take off my pants?"

"Yes."

He took off his shoes, pants, and underpants. He had very thin, hairy legs, long, skinny feet, he had to be at least a size 11. He kept on his linen jacket, shirt, tie, and, right below, the erect member that stuck out past legs and bare feet like a quarrelsome tenant who's been disturbed. We were both ugly, lucky there weren't any mirrors.

"Should I lie down on the floor?" I asked.

"What do you mean, there's the bed."

He headed toward an open door, I saw his small ass, the sunken buttocks. There was an unmade bed and nothing else. This time he didn't pull up the blinds, he turned on the light. I asked:

"You're not going to wash?"

"I washed this morning."

"Your hands at least."

"Are you going to wash yours?"

"Me, no."

"Then I won't, either."

"All right, I'll wash mine, too."

"Gianni, see what's happening to me?"

His penis drooped, shrinking.

"If you wash, won't it wake up again?"

"Sure, O.K., here I go."

He disappeared into the bathroom. What a lot of fuss I was making, I would never have imagined behaving like this. He came back with a little thingy dangling between his legs. I gave it a sympathetic look.

"It's cute," I said.

He scowled.

"Just say straight out if you don't want to do anything."

"Yes, I want to, now I'll wash."

"Come here, it's fine like that. You're a lady, I'm sure you wash fifty times a day."

"Can I touch it?"

"Good of you."

I went up to him, I took it gently. Since he had been unexpectedly patient, I would have liked to be expert and touch him in a way that would make him happy, but I didn't know what to do precisely so I just held it in my hand. All it needed was a few seconds to swell up.

"I'll touch you a little, too," he said in a slightly hoarse voice.

"No," I said, "you don't know how to do it and you'll hurt me."

"I know very well how to do it."

"Thanks, Rosà, you're nice, but I'm just not sure."

"Giannì, if I don't touch you a little, then you'll really hurt."

I was tempted to consent, he surely had more practice than me, but I was afraid of his hands, his dirty nails. I made a clear gesture of refusal, I let go of that excrescence, I lay down on the bed with my legs squeezed together. I saw him high above me, bewildered eyes carved into a happy face, he was so well dressed on top and so rudely naked from the waist down. For a

490

fraction of a second I thought of how my parents had prepared me carefully since I was a child to live my sex life with awareness and without fears.

Now Rosario had taken hold of my ankles, he was spreading my legs. He said in an emotional voice: what a nice thing you have between your thighs, and he lay cautiously on top of me. He looked for my sex with his, guiding it with his hand, and when it seemed to him to be in the right place he pushed gently, very gently, then suddenly gave an energetic thrust.

"Ow," I said.

"I hurt you?"

"A little. Don't get me pregnant."

"Don't worry."

"You finished?"

"Wait."

He pushed again, positioned himself better, pushed some more. From that moment all he did was pull back a little and then go forward again. But the more he persisted in that movement, the more it hurt, and he realized it, he murmured, relax, you're too tight. I whispered: I'm not tight, ow, I'm relaxed, and he said politely, Gianni, you have to cooperate, what do you have there, a piece of iron, a lockbox. I clenched my teeth, I murmured: no, push, come on,

491

harder, but I was sweaty, I felt the sweat on my face and chest, he himself said you're so sweaty, and I was ashamed, I whispered: I never sweat, only today, I'm sorry, if it's repulsive to you forget it.

Finally, he entered me, with such force that I had the impression of a long rip in my stomach. It was an instant, he pulled away suddenly, hurting me even more than when he had entered. I raised my head to see what was happening and I saw him on his knees between my legs with his penis bloody and dripping with semen. Although he was laughing, he was really angry.

"Did you do it?" I asked weakly.

"Yes," he said lying down next to me.

"Thank goodness."

"Yeah, I'll say."

"It burns."

"Your fault, we could have done better."

I turned toward him, I said:

"That was how I wanted to do it," and I kissed him, sticking my tongue as far as possible past his teeth. A moment later I ran to wash, I put on underpants and jeans. When he went into the bathroom, I unhooked the bracelet and placed it on the floor, next to the bed, like a bad-luck charm. He drove me home, him dissatisfied, me delighted.

The next day I left for Venice with Ida.

On the train, we promised each other to become adults as no one ever had before.

ABOUT THE AUTHORS

Elena Ferrante is the author of *The Days of Abandonment,* which was made into a film directed by Roberto Faenza, *Troubling Love,* adapted by Mario Martone, and *The Lost Daughter,* also adapted for the cinema and to be directed by Maggie Gyllenhaal. She is also the author of *Frantumaglia: A Writer's Journey* and a children's picture book illustrated by Mara Cerri, *The Beach at Night.* The four volumes known as the "Neapolitan quartet" (*My Brilliant Friend, The Story of a New Name, Those Who Leave and Those Who Stay,* and *The Story of the Lost Child*) were published in English between 2012 and 2015. *My Brilliant Friend,* the HBO series directed by Saverio Costanzo, premiered in 2018.

Ann Goldstein has translated into English all of Elena Ferrante's books, including the

New York Times bestseller, *The Story of the Lost Child,* which was shortlisted for the MAN Booker International Prize. She has been honored with a Guggenheim Fellowship and is the recipient of the PEN Renato Poggioli Translation Award. She lives in New York.